Hiding in Plain Sight

Susan Lewis is the bestselling author of thirty-eight novels. She is also the author of *Just One More Day* and *One Day at a Time*, the moving memoirs of her childhood in Bristol. She lives in Gloucestershire. Her website address is www.susanlewis.com

Susan is a supporter of the breast cancer charity, Breast Cancer Care: www.breastcancercare.org.uk and of the childhood bereavement charity, Winton's Wish: www.winstonswish.org.uk

Also by Susan Lewis

Fiction

A Class Apart
Dance While You Can
Stolen Beginnings
Darkest Longings
Obsession
Vengeance
Summer Madness
Last Resort
Wildfire
Cruel Venus
Strange Allure
The Mill House
A French Affair
Missing
Out of the Shadows
Lost Innocence
The Choice
Forgotten
Stolen
No Turning Back
Losing You
The Truth About You
Never Say Goodbye

Too Close to Home
No Place to Hide
The Girl Who Came Back
Believe In Me

*Books that run
in sequence*
Chasing Dreams
Taking Chances

No Child of Mine
Don't Let Me Go
You Said Forever

Behind Closed Doors
The Moment She Left
Hiding in Plain Sight

*Series featuring Laurie Forbes
and Elliott Russell*
Silent Truths
Wicked Beauty
Intimate Strangers
The Hornbeam Tree

Memoir
Just One More Day
One Day at a Time

Hiding in Plain Sight

arrow books

1 3 5 7 9 10 8 6 4 2

Arrow Books
20 Vauxhall Bridge Road
London SW1V 2SA

Arrow Books is part of the Penguin Random House group of companies
whose addresses can be found at global.penguinrandomhouse.com.

 Penguin
Random House
UK

First published in Great Britain by Century in 2017
First published in paperback by Arrow Books in 2018

www.penguin.co.uk

A CIP catalogue record for this book is available from the British Library.

ISBN 9781784755607
ISBN 9781784756758 (export)

Typeset in 11.83/15.06 pt Palatino LT Std by Jouve (UK), Milton Keynes
Printed and bound in Great Britain by Clays Ltd, St Ives Plc

 MIX
Paper from
responsible sources
FSC® C018179

Penguin Random House is committed to a
sustainable future for our business, our readers
and our planet. This book is made from Forest
Stewardship Council® certified paper.

In memory of Georgina Hawtrey-Woore, a truly talented editor and cherished friend, already missed by many and loved by all

She'd dreamt about nothing else for years.

That was when she'd been able to dream.

Now here he was, standing in front of her, shaking so hard she'd surely have been able to hear his knees knocking if the wind weren't so fierce.

His once handsome, now dissolute face was a white, stricken moon in the dark night. His hair was tossing around like trapped straw in a gale. He'd have run if he could, but the men either side of him – nameless, faceless and handsomely paid – were preventing it.

They were watching her too. Neither of them spoke. They were silent, solid, knew why they were there, knew that after they must silently disappear.

A fleeting memory of little Michelle Cross on a busy street flashed into her mind and was gone. She'd been there one minute, gone the next – to the arms of the Virgin Mary.

The Virgin Mary.

She could see he was shouting, crying, begging, but

the wind was snatching his words away, hurling them like feathers into the stormy night.

The cliff edge was so close.

A hundred feet below the sea was a foaming, furious black mass, heaving colossal waves on to the slick, jagged rocks.

She wondered if he'd ever dreamt about her.

Had she troubled his mind at all since he'd last seen her?

She knew she must have. How had he felt?

Guilty? Afraid? Vulnerable?

Certainly not as terrified as he felt now.

He'd no doubt hoped he'd never see her again.

But here she was, standing before him on this deserted tourist spot at the edge of the world, and he knew why.

What he didn't know, yet, was whether she was going to let him live or die.

Chapter One

These meandering, cobbled streets in the heart of Provence, laced through with sleepy canals and narrow, filigree footbridges were known as the Venice of France. Surrounded by the River Sorgue, with glittering waterways, tree-lined banks and many splendid mossy mill wheels, the area was home to a whole host of pavement and waterfront cafés, along with antique shops of every period and description.

It was through one of the leafy arcades that Andrea – Andee – Lawrence was strolling, aware of the ghosts she couldn't see, but sense: children, old women, thieves, sociopaths, philanthropists, spurned lovers, victims of grisly murders. Their spirits were as light and intangible as the wispy clouds overhead; their stories embedded in a forgotten time.

Andee Lawrence wasn't French, but with her effortless elegance and dark, compelling looks she could easily have passed for a wealthy Parisienne, here to while away a few hours before other demands claimed her. In fact, she was a British ex-detective turned occasional freelance investigator, who'd lately developed an interest in – and talent for – interior design. She was also the mother of two, Luke aged twenty-one and Alayna nineteen; she was separated from her husband, Martin, and was now enjoying a new relationship with antique dealer and property developer Graeme Ogilvy, who'd brought her to France.

Other than her striking looks, there was nothing to set her apart from the other browsers who'd come to L'Isle-sur-la-Sorgue today – not a Sunday in the middle of summer, but a Wednesday in early June. Sundays were crazy days when hundreds, thousands, of stalls cluttered the streets and eager bargain-hunters, tourists and vendors outnumbered even the ghosts of former times.

No one, least of all Andee, was aware of fate trailing her today like a sinister bridesmaid. She was experiencing no sixth sense, no unease, nothing untoward at all, only the pleasure of wandering from one small emporium to another, as entranced by the treasures and oddities as she was by the nuances of possible stories.

She'd left Graeme a few minutes ago discussing delivery of a neglected *bergère* chair to the villa they were here to renovate and furnish for a wealthy Spanish client. Their instructions were clear. Nadia Abrego, the Catalonian beauty who could roll out several more surnames and possibly even titles if she so wished, had provided them with photographs of the Renaissance chateau she wanted copied as closely as possible. The villa was an inheritance, apparently, from a recently deceased great-aunt.

The day was warm, the sounds of traffic, haggling, laughter, music were drifting like charms through the still air, passing by lace tablecloths and sombre tapestries, brushing scabbards and teapots, tangling an invisible web around people and relics of the past. A Frenchman in a beret and red neckerchief was posing for photographs with tourists, while an accordionist on the corner of Quai Jean Jaures was pumping out jolly tunes and winking at his admirers as they tossed coins into his waiting cap. As Andee crossed the Pont de la Rivière with its intricate iron balustrades and worn wooden treads, the aroma of freshly baked baguettes floated its temptation out of a nearby *boulangerie*, while the clink of glasses from pavement cafés provided its own irresistible lure.

Taking out her phone she sent a text to Graeme.

Fancy a glass of rosé? Meet you at the cafe next to Hubert's Antiques.

Graeme knew the heart of this small town so well that he'd have no trouble finding her, especially as Hubert was a friend of long standing.

She didn't notice the car approaching as she prepared to cross the road, she only knew it was there when it came to a stop in front of her, blocking the way. She was about to go round it when the rear window descended to reveal a blonde, middle-aged woman wearing dark glasses and crimson lipstick.

'Are you lost?' Andee asked, in French.

The woman smiled and removed the glasses.

Long, strange seconds ticked by before the woman said softly, in English, 'Remember me?'

Shock was twisting Andee's heart into a terrible knot. It couldn't be. It simply wasn't possible. And yet those eyes, the colour and shape, the cheekbones, the retroussé nose . . .

Apparently satisfied that she'd been recognised, the woman tapped the driver's shoulder and the car moved on.

Andee watched it go, too stunned to move, even to think beyond the shock that had trapped her in an unworldly grip.

'Are you OK, madame?' a voice asked from behind her.

She turned to find a concerned man watching her.

'Would you like to sit down?' he offered, pulling up a shabbily upholstered parlour chair.

Andee meant to thank him and move on, but her legs had turned weak. All she could do was sink into his kindness.

'It is 'ot,' he observed in heavily accented English. 'I find you some water.'

As he disappeared inside his shop Andee stared along the street searching for the silver Mercedes, but like the figment of a dream, it had vanished into thin air. She should have run after it, and would now if she had any idea of the direction it had taken. She tried again to make herself think, but her mind remained locked into that brief, earth-shattering moment of recognition.

Remember me?

How could Andee forget? Even after all these years she'd have known the woman anywhere, yet . . . How could it be? It simply wasn't possible.

The woman in the car was dead, so how could she possibly be here?

Andee was with Graeme now, sitting beneath the parasols of a favourite canal-side café next to Hubert's Antiques. She was watching his shrewd dark eyes dilating with shock as he connected with what she'd just told him.

'Are you sure?' he asked, then apparently annoyed with himself, 'Sorry, of course you are, you wouldn't be saying it if you weren't.'

Feeling for him, Andee said, 'Don't worry, I keep asking myself the same question.' She glanced up as a waiter brought a *pichet* of rosé to the table with two glasses. She couldn't remember when she'd last been in such need of a drink.

'I guess you didn't catch the car's number plate?' he ventured.

She hadn't even thought to look. 'It happened so fast. I can't even tell you if it was French.'

'Left-hand drive?'

Andee thought about it. 'She was in the back. She had to reach over to tap the driver, so I'd say it was right-hand, but I – I can't be sure ... I couldn't stop looking at her.' She finally understood now what it felt like to be a witness to something that happened so fast and unexpectedly that the memory could barely cope.

Clearly as bewildered and stunned as she was, though probably not as badly shaken, Graeme stared hard at the wine as he poured it.

'I don't know what to say,' she murmured after taking a sip. 'I don't even know what to think.' Her eyes were darting about the street, falling on random women, cars, empty windows behind lacy balconies where someone could be hiding, watching, waiting . . .

Why was she thinking that?

Because the car, the woman, had appeared out of nowhere?

How had she known where to find Andee – and at that precise time?

The questions rushing through her mind were as uncomfortable as they were impossible to answer. The woman must have been stalking her, but for how long, and why?

'How on earth did she know you were here?' Graeme demanded, echoing Andee's thoughts.

Their eyes met. His handsome face was taut with concern as he tried to make sense of what had happened.

'I'm already starting to doubt myself,' Andee confessed. 'It might not have been her.'

'So why would she ask if you remembered her?'

Andee drank more wine as though it might sort the craziness in her head.

'If she'd been a child, I mean a small child, two or three, when she disappeared,' Graeme continued, 'she'd have changed . . .'

'She knew I'd recognise her,' Andee cut across him. 'She stopped only for that, and then she drove on. Why did she drive on?'

Offering the only answer he could, Graeme said,

'Whatever the reason, she's decided she wants you to know she's alive.'

Andee's head started to spin. Almost thirty years had passed since her younger sister, Penny, had vanished from their lives. At the age of fourteen she'd left them with nothing more than a one-page letter, sent weeks after she'd gone. Everyone had long believed it to be a suicide note.

Dear Mum and Dad, I probably ought to say sorry for leaving the way I have, but maybe you already don't mind very much that I'm not around any more, so instead I'll say sorry for always being such a disappointment to you. I know Dad wanted a son when I was born, so I guess I've been a let-down to him from the start, and I don't blame him for always loving Andee the most because she's much nicer-looking than I am and likes sports, the same as him, and is really clever so it stands to reason that he'd be really proud of her. I know I shouldn't say this, but sometimes I hate her for being so much better than I am at everything. No one ever seems to notice me when she's in the room. It's like I become invisible and I know she wishes I would go away. So that's what I'm going to do.

I don't know what else to say, except sorry again. I expect you'll all be much happier without me. Please tell Andee she can have whatever she likes of mine, although I don't expect she'll want anything at all.

Your daughter, Penny

Although Penny hadn't actually said she was going to kill herself, it had certainly sounded that way.

However, because of the doubt and failure to find a body, Andee and her parents had never quite been able to give up the hope of one day finding her. It was the reason Andee had followed her father into the police force instead of going to uni, in the naïve belief that she might succeed in finding Penny where others had failed. By then Penny's disappearance had turned their father into a shadow of his former self. He'd never been able to get over it, and had died without ever knowing what had happened to his younger daughter.

Andee's mother was still alive, and Andee knew that she thought about Penny almost every day. Each case of a missing child that appeared on the news moved them both as deeply as if it were happening to them all over again. It was part of the reason Andee had finally given up her job as a detective. Every search she became involved in for a missing child drew her focus back to Penny, and dealing with other people's tragedies, finding bodies, uncovering murders, having so few happy endings, she'd come to realise, was keeping her own tragedy alive.

'What do you want to do?' Graeme asked gently, bringing her back to the present.

She looked at him, so lost for an answer that she almost laughed.

'We can lunch here, or go back to the villa,' he said.

Her gaze drifted along the street, as though lured there by the invisible Mercedes. 'The ridiculous thing is,' she said, 'I'm feeling afraid to leave in case she comes back.'

'Do you think she will?'

Andee shook her head; she had no idea.

He reached for her hand. 'Let's go,' he said. 'We need to talk this through and here's not the right place.'

An hour later they were on the vine-covered terrace of the villa they'd rented for the two months they were planning to be in Provence. It was just a few kilometres from the stunning medieval village of Gordes, surrounded by lavender fields and vineyards and partly sheltered from the warm mistral winds by the magnificent Mont Ventoux.

The villa's sprawling gardens were alive with the incessant scrape of cicadas. On the table in front of them were prawns, pâté, cheese, ham, beefy tomatoes, and succulent peaches collapsing from their skins. Graeme had opened more wine, but neither of them ate or drank. Andee's shock at seeing her sister hadn't lessened, and in fact was only increasing as disbelief, confusion and a horrible unease stole through her.

'Why did she do that?' she demanded in frustration. 'What was the point of showing herself to me, then simply driving off?'

'I still can't fathom how she even knew you were there?'

The fact that neither of them could answer these questions didn't matter, because it seemed clear that Penny *had* known; had indeed timed her return – if it could be called that – with the kind of precision that was as calculated as it was disturbing.

'What about your mother?' Graeme said, batting a

fly from the food. 'She's the only one I can think of who might have told Penny where to find you.'

Andee was already shaking her head. 'If my mother had heard from her she'd have called me straight away.' Her frown deepened as she said, 'Should I tell her about this?'

He reached for his wine glass as he thought. 'If she doesn't already know, then perhaps not yet,' he cautioned. 'Let's see if your sister approaches you again.'

Relieved that he didn't seem to doubt her, although she kept doubting herself, Andee checked her mobile. She had no idea if Penny knew her number, but she was ready to believe she might.

No messages of any sort.

To Graeme she said, 'Over the years I've imagined seeing her again in so many ways. The police bringing her to us; her turning up on the doorstep one night; randomly running into her on the street; seeing her on TV. I guess I've thought most of all about how we'd cope if her body was found. I never envisaged anything like what's just happened.' She shook her head in bewilderment. 'I keep asking myself why be so . . . *mysterious* about it? It's like she wants to tease, or even unnerve me. If that's true, she's succeeding.'

At the sound of a car passing along the shady lane beyond the villa's high stone walls, Graeme turned his head.

Andee listened, tense, half expecting the car to stop at the gates, but it didn't.

'Do you think we should contact the police?' he suggested carefully.

Her eyes went to his. 'I guess you mean the English police.'

'If she's no longer missing . . .'

'But what can we tell them? A random sighting in a foreign country of a woman who might, or might not be her.'

They both looked at his mobile as it rang.

Seeing it was Nadia, their demanding client, Andee said, 'You should take it. I'll clear these things away.'

As he clicked on and wandered through the olive trees towards the pool, Andee could hear him assuring, agreeing, advising while she continued to sit where she was, soft splashes of sunlight falling through the overhead vine to dapple her bronzing skin. The heady scents of honeysuckle and jasmine floated on the warm breeze, lending a potent sense of unreality to the strangeness she felt inside. She had no way of assessing or comparing it to anything, no idea how to articulate it, or even how to escape it. It was as though the world had carried on turning, leaving her at a standstill in the midst of a vortex that could so easily sweep her up again, though when or how, she had no way of knowing.

She tried casting her mind back to the time Penny had vanished, already knowing that the intervening years had blurred and buried the memories so deeply that their reality was all but impossible to reach. Of course they'd been different people back then, children, she sixteen, Penny fourteen. She recalled Penny as moody, insular, and erratic, but she could picture her laughing too, her funny fresh face with its freckles and rosy complexion, and her riotous giggle that had been so infectious. As a younger child she'd been mischievous and daring, they'd had fun, but Penny had frequently been sad or angry, spiteful even, and they'd fought often, the way sisters did. Andee had had no idea until the letter arrived that Penny had felt unwanted by her family, and worthless to the point that no life at all was better than a life with them.

But apparently she hadn't chosen no life at all.

Andee looked at her mobile again, and felt the need to talk to her mother, or one of her children, or even Martin, her ex, who hadn't known Penny, but had come into Andee's life soon after the disappearance. Her eyes drifted to where Graeme was seated on a lounger next to the pool. He was still talking to Nadia, the shock of the day no longer at the front of his mind. Andee didn't feel offended by that, only slightly cut off, as though this issue, this dilemma, this craziness, had her trapped in a place she could neither define nor escape.

Remember me?

The question echoed in her mind, softly spoken with a smile, and a kind of knowing that had seemed, she thought now, almost malicious. Maybe she was making that up. The eyes were the same blue-green as Andee's, their shape more oval than almond. Her face had barely altered, only aged, with prominent cheekbones and a determined jaw that might have appeared masculine were it not for the rosebud mouth and girlishly upturned nose. Her hair had been razored around the neck, like a boy's, with a thick blonde sweep on top that fell neatly over one eye. It wasn't the colour she'd been born with, but the change hadn't disguised her at all. The sighting had lasted for no more than a few seconds, yet Andee could still see her as clearly as if she were in front of her now.

Her sister was alive.

It was almost impossible to make herself believe it. She had no idea where Penny was, or even *who* she was now. She felt a desperate need to do something, but what? In the end, she had to accept that all she could do was wait and wonder if Penny was planning to show herself again.

Andee's mother rang just after eight that evening, while Andee and Graeme were in the kitchen listening to jazz on the radio and trying to focus on the plans for Nadia's villa.

As soon as she saw it was her mother, Andee's sixth sense kicked in with alarm and caution. She knew what the call was going to be about, but she kept her tone cheerful just in case she was wrong. 'Hi, how are you?' she asked.

With no preamble her mother said, 'I hope you're sitting down, because I've just had a call from . . . from someone who sounded just like you. She said . . . she said she was Penny. Can you believe that? I don't know whether to believe it. I thought it was you, but I know you'd never play such a horrible trick.'

Feeling for how shaken her mother clearly was, Andee held the phone so Graeme could hear and asked what else Penny had said.

'You're not sounding shocked,' Maureen accused, and Andee could almost see the uncertainty, perhaps even fear, clouding her mother's gentle blue eyes.

'I'll explain in a minute,' Andee told her. 'Just tell me what else she said.'

'She wants to see me. Oh dear God, do you think it's really her?'

Instead of answering, Andee said, 'Did she say where or when she wants to see you?'

'She's going to call again in the next few days to set up a time to come to the house.'

Surprised by that, Andee said, 'Does she know where you live?' Her parents had moved from Chiswick – Penny's childhood home – to Kesterly-on-Sea almost twenty-five years ago.

'I didn't ask. It all happened so fast. I could hardly believe I was having the conversation . . . Andee, I feel . . . I don't know how I feel, but you're not helping, because I'm sure you're holding something back from me.'

There was no point in lying. 'I saw her today, in L'Isle-sur-la-Sorgue,' Andee told her. 'Not to speak to, there wasn't time, she drove off as soon she was sure I'd recognised her.'

Maureen was silent, and Andee wished with all her heart that she could be with her mother now. She might be unflappable most of the time, able to deal with most things life threw at her, but this was too much for her to handle alone. 'What's happening?' Maureen asked shakily. 'I don't understand.'

'I don't either,' Andee responded. 'All I can tell you is that she pulled up in front of me, asked if I

16

remembered her, and as soon as she was certain I did she drove off.'

'But . . . I don't . . . Why would she do that?'

Having no answer, Andee asked instead, 'Did she call your mobile or the house phone?'

'The house phone, and yes I rang 1471, but the caller's number had been withheld.'

Andee looked at the note Graeme had passed her and asked her mother the question. 'Have you told anyone else about the call?'

'No. I rang you straight away. If you're sure it's her . . . I mean . . . Do you think I should contact the police?'

Andee's eyes returned to Graeme's as she said, 'Probably, but we won't do it yet. We don't know anything for certain, so let's see what happens.' She grimaced regretfully at Graeme as she added, 'I'm coming back.'

'It's OK,' he mouthed.

Maureen was saying, 'I must admit, I'll feel happier if you're here when she comes. If she comes. Do you think she will? Are we even having this conversation?'

'It'll be OK,' Andee tried to reassure her. 'If you're feeling nervous you should go and stay with Carol until I get there.' Carol was Maureen's closest friend and Andee's 'ex' mother-in-law.

'Carol and the family are in Spain,' Maureen reminded her.

And Graeme's sisters Rowzee and Pamela, also good friends of Maureen's, were driving a camper van around Europe with Pamela's boyfriend, Bill, attempting to keep them on the road and out of trouble. 'Blake and Jenny must be around?' Andee queried, referring to Graeme's business partner and his wife, who had recently become Maureen's neighbours.

'Yes they are,' Maureen confirmed, 'but I don't want to bother them. I'll be fine. I mean, I can't imagine she intends us any harm, can you?'

'No, of course not. Why would you say that?'

Maureen hesitated. 'I don't know,' she murmured. 'I suppose it's the way . . . I keep thinking . . .'

'Thinking of what?' Andee pressed.

'Nothing. I guess I'm just . . . all shaken up. Finding it hard to get my head round things.'

Feeling the need to be with her, Andee said, 'I'll book myself on a flight into Bristol tomorrow. Can you meet me at the airport?'

'Of course. Just let me know what time to be there.'

After ringing off Andee turned into Graeme's embrace and rested her head on his shoulder. 'I'm sorry,' she whispered, 'but if my sister has come back . . .'

'There's nothing to be sorry about,' he assured her. 'You should be with your mother, and I can manage here – at least in a business sense.'

Andee pulled back to look at him, and felt the pleasure of being with him trying to insist that she stay. 'We were having such a good time,' she murmured.

With the dryness she loved he said, 'I'm taking it we will again.'

She looked at him, feeling a reassuring sense of closeness surrounding them. Though they'd known one another for several years, it was only in the last few months that their relationship had developed into the intimate and easy connection that made it so pleasurable for them to spend time together. During the past week, since arriving in Provence, they'd begun to explore the idea of her moving into his elegant town house in Kesterly-on-Sea when they returned home. It was something they both wanted, and neither of them saw any reason why it wouldn't work, given how much time she was already spending there.

Andee began to wonder if this sudden surprise from Penny might have an effect on that. Though she couldn't immediately see how, she realised Graeme could be asking himself the same question. Whatever was going through his mind, she knew he was concerned on her behalf about this sudden shock life had thrown her. He was a man of genuine compassion and sensitivity, combined with easy humour and the kind of generosity that made her heart swell with admiration when she saw his kindness towards those needing help. He could be fierce too, and very determined, especially in business, and he made a convincing show of tolerating no nonsense from his two much older sisters, who completely adored him, or from his sons. In their twenties, and independent as they liked to consider themselves, they rarely did anything without seeking their father's approval first.

Smiling, she reached for the wine and refilled their glasses. 'If this is really happening,' she said, 'then it's going to turn the world upside down. How can it not? Someone walks back into your life after almost three decades . . . And not just someone . . .' She sighed as she tried to gather some sense from the confusion. 'I wonder what she's like now. I mean what sort of person she is, and where she's been all this time.'

'You'll soon be able to ask her.'

Andee's eyes narrowed as she pictured the woman she'd seen earlier. 'She didn't look like someone who'd been taken from her family against her will; shut away, imprisoned, enslaved for years on end,' she said. 'That's what usually happens when someone, especially at the age she was back then, disappears without trace. They're taken and held captive, and only a few manage to escape alive.'

'Well she's alive, we know that much.'

Andee nodded. 'And presumably on her way to the UK, if she's planning to see my mother in the next few days.'

Chapter Two

By the time Maureen collected Andee from the airport the following afternoon she'd lived through the shock and strangely suppressed elation of hearing from her younger daughter for a second time.

'Apparently her name's Michelle now,' she informed Andee as they drove out to the A38. 'Michelle Cross. I feel I should know the name, but I can't think from where.'

It rang a vague bell for Andee too. She turned to her mother, not quite knowing what to say.

Maureen's eyes stayed on the road ahead. She looked as she always did, calm, composed, a supremely elegant woman who wore her seventy plus years as though they were a mere sixty. Her expression was hard to read, but Andee knew that behind the bright, watchful eyes and gently lined complexion her mother was in turmoil. How could she not be, considering the enormity of what was – or could be – happening?

'What else did she say?' Andee asked.

'She'd like to come on Thursday at three if it's convenient for us.'

'Us?' Andee echoed. 'Did you tell her I was going to be there?'

'No. I decided she presumed you would be.'

'Even though she knew I was in France?'

Maureen speeded up to overtake a tractor. 'I've no idea how to answer that,' she said. 'I only know I never imagined it happening like this.' Andee didn't miss the tremor in her voice, and noticed her hands tightening on the wheel. 'The truth is, I'd stopped imagining it happening at all,' Maureen admitted, wretchedly. 'I thought, if we ever saw her again . . . I thought it would be a body.'

Andee wondered how long ago they'd started thinking that way. But no matter how many years had passed, the Lawrences' hope of Penny's safe and happy return had never entirely gone away.

Was the joy of that hope burning again now, and Andee was failing to feel it? Naturally she wanted to see her sister, more than anything, but whoever she was now, Penny, Michelle, she was going to be a stranger. Her adult years weren't entwined with her family's; they were all hers, untouched by the Lawrences. She had a story, a history completely separate from the world she'd been born into. It was possible she had her own family now. Two, three or more children as old, maybe even older than Andee's. What about the father of her children, if they existed?

Considering how long it had been there were likely to be many stories.

Everyone's lives were like that, going from one major event, to a smaller maybe happier time, only for disaster or triumph to strike again. The years were like chapters, some long, some short, with new characters and old drawn into the dramas, and each tale superseding the last.

'I wonder if she knows that Daddy's dead?' Maureen said quietly.

Andee had been thinking about her father throughout the journey here, wishing with all her heart that he was still with them, that the trauma of losing a daughter hadn't sent him to an early grave. He'd always been their rock, the one they'd turned to in a time of crisis. There was nothing he couldn't do or fix, nothing he didn't understand, no one who wasn't a little in awe of him. As a detective chief superintendent with the Metropolitan Police he'd commanded a great deal of respect, but at the same time he'd been known for his fairness and compassion. He had been seen as a pillar of the community, until his younger daughter had disappeared and the rock had eventually began to crumble under the weight of helplessness and grief, until finally it had been eroded completely.

How was Penny going to feel when she found out?

Maybe she already knew.

It wasn't a good feeling to think of her sister watching them from the shadows, knowing what was happening to them yet never showing herself. It surely hadn't been like that? More likely someone had told her – taunted her even – with details of what her family was doing, holidays she could never enjoy, a father she'd never see again, a new home she'd never get to know ... Except she had known the Kesterly home, because it had belonged to their grandparents before their parents had taken it on. It had been where she and Andee had often spent their summer breaks when they were small.

'Does she want us to call her Michelle?' Andee ventured.

'I'm not sure.'

'Do you think you'll be able to?'

Maureen hesitated. 'I guess it'll depend . . . I mean, after all this time, if she feels like a stranger then perhaps calling her Michelle won't be so hard.'

Andee regarded her mother carefully. 'You're managing to sound very philosophical,' she commented warily, 'but I know you.'

Maureen cast her a glance. 'I'm not sure how else to be,' she confessed. 'If I'm truthful I keep thinking it's going to turn out to be a hoax, or that I'll wake up in a minute and discover it's a dream. It can't be her, surely.'

It was how Andee felt, and yet here she was, back from France having already seen her sister, even if for a mere few seconds. It had been long enough for her to know.

After a while, Maureen said, 'Did Graeme mind you leaving?'

'He understood that I needed to be here.'

Maureen reached for her hand. 'Thank you for coming. I don't mind admitting I'd be finding it very difficult if I was on my own.'

Feeling a surge of love for her mother, and a deep sense of protectiveness, Andee lifted their joined hands to her cheek. They'd always been close, and should anyone ask her to name her best friend she knew her answer would probably be Maureen.

Second in line would be Rowzee, Graeme's older sister, who had sweetness, vitality, mischief and miracles all over her. She and her merry little dance with terminal cancer were a source of endless fascination for the medical profession, and sparked up so many emotions for those who loved her that the easiest refuge was in denial. It wasn't happening, Rowzee wasn't going to die, so now let's get on with life.

How blessed Graeme was in his sisters, whose far greater age had made them more like mothers while he was growing up; now they were getting to be like troublesome teenagers.

As though reading her mind, Maureen said, 'Do you know when Rowzee and Pamela are due home?'

'Not for a while yet,' Andee answered, checking her mobile as a text came through. It was Graeme wanting to know if she'd landed safely.

After messaging him back, Andee said, 'Have you told anyone about this since we spoke yesterday?'

Maureen shook her head. 'I know this is going to sound odd, but it's like I'm afraid to.'

Andee sort of understood.

'I'm afraid no one will believe me,' Maureen expanded. 'They'll think I'm getting delusional in my old age. I've even wondered it myself.'

Andee smiled.

'What does Graeme say?'

'He's as shocked and mystified by it as we are. He asked me to tell you that if you're worried about anything and you feel I'm not listening or responding appropriately, you're to call him any time of the day or night.'

Maureen's eyes lightened with humour. 'Did he really say that?'

'His exact words; give or take.'

'Then he knows you well.'

Andee regarded her sardonically. 'Because I'm given to responding inappropriately?'

'If we're putting it politely,' her mother countered.

Laughing, Andee checked her mobile again and seeing it was her daughter Alayna on the line, she quickly clicked on.

'Hey Mum!' Alayna cried in her sing-songy, I'm-a-supercool-student way. 'I just saw that a couple of the *Strictly* dancers are appearing at the Hippodrome, here in Bristol, at Christmas so I thought I'd get some tickets for Grandma's birthday treat. I'm checking with you first though to make sure you haven't already done it.'

'I haven't,' Andee confirmed.

'OK, so you'll come too, and drive her? We know she's not keen on driving at night. I can check out some Airbnb places for you, if you like. It'd be great if you stayed over so we can go for dinner and breakfast and do other stuff, like shopping so I can spend all your money.'

Wryly, Andee said, 'I'm fine thanks my darling. I hope you are too.'

'Yeah, dead cool, and you're very funny. How's Provence?'

'Actually, I'm in England.'

'I thought it wasn't a French ringtone. So why are

you back already? Weren't you supposed to be going for two months? Oh my God, don't tell me you've broken up with Graeme. I've only just got used to you being with him. Are you very upset?'

Rolling her eyes, Andee said, 'Graeme and I are still together, but there's some business I have to attend to back here, so Grandma just came to pick me up from the airport.'

'Are you saying you guys were in Bristol and you didn't come to see me? How am I supposed to get over that?'

'We assumed you'd be busy.'

'You should have rung, just in case. Anyway, don't mention the tickets if Grandma's there because I want it to be a surprise.'

'It's a lovely idea, and yes to everything.'

'You are so totally amazing, did I ever tell you that?'

'Not often enough.'

With a splutter of laughter, Alayna said, 'So what business have you got back here? Please don't tell me someone else has gone missing. You're supposed to have left the police because you didn't want to get involved in those searches any more, but everyone still keeps coming to you.'

Having already decided that now wasn't the time to tell Alayna what had really brought her back, Andee made up something about a client of Graeme's needing some special attention. She could always be truthful later, when she had a clearer idea of how things were going to progress with Penny. Michelle.

'OK, well if anyone's good at special attention it's

Grandma, so you should take her with you. Have you spoken to Luke, our man in Africa, lately?'

'Not since last weekend. Have you?'

'No, but he messaged me yesterday to say they had a run-in with poachers the night before last. Pretty scary stuff, if you ask me, but you know what he's like, I bet he loved it.'

Knowing for sure that her son was enjoying every minute of his time on a South African game reserve, Andee said, 'Did he say if the baby rhino's been born yet?'

'No, which means it hasn't or he'd have sent pictures. Dad's planning to go out there, did he tell you? We could go too if you felt like it?'

'I thought you were working all summer to earn some money.'

'Yep, I am totally doing that. Anyway, have to run, I'm already late for my next lecture. Only two weeks to go and summer officially starts. Yay! Love to Grandma, and to you. Kisses,' and she was gone.

'She makes me feel exhausted just to hear her jabbering,' Maureen commented, as they joined the M5. 'Is she all right?'

'I think we can rest easy.'

'And Luke? Has she heard from him?'

Deciding not to mention the poachers, Andee said, 'Apparently Martin's planning to go out there.'

'He's in Spain with his mother.'

'For now, but he was always intending to fly out and see Luke, so why don't you go and join Carol when he's gone?'

Maureen glanced at her. 'Are you trying to get rid of me?' she challenged.

'No, but I know you. You really wanted to go, but ended up deciding to stay behind in case one of the children changed their plans, so someone would be at home for them. They're twenty-one and nineteen, Mum. You don't have to arrange your life around them.'

'I know you're right, but it feels wrong for none of us to be in Kesterly. Anyway, given what's happening, it's a good job I did stay at home.'

Thinking again of Penny and how easy it would be for her to take over their mother's life from here on, maybe even Andee's too, Andee attempted to put herself in Maureen's shoes. It was one thing losing a sister, and God knew it had been bad, but losing a daughter ... How would she feel if Alayna vanished without a trace and suddenly turned up so many years later? It would make her feel sick with shock and apprehension, riven with curiosity of course, and no doubt insanely relieved and excited; it might also cripple her with guilt. She'd feel ashamed of having moved on without her, and afraid of somehow letting her down again; or of not being good enough; of doing and saying the wrong things; of being unable to make things up to her.

Andee felt all these things herself, was becoming more stressed by them as time ticked on, so she could only guess at how much worse it was for her mother.

'I was wondering,' Andee said, when finally they approached Kesterly seafront where early summer visitors were braving a feisty downpour, 'if I ought to have a chat with Gould about things.'

As Maureen slowed behind the tourist train Andee sensed her tension. 'You mean your old boss, Detective Inspector Gould?' Maureen said evenly. 'I'm not sure either of us is ready for that yet, are we?'

'It would be off the record,' Andee assured her.

Maureen's gaze drifted across The Promenade to where spirited waves were flinging themselves against the bay's flanking rocks. Andee suspected she was thinking about all the press attention that was likely to erupt once the news was out. Her mother had lived through it all those years ago, and it had come close to giving her a breakdown. She wouldn't want to go through it again. 'He doesn't know anything about the case,' Maureen said. 'It wasn't handled here, besides he's far too young. He wouldn't even have been in the force at the time she disappeared.'

'I realise that, but he's a friend, someone who can advise us if we need it. Maybe advise Penny too.'

Maureen's face was growing paler. 'I think we should wait and find out from Penny what she wants to happen,' she replied.

Deciding not to press it, since she wasn't sure herself of the best course to take, Andee said no more as her mother drove them up on to the northerly headland and along the steep, winding roads towards home.

The random sprawl of quaint grey stone cottages brightened by flower baskets and rose-covered porches, along with the handful of newer red-brick bungalows that made up the residences of Bourne Hollow, were gleaming wetly in a sudden burst of sunshine as

Maureen and Andee drove into the hamlet. At its heart was a neatly mowed patch of green shaped vaguely like a kite with a children's play area and sandpit at one end, several carefully tended (by Maureen) flower beds at the other, and half a dozen or more memorial benches parked invitingly around the edges. The Smugglers' Arms, a centuries-old whitewashed inn, was on the north side of the hamlet with a garden full of picnic tables and parasols spilling out on to the street, while the Bourne Hollow convenience store-cum-café and newly opened gift shop nestled together on the western tip. The old smugglers' tunnels that laced through the heart of the headland had mostly been filled in by now, but two were still offering guided tours for those bold enough to make the descent – and confront the ghosts.

The Lawrence family home, Briar Lodge, rambled sedately along the eastern end of the green with tall brick chimneys at each end, several slate roofs at different levels and a low stone wall to mark the garden boundary. It had started life back in the eighteen hundreds as a hunting retreat for a wealthy merchant from Bristol, but these days, with its Victorian-style extensions and large sash windows, it was a much lighter, more homely version of its original incarnation.

After pulling up behind Andee's car in the drive at the side of the house Maureen continued to sit at the wheel, holding on to it as though unwilling to let go.

'Are you OK?' Andee asked gently.

Maureen nodded stiffly. 'I think so . . . I just . . .'

'Take a moment,' Andee advised. 'We don't have to rush anywhere.'

Maureen inhaled deeply and slowly let the breath go. 'It's going to be all right,' she whispered to herself.

Andee stroked the back of her mother's neck. 'Of course it is,' she assured her.

Maureen started to nod without seeming to realise she was doing it. She gave a slight twitch and put a hand to her head. 'I wish Daddy was here,' she said.

Andee did too, but he wasn't. Trying to be upbeat, she said, 'We have each other, and think what it's going to be like for Penny seeing us after all these years.'

Maureen's face was bleak and colourless as she turned to Andee. 'You're right,' she replied. 'It's going to be much harder for her.'

Though Andee had conflicting thoughts about that, all she said was, 'Let's go and make some tea.'

Maureen led the way through a side door into the large kitchen-cum-sitting room that never failed to exude the irresistible cosiness that made everyone, family and visitors alike, reluctant to leave.

To Andee the place seemed hauntingly empty as they went about putting on the kettle and taking out mugs. It was as though, she thought, something indefinable had shifted. The house no longer seemed entirely theirs, as if it was preparing for new chapters in its existence, and she supposed it was.

'I should feel ecstatic,' Maureen suddenly declared. 'I think I do. Somewhere inside me I'm sure I do, but I'm so nervous, Andee. Why did she want us to think she was dead? The note she sent . . . We all thought . . .'

'We all thought the same,' Andee comforted her, 'but in our hearts, with there never being a body . . .'

'We never gave up hope of this day. But now it's here . . . Do you think someone forced her to write the note?'

'It's possible. Even likely, now that we know she's alive.'

'What if she hates us for not being able to find her? What am I . . . ?'

'Mum, stop,' Andee interrupted gently. 'She's not going to hate us . . .'

'But where has she been all this time? What's been happening to her? How did she find us? Tell me, how did she look?'

'She looked like a normal woman in her early forties. There was nothing to set her apart.' Andee tried to sound reassuring.

Maureen clearly needed more.

'She was quite stylish, well groomed,' Andee expanded. 'Her hair is blonde now, but her features are just the same, only older.'

'And her eyes?'

'The same colour as mine.'

'Does she still have freckles?'

'I don't think so.'

'What sort of car was she in?'

'A silver Mercedes which was being driven by somebody else. I've no idea who because I didn't see them.'

'I don't understand why she just drove off.'

Andee shook her head. 'Nor do I, but I expect she'll explain when we see her.' Though she didn't feel exactly confident of that, she wasn't going to say so to her mother. The last thing Maureen needed now was to try and cope with her elder daughter's misgivings.

'The truth is,' Andee said to Graeme later on the phone while her mother was having a lie-down, 'I've got no idea how I feel about seeing her again, because it changes by the minute.'

'It would when you've no way of knowing what to expect,' he replied.

'It's more than thirty years since your father died,' she ran on, 'so imagine how you'd feel if you suddenly found out he was still alive and wanted to see you.'

'I've tried putting myself in that very place,' Graeme admitted, 'and I know I'd be as thrown and as anxious as you are, excited too, of course, because he was a great guy. But pretending to be dead, deliberately removing himself from our lives, which is what it would mean in his case . . . I don't know if I could forgive that. But if we're looking at it that way, we're suggesting your sister was instrumental in her own disappearance. Do you think that could be the case?'

'No, no, of course not. She was only fourteen and she was depressed at the time, something we should have paid more attention to. But that doesn't explain why she's waited all these years to come back to us now.'

'Teenagers and depression can be a lethal combination, that's for sure. Have you thought any more about contacting the police?'

'My mother thinks we should wait to find out what Penny wants to do. Incidentally, she calls herself Michelle now. Michelle Cross.'

'And you've already Googled the name?'

'Mainly because I thought I recognised it, but no one came up to jog my memory, nor was there anyone who could conceivably be her. I might try again later, or I might just wait until she comes.'

'The day after tomorrow?'

'It's going to feel like an eternity, and heaven only knows what I'll do with my mother for all that time. We've no way of contacting her to ask if it can be sooner, so looks like we have to do it her way, and you can probably imagine how I feel about having someone else pulling my strings.'

Drily, he said, 'I can, but you have to consider that this probably isn't easy for her either.'

Hearing a repeat of her own words, Andee found herself relaxing for a moment, but was soon bristling again. 'It was easy enough for her to approach me in L'Isle-sur-la-Sorgue and ask if I remembered her,' she reminded him.

'OK, point taken. So how *are* you going to fill the time between now and when she comes?'

Hearing her mother on the stairs, Andee said, 'I'm sure we'll think of something. Tell me now, how are things going your end?'

Taking his cue, he said, 'Not bad. I've managed to pin the builder down at last. He's meeting me at Nadia's place on Friday at ten. I'll be there for most of tomorrow and Thursday with the cornice restorers and roofers. When you have a minute can you text or email me the details of the mirror chap you found on Avenue des Quatre Otages?'

'Actually, I left his card in a tray by the front door so you should have it.'

'Andee,' Maureen said quietly.

Andee turned to find her mother staring down at her mobile. 'I have to go,' she told Graeme. 'I'll call you later,' and taking her mother's phone she read the text that had clearly shaken Maureen quite badly.

Hi Mum, hope you're well. Really looking forward to seeing you. Do you remember Smoky, the kitten? He was so sweet, wasn't he? I wonder what happened to him? So many memories, lots to talk about, can't wait to hear all your news. Andee's too. Love Michelle.

Andee looked at her mother. 'When did it arrive?' she asked.

'A few moments ago. The jingle woke me.'

Andee went through to the sender's number, stored it and returned to the message. 'Smoky the kitten?' she asked her mother.

'I'd forgotten all about him,' Maureen replied. 'We gave him to Penny for her birthday one year, do you remember? She must have been eight or nine. He disappeared a few weeks later . . .' Her voice trailed off as her eyes stared glassily into the past.

'Mum?' Andee prompted gently.

Maureen looked at her.

'Are you all right?' Andee asked.

'We searched and searched,' Maureen told her. 'In the end we decided someone must have taken him.'

Andee kind of remembered, and frowned as she looked at the message again. Why bring it up now? 'She hasn't mentioned wanting to hear Daddy's news,' she observed.

'So maybe she knows he's gone.'

Experiencing a sudden surge of frustration, Andee went to the fridge and took out a bottle of wine.

'A large one for me,' Maureen said, sinking down at the table.

'How did she get your mobile number?' Andee demanded. 'You say she called the house phone before.'

Maureen shook her head as Andee passed her a glass and sat down too.

Picking up her mother's mobile again Andee tried calling the number, and wasn't surprised to find herself greeted by an announcement stating the mailbox was full and unable to take any more messages. She was faintly relieved, since she hadn't considered what she was going to say. Returning to the text she tapped in a reply, speaking the words aloud. *I'm looking forward to seeing you too. Where are you staying?*

Putting the phone down between them, Andee sipped her wine and stared at the mobile as they waited for a response.

Long minutes ticked silently by.

'She's not going to answer,' Maureen predicted.

Andee messaged again. *Do you have my address? Shall I send it to you?*

Still no reply.

'Maybe she's turned her phone off,' Maureen ventured, 'or she's in a bad reception area.'

Since either was possible, Andee put the phone aside and refilled their glasses. 'Even though she looked the same,' she said, 'apart from the hair, I'm still finding it hard to connect the woman I saw in France with my timid little sister.'

'She wasn't timid,' Maureen said emphatically.

Andee was surprised by this. It was how she remembered Penny, for the most part, but maybe that was because she'd shut out everything else. Memory often did that to a missing or dead person; it rubbed away the faults and turned qualities into almost saintly distinctions.

'You're both different people now,' Maureen reminded her.

While conceding the point, Andee said, 'The woman I saw seemed very confident, very sure of herself. That wasn't Penny.'

Maureen stared into her glass as she sank into her own thoughts, leaving Andee to wonder what they were, if she would even share them. She was about to ask when Maureen said, 'I sometimes wonder how well you knew her.'

Taken aback and slightly affronted, Andee waited for her mother to continue, but Maureen only sighed and drank more wine.

Andee found herself remembering the part of Penny's letter that had haunted her with the harshest of guilt for all these years. *I know I shouldn't say this, but sometimes I hate her for being so much better than I am at everything. No one ever seems to notice me when she's in the room. It's like I become invisible and I know she wishes I would go away. So that's what I'm going to do.*

Which meant that whatever had happened to Penny had been Andee's fault, or so she'd believed for most of her life.

Perhaps her mother did too.

Did she still believe it?

'Why do you think I didn't know her?' Andee asked guardedly.

Maureen shook her head slowly. It was a while before she said, 'You were just very different.' *Not close the way sisters should be; you were never very interested in her.* Though Maureen didn't say the words Andee could hear them, and felt undone by how wretched, even resentful they made her feel.

'We had so little in common,' she said. 'I loved sports, she hated them; I didn't have much of a temper, hers was terrible; she laughed at things that weren't funny, at least not to me, and we were young. We had different friends, different interests. There was nothing unusual about that.' She wished she didn't sound so defensive.

'No, of course not,' Maureen agreed.

'Then what are you saying?'

Maureen sighed. 'I'm not sure,' she replied. 'I guess, her being in touch is making me remember a lot of things I haven't thought about in years. It must be happening for you too.'

Of course it was; however, the moody sister she'd loved and yelled at, played with and rejected, cuddled and slapped, was impossible to connect with the woman she'd seen in France. The fourteen-year-old girl had gone for ever, so there was no point thinking about who she'd been then. It was who Penny was now that mattered, and how they were going to go forward once she was back in their lives.

Chapter Three

The following morning, after speaking for some time with Graeme on the phone, Andee arrived downstairs to find a note from her mother saying she'd gone to her yoga class.

Why don't you meet me at the Seafront Café for coffee at eleven? she'd added in a PS. *Text to let me know. I'm on library duty between twelve and three.*

Relieved that Maureen was keeping busy, Andee messaged to say she'd be at the café, and realising she should find something to do as well she rang Blake, Graeme's business partner, to find out if he needed any help at the shop.

'How soon can you get here?' Blake replied eagerly. 'Jenny's due back around eleven, but I need to go out now to make a delivery I promised yesterday.'

'I'm on my way,' she assured him, and retrieving her keys from the dresser drawer, she grabbed an apple from the fruit bowl and locked up behind her.

To her surprise, as she started to reverse out of the drive she found a motorcyclist blocking the way. Giving a brief toot on the horn to alert him to her need to exit she watched him in the rear-view mirror, certain he'd move out of the way, but he didn't.

Assuming he hadn't heard her through his helmet she tooted more firmly, but all he did was rev his engine and stay put.

Wondering what his problem was, she was about to get out of the car when a group of hikers strolled out of nearby Sheep Lane and he suddenly took off around the green.

A few minutes later Andee was driving along the narrow country road that snaked and dipped across the headland towards the edge of town, when she realised the motorcyclist was behind her. She couldn't be sure if he was purposely following her, but she had a feeling he was. Then he was so close that she was afraid to brake in case he went into the back of her. She speeded up and only just managed to swerve into a passing space as another car came around a bend towards her.

Once the other car had gone she waited for the motorcyclist to overtake, but he simply sat on her tail apparently waiting for her to move first. She stayed where she was, watching him in the wing mirror, realising he was trying to intimidate her. That she couldn't see his face through the black visor of his helmet was as annoying to her as the fact that he was too close for her to get his registration number.

Making sure her doors were locked, she lowered the driver's window and waved him on.

He stayed where he was, and revved aggressively.

Andee's police instinct kicked in and, suspecting

that this might be a mugging, she put her car into reverse and waited for him to spot the lights. Though he must have seen them he still didn't move, so pressing a foot on the accelerator she began edging back. Only when her bumper connected with the front wheel of his bike did he suddenly swerve out into the road and race past with a deafening roar.

He might have thought he was too fast for her to get the number, but if he had, he was wrong.

After entering it into her phone she drove on, half expecting to find him waiting around the next bend, but ten minutes later she was driving into town still apparently free of him.

As soon as she was parked she rang Barry Britten at Kesterly police station. Since ending her days as a detective sergeant with the Dean Valley force she'd stayed in regular contact with her former colleagues, mainly thanks to the freelance investigations she'd been persuaded into by Helen Hall, one of the town's more prominent lawyers. Whether her old boss, DI Terence Gould, had instructed his team to help her where they could, or whether they were just happy to anyway, she had no idea. She guessed the former, since Gould was regularly on her case to come back into the fold.

That certainly wasn't a part of her plan these days. She was very happy working with Graeme – she'd even completed a six-week Introduction to Interior Design course at the local college, and was intending to return for further instruction after the summer break. No, searching for missing people, especially children, was definitely behind her.

What lay ahead, with her sister coming back, was another matter altogether.

After giving Barry the motorcycle's details, she walked through the busy arcade towards the cobbled square where Graeme's antiques shop was located. The thought of Penny and what might happen in the next few days was making her feel very strange inside, and now this business with the motorcycle was throwing her off even more.

She didn't really think the motorcyclist was anything to do with her sister, but for a moment during their standoff the suspicion of a connection had been there. Even now the thought was wheedling its way around her normally trusty common sense, as though trying to insist there was no such thing as coincidence, when she knew very well that there was.

But why on earth would Penny, or anyone else come to that, send a motorcyclist to try and intimidate her? It was ludicrous even to think it.

Taking out her phone as it rang, she saw it was Barry and clicked on.

'The bike was stolen,' he told her. 'We've had a spate of thefts in the area. Kids mostly. They use them to mug people stupid enough to get out of their cars to find out what's going on.'

Since that had been her first suspicion Andee relaxed, and after thanking Barry she rang off, chiding herself for the uncharacteristic paranoia that had attributed the incident to her sister. Just because Penny had made contact the way she had in France, and was behaving oddly over texts and phone calls, didn't mean the motorbike had anything to do with her. Penny might be a stranger, but she wouldn't be out to intimidate Andee in that way.

Maureen was sitting on a bench in the changing rooms of the Downley leisure centre, only distantly aware of the thump and whirr of the spinning class going on in the studio next door. Her combined yoga and Pilates session had started several minutes ago, but she had yet to change into her leotard and leggings, or even open her locker.

She was staring blindly towards the mirrors and dryers, none in use at the moment, no one there to distract her from seeing back through the years to their lives in Chiswick, before Penny had vanished. And as the stress and anxiety of those times emerged from the past, the despair, the love and confusion followed by horror and grief began to feel as real now as they had been then.

Do you remember Smoky, the kitten? He was so sweet, wasn't he?

Why had Penny brought him up now, and in the way she had? Yes, Maureen remembered him. How could she ever forget?

The questions, the sickening shock of what had happened to the kitten were all over her, pushing any sense of today aside. She could see the dear little creature as clear as day, curling up on Andee's bed, and Penny becoming incensed by the disloyalty, even though Andee hadn't been there.

'He's not hers, he's mine,' she'd shrieked, snatching him up.

Startled and frightened, the kitten had scratched her, and Maureen had never forgotten the look that had come into Penny's eyes.

Remembering that time, Maureen felt her throat turn dry.

Yesterday, having wondered how well Andee had known her sister, Maureen had to admit that there were times she'd doubted how well she herself had known Penny. She'd loved her, of course, with all her heart; there had never been any doubt about that, at least not in her mind, but in Penny's . . . Had she ever really known what was going on in Penny's mind? One day she would be like any other girl her age, the next she could be sulky and withdrawn, defensive or aggressive, even violent.

She and Andee had argued a lot, even fought physically at times. Andee had always been the first to make up, while Penny, appearing quick to forgive, had been unable to hide, at least from Maureen, the way she was still brooding inside. She'd been full of contradictions and self-doubt – and consumed by a longing to be more like her sister. She'd adored Andee, while resenting her deeply. As Andee had progressed through her teens she had become increasingly irritated by Penny's sulks and outbursts. She'd accuse her of self-pity, and tell her to get a life or she'd never have any friends.

Penny hadn't always been without friends, though it was true she'd never managed to keep them for long, even when she was small. However, Maureen could remember pre-teen sleepovers at their house when she'd hear Penny giggling along with the others, sharing secrets, trying out make-up and creeping downstairs to raid the fridge for a midnight feast. She'd seemed happy and carefree during those times, just like any other young girl her age. Maureen had listened to them chattering away about pop bands and boys and who they were going to marry when they were older. Penny's crush had usually been on someone Andee was interested in, another source of irritation for Andee that had often ended in tears.

Penny was thirteen the first time she'd taken off. She'd said she was going to stay with a new girl at school called Madeleine, but it had turned out that Madeleine didn't exist and for three days no one knew where Penny was. Maureen still didn't know for certain where she'd been during that time, but she was sure her husband, David, had found out. He'd brought Penny home and taken her into his study for a very serious talking-to. Penny had come out swollen-eyed, angry and determined not to be contrite. She'd apologised to her mother, clearly because she'd been told to, and no one had referred to it again until the next time it happened.

'You have to tell me where she's going,' Maureen had shouted at David after he'd brought Penny home again.

'The least said soonest mended,' he snapped. 'She's grounded for the next month and all privileges are to be taken away.'

Penny had been furious with her father, but he'd remained unmoved even after she'd calmed down and tried to apologise.

'She's crying out for attention,' Maureen had told him, 'can't you see that?'

'Well she won't get it if she runs away,' he pointed out. 'Please don't try to take her side, Maureen. I can assure you I'm not being unreasonable, and she knows it.'

Neither Andee's nor Maureen's efforts to persuade Penny to tell them where she'd been had ever worked. Penny remained as close-lipped about it as her father, while her eyes seemed to glitter with the power of knowing something they didn't. That was until the sense of triumph finally turned to tears, and a horrible, black depression swallowed her into a pit of mumbling despair.

'Maureen? Are you all right?'

Startled, Maureen looked up to find a younger, sweet-faced woman stooping over her, her gentle blue eyes showing concern. 'Sorry,' Maureen muttered, collecting up her bag. 'Miles away.'

'You look pale,' the woman persisted. 'Can I get you something?'

'No, no really, I'm fine.' She knew this woman, but what was her name? She looked around, and found herself unable to connect with where she was.

'Maureen? What is it?'

Maureen shook her head. 'I should go,' she said, and leaving the woman staring worriedly after her she rushed outside to find her car.

'Another coffee while you wait?'

Andee glanced at her watch and looked up at Fliss, the owner of the Seafront Café, whom she'd known for years and liked a lot. 'I guess I could,' she replied. 'I don't know what's keeping her. She definitely said eleven and it's half past already.'

'You've tried calling, obviously?'

'And left several messages. It's not like her to be late.'

'Well, the road's up over by the leisure centre, so she could be stuck in traffic.'

Andee smiled gratefully and pushed her mug across the table. 'Better make it decaff this time,' she said, realising that her appetite for a biscotti or even a muffin had been swallowed up by concern.

Considering how uptight and distracted her mother was feeling right now, the failure to turn up, or message to say she was on her way, was worrying Andee more and more as the minutes ticked by.

She rang Graeme, needing to talk to someone, but she was pushed through to voicemail and the same happened when she tried her mother again.

Alayna texted to say she had the tickets for the *Strictly* show, and a few minutes passed as they went back and forth with details. Next came a message from the lawyer, Helen Hall, asking if they could get together when Andee was back from France. It was quickly followed by a text from Graeme's sisters attaching a photograph of themselves waving to her from a gondola in Venice.

Remembering that Luke had emailed earlier asking if his pictures of the baby rhino had arrived, she replied saying she hadn't seen them yet but would open them as soon as she got back to her computer.

By now it was a quarter to twelve. She'd finished her

second coffee and anger at herself was climbing all over her concern. Why on earth hadn't she put Penny's number into her own phone as well as her mother's? What a stupid oversight for someone like her. Except what was she saying here, that Penny had come along and kidnapped their mother?

No, she wasn't thinking that at all. However, it was possible that Penny had been in touch again and the two of them had made an arrangement to meet.

Her mother would have let her know if that were the case.

Maybe Maureen had gone to Graeme's shop, though why on earth she'd do that when she had no idea that Andee had been helping out between nine and eleven, Andee had no idea.

'Blake,' she said into the phone, 'I don't suppose my mother's wandered over your way, has she?'

'I haven't seen her,' he replied. 'Should I be looking out for her? It's Andee,' she heard him tell someone with him. 'Have you seen Maureen this morning?' To Andee he said, 'Hang on, Jenny wants to speak to you.'

A moment later Blake's wife was saying, 'I saw your mother at the gym earlier. I'd just come out of my spin class and found her sitting on her own in the changing rooms.'

Feeling a twist in her heart, Andee said, 'Did you speak to her?'

'Yes, but to be honest she didn't seem . . . I'm not sure . . . Well, she didn't seem to know who I was.'

Getting to her feet, Andee said, 'Was she still there when you left?'

'No, she rushed off saying she had to go.'

'She was due to meet me at eleven and she hasn't shown up,' Andee told her.

'Oh no. Is there anything I can do? Maybe she went to the library. Isn't it her day? It's just around the corner, shall I pop and see if she's there?'

'If you wouldn't mind,' Andee replied, handing some money to Fliss. 'I'll head over to the shop and meet you there.'

By the time Andee got through the bustle of the Inner Courtyard to Graeme's shop, Jenny had already rung to let her know that Maureen was at the library.

'Did she seem all right?' Andee asked, relief flooding her.

'Better than earlier,' Jenny replied, 'but to be honest I don't think she remembered seeing me, because when I asked if she was feeling better now she seemed surprised, as though she wasn't sure what I was talking about.'

Andee's insides turned over as she once again considered the turmoil her mother was in, far worse than Andee's own.

'What is it?' Jenny asked, as Andee sank into a Queen Anne walnut wing chair on the visitor's side of Graeme's desk. 'Something's going on. Is there anything I can do?'

Andee gazed around the shop, seeing but hardly registering the myriad treasures that had found their way down the years to pause here before setting off on the next stage of their journeys. She wished with all her heart that Graeme would walk through the door now. She was very fond of Jenny, and she longed to confide in her, but she knew, because of what Jenny and Blake had been through, that it would be an incredibly selfish thing to do. The Leonards' daughter, Jessica, had disappeared without trace for over two years, so they knew very well what it was like to experience that kind of fear and heartache. It was only after they'd called on Andee to help find her that the truth had emerged, but not in time to save the girl. She'd died the very day she'd gone missing, not murdered by a monster, but as the victim of a tragic accident that hadn't been reported.

Terrible though it was, the Leonards had had their closure, and were now doing their best to move on. Hearing about Penny was unlikely to help them with that, no matter how genuine or willing they might be in their offers of support.

'Andee?' Jenny gently urged. 'You're looking a bit like your mother did this morning. I don't want to pry, but if something's wrong . . .'

'No, it isn't, really,' Andee assured her. 'It's just that I saw this woman in France . . .' What was she saying? Why were these words coming out when she hadn't intended them to? 'My mother received a call, and a text. It turns out my sister, Penny . . .'

Jenny frowned in confusion. 'What about her?' she prompted.

'She's alive,' Andee stated, unable to stop herself.

Jenny's kindly blue eyes dilated with shock.

'It was her,' Andee continued, 'the woman I saw. I was in no doubt of it.'

'But what happened?'

Andee explained about the car that had pulled up to block her way. 'Then later the same day my mother rang to say she'd heard from someone who sounded just like me. We know how sisters sound alike.'

Jenny dropped into Graeme's leather-padded chair, clearly lost for words. 'So this is why you came back early?' she finally managed.

Andee nodded. 'Please don't mention it to anyone, apart from Blake, of course. I guess everyone will know soon enough, but for the moment my mother and I feel it's best to see her without the complications of police or media pressure.'

'Of course. Do you have any idea where she's been all this time? Or when you're likely to see her next?'

'No to the former. She's coming to the house tomorrow at three.'

Though apparently still thrown, Jenny regarded her carefully. 'How do you feel about it?' she asked, clearly sensing that Andee was far more disturbed by the way things were unfolding than relieved or joyful.

Andee shook her head as she sighed. 'Not how I'd expected to if it ever happened,' she confided, 'and nor does my mother. It's thrown us completely, mostly because of the way Penny's going about it. It's like . . . I don't know what it's like: it just doesn't feel good.'

'Does that mean it has to be bad?'

Andee shrugged. 'I guess not, but I keep seeing the car driving off as soon as she was sure I'd recognised her. She didn't want to engage any further, that much was clear. It was like she'd put down a marker, or played some sort of tease. And yesterday, she sent my mother a text asking if she remembered a kitten she'd had when she was small that disappeared and was never found. Much like she disappeared when she was fourteen – and was never found.' Her bemused and troubled eyes went to Jenny's. 'I'm asking myself, why bring that up about the kitten? Of all the things that happened when we were young . . . Why pick on that?'

'Maybe it was an attempt to establish that she really is your sister?' Jenny suggested. 'A shared memory, something no one else is likely to know about.'

'That would make more sense if she thought I was in any doubt about who she was. She knows I recognised her . . .'

They both looked up as someone came in to enquire about a Stölzle green glass bowl in the window.

As Jenny admired it with the woman and gave her some history on it, Andee checked her phone for messages, and finding one from Graeme she sent a quick text back saying she'd ring later.

'What's really bothering me,' she said to Jenny when they were alone again, 'is how she knew where to find me. If she'd turned up here, in Kesterly, that would be one thing, but in France . . .'

A few minutes ticked by as they sat with the mystery of that. In the end, Jenny said, 'Are you saying you think she's having you watched?'

Andee sat back, a hand to her head. 'I've no idea what she's doing,' she declared, 'but she apparently knew where to call my mother – we moved from Chiswick over twenty years ago – and she even has my mother's mobile number. How did she get hold of that?'

Having no answer, Jenny simply looked at her.

'I guess,' Andee said evenly, 'I'll just have to ask her – if she turns up, that is. If she doesn't . . .'

'What will you do?'

'The truth? I've absolutely no idea.'

Chapter Four

The following afternoon Andee and Maureen, appearing calmer than Andee suspected she felt, were staring at each other across the kitchen table, where a homemade coconut cake – Penny's favourite when she was young – and the best china were neatly set out as a welcome. It was only ten minutes to three, but they'd been ready for over half an hour, and now they'd finally run out of words that hadn't already been spoken dozens of times that day.

First thing this morning Maureen had said, 'I texted her the address. She'll probably remember it was Granny and Grandpa's place when she sees it.'

Feeling certain Penny already knew where they were, Andee said, 'Did she ask for it?'

'No, but I thought I should send it anyway, just in case she thinks we're still in Chiswick.'

Deciding not to point out that the first call had come to this house in Kesterly-on-Sea, which didn't have a London number, Andee said, 'Did you get a reply to the text?'

Maureen shook her head.

Andee stayed silent, not trusting herself to say anything impartial. Her mother was already stressed enough, she didn't need her elder daughter's anger adding to it. But Andee couldn't understand why Penny seemed to be toying with them.

At ten o'clock they'd driven into Kesterly so Maureen could get the ingredients for the cake as well as pick up some things for dinner in case Penny decided to stay for the evening – maybe even the night.

'Do you think I should get a room ready for her?' Maureen had asked during the drive home.

Finding it hard to imagine the woman she'd seen in France settling into their chintzy little guest room, Andee said, 'Do you want to?'

Maureen didn't answer. She was distracted, anxious, and Andee understood that, so she let the matter drop and continued to gaze out at the bay where a score of small sailboats were bobbing about the waves like sprightly ballerinas.

Now Maureen said, 'Maybe I should find some old photographs of her and put them on the mantelpiece with the rest of the family. She might find it hurtful to see she's not there. Do you think it was terrible of us to take them down? It was just so painful seeing her never getting any older . . .'

Andee looked at the framed shots of herself and the children, her mother and father, her grandparents and Maureen's nieces and nephews. There always used to be one of Penny, aged about ten, grinning widely and looking adorably mischievous. It was, Andee realised, how she'd come to remember her sister, since it was the only way she'd seen her for the fifteen or so years that it had been on display. It was as though she'd frozen in time, not as the fourteen-year-old who'd featured in the shots the police had circulated during the search for her, but as a younger, cuter version of the moody teenager with mussed dark hair and shocked, staring eyes.

'Do you still have any photos of her?' Andee asked.

'Of course. They'll be in the attic with the family albums.'

'So shall we get them down?'

Maureen regarded her warily. 'I can tell you don't think it's a good idea.'

Andee didn't, but wasn't sure why. Perhaps she didn't want to be too eagerly welcoming with Penny, after all this time.

'Are you looking forward to seeing her?' Maureen asked after another pause. Without waiting for an answer, she said, 'I wonder how she's feeling right now. Do you think she has far to come?'

Since Andee had no idea, she got up from her seat at the table and pulled her mother into a tender embrace.

'I wish Daddy was here,' Maureen said, for what must have been the hundredth time. 'Or do I? I wouldn't want him getting cross with her the way he used to. Except he wouldn't. He'd be nothing but relieved to know she was safe, and it won't be her fault that she hasn't been in touch for all these years.'

Though ready to accept that there might well have

been a period when Penny hadn't been in charge of her own destiny, Andee simply couldn't feel convinced that it had continued for the entire time she'd been gone. Certainly the woman in the Mercedes hadn't shown any signs of being controlled by anyone but herself.

'What if she doesn't come?' Maureen said now, gazing at the cake.

'We'll call Blake and Jenny and have a party,' Andee quipped.

Maureen's eyes shot to hers, and at last she managed a smile.

Smiling too, Andee said, 'If she does come, I'm wondering how we should greet her. With a nice big hug for the long-lost daughter/sister? A polite handshake for a stranger? How about a salute?'

'Stop it,' Maureen chided.

'Do we say hello Penny or hello Michelle?'

'I think I shall call her darling, or nothing at all, until we can work that one out. I wonder if she'll call me Mum? She did when she rang.'

Andee tensed as the clock in the hall chimed the hour.

Maureen glanced at her watch. 'It's a couple of minutes fast,' she reminded Andee.

Andee picked up her mobile as a text arrived.

Sorry, running about ten behind. Be there soon. M aka P Xxx PS: I took something of yours when I left, I wonder if you know what it was ☺

Andee's first thought was, 'So she has my mobile number too.' Her second thought, 'Does she think this is a game?' She passed the phone to her mother and went to fill the kettle.

'Do you know what she took?' Maureen asked.

Andee shook her head. She was feeling angry again; the sense of being controlled, or played, was seriously getting to her. Why on earth wasn't this gearing up to be the joyous family reunion she'd always imagined if her sister came home, the way her mother deserved it to be?

'She's upset you,' Maureen declared.

Throwing out her hands, Andee said, 'I just wish I knew what was going on with her. First that bizarre episode in France, then the text about the kitten, now this . . . Why is she running ten minutes late? Is it deliberate, to show some sort of power over us?'

'Maybe she came by train and has to wait for a taxi. She should have rung, we could have picked her up.'

Andee looked at her mother and felt a sudden urge to tell her they were going out, that they wouldn't be here when, if, Penny decided to show, because they had other things to do. Of course Maureen would refuse if she tried, so she didn't even attempt it. 'What did you mean yesterday,' she challenged, 'when you said that I didn't know Penny?'

Maureen gave a jerky sort of shrug as she gazed at the cake. 'I just meant that you two were very different,' she mumbled.

Reluctant to press her mother, but doing it anyway, Andee said, 'I think you meant more than that, so is there something you're not telling me?'

Maureen's eyes came up to hers, showing how helpless and anxious she felt. 'Please don't be angry,' she implored. 'We don't want to be in bad moods when she gets here.'

'I'm not angry,' Andee lied, although frustrated might have been a better word.

'The trouble is you're used to being in charge,' Maureen pointed out, 'but sometimes, and this is one of them, you have to ease up and just go with the flow.'

Amused by the way they were taking turns to bolster one another, Andee returned to the table and looked at her phone again. 'I should be feeling excited,' she said frustratedly, 'I want to believe that everything's going to be just wonderful, but it's not happening.'

'You're like Daddy. You never automatically trust anyone or anything. It's a part of having been a police officer.'

'Are you saying that you trust what's happening here?' Andee demanded. 'That you believe it's going to be wonderful?'

'I'm trying to,' Maureen insisted. 'And it is wonderful that she's alive. You have to admit that.'

Knowing she wouldn't be ready to explore how she felt until after she'd seen her sister, Andee sat down and regarded her mother keenly as they continued to wait. The fact that Maureen had avoided her question about knowing more than she was letting on hadn't escaped Andee, but now wasn't the time to push it any further. However, if Maureen thought they wouldn't return to it she was gravely mistaken, particularly when Andee had always believed she knew everything there was to know about her sister's disappearance. She'd seen the police files, had even carried out an investigation herself some ten years after the initial, exhaustive search, so what else could there be to know? But her mother's comment yesterday had made Andee feel that there *was* something else. If so, it hardly made any sense for her mother to be holding it back, especially from Andee, but Maureen was nervous about something, that much was clear.

It was just after three fifteen when they heard a car pulling up outside.

Maureen's eyes shot to Andee's. Her face had paled.

With her insides knotting, Andee said, 'Do you want me to go?'

'We both should,' Maureen replied, and got to her feet.

Feeling strangely disconnected from what was about to happen, as though she was watching rather than participating, Andee led the way along the hall, past her father's paintings that decorated the cream-coloured walls, to the rarely used front door. He'd painted the landscapes during the worst of his grief, a form of therapy designed to distract him, and in a small way it had seemed to help.

Though Andee had no deep-rooted belief in the afterlife, she couldn't help wondering if he was watching them now, and if he was, what he was thinking. Did he feel, as she did, that it would be better if their meeting weren't happening like this, or was he quietly rejoicing that his girls were finally about to be reunited?

No one had rung the bell or knocked on the door, but someone was outside, Andee could see their shape through the frosted glass. She turned to her mother. Maureen's eyes were bright with emotion. Her hands were bunched at her throat. She looked older all of a sudden, and smaller. She gave Andee a weak smile of encouragement, and feeling as though she was going through the motions of a long-rehearsed scene from some dystopian play, Andee swung the door wide and found herself face to face with the woman she'd last seen in the back of a Mercedes.

She wasn't as tall as Andee had expected – though Penny had never been tall – or quite as composed as she'd seemed that day in France, but the blonde hair was as immaculate as the make-up, and the outfit as expensive as the leather bag over her arm. Her smile seemed hesitant, even slightly shy, while the curiosity and eagerness in her aqua eyes sent Andee spinning back through the years.

Different and unexpected as she was, any lingering doubt that this was her sister vanished along with whatever Andee had intended to say.

'I'm sorry I'm late,' Penny said, and Andee, disoriented by her own emotions, turned round as her mother sobbed.

'I can't believe it,' Maureen gulped, holding out her arms. 'Oh my goodness, my goodness,' and as she folded her younger daughter into the agonised tenderness of her embrace, Andee watched from inside a profound sense of unreality. She glanced outside and saw a silver Mercedes at the gate with a suited man in the driver's seat. Presumably the same car, the same driver that had been in France.

'Andee,' Penny murmured holding out an arm.

Realising she was being invited to join the hug, Andee stepped obediently into it.

'Mummy, my very own mummy,' Penny smiled through her tears as she clasped Maureen's hands to her chest. 'I can't tell you how good this feels, how I've dreamt about this moment ... Is it really happening?'

'You look so ... So ... grown up,' Maureen spluttered with a laugh. 'In my mind I kept seeing you as a teenager, and now here you are ...' She looked at Andee, and Andee remembered to smile.

'My beautiful big sister,' Penny enthused, gazing directly into Andee's eyes. There was something behind the tenderness in Penny's, a kind of wariness, or amusement, or an emotion too well masked for Andee to read. 'You've hardly changed,' Penny ran on, 'apart from to get even more beautiful. I always knew you would. And you're tall, just like Daddy.'

Was there resentment in her tone? Their difference in height had always been a sore point for Penny. There was none that Andee could detect.

Andee simply smiled again and closed the door.

'Is anyone else here?' Penny asked, glancing down the hall.

'No, we haven't told anyone,' Maureen replied. 'We weren't sure you'd want us to yet.'

Penny said, 'So no one's been here – ahead of me?'

Curious, Andee countered, 'Like who?'

Penny laughed. 'I've no idea, but I do think it's important for us to have this time to ourselves, don't you? There's so much catching up to do, and we really don't need all the distractions of the police and media. After all, this isn't anyone's business but ours.'

Andee didn't disagree, but she was preoccupied with wondering if Penny really thought the press and authorities were ahead of her, or if her question had been about someone or something else entirely.

With a playful twinkle Penny turned back to Maureen. 'There's so much I want to ask you, and tell you, the question is where to begin?'

In spite of having several suggestions for that, Andee gestured for everyone to go inside.

'We've got tea and coconut cake,' Maureen announced as they went into the kitchen, clearly waiting for Penny to comment on how wonderful it was that her mother had remembered.

Penny said, 'I'm sure I'm too excited to eat a thing.'

Hiding her disappointment, Maureen tried again. 'Maybe we should be having champagne. Oh my, I still can't believe . . . Is it really you? I know it is. Andee's right, you haven't changed . . .'

'Apart from to get older,' Penny said wryly. She was looking around the room, taking everything in. 'You've redecorated, and the furniture's different, but it's still taking me straight back to my childhood and all the school holidays we spent here with cousin Frank. How is he? Are you still in touch with him?'

'Of course,' Maureen assured her, starting towards

64

the family photos then apparently changing her mind. 'He's married now, and his children are all grown up, like Andee's.'

'You have children?' Penny directed at Andee, appearing delighted. 'Of course, I should have known you would. What're their names? How old are they?'

'Luke's twenty-one and Alayna's nineteen,' Maureen told her proudly. Andee remained silent, appraising Penny, and letting her mother do the talking.

'So have they left home?' enquired Penny.

'Oh yes, a while ago,' Maureen replied. 'But we still see them quite often and they're in touch all the time. Luke's currently in Africa helping to save rhinos, and Alayna's at Bristol Uni studying English and drama. She's planning to go off travelling for a year when she finishes.'

Penny's eyebrows rose with interest.

'She decided to take her gap year after she graduates,' Maureen explained. 'She's working and saving very hard to finance her trip.'

Deciding this was enough about her children, Andee said to Penny, 'What about you? Are you a mother?'

Penny laughed and rolled her eyes. 'I'll tell you all about it,' she promised, 'but first shall we sit down and have a cup of tea?'

Andee filled the teapot while Maureen fussed about with napkins, listening and chuckling as Penny fondly recalled how she and Andee, with their cousin Frank, used to ride their bicycles down to the caravan parks of Perryman's Cove, known locally as Paradise Cove, to make friends with kids from all over the world.

'The world?' Andee echoed, bringing the pot to the table.

'OK, the country,' Penny conceded, 'but there were a couple of kids from Germany once, as I recall, and you must remember that hilarious hippy family from Ireland.'

Actually, Andee did remember them, the Irish and the Germans, and she wondered if this was an attempt on Penny's part to prove she wasn't an impostor.

'You fell in love with one of the Irish boys,' Penny teased. 'He was completely gorgeous. All the girls fancied him, and we were devastated when his girlfriend turned up for the second week. What was his name?'

'Actually, it was a Welsh boy, Evan, whose girlfriend turned up for the second week,' Andee reminded her.

'Oh, that's right, but it was the same year, I'm sure of it. What was the Irish boy's name?'

'I can't remember.'

'Well, it was a long time ago, and we were falling in and out of love all over the place back then. How could we possibly remember them all?'

'I had no idea you were having so many romantic adventures,' Maureen commented wryly.

'Oh, it was all perfectly innocent,' Penny assured her, adding with a wink at Andee, 'until it wasn't.'

Wondering why she'd added that when it had never been anything but innocent, Andee poured the tea while blushing Maureen cut the cake.

'So fancy you living in Granny and Grandpa's house now,' Penny remarked, looking around again. 'I can't tell you how thrilled I was when I found out. It would be awful to think of strangers here.'

'Exactly when did you find out?' Andee enquired mildly.

Penny frowned as she thought. 'Quite recently,' she admitted. 'I guess it was in one of the first reports I received.'

Andee's eyes flicked to her mother.

Penny laughed. 'I'm sorry, I have to confess that I hired someone to find out all about you. I felt I had to before I got in touch so I could work out whether or not I'd be welcome. Of course as soon as I was told you'd been a detective, Andee, I knew you'd be sceptical, ready to pick apart anything I said, and I honestly don't blame you. I'm sure I'd be the same if the tables were turned. All these years and no contact, you must be asking yourself why suddenly now?'

Andee waited for her to answer the question.

'I've wanted to be in touch many times,' Penny told their mother. 'I've hated holding back, but it's taken until now for me to feel confident about approaching you.'

'But you're my daughter,' Maureen exclaimed, 'there was never any reason to hold back.'

Penny smiled and lowered her eyes to her plate. As she lifted a dainty fork to eat Andee noticed that her hands were covered to the base of her fingers by a glove-like extension to her silk sleeves. She was wearing an exquisite gold band studded with yellow sapphires or diamonds on the third finger of her left hand, and a more subtle assortment of rings on the other, but there was no disguising the cracked and flaking soreness of her skin. Penny had never suffered with eczema as a child, but she apparently did now. 'I needed to be in the right place, up here, to answer your questions,' she said softly, tapping her head.

'And you feel you are now?' Andee asked.

Penny nodded slowly, still not looking up. 'I think so. It won't be easy, for any of us, and I kept asking myself if it wouldn't be better just to let things go on as they were. You're used to me being gone. The space I left has long since filled up, and I've made a new life for myself . . . Why disrupt it?'

Why indeed, Andee was asking herself. 'But you decided to,' she said shortly, 'and now here you are.'

Apparently unfazed by Andee's manner, Penny sighed softly as she reached for her mother's hand. 'Yes, here I am,' she said. 'We've got so much time to make up for, so many stories to share.'

Though Maureen was smiling, her eyes were uncertain as they moved briefly to Andee's.

Understanding that her mother wanted her to continue asking the questions, Andee said, 'Naturally, the first story we'd love you to share is what happened to you all those years ago. Where did you go? Why could no one ever find you?'

'Mmm,' Penny murmured, nodding her head as she gazed absently down at her cake. Then quite suddenly she gasped. 'This always used to be my favourite. I can't believe you remembered. I haven't had it in years. Did you make it?' Her eyes were bright with surprise and affection as she looked at her mother.

'Yes, I did,' Maureen told her, flushing with pleasure. 'I'm not sure it's as good as I used to make it . . .'

'Oh, I'm sure it is,' and digging in with her fork Penny helped herself to a generous mouthful. 'Mmm, it's perfect,' she insisted, showering a few crumbs. 'Oh God, it's bringing back so many memories.'

Andee said, 'Such as where you went all those years ago, and why no one could find you?'

Maureen stared an admonishment as all the joy seemed to drain from Penny, and she put her fork down again.

'That was a strange time,' she said quietly, 'and it was so long ago that it feels now as though it happened to somebody else.'

But it didn't, it happened to you, Andee wanted to point out, *so now please tell us what we need to know.*

'It's not a good story,' Penny admitted, gazing into the distance, 'and definitely not one for us to start with. It'll bring us all down and I think today should be about celebrating our reunion, don't you?'

Andee would have pressed her, had Maureen not said, 'You're right, dear, it should be a celebration, and if it upsets you to dwell on those times . . .'

'It does,' Penny confessed, 'quite a lot, but I've had counselling, and fortunately for the most part I've managed to put it behind me. I'm afraid I still have nightmares from time to time, but I have such a lot to feel thankful for now.'

They waited for her to elaborate, but she didn't. Seconds ticked by, until Maureen said brightly, 'Well, you look marvellous.'

Penny smiled. 'Yes, my life is very different now to what it was when I first went away, but a lot of years have passed, and things always change.'

'So what do you do now?' Andee enquired.

Penny shrugged as if to say, where to begin? 'I have an import-export company that we run from London,' she replied. 'A real estate and property management company, also based in London. Two medical centres, one in Connecticut, the other in Houston. A travel agency that we run out of Stockholm,' her eyes danced playfully, 'and as of about a year ago we have a highly exclusive online dating agency.'

Maureen was clearly as stunned as she was impressed.

Andee said, 'We?'

'I have a number of partners,' Penny explained, taking out her phone as it rang. After checking who it was she said, 'Will you think me terribly rude? It's a call I've been waiting for and I really ought to take it. I'll be just a minute,' and clicking on she announced herself, 'Michelle,' as she got to her feet and began speaking in a language Andee couldn't even identify, much less understand.

'Nej, han har inte varit här.' (No, he hasn't been here.) *'Ja, jag är säker.'* (Yes, I'm sure.) *'Hur tror du det känns att vara tillbaka här?'* (How do you think it feels being back?)

Penny laughed in a vaguely bitter way. *'Allt är ett spel, det bara beror på hur man spelar det.'* (Everything's a game, it just depends how you play it.)

Andee watched her mother's eyes following Penny out of the back door on to the patio. They had no idea what had been said, or who Penny had been talking to.

The phone call, the incomprehensible language was emphasising more than ever what different worlds they inhabited.

Turning to Andee, Maureen murmured, 'She's obviously doing very well for herself.'

Andee said, archly, 'And managing not to tell us very much.'

Maureen's nod was slow, pensive.

'Especially about the time she disappeared. Do you have any idea why she's being so reticent?' Andee asked.

Hearing the challenge, Maureen looked at Penny again as she said, 'She just told us, she'd rather not talk about it, and if it was that bad who can blame her?'

'Mum,' Andee said darkly.

'Please don't be like that,' Maureen protested. 'She's hardly been here . . . Ssh, she's coming back.'

Andee watched her sister return, tucking away her phone and breaking into a smile. 'All sorted,' Penny declared, closing the door behind her, 'but I'm afraid time is running out and there are several more calls I need to make.'

'You can use the front room,' Maureen offered. 'You'll be nice and private in there.'

Penny tilted her head fondly. 'That's so kind of you, but I've booked myself into the Kesterly Royal for tonight. It'll be easier if I work from there. I was hoping we could meet again tomorrow before I go back to London?'

'Yes, yes of course,' Maureen agreed, glancing at Andee. 'We'd love that, but it's been so short today. Are you sure you can't stay any longer?'

'I wish I could, really I do, but I'm afraid my time isn't my own. Could we meet for lunch tomorrow? I hear the Royal has a very good restaurant overlooking the bay.'

'The Palme d'Or,' Maureen told her.

Penny came to hug her. 'I'll book a table for one o'clock. I hope you'll join us, Andee.'

'I wouldn't miss it,' Andee assured her, and after coolly returning her sister's embrace she remained in the kitchen while her mother went to the front door.

'She's got a chauffeur,' Maureen stated when she came back.

Andee raised an eyebrow as she slid Penny's teacup into a plastic bag. She might not doubt that the woman who'd drunk from it was her sister, but Detective Inspector Gould would almost certainly want to run a more scientific check.

Maureen was staring at the chair Penny had vacated. 'Did I just dream all that?' she murmured.

'Have some more tea,' Andee advised.

Sitting down, Maureen pushed her hands through her hair as Andee poured.

Andee allowed several minutes to pass before she spoke in a quiet, but steely voice. 'I really don't know what's going on with her,' she said, 'but why is she in touch with us now after allowing us to think she was dead for so many years? I think there's more to it than her being ready to reconnect.'

Maureen flicked a glance her way, but said nothing.

'Mum, please talk to me. I feel like you're keeping something back . . .'

Maureen shook her head.

Andee took a breath. 'As you said yourself, I never automatically trust anyone or anything, but you usually do. And the fact that you've been more nervous than excited about seeing Penny is telling. I'm getting the sense that you know more about her disappearance than you're letting on, and it's tearing you apart.'

'OK, OK, but it's not what you . . . Actually, I don't know what you think, but it's been so long since we talked about her, I mean really talked about her, and you've either forgotten, or chosen to forget what she could be like.'

Accepting that was at least partly true, Andee waited for her to continue.

'It's not unusual,' Maureen told her. 'When someone dies, or disappears the way she did, you only remember the good things. It's human nature; it's the same for everyone. You put all the other things out of your mind. I told myself she was just a child, that they had nothing to do with why she went, and I still don't know that they did.'

'What other things?' Andee asked.

'You really don't remember?'

'Why don't you just tell me?'

Maureen swallowed hard and ran her hands over her face. 'Well, there were times,' she began, 'that I felt your sister did things deliberately to make herself . . . to annoy or even to hurt people. She didn't seem . . .' She shook her head. 'She never really seemed sorry when she said it, or to care if she was punished. She'd put on a show of being upset . . . Sometimes I think the tears were real, but there were other times . . . I don't know, it was like she was behaving the way we thought she should rather than the way she felt.'

'Did you ever talk to Daddy about her – behaviour?' Andee asked.

'Actually, we talked about it endlessly before she went and after she'd gone. We never knew if the depressions were genuine, or if they were something she'd read about and decided to pretend were afflicting her. I mean, obviously something was wrong or she wouldn't have been the way she was, or run away as often as she did . . .'

'Did you ever find out where she went?'

Maureen shook her head. 'I think Daddy knew. He never told me, he thought it was best for me not to know . . .'

'But she's your daughter! How could it be best for you not to know?'

'Times were different back then and your father was very . . . protective.'

'How was holding information back from you protecting her?'

'It wasn't just her he was protecting, it was me, and you.'

'From what?'

'I didn't ask.'

'Not even when she didn't come back?'

'If your father had wanted me to know, if he'd felt it would help in some way to find her, he'd have told me.'

Stunned by such blind faith, and lack of maternal strength, Andee said, 'So where do you *think* she went all those times?'

Maureen sighed. 'I told myself she was with homeless people, and I think she was . . .' When she broke off, Andee used silence to demand more, but Maureen stayed silent too.

'Mum, you obviously believe something else, even if you never knew it for certain.'

Maureen's cheeks coloured. 'OK, I think he found her with men,' she admitted finally.

'What men?'

'I don't know.'

'I think you do.'

'I swear I don't.'

Andee was ready to scream. 'Why did you never tell the police what you suspected?' she cried. 'It wasn't in any of your statements . . .'

'Your father knew what I thought . . . what I was afraid of. Andee, please don't shout at me. If there had been . . .'

'Mum, Penny was thirteen the first time she disappeared, and only fourteen when she went for good. That makes her . . .'

'I know what you're going to say, but I'd rather not have it spelt out, thank you very much.'

Andee clutched her head. 'I can't believe you're only telling me this now . . .'

'We thought she was dead. Why would I try to make you think badly of her when it wasn't going to bring her back?'

'You know I investigated her disappearance. You could have told me then.'

'Maybe, but you didn't ask . . .'

'I most certainly did. We went over and over your statements . . .'

'OK, you did, but if there had been any men you can be sure your father would have found them. Now, if you don't mind, I'd like a very large glass of wine, and perhaps we can sit quietly for a few minutes while I try to gather my thoughts.'

They were still sitting at the table, silently reeling from the past few minutes, when Maureen's mobile rang. Seeing it was Carol, her closest friend and Andee's mother-in-law, calling from Spain, Maureen hesitated.

'Should I tell her about Penny?' she asked Andee.

Andee baulked at the very idea. Until she'd managed to straighten things out in her mind she didn't want anyone else's thoughts or reactions to cloud it, and certainly not her estranged husband's, who was currently in Spain with his mother. Carol would be bound to tell him. 'Let's see how tomorrow goes first,' she cautioned, and leaving her mother to it, she took herself up to her room to make some calls of her own.

The first was to the Kesterly Royal Hotel, who politely informed her that they had no one booked in for that night by the name of Michelle Cross, or Penny Lawrence. The second was to her old boss, DI Terence Gould, asking him to call back when he got her message. The third was to Graeme.

After filling him in on the details of Penny's visit and brushing over the scene she'd had afterwards with her mother, Andee said, 'So now, you tell me, why has Penny come back after all these years, when she appears to be doing very well, and has no apparent need of us? Because I certainly have no idea.'

Sounding as bemused as she did, Graeme ventured, 'Sentimental reasons? Even if she's doing well, maybe it doesn't mean anything if she has no family to share it with.'

'We don't know that she has no family. She didn't answer the question when I asked, which is odd, or certainly if she's a mother. Why not just say that she has children – or not?'

'So her return is something to do with conscience? She feels guilty about not letting you know she's alive, and now she's putting it to rights.'

'She's had a very long time to do that, and she's chosen not to. So I go back to my first question, why now? Incidentally, she admitted to hiring someone to find out about us ... And let me read you the text she sent before she got here earlier. "*I took something of yours when I left, I wonder if you know what it was.*"'

'Do you?'

'No.'

'Did you ask her?'

'I didn't get the chance. She wasn't here more than twenty minutes, and during that time all we really managed to get out of her was how successful she is, but even that was vague.'

'Do you believe it?'

'She was carrying a Hermès bag, and wearing some expensive-looking jewellery. Oh, and she was driven here by a chauffeur. I'm pretty sure it was the same car that I saw in France.'

'Did she explain about that? Why she just drove off?'

'I'll make sure she does the next time we meet, which is supposed to be at the Palme d'Or tomorrow.' Making a mental note to check if there was a reservation, Andee said, 'I called the hotel just now and they don't have anyone staying there under the name of Michelle Cross or Penny Lawrence.'

'So you're thinking she might have another alias? Or she's staying somewhere else?'

'I guess anything's possible. I've left a message for Terence Gould to call me.'

Sounding surprised, he said, 'So you're going to involve the police?'

'Off the record, for the moment, because things are definitely not adding up for me. Why, for instance, did she seem to think that someone might have paid us a visit ahead of her?'

'Really? Like who?'

'I've no idea, but my gut is telling me it could be why she came.'

'Which leads us to what, exactly?'

'Good question; I'll let you know when I have an answer. Oh, and she pretended not to know that I had children, when it surely must have come up in one of her reports. I'd love to know how in-depth they are and how long they've been going on.'

'Indeed. What did you call her, by the way? Michelle or Penny?'

'I don't think we called her anything, but she called herself Michelle when she answered the phone. After that she spoke in another language and before you ask, I've no idea what it was. Definitely not French or Italian. Could have been Dutch. Actually, she mentioned having a business in Stockholm.'

'What sort of business?'

'A travel agency.'

'Called?'

'She didn't say. I wonder if she'll make it for lunch tomorrow? I have a feeling she won't.'

'Well, I guess you'll find out when you get there, presuming she's not in touch sooner. Don't forget to let me know if she is.'

Chapter Five

Maureen received a text at nine the following morning.

Hope you had a good night. Too excited to sleep much myself. Would it be possible to come and see you at eleven? Have to return to London earlier than expected and I don't want to leave without seeing you. There's still so much to catch up on. Love Penny/Michelle.

After reading it Andee handed the phone back to her mother. 'Interesting that she's asking to come when I won't be here,' she commented.

Maureen looked startled. 'But how on earth would she know that you're going to the shop this morning?'

Having no sensible answer for that, Andee said, 'Let's put it down to paranoia, and I'll change my plans.' The fact that she'd arranged to see DI Gould wasn't one she'd shared with her mother, and wouldn't until she'd heard what he had to say.

Clearly relieved not to have to deal with Penny alone, Maureen mumbled, 'Thank you,' and sat quietly staring at the table, blinking only when Andee put some toast in front of her. 'Are you going to ask her if she stayed at the Royal?' she ventured.

'If I get the chance, but there are other questions I'd like answers to first. I'm sure you would too?'

Maureen simply sighed. She was looking tired this morning and distracted, which was hardly surprising when her mind, her thoughts, were running around in jumbled and difficult circles.

'Would you like me to see her on my own?' Andee offered.

'No, no, I should be here. I *want* to be here.' Maureen's eyes came up, and her face seemed pinched and sallow as she said, 'If you can, I'd like you to find out where she went when she left all those years ago. I know she says it's painful for her, but it was painful for us too.'

'Of course,' Andee replied softly. 'Do you happen to have any theories you'd like to share with me before I go there?' she asked.

To her surprise Maureen said, 'Yes, I do, but I'd rather hear what she has to say first.'

Andee sat down slowly, keeping a hand on her mother's shoulder as she controlled her frustration. 'Let me get this straight,' she began, 'yesterday you said you thought there might be men involved, and now you're saying that you had an idea *where* she might have gone?'

Maureen looked so uncomfortable and apprehensive that Andee might have backed off if it weren't so important.

'Did Daddy know where she went?' Andee pressed.

Maureen shook her head.

Not sure if that was a no, or please don't ask, Andee

said, 'Did he know that you had suspicions of where she might be?'

Maureen stared down at her plate; her hand was shaking. 'Yes, he did,' she mumbled, 'but nothing ever came of it.'

'So he followed up on your suspicions?'

Maureen nodded.

'Where are we talking about?'

'I don't know. I mean, it wasn't . . . It was who . . . I was afraid of who she was with.'

Andee sat back in her chair, needing some time to assimilate the enormity of this. Probably the hardest part of it was the fact that nothing like this had shown up in the police files, which could only mean that her parents – her *father*, whose integrity she'd never doubted – had held things back from the investigation. 'So *who* are we talking about?' she asked carefully.

Her mother didn't answer.

'Pimps? Traffickers?'

'No, no, nothing like that.'

Unable to think of anything else, though realising that her mind was coloured by experiences in the force, Andee stared hard at her mother.

'I know that look,' Maureen told her, 'but I'm not going any further with this until after we've heard what Penny has to say. It could be I'm wrong, and if I am . . . Well, I'd rather . . . I'd rather not speak ill of the dead.'

Andee reeled. 'Are we talking about Daddy?' she demanded incredulously.

'No, of course not. It's just . . . Well, I think I've said enough. I'd like to have some breakfast now.'

Andee's eyes didn't let go of her mother's face. Were it anyone else in the world she'd never have backed down, not that she was doing so now, but she was reluctant to try and force answers out of her mother when she looked about ready to fall apart.

'What on earth does she mean she doesn't want to speak ill of the dead?' she cried down the line to Graeme, with the bathroom door closed and shower running to drown out her voice. 'Who the heck's she talking about? She says it's not my father, but I can't think of anyone else.'

'OK, this is a long shot,' Graeme replied after giving it some thought, 'but what about your grandparents? They're both dead, and died after Penny went . . .'

Andee was shaking her head. 'They were devastated when she disappeared. They never got over it. Grandpa even stopped speaking . . . It was awful, especially for my father. He'd lost his daughter, and then he was seeing his parents deteriorate in front of his eyes.'

'Were they living in Kesterly at the time?'

'In this very house, which is where Penny and I spent most of our school holidays until the time she vanished. I came the following year with my cousin Frank, and I think the year after that. It wasn't the same, obviously. We were miserable and scared and Granny and Grandpa didn't really know how to handle us. Then my parents sold up in Chiswick and moved here. No one was coping well and my father, who was probably more broken than any of us, wanted to try and hold us all together.'

Sighing, Graeme said, 'We saw what Blake and Jenny went through when their daughter disappeared, but eventually, thanks to you, they had an answer, or closure as some would call it. For your family . . . So many years . . .'

'But we know Penny's alive now, which should be all our prayers coming true, except it's starting to feel as though some kind of nightmare is just beginning.'

It was a little before eleven when the chauffeur-driven Mercedes pulled up outside Briar Lodge and Penny, looking spruce and elegant, got out of the back. She was wearing cream-coloured slacks and a matching shirt with long sleeves cut to cover her hands – she must have them made specially, Andee decided.

As Andee watched her glancing around the hamlet, taking in the scenery and sea air, she was thinking of the ghosts that could be watching too, her father, her paternal grandparents, and her mother's mother who'd suffered along with everyone else when her youngest grandchild had disappeared without trace.

Had her grandparents known more than they'd ever told?

'I hope the change of plan isn't a problem?' Penny grimaced playfully as she kissed Andee on both cheeks. She smelled of expensive perfume, and peppermints, and as she touched her hands to her cheeks Andee couldn't help wondering if it was a deliberate gesture to show she wasn't wearing any rings today.

Andee stood aside for her to go in, saying, 'Mum's in

the kitchen,' and after quickly clocking the registration number of the Mercedes she entered it into her phone and went to join them.

Finding them locked in a tearful embrace, Andee went to fetch the coffee pot and three mugs. As she poured she said to Penny, 'Do you take yours black or white?'

'Oh, I'm sorry, I don't drink coffee,' Penny apologised, 'but please don't mind me. I'll be very happy with water.'

'We can make tea,' her mother offered. 'It won't be any trouble.'

'Water's fine,' Penny assured her.

Filling a glass from the tap, Andee put it on the table and passed her mother a coffee.

'Lovely,' Penny declared after taking a sip of Kesterly's finest. Smiling at Andee she said, 'By the way, did you work out what I took of yours when I left?'

Andee hid her irritation as she shook her head. In truth she hadn't given it much thought, largely because she'd wanted to resist being pulled into some sort of mind game, presuming that was what it was.

Penny laughed. 'I really thought you'd have realised, but there again I don't suppose it was amongst your most treasured possessions.'

Maureen looked from one to the other. 'Are you going to tell us what it was?' she prompted Penny.

Penny seemed to consider it, then apparently decided against it as she said, 'I didn't stay at the Royal last night. I thought I'd try the Kingsmere opposite the marina instead. It was very comfortable, in fact quite respectable for a four star. I wouldn't have a problem recommending it to anyone coming this way.'

Not particularly interested in her TripAdvisor review, Andee said, 'Are we allowed to ask what's taking you back to London so soon?'

Appearing surprised, Penny said, 'You're allowed to ask anything, and the answer is business, of course.' She checked her phone even though it hadn't rung. 'A problem's come up that we didn't foresee,' she confided. She appeared slightly strained as she added, 'We'll get it sorted, of course.' At that moment her phone rang and she quickly clicked on. 'Yes?' she barked shortly. She listened, keeping her eyes down, until eventually she said, 'OK, stay on it . . . I should be there by four.'

As she rang off she looked as though she'd like to swear before her expression brightened and she was smiling again. 'Things rarely run smoothly, do they?' she commented wryly.

'Is there anything we can do?' Maureen offered.

Penny laughed as she said, 'I'm not entirely sure what to do myself, but don't let's think about it now. It's not . . .' She broke off as her phone rang again. 'Yes, I was informed last night,' she told the caller, 'and yes I'm coming back to London. This afternoon. *Nej, naturligtvis vet jag inte var de är. Då hade jag ju inte varit här. Jag måste gå nu.* (No, of course I don't know where they are. I wouldn't be here if I did. I have to go now),' and she abruptly ended the call. 'I'm sorry,' she grimaced, 'I'll turn it off or this will keep happening.'

'It sounds serious,' Andee commented.

Penny hesitated, seemed on the brink of saying something, then appeared to change her mind. 'It could become so, if we don't get ahead of it,' she declared, 'but please let's forget it for now and use what time we have to carry on getting to know one another.' She gave an amused, incredulous shake of her head, using the moment, Andee felt, to refocus herself. 'My mother and my sister. I have family. Of course, I've always known it, but being here, seeing you again after all these years . . . I should have come sooner. I wish I had, but I was so afraid you wouldn't want to see me.'

'We've always wanted to know what happened to you,' Maureen assured her, clearly distressed that she could think otherwise. 'It's dominated our lives.'

Penny looked from her mother to Andee and back again. 'Well, I can believe you were probably upset and even worried at first, after all I was only fourteen, but as time went on . . .'

'Upset? Worried?' Maureen cut in incredulously. 'We were beside ourselves. We thought you were dead. The note you sent . . .'

Penny frowned.

Andee's senses were suddenly alert.

Maureen said, 'The note that turned up after you disappeared. The things you said . . .'

Penny waved a dismissive hand and sighed. 'I remember it now,' she said, 'and it wasn't my idea. I just went along with it because it seemed like the right thing to do at the time. If you thought I was dead you might stop looking.'

Clearly appalled, as much by the tone as the words, Maureen could only stare at her.

Just as shocked, Andee kept her tone even as she said, 'So you send a note, intending to make us think you were dead . . .' She was finding this hard to take in. Who did something like that?

Appearing contrite and even managing to sound it in spite of her words, Penny said, 'I'm sorry to say I'd had enough of being in this family. You were the golden girl, I was the burden, the difficult one; the one who just wouldn't conform – at least not to the way *Daddy* wanted things. He might have been happier if I'd been born a boy, I couldn't have got into so much trouble – or that's what he told himself, I'm sure.'

'Your father loved you,' Maureen insisted hoarsely.

Penny's eyebrows arched. 'I think we both know that's not true,' she argued with an oddly disconcerting smile.

'It was losing you, never knowing what had happened to you,' Andee informed her, 'that took him to an early grave.'

At that Penny lowered her eyes and allowed several moments to pass before she said, 'I'm sorry that you think that.'

Momentarily lost for words of her own, Andee waited for her to elaborate on what the hell she was meaning, but Maureen was the next to speak.

'Penny, where did you go when you left?'

Penny's eyes rose to her mother's. For what seemed like an eternity she simply regarded Maureen as she dealt with whatever thoughts were behind her intense, unreadable eyes. 'Do you really want me to answer that?' she asked finally.

Maureen visibly blanched.

'Just tell us,' Andee snapped.

Penny's gaze flicked to her, and returned to her mother. 'It's up to you,' she said. 'If you want to know . . .'

'Your father checked,' Maureen broke in shakily. 'The police, everyone . . . It's not where you were.'

'They looked in the wrong places, but Daddy found me, once. He stared right at me, then he turned around and walked away.'

'No!' Maureen cried. 'He'd never have done that.'

Penny didn't argue.

'What is going on?' Andee demanded of them both. 'Where were you, Penny? Who hid you? Someone, others, had to have been involved . . .'

'Oh, someone was,' Penny confirmed. 'His name was John.'

Maureen flinched, and clasped her hands to her face.

'John who?' Andee pressed.

Getting to her feet, Penny said, 'I'll leave Mum to tell you. Oh look,' she exclaimed, gazing out of the window, 'you have a cat. How lovely.'

'It belongs to next door,' Andee informed her.

Penny nodded. 'That makes sense. I don't suppose you'd ever want another after what happened to Smoky.'

Maureen looked as though she'd been struck. 'Where are you going?' she asked desperately. 'I thought . . . I've made some lunch.'

'I need to go,' Penny told her. 'You two have things

to discuss. I'll be in touch,' and moments later the door closed behind her.

Andee regarded her mother's ashen face. The air in the room seemed to have contracted, as though Penny had somehow taken it with her. 'So who is John?' Andee demanded, trying to keep her voice even.

'I can't do this now,' Maureen replied, clearly deeply upset as she got to her feet. 'I need to think. Please don't press me, Andee. It won't help.'

'Then what will?' Andee shouted. 'You're going to have to tell me at some point . . .'

'Just not now!' her mother snapped, and leaving Andee staring after her she ran upstairs and shut herself in her room.

She didn't come out for lunch, or accept a cup of tea. When Andee called out, all she would say was, 'I'll be fine. Please just leave me alone.'

Andee was so angry she wanted to beat the door down, but knowing it would only stress her mother more to be terrorised she kept herself in check and waited.

Eventually, still pale and visibly shaken, Maureen appeared downstairs and announced she had to hurry or she'd be late for one of her regular WI teas at Kesterly town hall.

'And you think that's more important than what's going on here?' Andee queried tersely.

'I'm not arguing about it,' Maureen replied, picking up her keys and handbag.

'So when will you be back?'

'In time for dinner, but I won't want much. There's some fresh pasta in the fridge if you'd like that.'

More worried now than frustrated, Andee said, 'Mum, I'm not sure you should go anywhere while . . .'

'Don't fuss, Andee. I need to get out of the house and do something . . . normal. So please let me be.'

'Then let me drive you.'

'I'm not an invalid. I'm capable of driving myself.'

If it had been possible, Andee would have stopped her, but without getting physical there was nothing she could do. Nor was she able to go and see DI Gould, for he'd texted to say he was at a conference somewhere in Devon this afternoon, not due back until tomorrow.

Deciding to call Penny, Andee found herself bumped through to voicemail. Abruptly she said, 'I don't know what you were hoping to achieve this morning, but Mum's very upset and I need to know what's going on. Call me when you get this.'

Two hours passed with no response.

In the end, in need of some air, Andee took herself over to the pub where she sat at an outside table with a shandy, barely aware of the world going by as she tried to deal with the unsettling, even alarming turn events were taking. Her past, and all the perceptions she'd had of people and things that had happened, the beliefs in those she loved, the guilt that had weighted her for years over Penny, the longing she'd felt for a sister she'd wanted so desperately to share things with, none of it seemed rooted in reality any more. And why was her mother so reluctant to talk to her, when it was clear that she needed to lean on her now more than she ever had? For some reason Maureen wasn't allowing herself to do that.

Becoming vaguely aware of a car slowing as it passed, Andee watched it absently, registering a young couple in the front who seemed to be staring at her. Were they friends of Luke's or Alayna's? She didn't recognise them, and when they didn't wave she simply assumed they were tourists and tracked the red Corsa round to the other side of the green, where it came to a stop a few yards from the entrance to the Smugglers' Cave. No one got out, and Brigand Bob, all kitted out in his usual scary smuggler's gear, was too busy seeing in a tour group to move the car on. Bob was very strict about parking, and the area around the green, especially outside the cave, was strictly off limits to anyone, except the disabled.

Maybe there was a badge in the car that she hadn't seen.

'Fancy another one of those?'

Shading her eyes, she looked up to find Graeme's partner, Blake Leonard, standing over her, and felt a rush of gladness to see him. If it couldn't be Graeme himself appearing out of nowhere, then Blake was an excellent second best.

'No more shandy,' she replied, 'but I'd love a glass of Sauvignon.'

'Coming up. Crisps, nuts, scratchings?'

Realising how hungry she was, she said, 'Nuts would be good. Thanks. You're home early.'

'I had to go and see a client over on Temple Rise, so I

decided to call it a day rather than go back to the shop. Have you spoken to Graeme today?'

'Briefly this morning. Everything seems to be going well in France.'

'Will you be surprised to hear that he's asked me to keep an eye on you?'

Andee smiled wryly. 'I guess not, but please tell him I'm fine, and he shouldn't worry.'

With a dubious arch of an eyebrow, he said, 'Right, wine and nuts it is. Don't go anywhere, I'll be right back.'

Admiring how upbeat he managed to seem when inside she knew he was still grieving deeply for the loss of his daughter, Andee gazed across the green again. The red Corsa was still there, and the young driver was standing beside it talking to Bob. Next thing, the two men were shaking hands before the younger one returned to the car, while the smuggler ambled back to the cave.

In spite of feeling surprised that Bob was allowing the Corsa to stay where it was, Andee soon dismissed the thought as Blake returned with their drinks and settled down opposite her.

'OK, do you want to do small talk, business talk, or some other kind of talk that might explain why you're looking so worried?' Blake offered after taking the top off his Guinness. He was a remarkably good-looking man with sandy brown hair, clean-cut features and eyes that were as kind as they were knowing. 'I can also do no talk at all,' he added generously, 'but that doesn't seem like much fun.'

Knowing from his tone that Jenny had told him what

was going on, Andee said, 'My sister visited again this morning.'

Blake didn't look surprised. 'Jenny saw the Mercedes on her way out,' he told her. 'So how did it go?'

Heaving a deep, uncertain sigh, Andee said, 'I hardly know where to begin, apart from with the fact that my family has apparently been hiding something from me for years. And I don't just mean something, I mean information that I should have been told, that probably should have been in the police files, but never was.'

Frowning, he said, 'Do you know what it is now?'

She shook her head. 'My mother still won't tell me, and Penny isn't returning my calls.'

Clearly understanding how upsetting this was for her, he sat back in his chair and regarded her steadily. 'So do you have any theories?' he prompted.

'Not really. Penny mentioned someone called John. How many Johns do you think there are . . .' She broke off suddenly and stared at Blake. 'My mother had a brother called John,' she stated, only just remembering. 'We never really knew him, he was a bit of a black sheep, so no one ever talked about him, at least not in front of us children. I don't recall him coming to visit more than a handful of times. He was into gambling, I think, or drugs, maybe both . . . He had a dreadful row with my father once. I don't remember what was said, only that there was a lot of shouting and my father ended up throwing him out of the house.'

'Did you ever ask your father about it?'

'No, I was quite young at the time, maybe thirteen or fourteen, so I was probably afraid he'd tell me off for eavesdropping. But my mother told me later ... that's right ... that he'd wanted Daddy to lend him some money, and he'd started threatening him when Daddy refused.'

'A gambling debt?'

'Possibly.'

'So do you know where this villainous uncle is now?'

She shook her head. 'As far as I know no one's heard from him ... Hang on. He died. Quite a long time ago. I must have still been in my twenties and there was something ...' Her eyes sharpened as they went to Blake's. 'They found his body off the coast of Carmarthen, I think it was.'

Blake's eyebrows shot up. 'Well, the first question that comes to mind, is did he jump, or was he pushed?'

'I don't know. There must have been an investigation ... Maybe I need to look into it.' She was watching the red Corsa again. It was pulling away, heading out of the hamlet. 'Given my mother's reaction to the name John being mentioned this morning,' she said, 'I'm going to guess that her *brother* was somehow involved in Penny's disappearance.'

Blake said nothing, only watched her as she continued trying to pull things together. It was like attempting to complete a jigsaw in a fog with no idea if she even had the right, never mind all the pieces.

'Maybe she just assumed my father checked out her brother,' she said, 'but in reality it never happened. I know it sounds odd, but from some of the things she's said lately, there didn't seem to be a lot of proper communication going on between them at the time Penny went missing.'

'It doesn't sound odd to me,' Blake responded. 'Jenny and I all but dried up when Jessica disappeared. It's like you're afraid to talk in case something you say will raise hope where there is none, or stir up guilt, or blame . . . It's like navigating a minefield with something blowing up in your face every other step.'

Feeling for how desperate it must have been for the Leonards during those two agonising years of not knowing, Andee said, 'Well, whatever did or didn't happen with my uncle, we know that Penny was never found. Except she claimed this morning that she was. She said that my father saw her once, but he left her wherever she was and walked away.'

Blake blinked in shock. 'Do you believe that?' he asked.

Andee shook her head. Her father had been an unflinchingly honourable man who, more than anything in the world, had wanted to find his daughter and bring her home.

'So why would she lie?'

'Because she's messing with us,' Andee declared, certain it was true. 'Don't ask me why, maybe she's getting a kick out of it, but she definitely wound Mum up this morning, and I think it was intentional. In fact, I'm sure it was. The big question, though, is what is she really up to?'

Maureen couldn't think how this had happened. One minute she'd been driving home from the WI tea, the next she'd found herself here, on the wrong side of the headland with the car hopelessly stuck in a ditch.

She obviously hadn't been paying attention when she'd reached the fork at Pollard's farm, and had somehow managed to veer to the right instead of driving straight on towards Bourne Hollow.

There was nowhere to go from here, apart from over the cliff into the rampantly foaming sea below. Thankfully there was a barrier in place to stop such plunges from happening, or she might have done just that. Instead she'd tried to turn around on this narrow, rutted track and her back wheels had dropped into a gully, so were now spinning uselessly in thin air.

Her eyes scanned the mountainous landscape around her dotted with sheep and cattle, dissected by trees and hedgerows. Beyond there was only sky and sea, a vast swathe of perfect blue with the speck of a ship in the far distance on its way to the docks in Bristol. Seagulls screeched and dived through the air, and she could see, but not hear the merry lights of Paradise Cove curled into the hook of the bay. No matter how loudly she shouted or heartily she waved, no one there would be able to see or hear her.

What was she to do? There was no mobile phone reception here, and Pollard's farm was at least three miles back.

She gazed along the track, feeling hopelessly daunted by the prospect of such a long walk, too exhausted to do anything more than sink on to the grassy bank beside the car and drop her head in her hands.

Everything was crowding in on her, and she just knew that the next thing she was going to learn were gruesome details of all that her daughter had suffered at the hands of her brother and his cronies. She didn't want to go there. She simply couldn't bear it.

How had he hidden her?

Why had the police been unable to prove that he had her?

She knew so little of what had happened during that terrible time; she'd left it to David, knowing he'd had every available resource assigned to the search, that he'd have given his life to save his girl . . .

Daddy found me, once. He stared right at me, then he turned around and walked away.

It wasn't true; David would never have done that.

So why had Penny said it?

Maureen could only despise herself now for how weak she'd been back then. How could she, a mother, have allowed things to happen without asking more questions, insisting on more answers? It was no excuse that her husband had been far better placed than she was to understand, even oversee, the investigation. She shouldn't have been so trusting, should have forced them to let her be more involved, or at the very least more informed.

She was sure David had appointed a special team to interrogate John, for she could remember the relief she'd felt when she was told that her brother wasn't involved in Penny's disappearance. It wasn't that she'd ever been close to John, or cared about him enough to want him to stay in their lives, she'd simply needed to know that he hadn't carried out the veiled threat he'd once made to David.

Keep playing things my way, David, and I'll make sure everyone stays safe.

Oh Andee, Andee, she wailed desperately inside. She so badly needed to reach out to her elder daughter, and she would, because she had to, even though she knew Andee would never understand her mother's weakness, because Andee simply wasn't the sort of woman Maureen had been all those years ago. She was someone who took control, who wasn't afraid to stand up for herself and those she loved. If she wanted answers she'd get them, and Maureen was in no doubt that Andee would be expecting them now.

'Hello. Are you all right? Is there anything I can do?'

Maureen looked up, and her heart gave a twist of shock as her mouth opened and closed. 'Penny, what are you doing here?' she asked hoarsely. She wanted to pull away from the hand on her shoulder, but her limbs were like liquid, the world seemed to be spinning. 'Did you follow me? Why did you follow me?' she asked.

Penny looked confused and concerned. 'Have you had some sort of accident?' she said.

'It's proper stuck,' someone grunted from behind her. There was a man, with a beard and long hair inspecting the car.

'How did you know I was here?' Maureen asked Penny. 'I thought you were going to London.'

'Have you hit your head?' Penny enquired, coming down to her level.

Maureen drew back. 'Why did you go with him?' she asked. 'Did he force you?'

'We need to get help,' the man decided. 'Stay with her, I'll go and rustle some up.'

Maureen watched him start down the track, then

turned back to the woman beside her. She could see now that it wasn't Penny, and felt a surge of bile rush to her throat.

'I'm sorry,' she mumbled, trying to dab away her tears. 'I'm not . . . I got confused.'

'It's OK,' the woman soothed. 'It seems like you've had a bit of a shock. It's lucky we were passing, you could have been stranded here for hours. What happened? Did you get lost?'

'I took a wrong turn,' Maureen told her. 'Silly, because I live up this way, in Bourne Hollow, with my daughter, Andee. I should call her. She'll be worried.'

'Give me her number and I'll run after Simon. He can ring as soon as he's able. Will you be all right for a minute if I leave you alone?'

'Yes,' Maureen assured her, and after giving the woman Andee's number she lay down on the bank and closed her eyes.

Never, in all the years since Penny had disappeared, had she imagined herself one day wishing that she'd never come back, but it seemed that day had arrived, and she couldn't have felt more racked with guilt and remorse if she'd tried.

'Mum, wake up,' Andee urged gently.

Maureen's eyelids flickered as she rose slowly from the depths of a strangely dark sleep back to the sunlit world. 'Andee?' she said faintly, seeing Andee's face swimming about before her.

Easing her up, Andee said, 'Come on, let's get you home.'

Maureen looked around. 'Where are we?' she asked.

'Bearing Drop. You took a wrong turn and managed to get stuck.'

It was coming back to Maureen now, in slow, horrible waves. John, Penny, the search, the suicide note that hadn't been a suicide note at all, just a way of trying to get away from them all . . .

'We'll leave them to it,' Andee said, referring to Blake and the others who were helping him to bounce the Punto out of the ditch. 'Blake will drive your car back. I don't think there's any damage.'

Minutes later, as they were navigating the bumpy track back to the main road, Maureen mumbled, 'Why did she come? I don't understand it. After all these years . . . Why has it taken her so long?'

'Only she knows the answer to that,' Andee replied, 'but I intend to find out what it is, whether she's willing to tell us or not. Have you heard any more from her today?'

Maureen shook her head. 'Have you?'

'No, I tried calling, but she hasn't responded.'

Maureen gazed out at the passing hedgerows and hidden gates. 'We need to talk,' she stated, as Andee turned on to the road home.

'Yes, we do,' Andee agreed. 'And I need you to be honest and hold nothing back. Can you do that?'

Maureen nodded. 'Yes, I can,' she promised. 'We'll start as soon as we get home. And then I think we should go to the police.'

Chapter Six

An hour later Andee sat down at the table and raised her glass to her mother. 'To us,' she declared, putting both energy and affection into her tone.

With a tender smile Maureen clinked her glass and drank. There was more colour in her cheeks now, her eyes shone clearly; the ordeals of the day no longer seemed to be taking such a destabilising toll. If anything she appeared more together than Andee had seen her since Penny had returned to their lives. It was the relief, Andee realised, of having decided to let go of whatever she was holding back – had clearly been holding back for years.

At last, sounding slightly exasperated with herself, Maureen said, 'I keep trying to think of where to begin, but after so long it's become very jumbled.'

'Why don't you tell me if the John Penny referred to is John Victor, your brother?' Andee asked gently.

The light in Maureen's eyes dimmed.

Stepping through the partially open door, Andee said, 'And you suspected at the time that he might be involved?'

Maureen nodded. 'I was afraid he might be, because of something he once said to your father.' She paused as her mind swam with dark memories, secrets she'd kept buried for too many years. 'It was a horrible time,' she said quietly. 'John had been staying with my mother, Granny Victor . . . Do you remember, she used to live around the corner from us in Chiswick? Yes, of course you do. He hadn't seen her in almost five years. He hadn't been in touch either, not even for her birthday or Christmas. Then he turned up unannounced one day, and we soon found out that he was hiding from someone he owed money to. Granny wasn't in a position to help him and he knew it, but he told me that he'd ask her for it, even make her sell her flat, if I didn't give it to him myself. Of course I told Daddy – all the money I had belonged to both of us. He wasn't someone who'd give in to blackmail; he was very angry about it, but we knew, and so did John, how much it would upset my mother to discover that her beloved boy was in trouble, and she wasn't strong enough to deal with it. We'd already been told that she didn't have much longer to live, and because Daddy cared for her deeply, and was afraid of what desperation might make John do to speed up his inheritance, he agreed to let him come to the house so we could discuss things.

'They had a terrible fight, truly terrible, but Daddy ended up paying off the debt. He knew far better than I did the type of people John was involved with, the things they were capable of, and though his main concern was Granny, of course, he didn't want John's punishment or early demise on his conscience either.

When he handed the cheque over he told John that it would never happen again, and that after Granny's funeral he'd be on his own.

'John didn't seem in the least bit put out. If anything, he found it amusing. He said things like, "You know you can't resist me, and I'll come whenever I like . . ."' Maureen shook her head, as though still appalled and shamed by the scene. 'It was as he was leaving that he said to Daddy, "You know you really ought to watch out for those girls of yours, they're growing up fast, and that Penny's already a . . ." I can't remember the exact words he used, but there was no mistaking what he meant. He said, "Keep playing things my way, David, and I'll make sure she stays safe."'

Maureen sighed shakily, clearly as horrified by the threat now as she'd been at the time. That her own brother, the boy she'd played with growing up, who'd had the same parents as her, the same love and care, could threaten her teenage daughter that way . . . It was so beyond her comprehension that Andee could see how bitterly she still struggled with it.

Maureen forced herself to continue. 'Your father pushed him out of the door and slammed it hard in his face, letting him know that it would never be opened to him again. But by then Penny was already going off the rails; she'd started staying away from home, lying about where she was going and who she was with. The first time your father found her was probably the third or fourth that she'd taken herself off, but it was definitely the longest. Do you remember she told us she was staying with a friend called Madeleine? It turned out she was at Granny's and so was John. I don't know the exact details of what happened, Daddy didn't want to discuss it, but Granny told me later that she'd called Daddy herself because of the way Penny was behaving with John. It wasn't decent, she said, and she was afraid of where it would lead.'

Appalled, Andee said, 'What on earth did Granny mean? You don't think she thought Penny was sleeping with him?'

Maureen flinched. 'If not with him then with others he'd set her up with, possibly to help pay off his debts.'

Andee's eyes closed. It wasn't so much Penny she felt for as her mother, and the desperate, ravaging fear that her thirteen-year-old daughter was sleeping with anyone at such a tender age.

'It was what she wanted,' Maureen stumbled on, 'to go with men. She told Daddy that, but whether she meant it, or whether she said it to hurt him . . .' Her voice shook with emotions new and old, harsh and merciless. 'She was out of control. We didn't know what to do with her. When she asked to go on the pill I let her, because I didn't want the situation to get any worse than it already was. Daddy was furious when he found out, he told her she was grounded until she was sixteen, eighteen, I can't remember now. I only know that it wasn't long after that that she disappeared for good and I was always afraid that John had helped her in some way. And then the note came . . .'

Ashamed of how wrapped up in her teenage self she must have been not to have noticed any of this, Andee said, 'Well, we know now that he did help her.'

Maureen nodded awkwardly.

'What I don't understand,' Andee said, 'is why there's no record of him being questioned.'

'I can't explain that,' Maureen replied. 'Only Daddy could tell you, and obviously that's not possible.'

'Ah, but what is possible,' DI Terence Gould pointed out the following morning, after Andee had filled him in on everything so far, 'is that one or more of the officers working the case is still around to have a chat with. Can you give me any names?'

Andee's relief was so profound it was physical. 'So you'll help me?' she said, only realising now how much she'd been counting on it.

'Were you really in any doubt?' he countered, his large head tilted to one side as he regarded her with bright, steely eyes. He wasn't a man to be messed with, or taken for granted – or one who'd ever shied away from bending the rules in order to get to the truth. 'I'm guessing you want to keep it below the radar for the time being,' he went on. 'I'm good with that, but just run it by me again why you're so convinced this person is your sister.'

'She just is,' Andee said simply. 'She looks the same, sounds the same – my mother mistook her for me the first time she rang ... Look at photos of yourself at fourteen, you'll find you haven't changed that much either.'

'Bit weightier, and greyer,' he grunted, 'but I take your point. And your mother's equally convinced?'

'She is. She was going to come with me today, but

decided at the last minute that she wasn't up to it. She's willing to talk to you any time if you think she can be helpful.'

'Lovely woman, your mother,' Gould commented. 'Reminds me a bit of my own, but with more class.'

Amused, Andee said, 'I wouldn't let your mother hear you say that if I were you.'

'She says it about herself. Anyway, your sister's motive for being in touch after all this time? You're obviously convinced it's not about happy reunions, so any theories?'

Andee blew out a breath as she shook her head. 'At first I thought she might be wanting to show off how successful she's become, but there's definitely more to it.'

'Go on.'

'OK, the first time she came she wanted to know if anyone had visited ahead of her. When I asked like who, she just shrugged it off. The second time she had a good look round the hamlet before coming into the house, trying to make it seem as though she was soaking it all in, but my gut told me she was at least half expecting to spot someone.'

He nodded thoughtfully. 'OK, I've had experience of your hunches, or instincts as you'd rather call them, so I'm willing to run with it. I can see it's unlikely her motive is money related, since you say she seems to have a lot of it. So we can put that aside and return to it if it becomes relevant. Passion is always a big motivator, but I'm not sure it's fitting with this. You're definitely not persuaded by the family ties?'

Andee shook her head. 'She's putting on a show to try and convince us of that, but it's not ringing true for me, or my mother. In fact I'm pretty sure she's playing with us – for kicks or for some other reason, I've no idea. I told you about the kitten – that keeps coming up – and apparently she took something of mine when she left that she wants me to try and remember.'

'But you don't?'

Andee shook her head.

'So she's manipulative? Calculating? Sly?'

'Possibly all of the above, with a veneer of friendliness that's good, but not Oscar-winning.'

'Did you believe her when she said your uncle was involved in her disappearance?'

'We both did. I think he had to be, given what my mother told me last night, but there's nothing about him in the police files.'

'Which is indeed odd, because there should be. Did you ever talk to your father about revisiting the case?' Gould asked.

'I tried, but it wasn't easy for him. He was already going downhill by then, and I could see that reliving it was causing him problems.'

'Because he knew there were some irregularities and he didn't want you to find them?'

'The thought never crossed my mind at the time. Maybe it should have, but we're talking about my *father*. I knew how hard Penny's disappearance had been for him, and I'd never had any reason to doubt him – over that, or anything else.'

He nodded, clearly understanding a daughter's trust,

even if they were both now questioning it. 'What's that?' he asked as she put a plastic bag on the table.

'It's the teacup she used the first time she came to the house. I'm not in any doubt, but I brought it just in case anyone wanted to run a check.'

'If we do it now we'll alert the Met to the fact that she might have turned up, and I thought you didn't want that.'

'Just in case you have any doubts . . .'

'If you don't, I don't,' he retorted, airing a confidence that made her wonder if she ought to be back on his team, if only to repay him for his trust in her.

'I realise I'm asking a lot,' she admitted, 'and that this could all backfire horribly . . .'

'. . . on me.'

'On you,' she conceded, 'but I think we're agreed that it's important, at least for the time being, to find out why now, and what she's hoping to gain.'

His eyebrows rose in agreement. After a while he started to shake his head as the enormity of it coursed through him again. 'Twenty-seven years,' he murmured, reaching for his phone as it rang. 'I've never come across anything like this before – unless it's a dead body.' Clicking on, he said, 'Gould speaking.'

Feeling dreadful for thinking that a dead body might have been less traumatic for her mother, Andee glanced out of the partition window to where a number of her ex-colleagues were busy at their desks. She'd stopped to greet Leo Johnson and Jemma Payne on her way in, the DCs she'd worked most closely with during her time in CID. The new detective sergeant, Lydia

Mitchell, who'd replaced her, hadn't seemed especially thrilled to meet her, although from the grimness of her features she didn't seem especially thrilled by life.

'OK, so going back to your sister's presumed ulterior motive,' Gould continued after ending his call. 'We don't think it's money, so that's parked for now. Passion we've dealt with. When are you next seeing her?'

'We have no arrangement, and she's not returning my calls, but I'm sure she'll be in touch at some point.'

Seeming as certain, he said, 'How much have you found out about her business life?'

'I only have access to Google these days, and it's not offering me a Michelle Cross that matches the kind of profile she's given me.'

'Remind me again what her businesses are.'

'Import-export . . .'

'Which could mean anything, unless she said what she's importing and exporting? No, of course she didn't. Go on.'

'Apparently there's a property management company, based in London. Two medical centres in the States. A travel agency in Stockholm, and an online dating service. And before you ask, I've no idea if any of it's true.'

'If it is, it's pretty diverse. Did she happen to mention the names of any of these companies?'

Andee shook her head. 'The only name she's mentioned so far is John Victor who we know met his untimely end twenty years ago.'

He wrote it down and stared at it, as though an epiphany of some sort might emerge.

'I've checked and the verdict on his death was open,' she told him.

'How long after your sister disappeared did he go off the cliff?'

'Eleven years.'

'Where did it happen?'

'Apparently at a remote spot off the coast of West Wales. No suicide note. I need to get hold of a copy of the inquest.'

He nodded, clearly processing it all as he continued to stare at Victor's name. 'He didn't have a wife or kids, no other family?' he asked.

'None that I know of.'

'What about Penny? When you spoke to her did she mention a husband or children?'

'We asked about children, and she avoided answering. As for her marital status, all I can tell you is that she turned up the first time wearing what could have been a wedding ring, but the second time there was no jewellery at all.'

Gould's eyebrows rose. 'So I'm guessing your next step is to find an address for her or one of her companies. How are you going to do that?'

'I have the registration number of her car, which I was hoping to leave with you.'

'No problem. I'll bring Leo Johnson up to speed about everything when you've gone and let him do the necessary. Shouldn't take long. Meantime, I'll get on to the Met and find out who worked the case with your father. Any names you remember?'

'Gerry Trowbridge was always close to my dad.

I spoke to him at the time I revisited the case, but his daughter and grandson had just been killed in a skiing accident so I didn't push very hard. Anyway, I didn't have any reason to when I presumed it was all on file. I've no idea where he is now. He'll be retired, obviously. Alive and compos mentis, we can always hope.'

'If he isn't, he won't have been the only member of the team, but I'll put him first on the list. You realise I won't be able to come with you?'

She did, though she regretted it.

'OK, now fascinating as this is, and much as I'd like to sit here all day discussing it, I have to be somewhere.'

'But you'll speak to Leo before you go?'

'No, when I get back, but there's no harm in letting him have the reg number now. Oh, and should you happen to hear from your sister before we're next in touch, be sure to let me know.'

Andee was driving back to Bourne Hollow, her mind so full of the conversation with Gould that it took her a moment to realise her mobile was ringing. Seeing it was Martin, her estranged husband, she was tempted to let it go to messages. However, she dutifully clicked on and delivered a cheery hello.

'Hi, everything OK your end?' he asked, trying to sound upbeat and managing resentful.

'Everything's fine my end,' she confirmed. 'Are you having a lovely time in Spain?'

'It's relaxing and hot. My mother's worried about

your mother. She says she's not sounded herself the last couple of times she's rung.'

'Really? Well you can tell her that Maureen's fine, no cause for concern. And I have to wonder,' she continued, turning at the end of the busy promenade to head towards home, 'why your mother isn't calling me herself.'

'I needed to speak to you anyway. Alayna tells me you're back from France. Is everything all right with you and Graeme?'

Since Martin was still bitter over their break-up, and would love nothing more than to hear that her relationship with Graeme had failed, she had to bite down hard on her annoyance. 'Yes it is, thank you. I just had a few things to do here.'

'So you won't be staying long?'

'I don't want to be rude, Martin, but how is this any of your business?'

Ignoring the question, he said, 'I've told Alayna that I'm happy to make up her loss in wages if she'd like to come to Africa with me to see Luke. I think she'd be more inclined to accept my offer if you came too.'

Silencing a weary sigh, Andee said, 'You know very well that she's determined to finance her gap year herself. I think you should feel proud of that instead of trying to tempt her out of it.'

'She needs a holiday.'

'Why don't you let her decide? She's not a child any more. When are you flying out?'

'Next Tuesday. It's a fascinating and worthwhile

project he's working on that I might be interested in supporting.'

Deciding not to remind him of how negligent he'd been of his children's projects during the time he'd walked out of their lives to go and find himself, she said, 'Well, I hope you have a lovely time.'

'Why *don't* you come along? You're an animal lover . . .'

'Martin, just stop. It isn't going to happen and you're making it harder for everyone, the way you keep trying to use the children to bring us together.'

'It's what they want.'

'No it isn't, and anyway, it's not about them, it's about me and what I want, which is for you to understand that I'm in another relationship now, and that's the way it's going to stay.'

Chapter Seven

Early the next morning DC Leo Johnson rang Andee with the information she had requested about the Mercedes.

'I don't know how helpful this is,' he told her, 'but the vehicle's registered to a chauffeur-drive company in Knightsbridge. I'll text the address and phone number when we finish this call. I've also taken the liberty of looking into the company's ownership. It's a couple of blokes with the same family name, Balodis, so I'm guessing they're brothers, or father and son, something along those lines.'

'It doesn't sound English.'

'Your guess is as good as mine. I'll text the correct spelling with the other details when we finish the call.'

'Thanks. I take it Gould has already filled you in on things?'

'Some, and it's just about blowing my mind. I guess it must be having the same effect on you, times ten.'

'Something like that. Can I ask another favour while you're on?'

'Sure, shoot.'

'Can you get hold of a copy of the inquest report on John Victor?'

'Your uncle?'

'That's him. I'll text the dates and details I know. In addition to that, can you find out if he had any kind of police record, where he lived at the time of his death, what he did for a job, who his friends or associates were. Anything you can dig up that may or may not seem relevant.'

'I'll get back to you as soon as I have something.'

By ten thirty Andee was on a train to London, knowing that to get the kind of information she was after from Exclusive Chauffeur Drive she'd stand a far better chance if she turned up in person than if she tried to do it on the phone. Even so, it probably wouldn't be easy, since it was highly likely Penny had guessed she'd have the Mercedes traced, and had briefed the company to expect her. Had she needed to do that? There was simply no way of knowing.

A quick Google search had told her that the name Balodis was Latvian, which might have been the language Penny had used during her first visit. Since Andee knew not a single word of it herself, she had no way of recognising it.

It was after midday by the time the train pulled into Paddington, spilling fast-moving wheelie bags and important owners on to the platform to begin a race for the Tube, taxis and buses. As she moved with the crowd Andee was remembering what a thrill it gave her as a small child to come to this station; she'd always felt sure she'd spot her favourite bear if she looked hard enough.

She and Penny had had Paddingtons when they were young; she remembered them swapping bears because Penny had decided Andee's was bigger, or cuter, or more cuddly, or something that had made it better than hers.

'She's just a baby,' their mother had said when Andee had tried to hang on to hers. Penny had been two or three at the time. 'You don't mind swapping really.'

Strange the things that came to mind that had never seemed to have much significance before. She wasn't sure this memory did now, apart from the fact that it was an early example of Penny coveting what was hers, this time viewed in a different light thanks to recent events.

Since she was wearing flat shoes and carrying a light bag she decided the sunshine was too good to miss, so she set out on foot for Knightsbridge. On reaching Hyde Park she started across the grass, weaving amongst sunbathers and strollers, while trying, not very hopefully, to get hold of Penny.

To her amazement she got an answer on the third attempt.

'Andee! What a lovely surprise. How are you?'

Adjusting rapidly, Andee said, 'I'm fine. Actually, I'm in London, and I was hoping we could meet.'

Seamlessly, Penny said, 'Gosh, that would have been lovely, but even as we speak I'm on my way to Heathrow.'

'I see.' Why wasn't she surprised? 'Where are you going?'

'To the States. I'm afraid we have some clients who are in a bit of a state and it's my job to go and calm them down. But I should be back in a couple of days. If you're still around I'd love to see you.'

'I'm just here for the day. I was wondering when you were going to be in touch with Mum again.'

'Soon. Very soon. I just need to get this problem sorted first. It's such a pity you're going home today. I'd have offered you my apartment if you were going to stay longer, except it's having a makeover at the moment. However, I have a suite at a very nice hotel on Buckingham Palace Road. You're more than welcome to use it if you change your mind and decide to hang out in town for a while.'

'That's kind of you, but not this time, thanks.' During the awkward pause that followed Andee's gaze fell on a stray cat, wending its way through the bushes at the edge of the park. 'Tell me something, do you know what happened to Smoky the kitten?'

With a sad-sounding sigh, Penny said, 'Oh dear. Poor Smoky.'

Since that wasn't an answer, Andee waited.

'It was your fault, of course,' Penny told her. 'You shouldn't have tried to take him away from me.'

Andee's insides knotted. She had no memory of that, could barely remember the cat at all. 'So what did you do?' she asked, certain she didn't want to know the answer.

Without sounding in the least perturbed, Penny said, 'I broke his neck.'

Andee was sitting on a bench in the shade of a towering horse chestnut, still shaken by Penny's admission and needing to try and deal with it somehow. 'Mum, it's me,' she said when her mother answered the phone.

'Hello darling, are you there yet?' Maureen asked.

'Yes, I'm in Hyde Park. I've just spoken to Penny.'

Her mother's voice lost its buoyancy. 'Did she ring you?' she said.

'No, I rang her and this time she answered. Apparently she's on her way to the States, but that's not the reason I'm calling. I asked her about the kitten and she said . . . Did I try to take it away from her?'

'No, but the kitten seemed to prefer you and I suppose . . .'

When her mother didn't continue Andee said, 'She told me she broke its neck.'

When Maureen remained silent Andee's eyes closed at the gruesome, stomach-turning picture of a nine-year-old girl, her own sister, ending a kitten's life with her bare hands. 'How could she have done it?' she whispered incredulously.

'I don't know,' Maureen replied. 'It was very upsetting, a horrible, horrible shock when I found it.'

'Did you ever talk to her about it?'

'No, because I didn't want to accuse her in case she hadn't done it.'

'But you felt sure she had?'

'I kept trying not to believe it.'

Andee took a breath. 'Did she ever do anything else like that?'

'I don't know. I . . . There were things . . . She was always jealous of you, kept convincing herself that people preferred you to her.'

. . . sometimes I hate her for being so much better than I am at everything. No one ever seems to notice me when she's in the room. It's like I become invisible . . .

Andee felt her head starting to spin. 'How come I never realised any of this?' she asked bleakly.

'I think you did on one level, but you were older, more confident, and I guess you treated it more as an irritant than anything to be taken too seriously.'

Which would only have made it worse for Penny.

So was she responsible for Penny abandoning her family and putting her parents through utter hell?

No, only Penny could be responsible for that. She, Andee, wasn't going to fall into the trap of blaming herself, or of allowing Penny to get to her, however hard she tried.

A few minutes after ringing off from her mother she was updating Graeme. 'When I met with Gould yesterday,' she said, 'he suggested a couple of motives for why people do things, the first being money, the second passion. There are others, of course, including revenge, and I'm wondering if that might be what's behind Penny's return.'

The possibility of it silenced him.

Hearing herself say it silenced her, too.

'But for what?' he protested.

'I don't know. Imagined wrongs . . . The way her

mind works, it's . . . well, it's different . . . I just can't get a handle on what might be going on with her.'

'But to have held a grudge for so long? You know, I'm really not liking the sound of this. You need to speak to Gould again.'

'Perhaps she decided to punish us by staying away. Punish us for what, I'm still not sure. I'm not sure about any of this to be honest, but right now I'm going to see what I can find out at this chauffeur company.'

Exclusive Chauffeur Drive was at the end of a smart cobbled mews close to Belgrave Square, with vivacious begonias spilling from pots each side of its front door, and a small brass plaque bearing its name in elegant script above the bell. The opaque bay window to the right of the door glowed like cloudy silver in the afternoon sun, while what had once been an old-fashioned carriage entrance was now an olive green, square-panelled up and over garage door. It was closed, so it wasn't possible to see what vehicle, if any, was inside, but the garage didn't appear big enough to hold much more than a Smart and a motorbike.

Andee pressed the bell and glanced up and down the exclusive, quaintly crooked street. No one was around; it was as quiet as a rural idyll, right here in the middle of town. So quiet that she almost jumped as a voice came from a hidden intercom inviting her in.

Spotting a surveillance camera tucked under the guttering two floors up, she stepped into a postage-stamp lobby with a door to the right marked Private, another to the left signalling the garage, and a staircase straight ahead with a sign directing visitors up to reception.

'Hello,' a cheery female voice shouted down, 'have you been here before? If not, we're upstairs; if you have you know the way.'

The first level, with its surprisingly high ceiling and pale carpeted floors, turned out to be mostly open-plan, with a chic leather-fronted welcome desk, three arty sofas arranged around a glass and steel coffee table, a small bar with tall stools, and a large cardboard cut-out of an S class Mercedes.

'Hi, welcome to Exclusive, it'll be a pleasure to serve you in any way we can,' the beautiful, sparkly-eyed receptionist gushed. From her Slavic features and marked accent Andee guessed her to be Polish, and in spite of the sober dove-grey suit over a white silk shirt, she gave off the air of a mischievously happy life-lover. 'My name is Martyna,' she declared. 'Is it permitted to ask yours?'

Andee gave her name as Jenny Leonard, waited as Martyna repeated it, and was about to say more when a door behind the reception desk opened and a portly man with slicked-back hair, narrow eyes and a gold-glinting smile came out to greet her.

'Oto Balodis, at your service,' he told her, holding out a hand to shake. His grip was firm and cool, his smile was warm. 'Please tell us how we may best assist you, Ms Leonard.'

Deciding she wouldn't want to meet him on a dark night, Andee said, 'Actually, I'm hoping you can help me to find someone.'

He appeared surprised and intrigued. 'Please, take a seat,' he offered, directing her to the sofas. 'Martyna will bring us some refreshment.'

'Thank you,' Andee said as she sat down. 'Water will be fine for me.'

After nodding in Martyna's direction, Balodis said, 'So who is it you're looking for? Of course we will do our best to help.'

So gracious, and yet Andee could sense a certain wariness gathering. 'Well, it's the strangest thing,' she said chattily, 'but I was in the South of France recently, L'Isle-sur-la-Sorgue to be precise, when I saw an old friend of mine in the back of a Mercedes. She saw me too, but the traffic was crazy that day so she couldn't stop. Fortunately I managed to get the registration number of the car, and an old colleague of mine at the DVLA did me the favour of giving me your address. I hope you don't mind.'

Balodin's narrow eyes turned to slits. 'No, of course not. As I said, we are happy to help.' Funny, but he wasn't sounding all that happy.

'Here's the number,' Andee said, handing him a piece of paper. 'And the date I saw the car. My friend and I go back a long way. It's a real shame that we lost touch, our families were very close, but you know how these things happen. Time goes on, people get busy . . .'

Balodin was passing the registration number to Martyna.

Taking it, Martyna began entering it into the computer.

All charm again, Balodin said, 'I'm sure you under-stand that we can't give out our clients' details. It would be highly unethical and against all our principles. It is a very *exclusive* service that we operate here.'

Andee mimicked crestfallen. 'I was afraid you'd say that, it's just that I have something of hers that I'd really like to return.'

'Perhaps you can leave it with us and we'll pass it on. This is presuming the registration belongs to one of our cars, of course.'

Certain he already knew that it did, Andee grimaced. 'I don't have it with me, I'm afraid, and I'd really rather do it myself.'

Martyna said, 'According to our records, that car was in London on the date you've given me.'

'Oh, I see,' Andee said dolefully. However, since learning there was a chauffeur service involved, it had already occurred to her that the car she'd seen outside Briar Lodge might not be the same one Penny had used in France. 'Well, my friend's name is Michelle Cross . . .'

Balodin was getting to his feet. 'I'm afraid we do not have any clients by that name,' he interrupted.

'Perhaps the booking was in a company name,' Andee suggested.

Balodin said, 'Forgive me for repeating myself, but we are not in a position to discuss our clients.'

Intrigued by the brush-off, Andee stood up too. 'I guess she must be a client if she was in one of your cars . . .'

'But the car wasn't in France that day,' he reminded her, 'so you must be mistaken. Now, if you'll excuse me, I am due at a meeting in a few minutes. It was a pleasure making your acquaintance, and I'm very sorry that we haven't been able to help.'

Finding herself already on the stairs, Andee reassured him again that she understood his situation, and after thanking him for his time she took out one of Jenny's business cards. 'When you next speak to Michelle,' she said, 'would you mind giving her this?'

'As I said, we have no clients by that name.'

She watched him look at the card.

'Interior design?' he queried.

Andee smiled. He'd obviously been no more convinced by her claim to an old friendship than she had by him apparently running an everyday chauffeur service. However, the card had momentarily thrown him. 'If you're ever looking for anyone,' she offered.

He nodded distractedly and after asking Martyna to see 'our guest' out, he returned to his office.

'I probably shouldn't tell you this,' Martyna whispered as they stepped outside the front door, 'but it *was* one of our cars you saw in France, just not that one.'

Smiling her appreciation, while feeling certain the girl had been instructed to pass on the information, Andee said, 'And the client inside was Michelle Cross?'

Martyna shook her head. 'Not according to the file.'

Intrigued, Andee said, 'So who was it?'

Martyna glanced over her shoulder. 'I really shouldn't tell you . . .'

Going along with what she felt sure was a charade, Andee said, 'I'm just an old friend attempting to renew contact. I promise, I'm not out to cause trouble.'

Martyna dropped her voice again. 'She's a regular client of ours. Her name is Andrea Lawrence, so you see it couldn't have been your friend.'

Andee stared at her hard. Penny was using *her* name to ... To what? And did this girl know that *she* aka Jenny Leonard was the real Andrea Lawrence? 'Well, whoever Andrea Lawrence is,' Andee said, managing to sound no more than chatty, 'she looked very like my friend.'

'I'm sorry if you've had a wasted journey,' Martyna said, seeming to mean it.

'Oh it hasn't been,' Andee assured her. 'It was lovely meeting you. Have you worked here long?'

'Almost seven years. Actually, it was Mrs Lawrence who helped me to get my job. It's fantastic what she does. She helps so many people. I would not be where I am if it weren't for her. None of us would, including my bosses.'

Deciding to be fascinated, Andee said, 'So what does she do, Mrs Lawrence?'

'As I said, she helps people. Ssh, I'd better go back inside, but I wanted you to know that you were mistaken about your friend. Such a pity, I do hope you find her.'

Andee thanked her and set off back to the station.

'I have to admit,' she told Graeme on the phone, 'finding out that she's using my name really blindsided me. That's if she is. I'm pretty certain the receptionist was briefed to say what she did should I happen to turn up.'

'To what end?'

'I've no idea. The boss certainly didn't want to discuss Michelle Cross. I'm guessing, when I mentioned the name, that was the moment he realised I was the person he'd been tipped off about.'

'Whereupon he left it to the receptionist to deliver the bombshell that Andrea Lawrence was the client in the car?'

'Apparently. I'm intrigued by the do-gooder who helps people get jobs.'

'Do you believe it?'

'I've no idea what to believe, but right now I'm interested to see how long it takes for Penny to contact me, because I'm sure she'll have been told about my visit the minute I left the office.'

Maureen had just reversed from the drive at the side of Briar Lodge when a young lad around her grandson Luke's age suddenly appeared out of nowhere and held up a hand for her to stop.

Winding down the driver's window, she said, 'Are you looking for Luke?'

He shook his head. 'No, I . . .'

'Are you lost?'

'I don't think so. I'm sorry to interrupt you.' His voice was surprisingly soft and sounded quite cultured, maybe accented, and even at a distance she could see that he was extremely good-looking. 'I'm looking for Andee Lawrence,' he told her.

'She's my daughter,' Maureen replied. 'Is there something I can help with?'

He glanced over his shoulder to a red car that was

parked close by. 'If you're her mother,' he said, turning back to her, 'then you must be my grandmother.'

Maureen's eyes dilated as her heart gave a slow, strange contraction. 'You're . . . You're Penny's son?' she asked, in a whisper.

He nodded briefly and glanced at the car again. 'I need to talk to Andee,' he told her. 'She's a detective, isn't she?'

'She was,' Maureen managed to confirm. This boy, this stranger with his beautiful voice and shock of fair hair, was her grandson? 'I'm just going to pick her up,' she ran on, hardly aware of what she was saying. 'She's been in London today.' She started to get out of the car. She needed to hug him, or invite him in, or do something other than just sit there, but he stopped her with raised hands. He was looking at a white van coming around the green towards them. 'You're being watched,' he muttered.

Maureen blinked.

'I have to go,' he gasped, and before she could utter another word he ran back to the car, jumped in and drove around the green at speed.

Maureen gazed after him, too thrown to do anything more. She barely even registered Blake as he drew up outside his own house in the white van.

'Is everything OK?' he asked, coming to find out why she was standing next to her car with it parked half in, half out of her drive.

'I'm not sure,' she replied, still staring after the red car that had vanished over the brow of the hill. 'I've just had . . . The car that just drove off . . . Did you see it?'

He nodded. 'Was it someone you know?'

'The lad driving it just told me he's my grandson.'

Blake blinked with shock. 'You mean, Penny's son?'

'That's what he said.'

Blake looked across the green to where the hamlet entrance was quietly empty and shaded by a wind-blown holm oak. 'What else did he say?' he asked.

'That he needed to speak to Andee, then he saw your van and seemed to take fright.'

Clearly as baffled as she was, he glanced back across the hamlet as he said, 'Did you happen to get a number for the car?'

She shook her head.

'And he didn't tell you his name?'

'I'm afraid we didn't get that far.' She checked the time. 'I should go, Andee's train is due in at half past.'

Opening her car's passenger door he said, 'Come on, I'll drive,' and going round to the other side he got in and started towards town.

Andee was at Fruit of the Vine wine bar in the old town with her mother and Blake, feeling as stunned and baffled as they were by the mysterious visit from the lad claiming to be Penny's son. 'And he didn't say what he wanted to talk to me about?' she asked. 'Or give you a number for me to reach him?'

'There wasn't time,' Maureen replied. 'It all happened so fast. A van appeared, which was Blake's. He said something about me being watched and the next minute he was in his car and gone.'

To Blake Andee said, 'It was definitely a red Corsa?'

'It was,' he confirmed, sitting back as their drinks arrived.

'Did you notice a red Corsa parked on the green, close to the Smugglers' Cave, when we were at the pub the other evening?'

Grimacing, he said, 'I can't say I did, but I'm surprised Brigand Bob didn't try to move him on, you know . . .'

'He might have,' Andee interrupted. 'He certainly spoke to him, and then ended up allowing him to carry on parking there. Which means we have to speak to Bob to find out *why* he didn't move him on. The cave will be closed by now. Does anyone know where Bob lives?'

No one did.

Taking out her phone Andee pressed in Leo Johnson's number. As she waited for him to answer, she said, 'Did you notice if there was a girl in the car?'

Both Maureen and Blake looked perplexed.

'I thought I saw a girl with him on the green,' Andee explained, and put up a hand as she was connected to Leo's voicemail. 'Hi, it's Andee,' she announced. 'I need an address for Brigand Bob who helps run the Smugglers' Cave at Bourne Hollow. Call me when you can. If it's not this evening, don't worry, he'll be at the cave by nine tomorrow so I'll see him then.' As she rang off, she said to her mother, 'So did this boy happen to resemble Penny at all?'

'I didn't get that good a look,' Maureen replied doubtfully. 'His hair was fair, and hers was always dark when she was young, like yours. But of course he could take after his father.'

'Whoever that might be,' Andee muttered. 'What sort of age would you put him at?'

'Not much older than Luke, maybe twenty-three or four.'

After messaging Gould requesting another meeting in the morning, Andee was about to speak again when her mobile rang. Not bothering to hide her surprise, she said, 'This should be interesting. It's Penny.'

Chapter Eight

'Andee, I hope this is a good time,' Penny cried cheerfully.

'As good as any,' Andee replied smoothly. She hadn't yet told her mother about Penny calling herself Andrea Lawrence, and wasn't keen to if she could avoid it. Maureen was finding it hard enough to cope with things as it was, the prospect of any further mind games would only make matters worse. 'How are you?' she asked. 'I take it your flight's arrived wherever it was going.'

'Houston. Texas. We got in about an hour ago. I'm currently on my way into the city. So, how was your day in London? Are you still there?'

'No, I'm back in Kesterly. It was . . . productive.'

'You didn't tell me why you were there.'

'I was looking up an old friend.'

'And you found her? Him?'

'Kind of.'

'I have a lot of resources at my fingertips, if there's anything I can help with.'

'That's very kind of you. I'll remember that.' She

waited, wondering what the point of this call really was, for Balodis, or Martyna, had almost certainly informed her of the visit to their office, so what was she hoping to find out now?

To her surprise Penny said, 'Well, I should probably ring off. We've just arrived at the hotel. You have my number if you need me.'

'And you have mine.'

After Andee had ended the call, her mother said, 'What was that about?'

Andee sipped her wine and shook her head slowly, thoughtfully. 'A good question,' she replied.

'Does she know you went to the chauffeur-drive office?' Blake asked.

'I'm sure she does, but she didn't mention it. I used Jenny's business card, by the way.' Catching the expression on her mother's face, she wished she hadn't mentioned it. 'I told you this morning,' she said, 'that I was afraid if I gave my own name I might not get in the door. Penny will have been expecting me to trace the car, so there was a chance she had the people at the chauffeur-drive company on some kind of alert.'

Maureen either didn't remember or she simply didn't understand. 'Why would she do that?' she asked.

'Why is she doing anything?' Andee countered.

'You didn't ask about her son,' Blake pointed out.

'I wanted to see if she mentioned him first.'

'But she didn't?'

Andee shook her head again and refilled her glass. 'We've no idea what's going on here,' she sighed, 'but if he is who he says he is and wants to speak to me . . .

I'd like to give him the chance before . . .' Before what? 'Before I jump to any conclusions,' she decided.

'And if he turns out to be an impostor, someone sent by Penny to . . .' Blake broke off as Andee kicked him under the table.

Maureen was looking more bemused than ever. 'He came across as a nice enough lad,' she mumbled, 'but you can never be sure these days, can you?'

The following morning Andee was waiting outside the Smugglers' Cave when Brigand Bob, looking for all the world like an ageing Jack Sparrow in his tricorne cap, black frock coat and fancy breeches, came swashbuckling along the street ready to start the day.

Their chat lasted only a few minutes, during which Andee learned that the boy in the Corsa had asked if he and his girlfriend could park up for a while as his girlfriend was pregnant and feeling faint.

'Proper pale, she was,' Bob told her. 'And just a slip of a thing, with this great big belly . . .'

'I don't suppose,' Andee ventured, 'you happened to ask their names?'

Clearly astonished, he said, 'Why on earth would I do that?' Then, apparently remembering that she used to be police, he added, 'Should I have?'

'No, no,' she assured him. 'It's just that they came back here yesterday . . . Did you see them?'

'No, can't say I did. Why, what are they supposed to have done?'

'Nothing as far as I know, but he told my mother he wanted to speak to me. If you happen to see him again, could you try to get his name and maybe even a number?'

'I'll do my best. I could give him yours if you didn't mind me passing it on.'

After texting him the number Andee left him to his first tourists of the day, already straggling up the hill from the coach park, and went to get into her car.

As she drove into Kesterly her mind was darting about all over the place, though she was aware of how lack of sleep could alter perspective and even create a sense of paranoia. Heaven knew she'd been there during the night, when she'd become increasingly bothered by Penny's use of her name. What on earth was that about, and how often had she done it? Did she actually have documents such as a passport and driver's licence in the name of Andrea Lawrence? Apart from the chauffeur company, who had very possibly been instructed to give her name as a part of some warped little game directed by Penny, who knew her as that?

Then there was the mysterious appearance of a boy claiming to be Penny's son, with a pregnant girlfriend. What would he have done, or said, if he'd found Andee at home yesterday? Had he seen her the other evening at the pub? Maybe he didn't know what she looked like, although, given how frequently she'd appeared in the media, it wouldn't have been hard for him to find out.

So the boy either hadn't wanted to approach her the other evening, or he'd been waiting for instructions from Penny before making his next move.

After leaving her car in the underground car park on

Victoria Square, Andee splashed through the puddles of a sudden downpour over to Kesterly police station. Leo Johnson, looking as cute as ever with his mop of carroty hair and rash of cornflake freckles, was waiting to take her up to a fourth-floor conference room. Someone, probably Leo, had thought to order a Thermos of coffee, and when Gould joined them a couple of minutes later he tossed a greasy bag of pastries on to the table with an instruction for them to help themselves.

Gould and Johnson listened quietly as Andee updated them on the past twenty-four hours. Occasionally one or other of them made a note, or nodded, but mostly they scowled with concentration.

'OK,' Gould announced when she'd finished. He leaned back in his chair to retrieve the coffee pot from the buffet behind him. 'Leo has a copy of the inquest report you asked for, which contains some interesting background on the deceased Uncle John. We'll let you read that at your leisure, because I can't see how it'll impact what we're trying to find out now, which is why your sister has decided to return to the fold, if that's how we want to term it, and how frequently she's used your name.'

'Could it cause me a problem?' Andee wanted to know.

'On the face of it, it shouldn't. If she's committed any kind of crime while using it you'll presumably have an alibi, or sufficient grounds for denial, so I can't see anything to worry about. It's more a question of why she's using it. Leo, over to you.'

'After I got your email yesterday,' the young DC began, 'I made some preliminary searches and it turns out that your name appears as a director of Exclusive Chauffeur Drive. It's down as A.G. Laurence, with a "u", but it's as near as damn it.'

'Andrea Greta,' Gould stated, as if she didn't know.

'My maternal grandmother,' she informed them.

'Going further into the company documents,' Leo continued, 'it shows that A.G. Laurence provided the firm's start-up funding back in 2007.'

'Which is kind of what the receptionist told you,' Gould pointed out, 'that she helped her bosses get the company going.'

Andee looked at them, hoping they could come up with some suggestions of how this information might serve them, but apparently they were as lost for an explanation of anything as she was.

Moving them along, Gould said, 'Your nephew, her son, or whoever he is. As we have nothing to go on right now we'll just have to wait to see if he gets in touch again. If he does, I'd caution you to be careful, for the simple reason that we have no idea who he actually is, or what he wants.'

Worriedly, Andee said, 'Do you think my mother's vulnerable in the house when I'm not there?'

'I've been thinking about that,' Gould replied, 'and if there is somewhere you can take her that's a little less remote then it might not be a bad idea.' He took a sip of his coffee and referred to a printout in front of him. 'I'll email this to you,' he told her, 'but, in brief, I've heard back from the Met about your father's old colleague, Gerry Trowbridge. He was a DCS himself by the time he retired, nineteen years ago, but as you're no doubt aware he was a detective inspector at the time of the search for Penny. The good news is he's alive, the bad news is he lives in Wales.'

Confused, Andee said, 'Why is that bad news?'

'I've never got on with the Welsh,' Gould grunted.

Amused, she cast a glance at Leo, who was hiding his own mirth. 'Which is relevant how?' she challenged.

'It's not,' Gould conceded, 'but it's likely to mean you have to go there if you want to speak to him.'

'Well, it's hardly the other side of the world, and I happen to love Wales and the Welsh.'

Casting her a pitying look, he said, 'I tried calling him myself when I got the email, but so far I haven't managed to get hold of him so I can't tell you how willing he might be to talk to you.' He waited as she checked an incoming text.

As she read it her heart skipped a beat moments before her blood ran cold.

Good morning from Houston. Thought you might like to know that the young man who visited our mother yesterday is indeed my son, her grandson. His name is John Victor Jr.

Andee felt suddenly sick. She kept staring at the words, knowing what Penny wanted her to think and trying desperately not to think it. Was she doing this to be spiteful, to hurt her mother in some way, or was it the truth?

Taking the phone Gould read the message, swore under his breath, and passed it to Leo.

'My mother can't know about this,' Andee told them.

'Under no circumstances should she be told, whether it's true or not.'

Neither of them argued.

As Leo returned the phone, Gould said, 'I really don't like what's happening here. In fact, I don't like it at all.'

Andee was so shaken by the text that she couldn't face returning home right away. She needed to be alone to think and try to make sense of what was happening, if there *was* any sense, so switching off her phone she drove along the coast road, turning at Hope Cove to climb the hill to where Graeme's sisters lived, before driving on to the moor.

The weather wasn't at its best as she strolled away from the car, a low gloomy sky stretching out over the bay turning the sea a drab slate-grey and preventing the sun from showing the cliffs and heathland in their natural vivid colours. As she headed towards a deserted bench at a lonely lookout point, she found herself wondering if she was being watched. There was certainly no sign of this, but that was the whole point of surveillance, not to be seen or even sensed by the target. However, it would be hard for a watcher to blend into the landscape here, given that it wasn't possible to reach the spot without a car, and no one had known she was coming, or had been driving behind her for at least the last three miles.

With the breeze tossing her hair and the scent of salty sea mixing with pungent damp earth, she sat quietly staring at the distant choppy waves, picturing Penny as a child, trying to work out what had gone wrong, and why she, as the older sister, hadn't noticed things about her that perhaps she should have done.

What kind of person just walks away from a decent, loving home, no matter what problems there might be, and never comes back?

Not a normal one, that was for sure.

So her sister wasn't normal, at least not in a conventional way, but did that make her bad or crazy, or something much worse?

In her mind's eye she could see Penny during their holidays in Kesterly, laughing excitedly at some mischief they were up to, scampering about the beach in her blue cotton shorts and stripy top, climbing the rocks, foraging for crabs or seashells or whatever booty the tide had delivered. Andee could only remember her sister being happy here. She had scant recollection of their quarrels, though they'd happened, of course, but she had no memory of anything worse than the usual sibling tensions, and certainly not of Penny building a towering resentment that would drive her to inflict cruelty on innocent creatures.

However, there were times when *she*, Andee, had been cruel to Penny, either not wanting to share something with her, or take her to wherever she was going, or help her to look pretty. Teenage behaviour that she was ashamed of now.

'I want to look just like you,' Penny used to beg, 'then everyone will like me too.'

'Don't be ridiculous,' Andee had snapped. 'It's not

about looks, it's about personality and you just don't have one.'

The dreadful things she'd said to her, and she couldn't remember now how Penny had reacted, but she must have been hurt, who wouldn't be when spoken to like that?

'Will you teach me to dance the way you do?' Penny had asked.

'I don't have time, now get out of my way.'

'Have you kissed a boy yet?'

'It's none of your business.'

'I have.'

'Don't lie, you're only thirteen.'

'What's that got to do with it?'

Andee couldn't think why that particular conversation had come back to her now; she had no recall of being especially intrigued at the time. It was the kind of thing Penny used to say to make herself seem more interesting or mysterious without, Andee had assumed, a shred of reality behind it.

Yet according to their mother Penny had actually been sleeping with men at that age. It was what she'd wanted, Maureen had claimed.

Closing her eyes, Andee held her face up to the feathery rain, feeling the dampness in her hair, seeping between her toes and covering her hands. Was it loneliness that had driven Penny to be the way she was, a terrible certainty that her older sister was the favourite and that she wasn't wanted at all?

It didn't excuse what she'd done to their parents; nothing would ever excuse that.

'I've found something out that you don't know,' she'd told Andee not long before she'd disappeared.

'Good for you.'

'Don't you want to know what it is?'

'No.'

'It's about Mum's brother, Uncle John.'

'Sorry, couldn't care less.'

She'd assumed at the time that Penny was about to make something up, or maybe she'd been through their mother's letters and found some old scandal. Whatever, Andee genuinely hadn't been interested. Was that, insignificant as it had seemed at the time, what had finally prompted Penny to go?

She'd said it was her decision.

And what then?

Had she wanted to come back at any time but John Victor had refused to let her? Or had she been happy to stay with him?

John Victor Jr.

Andee's insides churned at the unthinkable suggestion.

With all her heart she wished she could speak to her father right now.

What had really happened back then?

Had he found Penny and walked away?

What clues was she, Andee, missing now?

What did Penny want?

The only person who could answer her questions was Penny, but with the way things were Andee felt no confidence in receiving straight, or even truthful answers. Penny simply wasn't the kind of woman Andee had

142

imagined her growing into; she wasn't someone Andee could feel any sort of affinity with at all. It would appear that, behind the sophisticated, friendly front she so effortlessly put on there was something deeply disturbed and malicious about her sister. Why else would she have reminded their mother about the fate of Smoky the kitten? What had been the point of that? What was she getting from it? And why make her decision to leave, and all the heartbreak she'd caused, sound as though it wasn't something that had remotely worried her? She must have known how hurtful that would be for her mother, though it didn't come close to how Maureen would feel were she to be told who'd fathered her grandson.

'Talk about being careful of what you wish for,' she said to Graeme as she drove back into town. 'All these years I used to dream about how wonderful it would be if she came back into our lives, and now here she is and I can't help wishing . . .' She didn't finish the sentence, he knew what she was saying.

'What have you decided to tell your mother about John Victor Jr?' he asked carefully.

'Nothing at the moment, but I guess I'll have to at some point, or there's a good chance Penny will. Do you think she's done it this way to set me the challenge of telling Mum?'

'If it's true, then given how she's operated so far, I'd say it's possible she wants you to do it for her.'

'Because it would churn my stomach, and once I've told my mother Penny's as likely to deny it, or say I misunderstood, or he isn't her son at all, meaning she'll have caused a lot of stress and upset for no good reason other than to give herself some sort of perverse pleasure.'

But what if she wasn't lying, and she really had had a son with her own uncle?

Slowing as she descended the hill to pass Hope Cove and the Mermaid pub, she said, 'I want to tell her not to bother us any more, that we're not interested in playing her games or finding out any more about her, but even if I did I can't imagine she's going to give up until she's achieved whatever she's come back for.'

'Which frankly is causing me some concern,' he said darkly. 'What are you doing now?'

'I'm on my way home. When I get there I'll contact Gerry Trowbridge to set up a time to go and see him, then I'm going to read the inquest report on John Victor.' Checking to see who was calling, she said, 'I have to ring off now, but I'll call again later if you're going to be around.'

'Dinner with Nadia,' he replied, sounding fed up about it, 'so I'll call you when I get back to the villa.'

Sorely wishing she was still in Provence with him, Andee clicked on to the incoming call saying, 'Hi darling, how're things?'

'Hey Mum. I'm cool,' Alayna replied. 'Did you see the baby rhino? She's soooo sweet. Oh my God, I wish we could adopt her. I think we should.'

'I'm sure it can be arranged.'

'Let's do it. Anyway, you need to check your phone because apart from Hermione – that's what we're calling the rhino – you'll find pictures of me in three different outfits. I so need you to tell me which I look the best in.'

'Is it for something special?'

'I've only got a date with this guy who's the hottest, most ripped, most amazing, coolest dude in town. I'm so excited, but I can't make up my mind what to wear. Sophie says it should be the white lacy top with peppermint jeans; Sanako reckons I look best in the yellow dress with daisies all over and Tamsin's going for the kind of grungy-looking string thingy over the red slip with the Roman sandals you got me the last time you were here. Can you look at them now?'

'I'm driving, but I will as soon as I get home. Actually, if you have the time you could do me a favour.'

'I never have time, but shoot.'

'I'm trying to find someone who we believe is staying at a hotel on Buckingham Palace Road in London. If you can get me names of all the hotels with that address, and their phone numbers, that would be great.'

'I can do better than that if you give me the name of the person we're looking for.'

Loving how she'd immediately jumped on board, while aware that she couldn't give Alayna her own name or Penny's, Andee said, 'She has several aliases, but let's start with Michelle Cross.'

'Got it. When do you need it by?'

'Before you go on your date?'

'No probs. Got to go now, love you,' and she was gone.

By the following morning Andee had read through the inquest report on John Victor's death and left a message for Gerry Trowbridge to call her back as soon as he could. She'd also received an email from Penny, using the name Michelle Cross, asking if she'd met John Jr yet.

Andee hadn't replied.

Let Penny think she'd been spammed, or ignored, either would do. A discussion about the boy and all it could entail wasn't one to have via email. She wasn't even going to bother wondering how Penny had got her email address.

She looked across at her mother as Maureen put aside the inquest report.

'Did it tell you anything you didn't already know?' Andee asked.

Maureen shook her head. 'Not really.'

Having expected as much, Andee said, 'For me one of the most interesting parts is the statement from the neighbour, Alison Brown. Did you know he was living in Shepherd Market up until the time he died?'

'We found out after. Until then we didn't know where he was.'

Andee reached for the report and turned to the part that had caught her attention. ' "He was really upset about something during the weeks before he disappeared," ' she read aloud. ' "He wouldn't tell me what it was . . . I assumed he'd got into some sort of trouble over money again – he was always owing money to someone – but he said that for once it wasn't that. He was definitely on edge. He kept checking to see if anyone was outside. He thought someone was watching him, and a couple of times he said, 'I saw her, I know she's out there.' Then he said, 'She wanted me to see her. She's doing this to freak me out.'

' "Did he ever say who this person was?"

' "No, but it was definitely a she."

' "And you personally have no idea who 'she' was or what she might want?"

' "He said once, 'It's about the kids.' "

' "Kids?"

' "That's all he said. I asked him what he meant, but he wouldn't tell me. He said, 'It's best you don't know or you'll be involved too and you really don't want that.' "

' "Did anything else happen during that time to concern you?"

' "Well, he kind of stopped going out and there was one time when he said, 'If anything happens to me, tell them it wasn't my fault.' "

' "What did you understand from that?"

' "I didn't know what he was talking about, but I guess he might have meant the people he owed money to, or someone he'd hurt in some way. For all I know he could have been talking about the police." '

Andee lowered the report and looked at her mother.

Maureen's face showed the strain she was feeling.

'So who was "she"?' Andee asked. 'This person he thought was stalking him.'

Hoarsely, Maureen said, 'You're thinking it was Penny.'

'It's possible. And who are the kids he mentioned?' Since neither of them could answer that, she went back to the report. 'The last time Alison Brown saw him was about a week before his body was found. She says he was getting into a car outside their building with a man who looked to be around fifty. He was tall, distinguished-looking, with white hair and wearing a long dark coat and round glasses. She didn't think JV was being forced, and she didn't see any sign of a woman.'

After a while, Maureen said, 'So what does that tell us?'

'Nothing on the face of it, but it'll be one reason why the verdict was open, because the man has never been traced. The other reason is that no one has been able to say why John Victor was in West Wales or give any insight into how he got there.' She read again. 'The police searched the clifftops for signs of a struggle, but with so much foot traffic in the area and bad weather at the time the findings were inconclusive.'

Maureen swallowed dryly. 'Do you think he was murdered?'

'Well, given that there was no suicide note or any evidence of him being suicidal at that time . . .' She broke off as Maureen's hands clenched tightly shut and opened again. Her breathing was unsteady; Andee could almost feel her stress building as she got to her feet and went to the window. 'Do you really think she's having us watched?' she asked, peering out at the back garden.

'If she is, it's unlikely that anyone's out there,' Andee replied. 'But I do think Gould's right, that we should move down into the town for a while. We can stay at Graeme's . . .'

'But what on earth do you think is going to happen? This isn't making any sense, Andee. Whatever you think is going on, she's my *daughter* . . .'

'That's who she used to be,' Andee came in gently. 'She's another person now, you've seen that for yourself, and until we know . . .'

'I'm not being pushed out of my own home. Blake and Jenny are just across the way, and the Villiers are right next door. I know he's deaf, but Susan's always in and out of the house. If anyone was behaving strangely around here, she'd be sure to spot them and let us know.'

Thinking of how the most effective form of surveillance was to blend with the environment, Andee said, 'Well will you at least go and stay with Blake and Jenny if I manage to get a meeting with Gerry Trowbridge?'

Maureen looked worried. 'Maybe I should go with you. I don't like to think of you all alone if you're being followed.'

'I'll be fine, I promise. I'm far more worried about how badly this is affecting you.'

Maureen seemed suddenly annoyed. 'I need to pull myself together,' she declared, straightening her back. 'I don't know why I'm letting it get to me, and I certainly don't need to go and hide myself away.'

Deciding not to argue any more for now, Andee went to give her a hug. 'Just don't agree to see Penny without me, OK?' she said, mindful of how shocking the news about Penny's son would be should Penny decide to drop in and break it while Andee wasn't around. 'Or anyone else come to that,' she added teasingly.

'You mean no talking to strangers.'

'That's exactly what I mean,' and going to check who was calling her mobile she saw it was Alayna and clicked on.

'Sorry I didn't get back before,' Alayna stated, 'bit of a late night last night.'

'How was the date?'

'That's not until Friday. So you definitely think the third outfit?'

'The grungy thing over a red whatsit with the Greek sandals,' Andee confirmed.

'Roman, but hey! Brilliant, that's what I thought too. But that's not why I'm calling. I've just emailed you a list of the hotels on Buckingham Palace Road. There are a bunch of them, but it turns out that someone called Michelle Cross is staying at the Forty One. It looks dead posh, so she must be a bit minted. What's she supposed to have done?'

'I'm not sure yet,' Andee hedged. 'You've done brilliantly, thank you. Grandma's here, have a quick chat with her while I go and see who's at the door.'

Thrusting the phone at her mother, and bracing herself for the unexpected caller, Andee closed the hall door behind her and went to answer a second ring on the bell.

To her amazement a deliveryman was brandishing an enormous bouquet of white flowers, mostly lilies and roses. 'Someone's birthday?' he smiled, handing it over.

'Are you sure these are for us?' Andee asked, searching for a card.

'Right there,' he said, pointing. 'And this is Briar Lodge? Mrs Maureen Lawrence?'

'OK, you're in the right place. Thanks very much. Do I need to sign?'

'No, you're good to go,' and with a cheery wave he returned to his van.

After closing the door Andee put the flowers on the stairs and tore open the card.

Dear Mum, I shall be visiting again very soon. Meantime, I hope you like these. Watch out for the roses, we don't want any blood shed now do we. With love, xxx

Fighting back a surge of anger, Andee quickly pocketed the note, and would have binned the flowers had there been a way to get them out of the house before her mother saw them. What the hell was Penny doing? Just what kind of message was this? It was intimidating, full of spite, like venom wrapped up in candy. And how were they supposed to react? It was as though they were in some sort of twisted game that only Penny knew the rules to, and only she derived any satisfaction from.

'Oh my goodness,' Maureen exclaimed, as Andee carried the bouquet into the kitchen. 'They're beautiful. Are they from Graeme?'

'I don't think so. There doesn't seem to be a card.'

Perplexed, Maureen searched amongst the blooms, and finding the cane that had supported the card she said, 'It must have fallen off in the delivery van. We should call to find out who's been so generous. Are you sure they had the right address?'

Without answering Andee plonked the bouquet in the sink and went in search of a vase.

151

'Oh, they're from Penny,' Maureen declared, reading from her phone. *'Hi Mum, hope you got the surprise I sent. Sorry haven't been in touch for last few days, but will get there very soon. PS: Watch out for those thorns.'* Maureen looked at Andee, clearly not sure how to react.

Covering her anger with a shrug, Andee left her mother to sort the flowers while she went upstairs to photograph the card. After texting it to Gould and Leo Johnson, she added the message, *What do you think?*

Within minutes she had a reply from Leo. *Blood shed? Sorry, but your sister's starting to creep me out.*

Just after came a text from Gould. *I read the inquest report last night. Do you think she might have been involved in death of JV?*

I do, she texted back in spite of having no grounds to go on.

Have you contacted Gerry Trowbridge yet?

Waiting for a call back. Why?

I've been hearing things.

What sort of things?

Too soon to clarify, but something's up. Just watch your step.

'OK, that does it, I'm on the next plane back,' Graeme declared when she updated him later.

Startled, Andee cried, 'No, no, you don't have to do that . . .'

'Oh, I do. I've got no idea – *you've* got no idea – what the hell is going on over there, and I'm not prepared to let you go and see this Gerry Trowbridge alone when Gould himself is telling you to watch your step. What's that about? To me it's smacking of some sort of cover-up that might be nearly three decades old, but someone still doesn't want it out there. Have you set a time with Trowbridge yet?'

'Yes, he rang me back just before I called you. He's in the Lake District for the next couple of days, taking a break with his brother and sister-in-law, but he'll be home on Thursday. He's asked if I can go on Friday.'

'OK, what time?'

'After ten in the morning. Apparently his wife has Alzheimer's and she goes to a group therapy session at nine thirty. He's recommended a place for me to stay the night before. The Bell at Skenfrith.'

'I know it. Is that where he lives? Skenfrith?'

'Apparently, yes.'

'Did you tell him Penny was back?'

'I did. He went silent on me. I thought he'd rung off, but then he said, "Yes, come and see me. It's time we had a talk."'

Chapter Nine

She could see Penny ripping into dolls with a knife, stabbing, tearing, gouging out eyes, slicing off fingers, amputating toes. The dolls were Andee's, no longer played with, passed on with love to her sister and destroyed by the inner demons that had powered Penny's growing jealousy. The violence of the dream was still so intense that the very air seemed to crackle and vibrate with it. Maureen was shaking, sitting up in bed, trying to breathe, to shut out the grotesque images that had no place in reality.

Or did they? Had it happened, or was it a figment of her tormented imagination?

It was the suspicion of Penny being involved in John Victor's death that had stirred up the terrible dream, Maureen was certain of that, but thankfully the images were beginning to fade.

Tears continued to run down her cheeks as she lay in the darkness with no sounds to disturb or distract her. Life had never been easy for Penny. She'd forever been losing friends, making new ones only to lose them too. Teachers found her helpful one day, distant and dismissive the next, and Maureen had always known they didn't like her. Other parents never seemed thrilled to see her, the way they often were with Andee, and Maureen had seen how hurt Penny had been by that. It had made her feel more protective of her youngest, but she'd clearly never done a good enough job.

Knowing she wouldn't sleep again for a while, she took herself downstairs to make some tea. She was still feeling shaky, inundated and disoriented. Having shut out so much for so long, it was as though it was all suddenly trying to come back at once, in her waking moments and in her dreams. Her poor mind was struggling to separate fact from fear, to sort dates and times, to know what had really been said and what hadn't, where blame lay and guilt had a rightful home.

Memory wasn't infallible, especially at her age. It had ways of colouring, distorting events that might not even be real.

'Are you OK?'

Maureen started and turned to find Blake in the doorway, looking sleepy and concerned. Remembering that he and Jenny had come to stay while Andee was in Wales, she felt glad he was there. 'Had a bit of a dream,' she confessed. 'I'm sorry if I woke you.'

Dismissing it, Blake said, 'Would you rather be alone?'

'No. I mean, please don't stay up on my account . . .'

'I'd like some tea, if you're making it.'

A few minutes later they were sitting at the table, gazing into their mugs with the early-morning seconds ticking by and the sound of a brisk wind whistling in the chimney.

'They were very different,' Maureen stated after a while. 'Andee was so easy whereas Penny . . .' With a catch in her voice she said, 'I loved her just as much, but I don't think I showed it or told her often enough.' Her tired eyes flickered briefly to Blake and away again. 'I couldn't reach her the way I could Andee. Sometimes she was like an adult before her time. She would look at me in a way that just didn't seem right for a girl her age. And yet she could be such a child, needy, insecure, and she'd put on baby voices . . . Her father hated it when she did that. He'd get cross with her, and she'd do it even more, either to annoy him, or because she couldn't help herself. I've never been sure.'

'She was obviously a complex child,' Blake said softly.

Maureen nodded, thinking that complex was putting it mildly, kindly. 'She'd lie and steal,' she confessed, 'mock people who were worse off than herself, and yet at the same time she could be the kindest, most generous person in the world. She'd come up with ways to make money for good causes, dance-a-thons, cake bakes, fancy-dress walks . . . Everyone used to flock to her then, wanting to be part of the fun. They were full of praise . . . I think she wanted it from her father most of all, but he wasn't good at expressing his feelings. He was proud of what she did, of course, but I don't think she could see it. All she saw was how proud he was of Andee.' Her eyes went back to Blake's as a cold dread ran through her. It wasn't the first time this random fear had come back to her, but this time it was so clear and persistent that she couldn't move past it.

Apparently sensing some sort of change, Blake remained silent, allowing her to decide whether or not she wanted to carry on.

Eventually, in a voice that was barely audible, Maureen said, 'I never met the child. She was in the same class as Penny, and everyone said what a lovely girl she was. They were on a school trip to Canterbury Cathedral and there was . . . there was a terrible accident . . . One of the girls tripped and fell off a pavement into an oncoming bus.'

Blake's breathing had all but stopped.

'Why,' Maureen asked helplessly, 'would Penny choose, all these years later, to use that poor little girl's name?'

Blake took a breath. 'Are you talking about Michelle Cross?' he asked quietly.

Maureen blinked and looked away. 'Yes,' she replied. 'Yes I am.'

Andee and Graeme had just returned from an early-morning hike along Offa's Dyke and were now slumped at each end of a cosy sofa in front of the inglenook fireplace at the Bell in Skenfrith. It was a welcoming old coaching inn at the edge of the village, where castle ruins imposed their grandeur from behind a derelict mill and the River Monnow flowed and gushed and meandered its way south to join the Wye.

Their reunion last night, after not quite two weeks, in one of the pub's luxurious guest rooms, had taken precedence over everything else, and during their walk this morning Andee had encouraged Graeme to share his memories of bringing his sons to the area, to fish, or canoe, or climb Coedanghred Hill, otherwise known as Heart Attack Hill. There would be time enough later to focus on her issues, she'd decided, and she was enjoying learning more about him.

She was also intrigued, as was he, by the young guy in leathers who'd arrived on a motorbike just after they had last night. He'd appeared for dinner with an iPod plugged into his jug ears and a phone never far from his fingertips. He'd barely acknowledged them, in spite of Graeme's cheery hello.

There was no sign of him now, nor of anyone else, as coffee was served along with a delicious assortment of pastries and a menu for more if required.

'Do you think it's safe to talk?' Graeme asked, clearly enjoying the cloak and dagger of it all.

Smiling, Andee said, 'We've got nothing to hide, so why not? What's on your mind?'

With twinkling eyes he said, 'I confess I'm intrigued to know what you're going to find out today. Did you tell Trowbridge I'd be with you?'

'I did and he's fine with it. He sounded very together, as a matter of fact; he didn't even seem to have a problem hearing, and he must be close to ninety by now.'

'What's important is how clear his memory is, and from the response you've got so far I think we can assume it's pretty well intact. Are you nervous?'

'A little.' She checked her phone as it rang. 'It's Blake,' she said, surprise turning quickly to concern. 'He and

Jenny stayed with Mum last night,' she explained, clicking on. 'Hi, is everything OK?'

'It's fine,' Blake assured her. 'Maureen's sleeping in. She had a broken night . . .'

'Did she hear from Penny?'

'No, it was a dream, but she asked me to let you know that she's remembered why the name Michelle Cross was familiar to her.'

As Andee listened to the explanation her insides turned to liquid. Of course. Why hadn't it come to her before? She might have been at another school when it happened, but she remembered the tragedy, she just hadn't remembered the child's name. Then, realising what her mother was really thinking, her head started to spin. 'Did anyone ever say that it might not have been an accident?' she finally asked.

'Your mother doesn't think so,' Blake replied, 'but apparently Penny had fallen out with the girl over something, Maureen can't recall what. She thinks it might have had something to do with Christmas.'

An hour later, aware of their fellow guest in leathers rambling at a distance behind them like a fascinated tourist, Andee and Graeme strolled through Skenfrith village where sweet peas tumbled over drystone walls, and the medieval church of St Bridget's with its dove-cote belfry and red sandstone walls watched over its visitors and residents with a benevolent air. The cottages were small and quaint; the sky overhead was blue, while the hills cradling the community's hollow were towering and green.

'I wonder if he knows Penny as Michelle Cross?' Andee murmured as the pale-haired man with apple cheeks and a bow-legged gait stopped to consult a map. Why on earth had Penny chosen that name when she, of all people, would remember what had happened? It wasn't good, in fact it was downright horrible.

'Shall we ask him?' Graeme suggested mischievously.

Though tempted, if only to let Penny know that her tracker had been rumbled, Andee shook her head and slipped her hand into his. She was so glad to have him here, and so moved by how close they'd been last night, and even now simply walking side by side, that she suspected she was falling quite deeply in love with him. And what a wonderful place it was to be.

After only a few minutes they reached the gate to the last small white house on the right. 'Not the bigger, smart-looking place that's next door,' Gerry Trowbridge had told her. 'I'm afraid ours is a bit run-down these days, but you'll recognise it from the birdhouse in the front garden, and the glorious bundles of buddleia that seem to be trying to take us over.'

As Graeme pushed open the gate Andee glanced back down the street to where their shadow appeared to be reading something in the parish hall window. When he looked her way she gave him a little wave and stepped in behind Graeme as a formally dressed, rangy man with wispy tufts of grey hair clinging to a balding scalp, droopy red cheeks and watery brown eyes came down the path to greet them. Were it not for his stoop he'd probably have been as tall as Graeme, but as it was he was closer to Andee's height, and seemed as fragile, yet durable as the cane assisting his progress.

'Andee,' he said warmly as Graeme moved aside to let her through. 'It's been so many years.' He clasped his arthritic hands around hers, and smiled into her eyes. 'I remember you well, my dear. Your father was always so proud of you.'

'Hello, Gerry,' she said, hoping it was all right to be informal. 'It's good to see you. You're looking . . .'

'Old,' he interrupted with a chuckle, 'because I am. I'll be ninety in a couple of years, if I make it till then. And you must be Graeme. Welcome, I'm very glad to meet you. Any friend of Andee's is a friend of mine.'

'Are you going to keep them standing around out there?' a voice called from inside.

'We're on our way,' he responded, adding so only Andee and Graeme could hear, 'My daughter-in-law. She insisted on coming to make sure you had uncracked cups to drink from and well-plumped cushions to sit on.'

'I'm Meryl,' a cheery-faced, chubby little woman with a melodic Welsh accent and pink-rimmed glasses informed them, as Trowbridge ushered them into what he called the best room. 'I live over by Abergavenny, so not far away,' she chatted on. 'I generally call in here a couple of times a week to make sure they're still breathing. It's a bit doubtful sometimes, but today's a good one. I won't stay, because I haven't been invited to, but there's a nice pot of tea on the table there, and I baked the biscuits myself.'

'She thinks they're delicious,' Trowbridge declared, 'and none of us have the heart to enlighten her.'

'You haven't got a heart,' she countered cheerily. 'Now, don't go overdoing things, I don't want to be calling an ambulance, they've got better things to be doing with their time than fussing about with you.'

Amused by the banter, Andee and Graeme said a reluctant farewell to the twinkling Meryl. Andee set about pouring the tea after Meryl had popped back to warn them not to let her father-in-law near the pot, unless they wanted to drink out of their laps.

'She's a cruel woman,' Trowbridge sighed as the door closed behind her, 'and I don't know where any of us would be without her. She's a saint with my wife, and I can tell you it needs a saint to be dealing with her at times. Terrible business, Alzheimer's, but I can't put her in a home. Not yet, anyway.'

'How long has she been ill?' Graeme asked.

'She was diagnosed six years ago.' With a shaking hand he brought a dainty cup to his mouth and flinched as the hot tea scalded his lip. 'But you didn't come here to discuss my problems,' he said, putting the cup down again, 'so I shall wade right in, if I may, and ask if you're sure it's Penny.'

'As sure as I can be,' Andee replied. Then added, 'Yes, it's her.'

'And where has she been for all this time?'

Having half hoped he'd be able to tell her that, Andee hid her disappointment as she said, 'You don't seem to doubt my word.'

'I don't,' he confirmed. 'Is this the first time she's made contact in all these years?'

Andee glanced at Graeme. 'It is,' she confirmed, adding, 'You sound as though you knew she was alive when the suspicion, or the general belief, was that she'd killed herself.'

'Mm,' he murmured thoughtfully. 'I was never convinced by that suicide note, any more than your father was. Of course, we couldn't discount it, it was definitely written by her, but there were other circumstances . . .' His rheumy eyes moved to Graeme and back to Andee. 'I'm sure you remember your uncle, John Victor,' he said.

Andee tensed as she nodded.

Trowbridge gave a grunt of dislike. 'I met a lot of worthless individuals during my time on the force, it goes with the job . . . He was right up there with the worst of them.'

'So she was with him when she left?' Andee prompted.

'Him and others.'

'How did you know?' Astonished that the police had known where Penny was, Andee bit her tongue, determined to hear the rest of the story first.

Sitting back in his chair, he steepled his gnarly fingers as he let his mind travel across the years to those distant days. 'The first time she went,' he began, 'she was only thirteen. I believe she'd told your parents she was going to stay with a friend, but when she didn't come back after a couple of days they found out the friend didn't exist. We, the police, were already organising a search when your grandmother rang your father to say that Penny was at her place. That was only good news until your grandmother told your father who else was there and what was going on. It was very upsetting for the poor dear, I remember how she tried to blame herself, as if anything like that could possibly be her fault. When we got there there was no sign of Victor, he'd taken off as soon as he found out his mother had called us, but Penny was still there. She told us she didn't want to leave. She was enjoying herself, she said, as if we ought to be pleased for her in some way.' Trowbridge shook his ancient head in dismay. 'Such attitude she had, and she was still so young. She kicked up badly when your father and I grabbed her and carried her out to the car.'

He sighed unsteadily and leaned forward to take another sip of his tea. 'I'm not sure how long it was before she disappeared again,' he continued, 'but the next time we knew where to look. Not her grand-mother's, she didn't go there, but she was with Victor all right, at a big house in Chelsea, and I mean big. It belonged to some Russian, I forget his name; it was a long time ago.

'He'd rented the place for his people, we were told, and by people no one was meaning family. Don't ask me where Victor fitted into the picture, I guess he was some sort of drone, you know, one of those types that the very rich and crooked usually surround themselves with . . . A court jester, a facilitator – who knew what his role was? He must have had one, because he was clearly at home there, and didn't seem in the least bit upset that we'd found him. I guess, when you're surrounded by thugs and hitmen and they're on your side, you can afford to be cocky.

'We didn't have to tell him why we were there, he told us. He even took us to Penny. There she was, lying on the bed, drugged or drunk, we didn't know which, and not wearing very much. She was just about conscious, enough to tell us to get the hell out, not using those words exactly, far more colourful. Thirteen years old and she was behaving like a . . .' He caught himself. 'She was like a woman twice her age, and she was clearly learning from the girls she was mixing with.'

'Who were they?' Andee asked.

'A lot were foreign. In fact, I think they all were, or the ones we met, and of course none of them could speak English, or so they claimed. We didn't press it, not then, we just wanted to get her out as fast as we could. She didn't come without a fight, but we got her home eventually and your father tried just about every way he could think of to deal with her. Nothing worked, because she just kept on going back. We always found her in the same place, and because the "people" didn't want any trouble they usually took us right to her and even helped us to get her out to the car. It damned near broke your father's heart, I can tell you. Well, it did in the end. We know that.'

'But if you found her all those times, how come you didn't the last time?' Andee asked.

'Because she wasn't at the house when we got there, and everyone swore they hadn't seen her. I've got no idea where she went, all I can tell you is what happened during our interviews with John Victor.'

'So there were interviews? Why aren't they on record?'

'Because your father and I decided to deal with him ourselves, in the hope that if we guaranteed to keep him and his friends out of it he could be persuaded to tell us where she was. He swore he didn't know, but we could tell he was lying. He knew all right, but we didn't even manage to get the cuffs on him before he said that if we even attempted to implicate him he would expose the sexual abuse she'd been suffering for years at home.'

Andee drew back in shock. She hadn't heard right, surely. Somehow she'd misunderstood, but she could see from the expression on Trowbridge's face that she hadn't. 'It isn't true,' she told him.

'I never thought it was, but we could see Victor was serious. She'd told him, or so he said, that her father and grandfather had been molesting and raping her since she was six years old. I'm sure I don't have to describe how that affected your father . . . I can tell you this much, Victor was lucky to come out of that interview alive.'

Andee sat back in her chair, so appalled she hardly knew what to say.

'Did you see her at that time?' Graeme stepped in. 'She claimed recently that her father saw her once and turned around and walked away.'

Trowbridge shook his head. 'I don't remember that,' he replied. 'As far as I'm aware, after the last time she disappeared none of us ever saw her again.'

'So how did you know that she'd back Victor in his claims?'

'Because she called your father and told him she would. I didn't hear the conversation; I only know that he didn't doubt she meant it. If he made her come home she'd tell the world what he'd been doing to her.'

'Jesus Christ,' Andee murmured, unable to imagine just how devastated and afraid her father must have felt at that time.

'You know what it would have done to your father's career,' Trowbridge went on, 'never mind to your family, if even a whisper of an accusation like that came out. You'll have seen it plenty of times. Innocent men's lives ruined by false accusations of child abuse. Even if he could prove himself innocent you'd always be the daughter of the child-molester cop, because that sort of mud sticks. People would look at you and wonder if you'd been molested too. He couldn't even be certain that you and your mother would believe in his innocence. Penny didn't want to be a part of the family any more, she'd given that as the reason, so maybe in your hearts you'd always wonder . . .'

'We never would have,' Andee told him forcefully. 'Not my father, or my grandfather . . .'

'I believe you, but it was hard to convince your father, especially when we still had no idea where Penny was or what she was doing. We couldn't even be sure, after the phone call, that she was still alive. And I guess he wasn't thinking too straight; the stress, the fear was tearing him apart . . . I tried to advise him, but I barely knew what to do myself.'

Andee tried to imagine what she'd have done faced

with such a harrowing dilemma, but there were no easy answers.

'A lot of rules were broken after that,' Trowbridge admitted. 'The higher-ups knew what was happening, we had to tell them and I'm glad we did, because it turned out they were no keener for one of their senior officers to be embroiled in a child abuse scandal than your father was to be at the centre of one. So he was given time to carry on playing things his way with Victor. Then the note turned up, and he decided it would be easier on you, and your mother in particular, to believe in the possibility of suicide rather than to have to deal with what he'd learned about Penny.'

Stunned, Andee cried, 'It was the wrong decision.'

Trowbridge didn't argue.

'So you stopped looking?' Graeme prompted.

'No, of course not, but in the backs of our minds there was always the fear that the letter was for real. There were never any sightings of her, and surveillance on Victor never got us anywhere apart from up a garden path. So perhaps she was dead. We know now that she wasn't, but where she went and what she's been doing for all these years, I'm afraid only she can tell you.'

Andee looked at Graeme, knowing there was more she needed to ask, but for the moment she seemed unable to unravel her thoughts or emotions.

Apparently understanding, Graeme said to Trowbridge, 'I take it you know John Victor's dead?'

Trowbridge nodded.

'Can you tell us anything about that? Do you think Penny might have been involved?'

Trowbridge's eyes remained focused on the middle distance as he said, 'It happened a long time after she disappeared, but anything's possible, and I certainly don't think his death was an accident. No one did.'

'Did you go to the inquest?' Andee asked.

'Yes, because your father asked me to. He'd retired by then, as you know, and taken you and your mother to Kesterly . . . In fact, you must have been in the force yourself by that time . . .'

'I was at detective school,' she confirmed. 'I remember the death. I didn't go to the funeral, or the inquest, but I've read the report. The neighbour, girlfriend, Alison Brown had an interesting story to tell.'

Trowbridge agreed. 'I expect you're wondering if the woman Alison Brown referred to, the one Victor kept seeing, or feeling was stalking him, was your sister. I wondered the same, so I spoke to Alison after the hearing but she was certain he'd never mentioned a name.'

'She said he mentioned children. Kids.'

'Yes, but I'm afraid I can't tell you anything about that.'

Andee said, 'My mother's been approached by a young man claiming to be Penny's son. Apparently his name is John Victor Jr.'

Trowbridge's eyes closed. He seemed to be struggling mentally with something deeply unpleasant. 'Have you spoken to him?' he asked in the end.

'No, but he says he wants to speak to me. I just don't know how to get hold of him.'

Seeming more upset than he had throughout the entire time they'd been talking, Trowbridge said, 'I wish I could be of more help to you, but I suppose the question of whether or not Penny's alive is no longer in doubt. Maybe that's something.'

'Maybe,' Andee murmured.

Graeme went to help as Trowbridge rose unsteadily to his feet.

'See if you can track down Alison Brown,' Trowbridge advised as he walked ahead of them to the front door. 'As I recall she found something in Victor's apartment that didn't get mentioned at the inquest, probably because no importance was attached to it. When she showed it to me . . . I remember it rang some bells. It was like something I'd read before, or heard someone say . . . I'm sorry, I can't remember the words now, but maybe she does, and you never know, they might mean something to you.'

Andee and Graeme were back at the Bell, sitting at a table in the bar with drinks and lunch menus between them. There was so much to think about, to try to understand and know how to process, that neither of them gave a thought to the fact that their stalker seemed to have disappeared.

'It's hard to imagine the kind of hell my father went through,' Andee said, staring into her wine. 'I don't blame him for making some wrong decisions. When you're in the thick of something like that, especially where family's concerned, it's impossible to know what to do for the best. I just wish he'd trusted us.'

'I don't think it was a question of trust,' Graeme responded. 'It was the burden you and your mother would have to carry that clearly worried him the most. The scandal, the heartache, the unforgiving memories some people have . . . You know how these things work. The world never seems to forget the sordid details of other people's tragedies, even if those details turn out to be lies.'

Yes, Andee did know, particularly where accusations of child abuse were concerned. She'd seen too many lives ruined by the malicious claims of others who had no care for anyone but themselves – no conscience or morals.

'And let's not forget,' Graeme continued, 'he would have been trying to protect Penny so that she wouldn't have to live with what she'd done, if she'd carried out the threat. She was very young, he would've believed her capable of change. He probably even expected it.'

Sighing sadly as she considered her father's terrible dilemma, Andee said, 'All those years we spent turning her into a saint in our minds, deliberately forgetting the bad things, only focusing on happy times, wishing she was still with us to share in a world that should have been hers. We had no idea she'd completely and deliberately rejected it. How is it possible for someone to be so cruel to her own family? Of course, people can, I know that, but I'm having a hard time accepting that it's happened to mine.'

171

Graeme was reading a text on his mobile, but looked up when she stopped speaking.

'Are you going to call her?' he asked, indicating to the waiter that they needed more time.

'Not yet, but I will, unless she calls me first.'

'And what are you going to tell your mother?'

'I'm still undecided about that, but I think it probably has to be the truth. It'll be too hard trying to hide it.'

Glancing at his phone as it rang, he grimaced an apology. 'Nadia. She's just texted so she's clearly keen to get hold of me . . .'

'Don't mind me,' Andee insisted, and reaching for the menu as he left the table she tried to concentrate on the appetising choices on offer, while her mind continued to whirl with everything she'd learned from Trowbridge that morning.

I've found something out that you don't know, she recalled the teenage Penny boasting all those years ago. *Don't you want to know what it is? It's about Mum's brother, Uncle John.*

What would Penny have told her if she'd bothered to listen, and if she had would it have made a difference?

Hearing Graeme laugh, she came back to the present.

'Don't worry, don't worry, it'll all be done,' he was telling Nadia. 'Yes, I promise. I'm not exactly sure when I'll be back, but everything's running to schedule . . . OK, ciao, ciao. Mm, same to you.'

As he rang off Andee almost asked what the 'same to you' meant, but managed not to. It was true that Nadia was an exceptionally beautiful woman, not to mention

172

rich, charming and flirtatious, but now definitely wasn't the time to start feeling worried when Graeme was here, with her, lending every bit of support he could to this bizarre and unnerving crisis that was consuming her world.

Had her father expected Penny to return one day? Had he even seen her before he died and never told anyone?

Chapter Ten

It was just after five that evening when Andee and Graeme drew up outside Briar Lodge, where they had to wait for a chauffeur-driven silver Mercedes to clear the drive so they could get in.

'Why didn't my mother let me know she was coming?' Andee demanded, sounding angrier than she actually felt.

'Maybe she turned up unexpectedly,' Graeme suggested.

Accepting that could be true, Andee got out of the car, still annoyed because this was not how she'd wanted the next encounter with her sister to happen. She'd rather have seen her alone first, or at least have had a chance to speak to her mother so she could prepare her, but that clearly wasn't going to be possible. 'I think the way to handle this,' she said as Graeme joined her, 'is to let Penny do all the talking and see where it gets us.'

Agreeing, Graeme pushed open the kitchen door for her to go ahead, and almost collided with her as Penny's greeting brought her to an abrupt stop.

'Speak of the devil, and here she is,' Penny gushed, arms wide as she came to Andee. 'Tell me, how was dear old Gerry Trowbridge? As informative as you'd hoped? Or has the poor soul lost his marbles by now?'

Andee's eyes shot to her mother, but the way Maureen quickly shook her head told her that Penny hadn't got her information here. So this was a blatant admission that she'd had Andee followed. Coolly accepting the embrace, Andee said, 'This is a surprise. Had you said you were coming?' Again she looked at her mother.

'I was in the garden,' Maureen told her. 'I didn't even hear the door. She only just got here, less than ten minutes ago.'

Realising her mother was both flustered and relieved that she was no longer having to handle Penny alone, Andee briefly softened her expression before saying to Penny, 'So when did you get back from Houston?'

With an airy wave Penny said, 'This morning. Panic allayed, or at least delayed. I only wish I could say the same for here, but that's another story. I'm going to guess that you're Graeme,' she said, treating him to an appreciative once-over as she reached for his hand.

'It's good to meet you,' he told her.

'Likewise. I hope we're going to get to know one another much better.'

Was she flirting, Andee wondered with no little ire?

Appearing oblivious to it if she was, Graeme offered to make tea while Andee followed her mother and Penny to the sofas where they'd been before she came in.

175

'So,' Penny prompted chattily, 'are you going to tell us how you got along with Gerry Trowbridge?'

Determined not to be rattled, or led, Andee said, 'I'd rather hear about why you chose to come now, when you apparently knew I wasn't here.'

Penny looked amazed. 'I'm sorry, I didn't realise I needed to check with you first, but I promise I'll be sure to do so next time. I hope I haven't caused a problem.'

Since she didn't appear to have done so, Andee let it drop and instead indulged in some wrong-footing of her own. 'Why did you use my name when you booked a chauffeur to take you to France?'

Penny looked startled, then laughed. 'Well, I suppose I was feeling ironic at the time,' she countered with a playful glance towards Maureen.

Andee waited for more, but no more came. 'That's not an answer,' she pointed out.

'Isn't it? I thought it was. Is it not permissible to feel ironic?'

'Are we going to have a sensible conversation,' Andee challenged, 'or are you here to waste our time?'

'Andee,' her mother scolded.

'It's all right,' Penny assured her. 'I can see Andee's cross with me, and I suppose I don't blame her. It's probably quite upsetting to discover that someone has been using your name, but it's not as if it was identity theft, or anything serious like that. It's just a little thing I do from time to time to keep us close.'

To keep us close! What the heck was that supposed to mean?

'Do you have documents in my name?' Andee demanded.

'No.'

Hoping it was true, Andee continued. 'And what about Michelle Cross? Is using her name something you do to keep yourself feeling close to her?'

Penny's expression turned mournful as she said, 'Poor, sweet Michelle. It was so tragic what happened to her. Losing her life before it had even properly begun. Yes, I use her name as a reminder, as a tribute almost, kind of letting her share in a life she missed out on. And before you ask, yes I do have documents in her name. She didn't need it any more, and when I required a new one hers was the first that came to mind.'

Faintly repulsed by that, Andee looked at her mother as Maureen asked, 'Why did you need a new name?'

Penny regarded her in a way that said *surely you know the answer to that.* To be clear, she replied, 'Everyone was looking for Penny Lawrence. It was the only thing we could think of to help me hang on to my new-found freedom.'

'Freedom?' Maureen echoed faintly.

'From all of you,' Penny explained. 'No one seemed to understand that I didn't want to come back. I was happy, for the first time in my life. I was living in John's world, doing things I loved with people I loved and who loved me.' Twinkling, she added to Andee, 'I expect Gerry Trowbridge has already told you all about it.'

Wishing this wasn't happening in front of her mother,

Andee said, 'Maybe you'd like to tell us yourself, in case he got it wrong.'

'Oh, I don't suppose he did.'

Maureen was watching them carefully, apparently trying to keep up.

'I'm presuming you don't want to spell it out in front of Mum,' Andee stated, 'so shall we . . .'

'I will if you want me to,' Penny interrupted.

Too stubborn to back off, Andee said, 'Then perhaps you can begin by telling us how you made your initial connection with John Victor.'

Maureen flinched as Penny threw out her hands in amazement.

'He was our uncle. You knew him as well as I did.'

Since that was patently untrue on the second count, Andee stared at her hard.

Apparently enjoying the silent treatment, Penny let it run for a while, before saying, 'It was quite simple, really. I knew he was the black sheep of the family, which was exactly how I felt, so I found his number in Mum's phone book and called to ask if I could go to see him. He said yes, we got along . . . Would you like the details of that particular part of it?'

Certain her mother wouldn't, and nor did she, Andee said, 'Whose idea was it for you to stay with him?'

'Mine. And his. Actually, everyone's. I fitted in. We were a happy-go-lucky commune living life to the full in a house on Glebe Place, in Chelsea. Do you know it?' She was looking at Graeme.

'The street,' he confirmed. 'Probably not the house.'

'But I'm sure you've been there.'

'I'm sure I haven't.'

Penny's eyebrows arched as she turned back to Andee.

Wondering what she was up to, Andee said, 'How long did you stay in that house?'

Penny frowned as she thought. 'Well, I was back and forth quite a lot between various countries and so on, and I was almost seventeen when I got sold, so that would make it close to three years.'

'Sold?' Maureen echoed in disbelief. 'What are you talking about?'

Penny's tragic look struck Andee as a tad overdone as she said, 'I'm afraid your brother ran into some financial difficulties, and selling me was how he solved them.'

Maureen looked at Andee, so aghast she had no idea what to say.

Unable to tell if Penny was being truthful, Andee said, 'Who did he *sell* you to?'

'Ah, well there begins a part of my life story that I'd really rather forget, but I understand that you need to know so I'll do my best. You see, I was already working as an escort – sorry, Mum, but you must have guessed.'

Maureen didn't deny it.

'The difference was, at the house on Glebe Place we girls were treated like princesses. We had everything we could ever want, money, clothes, jewellery, holidays . . . Men would fly us in private jets to their yachts, or their gorgeous villas in exotic places and lavish us with everything our hearts desired. We could

179

even say no if we weren't in the mood . . . It was a magical time. I really felt as though I belonged, and I was quite popular as well, being as young as I was.'

Seeing that her mother was shrinking inside, Andee said to her, 'Do you want to hear any more of this? If you don't I'm sure Graeme will take you over to the pub.'

'No, I want to hear it,' Maureen assured her, sounding hardier than she looked. To Penny she said, 'Was my brother acting as your pimp during that time?'

Penny frowned. 'That's a harsh word,' she chided. 'The way I'd put it is that he was very good at introducing me to people he thought would enjoy my company, and whose company I would also enjoy. He was very attentive to my needs. He even organised private dance lessons for me so I could expand my entertaining talents. I'm afraid I'm nowhere near as limber these days, but we are talking some time ago.'

Knowing precisely what sort of dancing she was referring to, Andee let her mother continue to study Penny's expressions and tone.

'So the entire time we were going out of our minds with fear and worry,' Maureen declared incredulously, 'you were right there, in Chelsea?'

Penny grimaced. 'Well, not then,' she admitted. 'It was all getting a bit fraught around the time I decided to take off for good, so John's boss Val, short for Valentin, flew me to his home on the Black Sea. You should see it, it's as grand as Buckingham Palace, or it was. I've no idea if it's still there, but . . .'

Cutting her off, Maureen said, 'So you knew what

you were putting us through, but it didn't matter to you?'

Sounding apologetic, Penny said, 'To be honest I didn't think you cared.'

'But if you saw the news, heard me making an appeal . . .'

'Actually, I stayed away from the news because it always brought me down. I find it very depressing, even now. Oh lovely,' she smiled as Graeme set a tray on the table. 'I'm getting quite thirsty doing all this talking.'

After waiting for their cups to be filled and for Graeme to settle into the chair her father had always used, Andee said, 'So you were sold. To whom?'

Penny's eyes went down, and the way she seemed to hunch into herself made her appear surprisingly fragile.

Was this an act, Andee wondered.

Maureen said, 'You don't have to tell us . . .'

'I was sold to some very bad people,' Penny murmured, not looking at them. 'Very bad indeed. I expect you came across their type, Andee, when you were in the police. Traffickers. They're the kind no decent people ever want to meet, and no one in their right mind would ever want to mess with. They didn't take care of us girls at all. The places they kept us . . .' She swallowed dryly and put a partly-gloved hand to her head. 'One mattress between three girls, paper peeling off damp walls, windows cracked and broken to let in the freezing air, bare floorboards, the kind of toilet facilities that made you gag to go near them. Sometimes we were lucky to get fed more than once a day, and the men they made us work for were animals.'

Andee could see her mother's colour draining.

'They gave us drugs, of course,' Penny went on. 'Hard drugs and often cut with something bad. Anything to keep us quiet and submissive.' Putting down her cup, she peeled back the gloved end of one sleeve to reveal her eczema-ravaged hand, and rolled it up further to show the scars she still bore from those days. Though faint now, there was no mistaking the old puncture wounds and purplish withering of the skin. 'My neck and feet don't make pretty pictures either,' she told them. 'Most of my hair fell out during that time, and several teeth – one was knocked out by someone who tried to stab me. It was its own kind of hell. I wanted to come home then, when I was lucid enough to remember I had a home. When I was sober I felt so sick and afraid that I wanted to die. We all did. We tried to escape, but we never could and the punishment when we were caught was terrible. Our handlers were brutal beyond anything I even knew existed. I can still remember some of their names, Rafal, Edouard, Mohammed . . .'

'Where were they holding you?' Andee asked, trying to break what might have been a rehearsed story, although the scars and even the tone were certainly convincing.

Penny didn't appear thrown. 'They moved us around so we never really knew where we were, north, south, England, Wales. I don't think we ever went overseas, but I can't say for sure. They used to pile us into the back of a van that had no windows, no air, and drive us for hours to the next place and keep us there until they decided it was time to move us on again.'

'Were there never any police raids? Someone at some stage must have been suspicious, even if they didn't realise exactly what was happening?'

'The only police that came weren't there to rescue us.'

The meaning of that was so clear that Andee almost regretted asking the question.

'In better moments I used to try and teach the other girls to speak English,' Penny continued. 'Most of them had been brought from other countries, lured in with promises of a better life and money enough to send back to their families. It was tragic and hopeless. We were so young, all of us. I knew they'd need to speak English if we ever managed to get away, even if it was only to ask for help. I remember one girl who was only twelve and so tiny she looked closer to ten. Her name was Helena. She'd left home with her sister, but no one knew where the sister was. I never found out where she was from; the first rape she suffered was so vicious it killed her before I could get that far. I've no idea what they did with her body, or any of the bodies they ended up with, because it wasn't unusual for someone to die. There were never any questions asked, no one even knew they were in the country.'

Knowing very well how those types operated, Andee said, 'How did you manage to survive it?'

Penny shrugged. 'I've no idea, but there were plenty of times I thought I wouldn't.'

'How long were you there?' Maureen asked.

'Four, nearly five years. And do you want to know how I got out? Now here's an irony for you, the man who put me there, who sold me to save his own skin, was the same man who brokered the deal to get me out. In fact, if I were feeling generous I could say he rescued me, but actually it wasn't really John Victor who did that, it was Sven and his wife Ana. They changed my life. I have them to thank for everything.'

Though keen to know more about these angels of mercy, if they existed, Andee was more interested right now to hear the vital part of the story that Penny had blithely missed out. 'Where was your son all this time?' she asked softly.

Penny's demeanour changed; her eyes sharpened with a wariness that hadn't been there a moment ago.

'If he's the age we think he is,' Andee continued, 'you must have had him when you were sixteen or seventeen.'

Penny's face was taut. 'My son is my business, no one else's.'

'But he's my grandson,' Maureen pointed out. 'That alone makes him my business. The fact that he came here . . .'

'Was an act of foolishness on his part and he knows it.'

'Foolish to want to meet his family?' Andee countered.

Penny didn't answer, and when it became clear no one else was going to speak, Graeme said, 'Where was he during the time you were . . . imprisoned?'

Minutes ticked by. The air was awful, tense and full of resentment. In the end Penny spoke as if the

184

question hadn't been asked. 'Did Gerry Trowbridge tell you about the time Daddy saw me and turned around and walked away?'

Stiffening along with her mother, Andee said, 'He says it never happened.'

Penny didn't appear surprised or troubled. 'I was still in Glebe Place,' she said, 'and I admit it probably wasn't the best way to see your daughter. I was high and not alone. The man I was with actually invited Daddy to join in.' She smirked sourly. 'He didn't know who the stranger at the door was, of course.'

Trying to blot the scene from her mind, Andee said, 'Did you speak to him?'

'I don't think so. I can't remember now. He was there one minute, gone the next.'

'If he knew where you were,' Maureen stated, 'he'd have brought you straight home. Or he'd have sent other officers in to get you.'

'He couldn't do that.'

'Why? I don't understand.'

'Mum,' Andee tried to interrupt.

'Please listen,' Maureen admonished.

Penny looked directly at Andee. 'Trowbridge told you.'

'Would you have carried out the threats?' Andee challenged.

'Of course.'

'What threats?' Maureen wanted to know.

Penny said, 'I told him I'd tell the world what he and his father had been doing to me for years.'

Maureen's jaw dropped; a moment later she was looking desperately at Andee.

'It's not true, Mum,' Andee assured her. To Penny she said, 'Why would you lie like that?'

'They abused me,' Penny declared, 'and our mother allowed it to happen.'

Stunned, Andee watched Maureen turn white as she got to her feet. With a shaking hand pointing towards the door, she said, 'Get out of my house. Get out right now and don't ever come back.'

Penny's eyes darkened with something terrible as she stood up. 'If you think this is over . . .'

'Get out!' Maureen screamed. 'You are no daughter of mine.'

Graeme rose quickly to steady her as Andee, not yet finished, followed Penny outside. 'Why are you telling these lies?' she hissed, spinning Penny back as she closed the door behind her.

'Lies?' Penny echoed smoothly.

'We both know that Daddy would never have laid a finger on you that way . . .'

'You tell yourself what you want to.' She was looking at her phone as it rang.

Grabbing it before she could answer, Andee said, 'Tell me this, does your son know who his father is?'

Penny's eyebrows arched, almost as though she was enjoying the challenge. 'Are you saying you'd tell him?' she asked. 'I don't believe you would, but you won't get the chance, because he knows what'll happen if he tries to come near you again.'

Having no idea what that meant, Andee glanced round as the door opened behind her.

'Ah, Graeme,' Penny smiled sweetly. 'Tell me, how's Nadia?'

'You know her?' Graeme responded, startled.

'Not as well as you do,' she replied, and taking her phone from Andee she went to get into her car.

'None of it's true,' Maureen insisted as soon as Andee returned. 'Why is she saying these things? Neither your father, nor his father, would ever . . .'

'I know, I know,' Andee interrupted, going to calm her. 'Nobody believes it, but according to Gerry Trowbridge Daddy was afraid people would and if they did he was even more fearful of what it would do to us, you and me . . .'

'But if he knew where she was . . .'

'She didn't want to come back. That was the whole point. She just told us, she was happy where she was. At least while she was in Chelsea.'

'But what happened after . . .'

'He wouldn't have known where she was then.'

'Oh, Andee. This is terrible. I wish . . . I don't want to say it, but I'm starting to wish she'd never come back.'

'Me too, but she's done it for a reason, and I'm damned sure that it's connected to her son.'

'Which means we have to find out more about John Victor,' Graeme stated, pulling the cork from a bottle of wine. 'She must have had the baby before he used her to pay off his debts. A child would never have survived what she went through, and the thugs who bought her wouldn't have wanted it around anyway.'

'So what happened to him?' Andee murmured, afraid that she might already know the answer.

Not until she and Graeme were alone did Andee voice her suspicions. 'Did John Victor keep the baby,' she wondered, 'or, God forbid, did he sell him too?' Taking out her phone she connected to Gould, and took a few minutes to update him on what she'd learned over the last couple of days. 'If you can spare Leo,' she said, 'I need him to find out everything he can about this Val or Valentin who owned the house on Glebe Place, and anyone else living there at the time in question. I'd also like to know the whereabouts of Alison Brown.'

'Remind me,' he prompted.

'She's the woman who gave evidence at the inquest.'

Chapter Eleven

Thanks to a shooting on the notorious Temple Fields estate, followed by a chaotic hunt for the gunman, it was over a week before Andee received any news from Leo. During that time neither she nor her mother heard anything from Penny, or her son. All that seemed to be happening, to Andee's annoyance, was that she was becoming ever more aware of how often Graeme spoke to Nadia on the phone. In spite of knowing that this was exactly what Penny had intended – plant a seed of doubt and let insecurity or paranoia or simple imagination take it from there – she was in danger of falling for it.

But the calls were frequent, the tone was usually fond and Nadia was clearly quite gifted when it came to making him laugh.

'It's a huge job, and she's paying him a fortune,' Andee informed her mother, as they waited for Graeme to finish yet another call before they wandered over to the pub for lunch.

'She's probably one of those needy types,' Maureen

commented, 'can't do or think anything without getting someone's approval first.'

Although this wasn't the Nadia Andee had met, she decided to let the subject drop rather than allow Penny's manipulation to occupy any more of her thoughts.

'I'll need to go back in a day or two,' Graeme informed them as they meandered across the green. 'The builders should be ready to move on to the next phase by the end of the week, so I ought to be there to supervise.'

'Have you asked Nadia if she knows my sister?' Andee wondered, as they settled down at one of the outdoor tables.

'No, I haven't. For one thing I wouldn't know which name to use for your sister, and for another it would make me feel I was dancing to her tune.'

Surprised and impressed by that, Andee said, 'So you thought the same as I did, that she was trying to get to me?'

'Of course, I *know* she is trying to get to you. And I'm glad to see it hasn't worked. Now, Maureen, what will it be? A glass of Picpoul?'

As he went into the pub Andee began texting Alayna, wanting to know how her second date with the ripped and amazing coolest dude in town had gone, when Graeme's phone vibrated. Glancing at it, she saw the message was from Nadia and had read it before she could stop herself. *Don't worry about the hotel. I'll see to it. Bisous chéri.*

As the screen darkened Andee looked at her mother, who had also read the text.

'It doesn't have to mean anything,' Maureen said carefully.

'I'm sure it doesn't.'

'He's a good man.'

'I know that.' Andee was trying to be patient.

'But she's rich and beautiful . . .'

'Says who?'

'You, but money won't sway Graeme any more than looks. For someone like him it's personality, character that counts.'

'Well, she's blessed in that area too,' Andee commented, waving out to Brigand Bob who'd just emerged from the Smugglers' Cave.

'I asked Bob yesterday,' Maureen said, 'if he'd seen the boy in the red Corsa again, but he hasn't.'

Andee had been thinking a lot about her nephew too.

'I wonder where he is, what he's doing,' Maureen sighed.

Andee said, 'If you're serious about not wanting Penny back here . . .'

Maureen's jaw tightened. 'Of course I'm serious. I'll never forgive her for what she said about your father, and to claim that I stood by and let it happen . . . What kind of person is she?' She raised a hand as Andee made to interrupt. 'I don't know and I don't care who she is,' she declared, 'but I do know that we don't need her in our lives.'

Although she was aware of how much it was hurting her mother to say that, Andee didn't argue. What she said was, 'But her son might need us, that's what you keep thinking?'

191

Maureen didn't deny it. 'Don't you?' she asked.

'Of course, and I'll find him, but to do that I'll either need to see Penny again or make some sort of breakthrough where John Victor is concerned, possibly both.' She checked her phone as it rang. Seeing it was Leo Johnson she clicked on. 'Leo,' she declared, relieved to get a call at last. 'Do you have any news on Valentin of Glebe Place, or John Victor?'

'OK, we know JV bought it going over a cliff. In Valentin's case it was cancer and he was back in Moscow by then. The Chelsea house was sold in '99 to some advertising type who's still there throwing his own lifestyle parties, but I don't think they fall into quite the same category as those of Valentin's day. Tracking anyone who lived in the house around the time your sister was there is going to be near impossible, given that there are no records to assist us. However, I've had a bit more luck where Alison Brown of inquest fame is concerned. It wasn't easy; she's Ally Jackson these days and is a very respectable solicitor for a firm based in Kensington. She, her husband and two kids live in Hammersmith, not far from the River Café she told me, as if I'd know where that is.'

'You've spoken to her?'

'I took the liberty of using my position with the force to ask if she'd be willing to talk about John Victor, and she said she'd be happy to, but she doesn't know any more than she told the inquest.'

'People always know more than they think,' Andee murmured. 'You're a star, Leo. Thanks very much. Will you text me her number and the address?'

'Sure. On its way. I told her you're a relative of Victor's, by the way.'

Andee couldn't object to the truth, much as she disliked it. She waited for Ally Jackson's address and phone number to come through and called right away. 'Hello,' she said to a voicemail, 'this is Andee Lawrence. I believe Leo Johnson told you I'd be calling. I'd be grateful if you could get back to me so we can set up a time to meet.'

As she was ringing off Graeme's phone vibrated again. Not a text, a call from Nadia. Andee's eyes went to her mother. She couldn't answer it, she had no right to. All she could do was wait to see how long it took Graeme to get back to her, which turned out to be almost immediately after he brought the drinks.

'I'll just be a minute,' he said, and taking the phone out of earshot he left Andee and Maureen wondering why he always seemed to have to speak to Nadia in private.

Whatever the reason, it was plain when he returned that he was worried or upset, possibly even angry. 'Apparently half the tradesmen have walked off the job,' he informed them.

'Why?' Maureen asked, confused.

'Nadia is not a project manager,' he replied, meaning, Andee suspected, that Nadia had managed to upset them all. 'I'll have to go back, or heaven only knows what sort of mess it'll end up in.'

Andee said, 'You should be able to get a flight in the morning. I'll drive you to the airport if you like.'

'Thanks. I'm sorry, but right now I think I'm needed a lot more there than I am here.'

Andee didn't correct him. How could she, when it appeared to be true?

It turned out that Ally Jackson's home was indeed close to Hammersmith's River Café, and since she'd told Andee there would be somewhere for her to park Andee had driven straight there after dropping Graeme at the airport.

'You're not letting me down,' she'd assured him as he got out of the car. 'It's just that your priorities are different right now, and I understand that. You can't put this project into any further jeopardy.'

It was true, he couldn't, and because she knew he wasn't deceitful or in anyway uncaring of what was happening in her world, she really did believe there were problems in France. She only wished she'd been able to go with him to help sort them out. Their first big project together and she was the one letting him down.

Pulling into the small forecourt that had once been a garden at the address Ally Jackson had given her, she closed the sunroof and turned off the engine. It was a humid, overcast day, the kind of weather that sapped energy and made everything seem flat and lifeless. However, the hanging basket next to the house number was as lively as an artist's palette, and the front door itself was a cheery cobalt blue.

'You must be Andee Lawrence,' a slender, middle-aged

woman greeted her warmly on answering Andee's knock. 'You found it all right. I'm Ally, please come in.'

Andee followed her along a beige-carpeted hallway, past a post and bar staircase cluttered with shoes and toys, and into a large, airy kitchen with three skylights in the ceiling, a set of bifold doors opening on to a small square garden, and a range of wall and base units that were clearly as expensive as they were artfully designed.

'I've made coffee,' Ally told her, her large, dimpled face and cat's-eye glasses making her appear both maternal and lawyerly, 'but have you had any lunch? I can easily set up a cold plate. We've plenty of ham and cheese.'

'I'm fine,' Andee told her, 'but thank you. And thanks for agreeing to see me.'

'I'm happy to help in any way I can,' Ally assured her, waving her to a leather and stainless steel chair at a matching table, where her computer and a stack of files were taking up most of the space. 'I'm working from home today,' she explained, quickly pushing everything to one side, 'and the kids are with my sister in Kew, so we shouldn't be disturbed. Having said that, I'm afraid I didn't know your uncle all that well, and it was quite a long time ago. Do you take milk and sugar?'

'Just milk, thank you. You were his neighbour, I believe?'

'For about a year. We were across the landing from each other, but we kept quite different hours. If you're wondering how I managed to afford to live in Shepherd

Market, my place was a tiny studio that my parents paid the rent on while I finished my studies.' Bringing the coffee to the table, she sat down too. 'His flat was much bigger; two bedrooms, might even have been three, but he was hardly ever there. Weeks on end would go by without any sign of him. I've no idea where he went, he never said and I didn't feel it was my place to ask.'

'Did he have any visitors when he was there? Or even when he wasn't?'

Ally shook her head. 'Not that I can remember.'

'Do the names Penny or Michelle ring any bells for you?'

Again Ally shook her head.

'OK, at the inquest you talked about how edgy and anxious he seemed during the weeks before he died. So presumably he was spending more time at the flat then?'

'Yes, he was.'

'Alone?'

'As far as I knew.'

'Did he ever tell you why he was worried?'

'No, but he definitely was. I told him, you can't keep coming over here banging on about how someone's out to get you and not tell me who. It was like he was turning paranoid, he kept saying things like I saw her, I know it was her, or, she's doing this to freak me out.'

'It was always "she"?'

Ally frowned. 'I'm pretty sure it was.'

'Did you ever see anyone yourself?'

'No. The street was always empty when I looked out. Or empty of anyone who seemed interested in him.'

'He mentioned children? Or kids.'

'More than once, but that was it. "It's about the kids," he'd say. Obviously, I asked him what kids, but it was like he didn't even hear me. He was in another world, another zone.'

'The last time you saw him . . .'

'He was getting into a car right below his apartment. The man with him was tall, white hair, glasses, but it was dark so I didn't get a very good look.'

'Was he forced into the car?'

'It didn't look like it. In fact, I forgot all about it until the call came a week or so later to say his body had been found. It really threw me, I can tell you. I liked him. I had no reason not to.' Her eyes drifted to the garden, and after a while she said, 'There's something I told the police after the inquest. It only came back to me then. I don't know if they did anything about it. To be honest, I'm not sure if there was anything they could do, it was so vague.'

Andee waited.

'I remembered that a couple of days before he went off in the car, he said he'd heard from . . . I think he said Sven, but I can't be certain, which is probably why the police ignored it.'

Sven. It was the name of the man Penny claimed had rescued her.

Allowing a moment to pass, Andee said, 'I met with someone the other day, a detective who was at the inquest. Gerry Trowbridge? Do you remember him?'

'Yes, kind of. He came to see me a couple of weeks after. He wanted to know if John had ever talked about someone called . . . Penny? You just mentioned that name. Who is she?'

'Someone John Victor used to know,' Andee replied blandly. 'Gerry Trowbridge said you showed him something . . .'

'Oh yes, I did. It was odd, or I thought it was. A bit creepy actually, considering what it said. I found it when I packed up John's stuff. No one else came to do it so the landlord asked me to clear the place so he could rerent it. Anyway, an envelope fell out of one of the books . . . I still have it, in fact I can show you.'

Amazed, and quietly intrigued, Andee said, 'That would be lovely.'

A few minutes later Ally was back from upstairs carrying an old box file from which she produced a heap of wedding invitations, funeral service leaflets, photographs, ticket stubs, newspaper cuttings – all obviously things from over the years that she'd decided to keep and didn't know what else to do with. Eventually she pulled out a worn white envelope with John Victor's name and a Shepherd Market address on the front, and a London postmark dated, Andee noted, about a fortnight before John Victor's body had been found.

'That's all that was in there,' Ally said as Andee took out a single yellowing page and unfolded it. 'Whether it came with a letter, or something else . . .'

Andee read the typeset lines, several of which had been underlined in ink. She frowned. She knew these words . . . She couldn't say from where at this moment, but it would come to her . . .

'It looks like a page from a book,' Ally commented.

Andee swallowed dryly. It was indeed, and as she realised which book, her heart started to pound. 'Can I . . . Is it possible to take a copy?' she asked.

'Of course. Or you can have it if you like. I've no idea what I'm going to do with it.'

Putting the page back into the envelope, Andee got to her feet. 'Thank you,' she said, 'you've been incredibly helpful.'

Appearing doubtful, Ally walked with her to the door. 'If you think I can be of any more help feel free to call,' she insisted, as Andee got into her car.

With a wave of further thanks Andee reversed out of the forecourt and turned towards the Hammersmith roundabout. Once there she took the A4 in the direction of central London and called Penny on her hands-free. The ringtone was British, telling her that Penny was at least in the country.

'Well, here's a surprise,' Penny drawled as she answered.

'I know what you took of mine when you left,' Andee told her.

Penny laughed.

'Are you in London?' Andee asked.

'I am.'

'I'll meet you at the Forty One hotel in an hour.'

Maureen had no idea that she was being followed around Waitrose, no sense at all of someone watching what she was putting into her trolley, or examining and replacing on a shelf. If the truth were told she was barely aware of where she was or what she was doing. She'd forgotten to bring her shopping list so she was picking goods at random, the kind of things she usually got, and some she'd never bought before.

She was thinking about Penny, seeing her not as she'd been during that terrible scene just over a week ago, with that awful look in her eyes, but as a small child, toddling along in front of the trolley, turning now and again to make sure her mother was still behind her.

Once she'd thought she was lost and Maureen and Andee had watched her looking around slowly, until she'd spotted another woman with a small girl and a trolley and had gone to join them.

How they'd laughed about it with the woman, and later with David.

Penny had done it again the next time they were out, and the next and the next. She'd just go off and join other families, looking for all the world as though she'd be happy to stay with them.

It was as if, Maureen was thinking now, she'd been testing her mother, wanting to find out if she would always come and get her.

When Penny was older she'd started telling stories of how she'd got lost, aged three, and the police had found her just as a creepy man was trying to force her into his car.

It had never happened.

Nor had Penny been one of twins, the other having apparently died at birth.

She'd never appeared on TV, or fallen overboard when they were on a ferry to France, or been made to stay in her room for a whole week without anything to eat or drink.

They used to call them Penny's tall tales.

This wasn't how Maureen could describe the monstrous lies Penny had told about her father and grandfather. Those vile accusations were nothing short of evil. And to say that she, Maureen, had stood by and let it happen . . . It was so shocking and so cruel that Maureen was still reeling from the horror of it.

What was the matter with Penny? She knew she was lying, and she knew that her mother knew it, so what was making her want to cause so much terrible pain?

She was in the car park by now, taking out her phone to read a text from Andee while loading her shopping into the back of the car.

Will call later to update you on things, but am now in central London waiting to talk to P. Did you find your glasses? Ax

Maureen's heart sank at the reminder. She'd searched high and low for her glasses earlier and still had no idea where she'd put them. It was just as well she had a backup pair, which she'd had no trouble tracking down in the drawer next to her bed, or she wouldn't have been able to leave the house.

She texted back, *I've invited Blake and Jenny for supper. What time should we expect you?*

Receiving no immediate reply, she popped the phone

back in her pocket and was about to close the boot when she became aware of someone standing beside her.

With a jolt of alarm she quickly stepped back, ready to hand over her purse, or her shopping, whatever he wanted.

'It's OK, I'm not going to hurt you,' he said softly.

Maureen stared at him. His eyes were a summer-sky blue, his features handsome and intense . . . It was the boy who'd claimed to be Penny's son. She felt a rush of panicked emotion. 'What do you want?' she asked shakily.

'Please don't be scared,' he said. 'I just need Andee to call this number.' He was handing her a slip of paper.

Maureen barely glanced at it. 'Why don't you call her?' she demanded. 'I can give you her mobile . . .'

'Please, just ask her to be in touch with this person. He'll explain everything.'

'Who is it? You need to tell me who it is?'

'His name is Sven. Tell her not to mention anything about this to Mich—Penny.'

As he hurried away Maureen called after him, 'Please wait.'

A blue Mini paused for him to get in and drove out of the car park. To Maureen's astonishment another car went after it, at speed, and both vehicles disappeared over the Kester bridge with horns blaring furiously all round them.

Maureen tried to pull herself together. There must be more she could do. She'd noticed a girl was driving the Mini, and that the registration number ended in VRT. She needed to write that down. She could remember nothing about the other car, apart from the fact it was white.

Quickly slamming shut the boot of her own car, she got into the driver's seat and rummaged around in her handbag for a pen. Not finding one, she decided to text what she could remember to Andee.

Girl. Blue Mini. VRT.

After giving herself a minute, she began driving slowly out of the car park, knowing there was something else she should do, but unable to think what it was. Her thoughts were all over the place, fragmenting and reforming into images and words that seemed almost meaningless.

For a moment she forgot where she was. She recognised nothing around her and had no idea where she was going.

Fear blossomed like a flame.

Her mind cleared and she drove on towards home, aware that her heart was racing and a cool sweat was breaking on her skin. How had the boy known where to find her? Why wouldn't he call Andee himself? What on earth was going on between him and his mother?

How could Penny have said those terrible things about her father?

Sickened all over again by the wickedness of the words, Maureen forced them from her mind and kept going.

On reaching home she took the shopping inside and set about making a cup of tea. She was focusing on the scene in the car park, and realising the boy had an unusual accent. It was American, but there was something else too. French, maybe? Or Italian?

Had the other car caught up with him?

Someone was texting her. Taking out her phone she saw it was Andee.

This could take a while. Will let you know asap.

What could take a while?

Realising she must tell Andee what had happened at Waitrose, she was about to text her back when she remembered the boy had given her a number for Andee to call.

Where was it?

What had she done with the slip of paper?

She rapidly checked her pockets, her handbag and purse, the shopping bags, the floor in case she'd dropped it on the way in.

No sign of it.

Rushing out to the car she searched the front seats, back seats and boot.

'Oh no,' she gasped wretchedly. She must have dropped it in the car park. How on earth was she ever going to find it?

Chapter Twelve

Andee might have guessed that Penny would keep her waiting, but two and a half hours with no text, no call, nothing at all to excuse or explain the delay, or even to confirm that she was on her way?

Maybe she wasn't coming.

It was clearly a power trip to show who was in charge, which might have irritated Andee had she not been filling the time so usefully – and in such luxury.

Her sister certainly knew how to pick her hotels. This, at Forty One Buckingham Palace Road, was about as exclusive as they came. With Her Majesty as a very close neighbour, it was for residents only. No passing members of the public were encouraged to enter, indeed there was no way of getting past the concierge unless you were expected. Penny, it seemed, had given instructions for her sister to be allowed in. She'd then been escorted to the Executive Lounge on the fifth floor, welcomed with the offer of a glass of expensive champagne, which she'd politely declined, served tea, given the Wi-Fi code and was now seated in a cosy niche in front of a grand fireplace in what could almost be a private sitting room.

Did all the residents' guests find themselves treated so well? Or did the name Michelle Cross conjure that extra magic?

By now Andee had used her phone to photograph the page Ally Jackson had given her and sent it to Gould, asking him to let her know when he'd read it and she'd explain. Not that she fully understood its relevance, but she certainly knew where the words had come from.

She'd also explored the Exclusive Chauffeur Drive website where she'd found Martyna's full name – Martyna Jez – before switching to Facebook to try and track her down there. It didn't take long. The girl was Polish, aged twenty-nine and from a place called Sanok close to the Ukraine and Slovakian borders. She was in a relationship with Todd Rushton, and had one hundred and fourteen 'friends'. There were no details on education or how long she'd been in the UK, nor was anyone listed under family.

A quick read through the latest postings told Andee that her initial assessment had been correct – Martyna was a party girl, very fond of cocktails and taking selfies with Todd at various bars and nightclubs.

A more detailed scan of older exchanges proved far more interesting. Several were with Polish friends, to be expected, while the rest were with girls from various other parts of Europe and beyond. The most intriguing aspect was the number of exchanges thanking Martyna for being the best thing that had ever happened to them.

So happy now. Loving this life. Could have been so differ-ent. Love you Martyna Jez.

Never dreamt I'd live anywhere like this. Love everything about it. So glad I signed up. Friend for life, Martyna.

I was so scared when I left, but I know now I didn't need to be. I hope anyone else who reads this and is feel-ing scared will take heart. Definitely nothing to worry about.

Thanks for asking about my mother. Treatment going well, hoping for more good news soon. Couldn't have done it with-out you.

There were many more comments in Polish, or other languages, making them impenetrable for Andee, but with all the emoticons and kisses attached they were almost certainly along the same lines.

So how, if this rash of postings was to be taken at face value, was the office manager of a chauffeur-drive company having such a positive effect on so many people's lives?

Though Andee found no mention of anyone who could conceivably have been Penny, she was mindful of what Martyna had said the day she, Andee, had gone to ECD. 'It's fantastic what she does. She helps so many people. I would not be where I am if it weren't for her. None of us would.'

Andee looked up as one of the receptionists came to speak to her.

'I'm sorry,' the girl said sweetly, 'we have just received a call from Ms Cross's office to inform us that she is unable to come and meet you.'

Having expected it, Andee said, 'Thank you. I'll give

her a call. Would you mind if I continued to work from here for a few more minutes?'

'No, you are very welcome. There is a business area up on the mezzanine, if that is helpful.'

Andee glanced up to where a highly polished railing was closing off an area of desks and computers beneath an exquisitely vaulted skylight.

'But if you prefer to stay here,' the receptionist hastily added, 'there is no problem. Can I bring you any more refreshment?'

'I'm fine thanks,' Andee assured her. Her mind was already going into overdrive, certain that Penny was messing with her again. Let her, it wasn't particularly intimidating, only annoying.

She'd talk to the receptionist again when she went to settle up for her tea, meantime she needed to speak to Martyna, preferably away from the ECD offices, and some official backup could be useful for that. Since she was within a stone's throw of Scotland Yard, she thought immediately of her old friend and colleague Tim Perroll. They'd attended detective school together and he'd worked with her during the time she'd revisited the search for Penny. She'd heard from his wife, in a recent Christmas card, that he was with SO15 these days, Counter Terrorism Command, so this was going to be a big ask. If she could even get hold of him.

Eventually, after being put through to several different extensions she found herself talking to a familiar voice that wasn't Tim's, but turned out to be Jan Shell, another old friend and colleague.

'It's great to hear you, Andee,' Jan cried warmly. 'It's been too long. We must get together.'

'Absolutely,' Andee agreed. 'I just need to get up to London more often. Or if you're ever in the West Country . . .'

'I'm sure it can be arranged. Anyhow, I hear you're looking for Tim. He's not around at the moment. In fact, he could be on leave . . . Hang on, I'll check.' A few moments later she said, 'I'm being told that he's in Portugal this week.'

Damn!

'I'll give you his mobile number, it'll be easier to get hold of him with that.'

After jotting it down Andee decided not to ask when he was back; she'd call and ask him instead.

A few minutes later, with the surprise of hearing from her and the reason for her call out of the way, Tim Perroll was saying, 'OK, still getting my head round the fact that she's turned up after all these years, but you can fill me in more when I see you.'

'So where are you? I was told you were in Portugal, but the ringtone was home-grown.'

'We should be on holiday, but Karen's mother had a fall so she's gone to York and I'm left here doing all the jobs I never get round to. Now, what is it exactly that you need me to do?'

Wishing she could hug him, Andee said, 'I want you to be my official escort when I go to interview someone, so I can say we're from the police, but actually it's going to be unofficial.'

'OK,' he said, drawing it out. 'Is this person dangerous?'

'Nothing I've come across so far would suggest it. She's female, by the way.'

'Ah, the deadlier of the species. So, tell me when and where I can be of assistance.'

Andee glanced at her watch. Almost four thirty. What time did Martyna finish work? 'Would this evening be too soon?' she asked.

'Fine by me.'

'You're my hero. I need to make a call first and I'll get right back to you.' After ringing off she connected to Exclusive Chauffeur Drive, and learned from Martyna, without letting on who she was, that the office closed at six.

'Can you get to Knightsbridge for five thirty?' she asked Tim when she rang back.

'I'll do my best, but it's rush hour. Where do we meet?'

'I'll text you the address.'

Realising she was unlikely to make it back to Kesterly until late that night, Andee rang her mother. 'Hi, are you OK?' she asked when Maureen answered.

'Yes, I . . . Um . . .'

Not liking the hesitation, Andee said, 'What's happened?'

'Nothing. I just . . . What time will you be home?'

'I won't make dinner. Are Blake and Jenny still coming over?'

'Yes. I . . . Andee, I have an awful confession to make. Please don't be cross. I'm still looking for it, I've even been back to the car park . . .'

'Mum, what are you talking about?'

'The boy,' Maureen answered. 'He came up to me outside Waitrose and asked me to give you a number to call, but I can't find the piece of paper he'd written it on.'

Realising who she was talking about, Andee's eyes closed in frustration. 'Did he say anything else?' she asked.

'He said it was a number for Sven . . . I remember the name because Penny mentioned it. He said not to tell her anything about it.'

And her mother had managed to lose the number. Aaaagh!

'I texted you,' Maureen told her. 'There was a girl driving the car he went off in, and the registration . . .'

'Oh, that's what that was about,' Andee cut in, having put it down to one of her mother's funny five minutes. 'You didn't get the entire number plate?'

'No, I'm afraid not. I'm obviously not as quick as I used to be.'

Understanding how wretched she felt, Andee said, 'There's been a lot to deal with lately. We've both been thrown off course . . . But if you do find that number, call me straight away. I'll let you know when I'm on my way home.'

As she ended the call Gould rang.

'What the hell is this?' he demanded when she answered. 'Satan, saints, all good, all bad? I don't get it.'

'It's a quote from John Steinbeck,' Andee explained. 'It's what he said about his character Cathy Ames in *East of Eden*, which is basically that if you believe saints are completely good, then you have to believe that someone can be completely bad.'

'Yeah, I got that much. And your sister sent this to John Victor?'

'I'm presuming it was her, and here's why I think it was. I was studying the book for GCSE at the time she disappeared. It never occurred to me that she'd taken it. She was never that interested in literature, and anyway losing it was hardly at the front of my mind. I just remember searching for it and giving up without really caring where it might be. Fast forward to a couple of weeks ago when you might remember she asked me if I'd worked out what she'd taken of mine when she went. I think this quote from Steinbeck is giving me the answer.'

Sounding bewildered, he said, 'OK, so what are we supposed to read into it?'

'Maybe that she considers herself to be like Cathy Ames, bad through and through?'

'And that's supposed to what? Intimidate you?'

'Not me, John Victor. He's who she sent it to, and the postmark on the envelope shows that it arrived ten days before he died. Of course there's nothing to say it was from her, and I doubt after all this time that forensics could do much with the page that's clearly been torn from a book, but I'll hang on to it anyway.'

'Right, so tell me more about this Cathy Ames character.'

'Well, from what I remember, she was very sexually advanced for her age, getting boys into trouble rather than the other way round. She burned her parents' house down, killing them both, and took off with all their money. She then went to work as a whore for a character called Edwards, I think – it's been a long time since I read it. He fell in love with her, but ended up beating her so badly he almost killed her. She was rescued by one of the Trask brothers who took her in and married her, but she got pregnant by the other brother. She tried to give herself an abortion and failed. I'm picking things at random here, I'd have to read it again to be more accurate. Anyway, after her twin sons were born she abandoned them and went to work in another whorehouse where she became the madame's favourite. She ended up poisoning said madame and inheriting the brothel, which she turned into a seriously sordid den of iniquity.'

Astonished, he said, 'And you were reading that aged sixteen?'

Andee had to smile.

'So how does it end?'

'Her sons find her. One of them is disgusted by her, the other . . . I can't remember exactly, but I'm sure she made the one who hated her the sole beneficiary of her will before she committed suicide.'

As Gould stayed silent Andee felt the words resonating inside her, while watching a couple come into the lounge and go to sit by the window. She wondered if they'd been sent by Penny to keep an eye on her. Presumably the receptionist had been doing that up to now.

'My mother's had another visit from John Victor Jr,' she informed Gould.

'Your sister's son. Do you think he has a twin brother?'

'I've no idea. You're looking for parallels.'

'Aren't you?'

'Yes and no. She didn't burn our house down and kill our parents, but she did, of her own volition, go to work as an escort, as she prefers to call it. I'm asking myself was John Victor the Edwards character, falling in love with her, then selling her on to get himself out of a fix?'

'I thought you said Edwards beat this Cathy up,' Gould put in.

'Beating up, selling . . . Either way, it's abuse.'

'And she, Penny, came back to make Victor pay?'

'It's possible,' Andee agreed.

'Which doesn't quite chime with the book.'

'Does it have to? Anyway, what I'm asking myself is did John Victor keep her son?'

'Do you think it's likely he'd want to, considering his lifestyle?'

'No, I don't, but there's a good chance he knew where the boy was. Penny was around twenty-one when she claims she was rescued from a life of virtual slavery by someone called Sven. She was twenty-five when John Victor went over a cliff. So where had she been for the intervening four years, and was this Sven the same person Ally Jackson saw Victor getting into a car with just before he died? I should return here to my mother's visit from JV Jr. Apparently he gave her a number for me to call. He said it was for Sven and that he doesn't want me to mention anything to his mother.'

'Well, that's interesting. So have you rung the number?'

'My mother's lost it.'

'You're kidding me, right? So how are you going to get hold of this guy?'

'At this moment in time I've absolutely no idea, but I'm working on it.'

Before leaving the hotel Andee paid her bill and at the same time managed to get an address for Michelle Cross.

'She just emailed asking me to meet her at her office,' Andee told the receptionist. 'The trouble is, I can't remember exactly where it is.'

'It's no problem,' she was assured, and a moment later she was handed a printout giving the name of the company, K.T. Holdings, and where it was located.

Belgravia! Addresses didn't come any fancier than that.

Since Andee was more or less in the neighbourhood she decided to make a brief detour on her way to meet Tim, going past the small park on Lower Grosvenor Place, right at Eaton Square and into Upper Belgrave Street. The imposing white Georgian terraces with their supremely elegant porticoes and numerous blue plaques – Alfred Lord Tennyson being the only name she recognised – were quite clearly homes to the unimaginably rich. She could find scant evidence of any businesses located here, although Google Maps was telling her that several embassies and high-commissions were located nearby.

When Andee reached the correct house number, she searched for a sign announcing K.T. Holdings, but there was none. The main entrance, with its shiny ebony front door and topiaried trees, didn't appear to have an entryphone, or even a knocker, which she found odd – how did anyone make contact with someone inside?

Presumably they weren't supposed to.

Wondering if Penny was watching from within, Andee took a long slow look over the tall sash windows up to the roof and blue sky beyond. She had no problem with Penny knowing that she'd discovered the name and location of K.T. Holdings, and once she'd passed the details to Leo she was hopeful of knowing a lot more.

Several minutes later she was at the other end of Belgravia approaching the mews where she'd asked Tim to meet her, and seeing his impressive six foot six frame packed out with bulging muscles and far too much testosterone already stationed on the corner looking for all the world like a drug dealer, she felt a rush of pleasure. She'd missed him, she realised. She'd always felt safe when he was around, as though nothing could possibly go wrong, although it had, plenty of times, but somehow he'd managed to make any disaster feel less problematic than it was. He'd been a friend, a brother, a partner . . . He'd been a very big part of her life.

'You're looking good,' he chuckled, his husky baritone as familiar as the swamping feel of his embrace. 'And I hear you're kind of available again these days.'

'I was,' she countered, thinking of Graeme and the fact that he hadn't called or texted since she'd dropped him at the airport earlier. She hadn't called him either so she was hardly in a position to make a big deal of that.

'OK bring me into the picture,' Tim prompted as she glanced along the mews towards Exclusive Chauffeur Drive. 'Why here? Who are we looking for? And what do we need to get from them?'

After explaining that her sister was apparently behind the chauffeur-drive company, effectively making her Martyna's boss, and showing him some of the posts on Martyna's Facebook page, Andee said, 'The girl should be finishing work any minute, and I want to have the kind of chat with her that makes it clear she ought to be helping me.'

'So what exactly are you suspecting her of?'

'There's some kind of cover-up going on, I'm certain of it, but of what and of whom . . . That's what I'm trying to find out.'

'Which is where I come in?'

'Exactly. You don't have to say anything, unless you think it's relevant, I just want to see how the girl reacts when she realises you're a police officer. What we need right now is somewhere to take her for a quiet chat.'

Perroll looked around, and spotting a restaurant awning about fifty yards down on the right, he said, 'I'm sure they'll be able to accommodate us.'

Knowing that his imposing physique coupled with the flash of his badge would indeed get them what they wanted, Andee smiled and checked her watch. All she had to hope for now was that Martyna finished on time and left the office alone.

It happened exactly that way.

At a couple of minutes after six Martyna, looking her executive best in a beige skirt suit and matching low heels, exited the office, locked the door and started along the mews towards them. She was so focused on her phone that she didn't even realise anyone was there until Andee said, 'Hello Martyna.'

The girl stopped, shocked and clearly becoming afraid as she looked at Andee, at Tim and back again.

'Remember me?' Andee asked, hearing the echo of her sister's words on that strange day in France.

Apparently Martyna did, for her colour deepened and her eyes showed unease as she said, 'Of course. You came to see us . . . Your name . . .'

'Is Andrea Lawrence.'

Martyna stared at her.

'I believe it's the name used by one of your directors,' Andee said kindly.

Martyna glanced worriedly at Tim. 'What . . . What can I do for you?' she asked. 'The office is closed now.'

'I just need to have a little chat with you,' Andee explained. 'It won't take long . . .'

'But I'm in a hurry. I have to meet someone.'

'No, you really do want to talk to us,' Tim assured her, 'and as Andee just said, it won't take long.'

Paling at the sight of his badge, Martyna turned back to Andee. 'I can't tell you anything,' she exclaimed. 'I swear . . .'

Stopping her with a raised hand, Andee said, 'How do you know you can't tell me anything without even knowing what I'm going to ask? Come on, we're just going to have a friendly few minutes in the bar down the road and before you know it you'll be on your way to wherever you're going.'

On entering the bar they were told that a private party was expected at seven, but once Tim showed his badge, they were assured of the place to themselves until the guests arrived. After choosing a cosy banquette away from the window Andee and Tim sat on one side, with Martyna opposite and a highly polished brown table with a Tiffany-style lamp between them.

'I have to confess,' Andee began, 'I've been reading your Facebook page.'

Martyna's eyes widened with a mix of what seemed to be confusion and wariness. 'I don't understand. Why would you do that?'

'I wanted to find out more about you, and the messages I read told me that you're a very good friend to have. You seem to have helped a lot of people.'

Martyna glanced at Tim. 'Is there any law against that?' she asked carefully.

'Well, I suppose that depends on what you're doing to help,' Andee replied.

Martyna swallowed. 'I help them to get jobs, and to find somewhere to live,' she said.

'But you work at a car-hire company, so how are you giving assistance in these other areas?'

A hot colour was spreading over Martyna's neck. 'I am not responsible for people who post on my page.'

'Are you saying you don't know who they are?'

'Yes, no. I mean . . . I don't *know* them. I just . . .'

'If you don't know them,' Andee said, 'how come

they're calling you by name and thanking you with such . . . ?'

'I have never met them, but they are not doing anything wrong. No one forces them to do anything they don't want to.'

Andee's eyebrows rose. Maybe now they were getting somewhere. 'Would you care to elaborate on that?' she invited.

Martyna was starting to look scared. 'I cannot tell you any more,' she cried. 'This is all I know, I swear it.'

'But you haven't told us anything.'

'Because I don't know anything.'

'But you do know that there's more than a chauffeur-drive business being run out of your offices, and you're a part of it.'

'I just . . . do what I am told. But it is not bad. There is nothing bad, only good.'

'So tell me what it is.'

Martyna stared at her with wide teary eyes.

Feeling sorry for her, and suspecting she wasn't fully aware of what she was involved in, Andee decided to come at things another way. 'How did you meet Michelle Cross?' she asked. 'AKA Andrea Lawrence.'

Martyna's mouth trembled. 'My sister introduced us.'

'Does your sister also work for her?'

'No, not any more.'

'What did your sister do when she did work for her?'

'She – she was . . . She did the same as me. She work at ECD.'

'And where is your sister now?'

A tear fell on to Martyna's cheek. 'I don't . . . I am not supposed to say.'

'You can tell me,' Andee said gently.

'No. It is . . . She is at home in Poland.'

'Are you sure?'

Martyna nodded. 'I can give you her number. I write it for you here. You can call if you like, but please don't tell her that I give you the number.' She tore a page from a small notebook.

Taking it, Andee said, 'What are you afraid of, Martyna?'

'I am not afraid. You don't understand . . .'

'Then make me understand.'

'It is a wonderful thing that she does. It helps everybody. It can change their life in so many ways.'

'So explain it to me.'

'No, I cannot. It is not for me to do this. You are not being kind. I wish to go now.'

'If it's legal,' Andee said, 'then where's the problem?'

Martyna regarded her helplessly, clearly having no idea what to say next.

Stepping in, Tim said, 'Do you want our colleagues in Immigration to start investigating you and your Facebook friends? You know what things are like here since Brexit . . .'

Andee almost winced. He'd never been subtle, but she had to admit it had provoked an interesting reaction. Martyna's face was white.

'They are not illegal immigrants,' she insisted. 'I swear it. They are all here . . . It is allowed for them to be here.'

'*All?*' he repeated mildly.

She looked panicky and started to get up. 'Please, you must let me go now,' she implored. 'I do not want to be rude, but . . .'

'Martyna,' Andee interrupted in a calming voice.

'No,' Martyna cried shakily, 'I cannot help you. I am sorry, but it is not a good thing you are trying to do to me.'

'Tell me something before you leave,' Andee said. 'Do you know someone called Sven?'

Martyna appeared genuinely puzzled. 'No. Who is this person?'

Andee ignored the question. 'And what about John Victor? Does that name mean anything?'

Though she shook her head, she didn't seem certain.

Since she was too new on the scene to have been around at the time of JV senior, it had to be JV Jr. 'Do you know how I can get hold of him?' Andee asked.

Martyna's eyes filled with more panic as they flitted to Tim. 'He is . . . No one knows where he is,' she replied. 'Everyone is looking for him.'

'Why?' Andee pressed.

'Because he is doing a terrible thing. He will ruin everything if we do not find him,' and before they could say any more she darted across the bar and out into the street.

'Do you want me to go after her?' Tim asked.

Andee shook her head.

After a while he said, 'So how much of that was useful?'

Andee was still assimilating. 'Tell me what you made of it,' she prompted.

'Well, she's scared, that much is certain, but of what and *why*, when she's claiming everything is good, is beyond me. Who's Sven, by the way?'

'That's something I need to find out.'

'So what's your next move?'

Good question. 'I'm waiting to learn more about K.T. Holdings,' she remembered. 'I found out earlier that it's the name of Penny's company.'

'What's the K.T. stand for?'

'This is a wild guess, but Cathy Ames in *East of Eden* was also known as Kate Trask.'

He shook his head as though to clear it. 'OK, you're losing me now. Where does this come in?'

After explaining about the book, she said, 'What's not chiming with the story at all are the claims that Penny, Michelle, whatever we want to call her, is a good person doing good things. To begin with it's definitely not the way she's behaving with us, her family, and it's not something that could ever be said about Cathy Ames, aka Kate Trask. In Steinbeck's words Cathy was a "psychotic monster with a malformed soul".'

Tim's eyes widened. 'And your sister's modelling herself on her?'

Andee sure as hell hoped not. She checked her mobile as it rang, and seeing it was Blake she took it.

'Hi Andee,' he said gravely. 'Everything's fine and she's home again now, but I'm afraid Maureen had a bit of a turn earlier . . .'

'What does that mean?' Andee demanded, gesturing for Tim to follow her outside.

'They said at the hospital that it might have been caused by stress . . .'

'Hospital? Oh my God! What happened?'

'She seemed to lose a sense of things,' he replied. 'It didn't last long, but we decided she needed to be checked out so we took her to A & E.'

'Thank you. Thank you. Where is she now?'

'Asleep, in bed. She asked me not to tell you . . .'

'You did the right thing. I'm still in London, but I'll be back tonight. Can you stay with her until I get there?'

'Of course. She's going to be fine, honestly. She was her old self again by the time we brought her home.'

Though relieved to hear it, Andee was still worried, for her mother hadn't been her old self since Penny had come back into their lives.

'Before you go,' Blake said, 'have you spoken to Graeme today?'

'No. Have you?'

'I've left messages, but he still hasn't got back to me. Must be busy. I'll try him again tomorrow. Drive safely now,' and he was gone.

'I'm taking it that was some kind of emergency,' Tim commented, as they started towards Knightsbridge.

'My mother,' Andee replied. 'Apparently she's all right now, but I should go home. Damn, I was hoping to find a cheap hotel, if such a thing exists around here, and spend tomorrow staking out K.T. Holdings.'

'Where is it?'

'Upper Belgrave Street. No, please don't offer to do it for me, I can't use up your holiday that way, Karen would never forgive me, and besides, I need to speak to Penny myself.'

During the drive home Andee tried several times to contact Penny, but her calls kept going to voicemail. In the end she left a message saying, 'You're clearly avoiding me, so I have to ask what you're afraid of? If I'm right about what I think it is, then you should be afraid.'

As she rang off she was frowning hard. The fact that she had no idea what her sister might be afraid of was neither here nor there. What mattered was that Penny needed to think Andee was getting close to the truth. It undoubtedly had something to do with John Victor Jr, who was apparently doing his very best to avoid his mother, and everyone else.

'No, he hasn't been in touch again,' Maureen admitted dolefully when Andee got home. 'I'm so sorry. I feel such a fool . . .'

'It's OK,' Andee soothed. 'And you shouldn't have waited up. Blake told me you were in bed. It's gone midnight . . .'

'I was awake anyway, and when I heard you come in I thought you might be hungry. There's a pasta salad in the fridge.'

In fact Andee was ravenous, so grabbing the salad and a fork, she sat down at the table while Maureen made some tea. 'Where are Blake and Jenny?' Andee asked through a mouthful of food.

'In the guest room. I told them they didn't have to stay . . .'

'They did. This is really getting to you, Mum, and I'm worried.'

Sighing, Maureen brought two mugs to the table and set them down. 'Is there any other way to find a number for this Sven person?' she asked.

'There might be,' Andee replied, more to try and comfort her mother than because she felt confident there was. 'I think I've figured out what Penny took from me when she left.'

Maureen's eyes showed interest.

'My copy of *East of Eden*.'

Maureen frowned. 'Why would she take that?'

Andree shrugged. 'To be a nuisance; to have something of mine. I've no idea what was going through her mind back then, any more than I have now. However, I learned something today that was interesting. Apparently everyone's looking for her son. I was told that he's doing a terrible thing and will ruin everything if he isn't found.'

Maureen stared at her in alarm. 'What on earth does that mean?' she asked.

Andee shook her head, realising too late that tiredness had prompted her to confide in her mother when she probably shouldn't have done.

'If I could find that note,' Maureen mumbled, looking around as though it was hiding somewhere nearby. 'He's coming to you for help, I'm sure of it, and now I've gone and . . .'

'We don't know why he's trying to contact me,'

226

Andee interrupted, 'but whatever the reason he'll very likely try again when he realises I'm not going to ring the number he gave you.' Even to her own ears this logic sounded feeble, and it clearly hadn't done anything to assuage her mother's fears.

'What if Penny finds him first?' Maureen asked.

Chapter Thirteen

The following morning, at her mother's insistence, Andee was on her way back to London, this time by train.

'I'm fine, I'm fine,' Maureen had promised as Andee hesitated over leaving. 'You don't need to fuss. I'll be with Jenny most of the day anyway.'

Since that was true, Andee was now able to focus on her reasons for going, and after texting Tim Perroll to set up another meeting she rang Leo to find out if he'd made any progress with KT Holdings.

'Have you tried Googling them?' he asked.

'Of course, but I didn't get anything.'

'Same here, and I haven't had time to delve any deeper. As soon as I have I'll get back to you.'

Deciding that nine thirty wasn't too early to contact Alayna, Andee pressed to connect, and only realised she'd used FaceTime when Alayna's sleepy young face and copious blonde waves filled the screen. No matter what was going on in the world, or her life, the sight of one of her children never failed to lift Andee's spirits.

'Hey Mum, what's up?' Alayna yawned, apparently jostling with someone behind her.

'Can you talk?' Andee asked carefully.

'Hang on.' Alayna turned away, said something Andee didn't catch to someone Andee couldn't see, and a moment later she was back. 'Sorry about that. He's always in here, it drives me nuts, or it would if I didn't love him so much.'

'Who are we talking about?' Andee wondered casually.

'Tartie Bartie. You remember him. He's forever having boyfriend trouble and he seems to think yours truly can sort it all out. Like as if. Anyway, I expect what you really want to know is how things are going with Jaylan.'

Jaylan? Of course, the new boyfriend. 'Tell me,' Andee encouraged.

'Oh, Mum, he is so amazing. I really like him. Actually, I think it might be love.'

Spotting the mischief in her daughter's eyes, Andee laughed. 'Remind me what he's studying,' she said.

'Law. And he's only got a room in a flat two streets from here, isn't that amazing?'

'I'm blown away,' Andee assured her. 'So how many times have you seen him now?'

'Last night was the third. We went to the Albion, a whole gang of us, and got totally smashed. I expect you really want to hear that. His mum's coming down from London the weekend after next, and he's dead keen for me to meet her. I can't wait to show him off to you and Grandma . . . How is she, by the way? I tried calling her yesterday but couldn't get an answer.'

'She's OK. Missing Grandma Carol and Graeme's sisters, but she'll survive. Try her again today, she'd love to hear from you. Now, there's something I'd like you to do for me if you have the time.'

'Hit me with it, Sherlock.'

'Sorry?'

'I'm Watson, you're . . . Never mind. Name it.'

'OK, so using Facebook, or any other social media sites you think might be relevant, I want you to do some research on someone called Martyna Jez, I'll text you the spelling. Make a list of all her friends detailing where they're from, if the info's there, where they live now, what they do as jobs, anything about them you think might be useful. I'm particularly keen to know if you think they're real.'

Blinking, Alayna asked, 'What, are you saying it could be some kind of showcase page?'

'It's possible. Do they exist?'

'I've no idea. I'll try to find out. So, am I allowed to ask why this Martyna's of interest?'

'She works for Michelle Cross whose name you'll remember . . .'

'The one who stays in swanky hotels.'

'That's her. I want you to see if you can find any mention of her on the pages you turn up. Or of someone called Sven, I don't have a surname. Another name that's important is John Victor, senior or junior.'

'OK, got it. Can't wait to hear what all this is about. How soon do you need it?'

'As soon as you can.'

'OK, I'll make a start this morning, I don't have to be anywhere until two. Are you on a train?'

'I'm on my way to London. How are you managing for money?'

'Fine, and you're sounding like Dad. Well, not fine, because I'm missing out on a week in Ibiza with Tamsin and Sanako, but if I take the time off I'll lose my job and I definitely can't afford to do that now I'm saving for my gap year. And before you offer to make good until I find another, the answer's thanks, but no thanks. Anyway, Jay's also staying in Bristol for the summer, he's got a job at Bordeaux Quay on the Harbourside, so I don't mind so much about not going to . . . Hey, listen, I have to go, he's trying to get through,' and the screen went blank.

Minutes later Leo rang.

'OK, I don't have long, but here's what I have so far on KT Holdings,' he told her, 'which actually isn't anything we don't already know, apart from the fact that there's no record of it at Companies House. So, whatever it is, it's not registered here. Could be offshore, in fact it probably is. However, something that is at that address, is a property management outfit called UBS – Upper Belgrave Street? – and they have a website. Correction, a web page with a fancy logo and mobile numbers for Martyna Jez and Todd Rushton.'

Intrigued, Andee said, 'According to Martyna's relationship status, those two are an item.'

'I know, so I tried calling his number, but all I got was "Hi, I'm Todd, good to hear from you, leave a message and I'll get right back." Same sort of thing on the girl's. From there I had a quick look at Todd Rushton's social media activities to see if there was any mention of the businesses. I drew a blank, I'm afraid, but if you ask me it's all so non-specific that it has to be shady.'

Since Andee was already convinced of that, she simply said, 'I don't suppose you came across the name Sven anywhere?'

'Not that I recall. Is he significant?'

'I think so. And no mention of my sister?'

'None that I could find, but I'll keep looking, trouble is my workload's piling up here, so I'm not sure when I can give it any more time.'

'You've done brilliantly already, Leo. Thanks. I'll keep on it myself and let you know what I find.'

'Well, I think Mr Todd Rushton is our first port of call,' Tim declared confidently after Andee had shared her latest information. 'Did your guy in Kesterly send you the number?' She nodded.

Reading from her screen he connected to Rushton's mobile and told the voicemail, 'Hi, the name's Tim Perroll. I hear you can help with investments, so if you could call me back that would be great.'

As they walked on towards Upper Belgrave Street Andee said, 'So knowing what we do now, which admittedly isn't much, what do you think it's all about? What's your hunch?'

He took a while to think. 'Still too vague,' he decided, 'but if I had to hazard something . . . When you first told me about it you mentioned a couple of clinics in the US. If we put that together with Martyna's claims that her boss is doing wonderful things, helping many people . . . OK, I'm going right out on a limb now, but it could be some kind of organ trade.'

Andee baulked. That hadn't occurred to her at all. Amazing how differently men and women thought.

'What's your gut telling you?' he asked.

'Not that,' she admitted, 'but now you say it . . . I guess it could fit. Small fortunes change hands for healthy organs.'

'And from what we've seen so far, the young people posting on Martyna's page would definitely fit into the category of healthy. Plus they seem to have hit some sort of jackpot, "loving this life", "so scared when I left, but didn't need to be", "treatment going well". I'm just saying, it's a possible.'

Since she couldn't match it with any rational theories of her own, Andee didn't argue.

'OK, so here we are,' he announced as they reached the address on Upper Belgrave Street. 'As you said, no entryphone, and no knocker, telling us the people inside are not interested in getting to know the people outside.' Taking out his phone he left Rushton another message.

'Hi, Tim Perroll again. I forgot to mention that I'm with the Metropolitan Police. We're outside KT Holdings on Upper Belgrave Street. It would be a good idea to let us in, or to call me back on the number you'll now have. We'll wait five minutes.'

As he rang off Andee said, 'What are we going to do after five minutes?'

'I'm sure you have a plan.'

Choking on a laugh, she said, 'I feel like I've been here before with you.'

He grinned and glanced at his phone as it rang. 'My brother,' he said, 'I'll call him back.'

Going to sit beside him on the front steps leading up to the porch, Andee said, 'I think in your next message you should say that we have reason to believe that illegal activities are being conducted from these premises. If no one lets us in we'll be forced to obtain a warrant and if there is still no cooperation the door will be broken down.'

'I like it. There's one thing we haven't tried yet, of course,' and getting up he mounted the rest of the steps and hammered his fist against the solid bastion of a front door.

'Now why didn't I think of that?' Andee commented drily.

Receiving no response, he returned to the pavement and looked up at the silent, unblinking house. 'It's impossible to tell whether anyone's inside. I wonder if there's a way in – or out – round the back?'

As he started off down the street Andee received a text and immediately called him back.

It was from Penny.

You don't know what you're doing. You need to stop.

After showing it to Tim, Andee texted back. *Tell me why.*

Several minutes ticked by. In the end Andee texted again. *Why are you afraid to see me?*

The response came quickly. *I am not in the country. Please stop hounding my staff. They can't help you.*

Andee gave herself a moment before messaging

again. *I don't believe that and we won't stop until we've got some answers. Tell me about Sven?*

You'll never find him so do yourself a favour and stop trying.

'Ask if her son's with her,' Tim prompted.

'Why?'

He shrugged. 'Why not?'

Andee did, and no answer came back. How quickly the balance had shifted. It had been Penny who had sought out Andee, and now she was trying to push Andee away. Clearly Penny hadn't contacted her and her mother to rekindle their relationship. It had always been about something else, something bigger.

Andee tried texting again, but still no response. 'I think we can deduce from the way the boy's approaching me through my mother that he doesn't want to talk to me himself,' she said. 'Is that because he's afraid his mother is having me watched – and we know that she is – so I'd lead her right to him? Or is he part of whatever twisted game she's playing?'

'Do you think he is?'

'No, actually I don't, but I guess we can't rule it out.'

'Why doesn't he just contact you by phone or email?'

Andee shrugged. 'You'll have to ask him that.'

Tim was looking up and down the street, trying to spot anyone in a car or on foot who might conceivably be tracking them. There didn't appear to be anyone. Taking out his phone he called Todd Rushton again. 'OK, your five minutes is up. We're heading round to your gaff – yeah, we know where you live – while we wait for backup to join us here in Belgravia. If you're in put the kettle on, there's a good lad. Dying for a cuppa.'

'Where does he live?' Andee asked, falling into step with him.

'No idea, but keep walking in case someone's watching.'

Apparently someone was, for as they reached Belgrave Square a silver Mercedes drew up alongside them, and a middle-aged man with greying slicked-back hair and horn-rimmed glasses lowered the rear window. 'I'm Peter Graze-Jessop, lawyer for KT Holdings,' he informed them. 'Is there anything I can help you with?'

Thinking fast and hoping for the best, Andee said, 'We're trying to find John Victor Jr.'

Graze-Jessop appeared amused. '*John* Victor Jr,' he repeated, as though enjoying the name. 'Yes, a lot of people are trying to find that young man. I take it you haven't seen him.'

Before Andee could reply, Tim said, 'Why are you looking for him?'

Graze-Jessop pondered the question. 'Let's just say he has something that doesn't belong to him and he really needs to give it back.'

'And that would be?' Andee prompted.

'He knows what it is. He also knows that no good will come out of what he's trying to do. Nor are you helping anyone by harassing Martyna and Todd. I believe,' he continued, 'your sister has already cautioned you to stop. You'd be wise to heed her words.'

Astonished and annoyed, Andee said, 'Please tell

my sister that I don't appreciate being threatened by her lackeys.'

Graze-Jessop glided right over the insult. 'You must make your own decisions,' he said, 'but please don't say you weren't warned,' and before she could respond he instructed the chauffeur to drive on. However, Tim was too fast for them. He was in front of the car before it had moved an inch, holding up his badge and instructing Graze-Jessop to step out on to the street.

Appearing vaguely ruffled Graze-Jessop complied, his hands ludicrously raised as though someone was threatening him with a gun.

'I don't know what your game is,' Tim growled into his face, 'but I do know this. Nothing legal needs the sort of cover-up you're involved in here. So despite your threats, we're going to find out what it is, and *please don't say you weren't warned.*'

Still not looking as shaken as Andee would have liked, Graze-Jessop returned to the Mercedes, spoke to the driver again and minutes later they were turning off the square in the direction of Knightsbridge. 'That was subtle,' she told Tim.

'I do a good line in it,' he quipped. 'Bastard's so smooth you can practically see the trail he leaves behind.'

Andee turned to look back down the street, wondering if anyone inside the house had witnessed the last few minutes. 'Where do you suppose she is?' she pondered. Taking out her phone she connected to Penny's number, and the ringtone confirmed that she was indeed out of the country. Deciding not to leave a message, she ended the call just as another came in. Seeing it was her mother she clicked on.

'Are you OK?' she asked.

'I've seen him again,' Maureen replied breathlessly. 'He was waiting outside reception when I left the gym. He seemed very upset that you hadn't rung the number yet, so I told him it was my fault. I said I was sorry. He was very nice about it and wrote it down again. He really wants you to call this Sven. I promised you would, so you must . . .'

'I will,' Andee cut in, 'but you need to give me the number.'

'Yes, of course. Here it is. I've got it right here.'

After taking it down and double-checking she had it right, she said, 'Was anyone else with him?'

'Not that I saw. He seemed very worried. He said I should tell you that time was running out and he really needs your help.'

'With what?'

'He didn't say, and he'd gone before I could ask.'

'Are you all right?'

'I'm fine. Jenny's with me. She saw him too. I looked out for the car but he cut into the woods, so I've no idea where he went from here.'

After assuring her mother she'd call back as soon as she had some news, Andee rang off and relayed the information to Tim. 'The number begins 0046. Do you know where that is?'

Googling it, he said, 'Sweden. With a name like Sven we should have guessed.'

Wasting no more time Andee pressed in the number,

and felt her heart starting to beat a little faster as she waited for a reply. Where on earth was all this going to take her?

When the ringtone stopped it was followed by silence, so she said, 'Hello? My name's Andee Lawrence. I was told to call this number.'

'Yes, Ms Lawrence, we've been expecting to hear from you,' a quiet female voice responded. Her English sounded perfect, spoken as it was with a Swedish accent. 'I'm afraid it is not convenient for Mr Sylvander to take your call at the moment. Is it possible for him to ring back on this number in half an hour?'

Seeing no point in arguing Andee said, 'Yes, that'll be fine.'

Having walked round to the Rubens Hotel to have coffee while they waited for the call back, Andee and Tim chose seats at the streetside window overlooking the Royal Mews, watching crowds of tourists coming and going.

As Tim spoke to his brother on the phone, Andee poured them coffee from a cafetière and returned to an email from Leo detailing the information he'd given her earlier. Two companies without websites or registered addresses, neither of them offering services that could be accessed, other than by calling Todd Rushton or Martyna Jez, and no mention at all of any US-based medical centres.

'Do you have any helpful contacts in the States?' she asked Tim as he finished his call.

'I've been thinking about that,' he replied, picking up

his coffee, 'but there's no one I'd feel comfortable trading favours with at this stage. We need more to go on.'

Having expected that answer, Andee checked her phone as it rang, and seeing it was Graeme she felt unsure about answering. Now wouldn't be a good time while she was waiting for Sven to call back; on the other hand they hadn't spoken for what seemed too long.

'Hi, how are you?' she asked, clicking on.

'I'm fine,' he replied, his tone slightly querulous and distracted.

'How are things going over there?'

'I wish I could say also fine, but the problems seem to be piling up. What about with you?'

So much had happened since they'd last spoken that she couldn't think where to begin, or why he'd be interested when he was so challenged by events over there. 'It's still quite complicated,' she replied. 'No sign of Penny, but we're working on it. Listen, I'm waiting for a call that I have to take. Can I ring . . .'

'It's OK. I'll try again later,' and before she could draw breath the line had gone dead.

Tim regarded her curiously.

Not sure whether she was offended or worried, Andee simply shook her head and returned to her phone, this time to read an email she'd just received from Alayna.

Hey, made a start and thought I'd send this through. Out of first twenty friends on MJ's FB page five are Polish, two Estonian, six Latvian, three Slovakian, and four Hungarian. All living in UK. Can't find what they do for work, or where they live, but all sounding very grateful to

Martyna. Are they for real? No way of knowing. If you scroll on down from these posts you'll find more, mostly from guys in their twenties, definitely not older, and saying more or less the same thing. Again, no idea if they're real. More soon as I can. Xxx

Andee showed it to Tim, and was about to comment when a call came in. Seeing the Swedish number she quickly clicked on.

'Ms Lawrence, Sven Sylvander here. I'm sorry to have kept you.' The voice was low, gravelly and very slightly fractured. 'I am presuming that Jonathan gave you this number. Do you know where he is?'

Jonathan? 'No. Do you?'

'I'm afraid not, but it's very important that we find him. Can you come to Stockholm?'

Andee blinked in astonishment.

'I'm afraid my health won't allow me to make the trip to London,' he explained, 'but we need to talk. I will arrange the air travel from this end and someone will be at the airport to meet you. Is tomorrow too soon?'

Andee looked at Tim as she said, 'That sounds fine.'

'Thank you. If you will be kind enough to give me your email address I'll have my assistant send you details of flight times. I shall look forward to meeting you.'

Chapter Fourteen

The following morning, feeling as though everything was taking a truly surreal turn, Andee was settled into a business class seat on the 7.40 flight to Stockholm from Heathrow. Given the short notice of the trip, she'd paid a quick visit to Oxford Street yesterday to gather up enough essentials to last for three days, though no one had told her she'd be away for that long. In fact, there had been no mention of a return flight at all, and the ticket she had was only one-way.

'Don't worry,' she'd told Tim when he'd pointed this out. 'I'm sure no one's planning to kidnap me, and I can always buy myself a ticket to get home if need be.'

He still didn't look happy. 'You don't feel you might be walking into some sort of trap?' he challenged.

It hadn't crossed her mind until he'd suggested it. However, now, as the plane soared off into the blue beyond, she was asking herself if she was crazy to be following a stranger's instructions to fly to a country she'd never visited before, as though this were some sort of game for which she knew the rules – which she patently didn't.

There was no point trying to second-guess things; she had absolutely no idea what to expect when she got to Stockholm, apart from a meeting with Sven Sylvander, and after that, presuming it happened, she'd just have to wait and see.

In an effort to distract herself from the continued taunt of misgivings she tried to focus on her mother, whose concern about this trip to Stockholm hadn't been so very different to Tim's.

'I wish Graeme was around to go with you,' Maureen had commented with a sigh. 'It doesn't seem right you having to go there when I'm sure this man could just as easily come here.'

'It'll be fine,' Andee had assured her. 'I just want you to stop worrying and let me know immediately if either Penny or her son get in touch again.'

Having wondered earlier if this trip was some sort of ruse to get her mother on her own, Andee had already texted Blake to ask him and Jenny not to let Maureen out of their sight. She'd also alerted Gould and Johnson of her movements and of course Tim knew, and would have come with her had his wife not been returning from York today.

Remembering that Alayna had emailed her a further update last night, she scrolled to it and felt her curiosity growing, along with confusion and unease, as she tried to make sense of it.

OK, girls first. Seems like seven of those I checked yesterday are living in London. No actual addresses, but that's not unusual, only a moron would give that sort of information on social media. They're still active on various sites, but nothing unusual about their posts since those a couple of months ago, apart from the fact that they no longer seem to be in contact with Martyna. I went back a bit further on a couple of pages and found some interesting entries about someone called 'Polina' who 'didn't want to go through with it'. Have attached a screen shot. See where someone says, 'Oh my God, that's terrible. No one will ever find her.' The responses are all weepy emoticons, apart from a couple saying that she had a choice so it's her own fault. Couldn't find anything to explain what it meant. The next weird, or interesting thing, is a post from someone called Inga reminding them that they should be using their private chat room.

Sorry, got to go now, Jay's waiting. No idea what any of this means, or how real it is. Will try to check.

Love you, A xxx

(PS – Will focus on the guys next.)

Making a mental note to forward this to Leo when she landed, Andee refused a second coffee and croissant from the steward and closed her eyes. Although none of this confirmed Tim's theory, it wasn't ruling it out either; in fact it was making her increasingly uneasy. But organ-trafficking? Really?

Feeling faintly queasy, she turned to gaze at the clouds. Nothing was making sense to her, from Alayna's social media report, to Martyna's comments about Penny, to John Victor Jr's – *Jonathan's?* – need for help.

After an easy pass through immigration Andee wheeled her new overnight bag through to Arrivals, where a portly, well-groomed woman of around fifty was displaying a board with her name on it. Going to her, Andee found herself responding to the warmth of the woman's smile with some enthusiasm of her own.

'I'm guessing you're Selma,' Andee said, as they shook hands.

'Indeed I am,' Selma replied, her gentle voice confirming her as the woman Andee had spoken to on the phone. She was also the 'assistant' who'd sent the email containing flight details. 'I am very happy to meet you. Please come this way. The car is not far.'

With the pleasing anticipation of being in a country she'd never visited before mixing with some apprehension, Andee took in her surroundings as she walked alongside Selma to a large black Mercedes, where a chauffeur was already holding open a rear door.

'Is this your first visit to Stockholm?' Selma asked, as they merged with the traffic heading towards the city.

'It is,' Andee confirmed. 'I read something recently about Sweden being in the top ten best places to live.'

Selma's smile was full of pride. 'It is a beautiful country, and Stockholm, as you will see, is a very special city. Maybe you already know that it is made up of many islands which are linked by, I think, forty-two bridges. This is why we call ourselves the Venice of the North. Our waterways are much wider, and very blue at this time of year. Plus, we have many quaintly cobbled streets, historic buildings and a magnificent palace in Gamla Stan, which is the old town. Of course there are also many boats and cafés on the waterfronts, and also some of the best restaurants in Scandinavia, possibly the world. And then there is the coffee.'

Andee's eyes twinkled.

'I am reading your mind,' Selma told her mischievously, 'which is why our first stop will be at a very special place which is not far from your hotel.'

Interested to hear that she would be in a hotel, Andee said, 'When will I meet with Sven?'

Selma grimaced an apology and glanced at her watch. 'I am afraid it cannot be today. I will explain over coffee, meantime, if you will forgive me there are some urgent calls I must make.'

Deciding now wasn't the time to object to being kept waiting, Andee simply gazed out of the window, having no more success in reading the passing signs than in understanding whatever Selma was saying on the phone. She truly was in a foreign country, excluded by the language and possibly even the culture; however, she wasn't feeling too anxious yet, only curious and even vaguely excited.

Checking her own phone as it rang, she saw it was Graeme and gladly clicked on. 'Hi, how are you?' she asked quietly.

'I'm fine. Where are you? That wasn't a British ringtone.'

'I'm in Stockholm.'

'*Stockholm?* Why?'

'It's a long story. I'll tell you later. Have you ever been here?'

'Yes, a few times. I used to go with a client to buy art at the Auktionsverket. How long are you going to be there?'

'I'm not sure yet.'

'I'm guessing it's something to do with Penny?'

'It is.'

'Are you alone?'

'Yes and no. I was invited by Sven Sylvander, who I haven't met yet. He's someone Penny's son wants me to be in touch with.' If Selma was listening she showed no sign of it.

'Is Penny going to be at this meeting?'

'I've no idea, but I don't think so. Are you managing to get things back on track at your end?'

With a sigh he said, 'Don't get me started.'

'Oh dear. How's Nadia behaving?'

'The way she usually behaves, passionately.'

Not sure she liked the answer, Andee said, 'Is she with you?'

'Yes. I mean, not at this moment, but she's at the villa every day now and I really wish she'd go back to Spain for a while.'

Liking that answer much more, Andee fell silent for a moment, not sure what else she wanted to say, but not wanting to ring off either.

'I miss you,' he said softly.

Swamped by feeling, she said, 'I miss you too.'

'I'd like to be the one to show you Stockholm. It's one of my favourite cities.'

'If you can get here . . .'

'If I could I'd be on the next flight.'

Forty minutes later, having journeyed along a motorway surrounded by more glorious pine forests than she'd ever seen in her life, to be greeted in the city by the most entrancing baroque architecture on just about every street corner, Andee was sitting outside a famous café in the Gamla Stan being invited to name her bean type, grind size and froth style.

The coffee shop was on a quaint, cobbled street adjacent to a waterfront with towering and colourful old houses soaring skywards, and a tantalising glimpse of the royal palace glistening in the bright midday sun.

When eventually their bespoke brews arrived Selma raised her cup and said, proudly, '*Valkommen till* Stockholm.'

'*Tack*,' Andee smiled, using the only Swedish word she'd managed to pick up from watching every episode of *The Bridge*.

'When we are finished I will take you to your hotel,' Selma told her. 'It is not so far from here, in the area known as Ostermalm, which is like your Kensington or Knightsbridge in London. You will probably enjoy to freshen up a little before we begin our tour.'

Andee blinked. *Tour?* 'Oh no, I really don't want to put you to any trouble,' she protested. 'I'm quite . . .'

'It is no trouble. I am happy to do it,' Selma assured her, 'and Sven insists that you should see something of our beautiful city before you leave. I'm afraid it isn't possible for him to see you today, because he is very sick. He has – how do you say *leukemi* . . . ?'

'Leukaemia?' Andee ventured, hoping she was wrong. Who'd wish it on anyone?

'This is correct,' Selma confirmed. 'Yesterday he was receiving chemotherapy. He insisted he would be strong enough to see you today, but of course it is not true. He needs another day to regain some strength.'

'Oh, goodness,' Andee murmured. 'I'm so sorry.'

'We are all sorry, because we love him very much and sadly he is not going to recover. The doctors are keeping him with us for as long as they can, but not so long that his life becomes unbearable.'

Andee couldn't think what to say as Selma sipped her coffee and waved to someone she knew. In the end she said, 'Have you worked for Sven for long?'

Selma smiled. 'Since I was twenty. He is a very good man to work for, which is why he is so much loved.'

Andee weighed up her next question, and decided simply to go for it. 'Do you know my sister?' she asked.

'Oh yes, very well,' Selma replied, clearly unfazed. 'We call her Kate, which is what she prefers. Others know her as Michelle, and of course to you she is Penny.'

Andee had got stuck at Kate – the evil Kate Trask from *East of Eden*? – until the mention of Penny. 'So you know who she really is?' she asked incredulously.

Selma simply added more sugar to her coffee.

'Is she here?' Andee wanted to know.

'No, we have not seen her since Jonathan disappeared.'

'Jonathan? Her son?'

'That's right. He has been in touch with you?'

'With my mother. He wanted me to contact Sven. Penny calls him John. John Victor.'

Selma's eyebrows rose.

Hoping for more of a response, Andee waited, but none was forthcoming. 'What did you mean when you said he's disappeared?' she asked.

'He is not in contact with Kate or Sven.'

'Why?'

'It is Sven who must answer this question. I am here to keep you company for today and make sure that you have everything you need.'

Realising that Selma would have her instructions and that nothing she, Andee, could say would make her sway from them, Andee decided to resign herself to the wait and simply enjoy her tour.

By seven that evening she had crossed so many bridges, admired so much stunning architecture and gasped at such an abundance of picture-postcard views, many from Heaven, a rooftop bar in the Sodermalm district, that she couldn't imagine why she'd never been here before. The city was far more fascinating – and friendly – than she'd expected, and she couldn't help wishing Graeme was with her so she could enjoy his stories of previous visits.

Since she was eager to talk to him, she waited no longer than it took to get to her hotel room and pour herself a large glass of wine before connecting to his number. To her frustration she went through to voice-mail, so after leaving a message for him to call as soon as he could, she sank into a plush armchair and opened her emails.

No more from Alayna, nor from Leo; however there was a curt note from Penny that immediately infuriated her.

For all these years I've left you alone, never digging into your life or trying to interfere with what you're doing. It would be to your credit if you would afford me the same courtesy.

'I can't believe the nerve of her,' she exploded to her mother when she got through. 'It's like she's completely forgotten that *she* got in touch with *us*. And how dare she say she's never dug into my life when she's so blatantly been having me watched. I don't suppose you've seen the boy again?'

'I'd have told you if I had. I keep thinking about him though, and wondering why he said time was running out. What on earth do you think he means?'

'I've no idea, Mum, but hopefully by this time tomorrow I'll be able to give you an answer.'

The following morning Andee was already waiting in the hotel lobby when Selma and the chauffeur arrived to take her to meet Sven. Having consulted a guidebook she was aware that the area they were travelling through – Ostermalm – was home to some of Stockholm's wealthiest residents, and this was very evident. The baroque and Renaissance buildings, immaculate in their upkeep and made glorious by ornate turrets, spires and onion domes, were as opulent and elegant as anything she'd seen in Paris or London, maybe even more so. She tried to imagine Penny moving around the area, speaking the language, meeting friends, shopping in the stylish boutiques, enjoying the history and charm. It wasn't easy, but given how little she knew of her sister's life that was hardly surprising.

Eventually they turned off a wide, busy boulevard with a tree-lined walkway down the centre of it into a quiet, triangular construct of exclusive mansion blocks. They came to a stop outside an ivory-coloured building with black wrought-iron balconies rising up over several floors, and a set of heavy black doors to mark the entrance.

'Sven also has a home at Djursholm, overlooking the sea,' Selma informed her as she put in a security code to enter the block. 'It is where he prefers to be, but his treatment means he must spend most of his time in town.'

Concerned for how sick he actually was, Andee said, 'Are you sure he's up to seeing me today?'

'Oh yes, he is looking forward to it.' Selma nodded her thanks to a security guard who was showing them into an elevator.

At the fifth floor the doors opened and they were greeted by a slightly bent old man with a complexion like tree bark and an expression that appeared half happy, half tragic, the result, Andee suspected, of a stroke. 'Thank you, Erik,' Selma said gently. 'You can tell Freja that we are here and will take coffee in the *lilla salongen* when she has it ready.'

'Of course. It will be my pleasure,' Erik responded with an awkward little bow.

Moved by the politeness of them speaking English, presumably for her benefit, Andee looked around the extraordinary circular entrance hall with its elaborate mid-European decor and wide marble staircase that curved up to the next level. There were statues and paintings everywhere, fresh flowers in large oriental urns and a rack filled with so many styles of walking cane that Sven – or someone in the household – must surely be a collector.

'Through here,' Selma invited, pushing open a large oak door with iron-studded hinges and, incongruously, but sweetly, a child's drawing of a house pinned to the front. Underneath the drawing were the words *Pappa's Den*.

'We found it the other day while going through some things,' Selma explained, 'and we decided to put it up again.'

The *lilla salongen* turned out to be a cosy, oak-panelled room with tall sash windows along one wall offering views over dense green treetops, a black and gold marble fireplace with a gilt-framed mirror over the chimney breast, and three matching sofas in mahogany leather forming an intimate square around a circular glass table.

'Sven will be with us shortly,' Selma told her. 'He favours this room above the others. It is less formal, he says.'

Andee was by now so riveted by the photographs on just about every surface that she was barely listening. Penny was in so many of them, staring out with watchful, almost solemn eyes, or seemingly trying to avoid the lens altogether. In some she was smiling, but only a few, and in others she was much slimmer and younger than she was now. Andee presumed the older man who often featured alongside her was Sven, and the young boy was surely John – Jonathan – at various ages. Selma also appeared, but the woman who really caught Andee's attention, apart from Penny, was a truly striking beauty. There was so much gaiety radiating from her in just about every shot that Andee felt a strong desire to meet her.

'Sven's wife, Ana,' Selma said softly, seeing Andee transfixed by the woman's appearance.

Before Andee could respond, a door beside the fireplace opened and the man from the photographs came to life. For a bizarre moment Andee felt thrown, for as strikingly similar as he was to his captured images, there was also an enormous change. The shock of white hair had gone, as had the swarthy complexion. His age-spotted head was completely bald, and the skin on his face was waxen and crusted. He was painfully thin and stooped, but his eyes, behind their frameless spectacles, were such a deep and arresting blue it felt almost as hard to look at them as it was to look away.

'Andee? May I call you Andee?' he asked, holding out an unsteady hand to shake. This was the voice she'd heard on the phone, low and gravelly and slightly hypnotic.

'Yes, of course,' she replied, feeling the knotted bones of his fingers as her own closed around them.

'Thank you for coming to Stockholm,' he said, holding her gaze in a way that felt authoritative yet reassuring. 'I am sure Selma has explained why it is not possible – or let us say it is not *easy* – for me to travel these days.'

'Yes, she has,' Andee replied, 'and I'm very sorry to hear what you're going through.'

He dismissed it with a wave of his hand, which he turned into a gesture for her to sit down. 'Ah, here is

Freja with our refreshments. I hope you'll forgive me for not taking anything myself – doctor's orders – but please enjoy the coffee, and Freja makes the most excellent *kladdkaka*, which I expect you know is a Swedish version of chocolate cake.'

Andee hadn't known it, but she was happy to try it, along with the coffee, which turned out to be excellent. As for the patisserie . . . She wondered how she was going to limit herself to only one slice.

'Selma will stay with us,' Sven informed her, as Freja set a bottle of mineral water and a glass on the table next to him. 'I don't think I'm going to collapse or die in the next hour or so, but just in case, it would be awkward for you to deal with it alone.'

The merriment in his eyes was so infectious that Andee had to smile.

'Now, I think we should come straight to the point of why you're here, don't you?' he said. 'Jonathan gave you my number, yes? Have you seen him?'

Startled by the suddenness of the question, Andee said, 'No, but my mother has. He gave her your number to pass to me.' She wondered whether to bring up the issue of the name, but decided to leave it for now. 'Why doesn't he approach me himself?' she asked.

Batting the air, as though there might be a fly near him, he said, 'Because he suspects his mother is having you watched, and I am sure he is correct about that.'

Andee's eyes widened. Apparently he didn't find anything inappropriate about this, or if he did he wasn't showing it. 'But there is always email, and the phone,' she pointed out.

'He believes his mother to be capable of monitoring all things.'

Andee held his gaze, an unspoken request for him to expand. When he didn't, she said, 'Is she?'

He smiled. 'I really have no idea, but I can tell you that she is very resourceful.'

'So what is going on? Why am I here?'

'To answer that I must tell you that I have not spoken to Jonathan in several weeks, but I imagine he has put us in touch because he wants me to ask you to help him.'

Andee's eyebrows rose. 'Why does he need help?'

Sven shifted uncomfortably, but waved Selma back to her chair as she made to get up. After sipping some water, he said, 'He has got himself into a situation that does not please his mother. It could end up causing her some . . . difficulties and she is very keen to avoid that. I'm afraid he can be as stubborn as she is.'

Realising she needed to back up slightly, Andee said, 'How did he even know about me?'

'Ah, yes. This is a good question. He knows because I told him, and once his mother realised I had done this she guessed he would go to you if things should go wrong between them. I confess this was my intention, although the current circumstances – I refer to the reason for his disappearance – were not in existence at the time I told him he had another family. I did it as a form of insurance. Once my cancer was diagnosed I needed to be sure someone would be there for him should things ever become . . . complicated, as they are apt to do with his mother.' He paused as Selma refilled his glass and passed it to him. 'He has come to you now,' he said, after taking a sip, 'because he feels that his situation is . . . It is becoming urgent. He should let me help, but he won't because of my health, and to be frank, I'm not sure he fully trusts me. This makes me sad, of course, but I understand it.'

Andee said, 'If you want me to help him, then you'll need to be more specific.'

Sven smiled and nodded. 'Of course, and I will be, but to explain properly means that first I must tell you about your sister.' He gave a ponderous shake of his head, suggesting dismay, even sadness. 'It still surprises me to think of her as part of another family, but of course, I've always known that she is.'

'If you've always known it then why didn't you . . . ?'

He raised a hand to stop her. 'I will tell you everything, from the beginning, and hopefully this will answer your questions.'

She regarded him carefully as, for several moments, he appeared to sink into his thoughts, until eventually his mesmerising eyes returned to hers. 'Kate came to us,' he began, 'Kate is what we call her. I hope that is not difficult for you?'

Andee shook her head, and wondered if he knew why Penny had chosen that name, if she'd even chosen it for the reason Andee suspected.

'Kate came to us when she was twenty-one,' he said. 'We found her . . . I should say we were told where to find her, by John Victor, who I know to be your uncle. He is also the man who sold us her twin sons four years before.'

Andee inwardly reeled. John Victor had *sold* Penny's *twin* sons. So there were two, just like in *East of Eden*.

'I realise you will think it a terrible thing that we bought two children,' Sven continued, 'but my wife was unable to have any of her own, and she so desperately wanted them. We could have adopted, of course, but it can take so much time and we weren't getting any younger. So we decided on a different route. It wasn't easy to find the right people to help us, but then I was introduced to John Victor . . .'

He paused and drank more water, and used a folded handkerchief to dry his lips. 'We were introduced, your uncle and I,' he continued, 'by a mutual friend whom I trusted and who assured me that Victor could help us. It turned out to be true, at least in one sense. At our second meeting Victor told me about a young girl who would willingly carry my child, so I paid him a great deal of money to keep the pregnancy and birth under the radar until it was time to bring the newborn – we didn't realise at the time there would be twins – by private jet, to our home in Connecticut. By receiving the child there and not returning to Stockholm for a while, it would be easier for us to pass the baby off as our own. So Ana faked her pregnancy, and one day we got a call from Victor to let us know that the girl had given birth to twins. It didn't matter. There was never any hesitation. We wanted them both. So Victor brought them to us, and Ana and I remained in America for the next two years, moving around quite a lot to avoid becoming too close to people, and of course to avoid awkward questions. After obtaining birth certificates and passports for the boys we brought them to our home in Djursholm.'

Andee was so stunned she hardly knew what to say. To think of two tiny babies, her own nephews, as the victims of such exploitation and bartering was so shocking and unacceptable that she simply couldn't deal with it right now.

'They thought, believed,' Sven went on, 'that we were their parents. Their birth certificates say that we are . . .'

Unable to stop herself, Andee said, 'Why would you call one of them after John Victor?'

Sven nodded soberly, apparently considering this a reasonable question. 'At the time he brought them to us he was our saviour. We felt very much in his debt, even though we had paid him a great deal of money. It was his wish that one of them should be named after him, so that is what we did, altering it slightly to Jonathan. We had no idea at the time what Victor was really like, although you would say that we should have, as no normal person would have been able to pull off what he had. I guess we only wanted to think about the boys and how blessed we felt, and how blessed they were too to have parents who wanted them so much, when their own mother had only given birth to them for financial gain.'

'Did you know that for certain?' Andee challenged.

Apparently chastened, he said, 'We took Victor at his word, and got on with our lives.' He stopped, took a shaky breath and drank some more water.

'The boys were four years old when Ana, my wife,

was seriously injured in a car accident and Alexander, Jonathan's twin, was killed.'

Andee felt the blow, and could see how deeply affected Sven still was by the tragedy.

Seconds ticked by. He was staring at nothing as he eventually said, 'When it became clear that Ana wouldn't walk again, that she'd be unable to do many things for herself . . . This was when she started to believe that we'd been punished for taking the boys the way we had. She became convinced that their mother hadn't wanted to part with them; even if she had, she might have changed her mind by now. She decided that we must try to find her, that she should be given the chance to be a mother to her son. I think she believed that only by doing this would she ever be able to forgive herself for the death of Alexander.

'So I contacted John Victor and for another considerable sum he told me where the mother could be found.

'It was appalling. The conditions she was being kept in were the worst I'd ever seen; I didn't even know that people lived like that. She wasn't alone; there were a number of girls there, and boys, barely existing in the kind of squalor I hope never to see again. She was so emaciated and sick that her captors were glad to be rid of her, but of course they made me pay. I didn't mind, I'd have given them twice as much, ten times as much, to get her out of there. She had no idea who I was; she was in no state to know anything. She just did as she was told, collected up the few possessions she had: a hairbrush that was clearly rarely used, a ragged selection of clothing; only one pair of shoes; a tooth-brush and a book.'

A book.

'*East of Eden*?' Andee asked quietly.

He nodded, though he didn't appear to find her accurate guess either surprising or relevant. 'I brought her here, to this apartment,' he continued. 'Ana and Jonathan were still in Djursholm. I didn't want them to see Kate, as we came to know her, until she was well. It took a long time to get her well. I hired a nurse to help take care of her. She had the best medical and psychi-atric attention, but it was still more than a year before she was able to converse without forgetting her words, or eat without vomiting, or even walk down the street without thinking someone was coming to get her. The psychological effects of her ordeal were profound.

'Eventually, when the doctors declared her well enough, I took her to Djursholm to meet Ana and Jona-than. By then she'd chosen her new name and we decided that she should also have ours, so she became Kate Sylvander. We did everything we could to get her started in a new life, and she did everything she could to help care for Ana.' He paused to take a breath. 'We could see right away that she was finding it difficult to bond with her son,' he said, 'and she showed no out-ward signs of upset when she was told about Alex. We understood that she had been forced to internalise her emotions for so long that she was still afraid to show them, so we simply continued as we were. Jonathan called Ana Mamma and me Pappa and that was the way it stayed.'

His luminous eyes came to hers, and seemed to leave his own thoughts behind to penetrate hers. 'You are wondering,' he stated, 'how much we knew of Kate's background when we brought her here.'

He was right, she was asking herself that, along with many other things.

'The truth is, we knew everything, because John Victor had told us before we entered into our agreement. He would not get his money unless he provided us with a full history of the mother. There could have been medical or psychiatric issues, and we needed to know what sort of legal complications we might face if she ever found the boys and wanted them back.

'In the event it was never a problem. After we took her in she was happy to stay with us. She felt safe, she said, as though she belonged. She and Ana became close, and I knew it would break Ana's heart to lose her, so there was never any question of her leaving and returning to you. It was her choice, never forced on her by us.'

His eyes remained on Andee's, slightly defiantly, showing that he'd known then, and knew now that he'd done wrong, but he wasn't sorry.

'You are wondering,' he said, reading her mind again, 'if she ever asked about you and your parents. The answer is no, she didn't. That isn't to say she didn't use the Internet to read about her disappearance, because she did, and she frequently Googled your name during the time you were with the police to find out what you were doing. But she never talked about you, at least not to me or Ana. We tried to encourage her, told her that we'd understand if she wanted to be in touch with you, but she insisted that she didn't. By then she'd begun working with me, helping to manage our properties here in Sweden, also those in London and the United States. She was very adept; a quick learner and as it soon turned out, a shrewd business-woman. I promoted her through the ranks of the company with far greater speed than I had with any-one else, which didn't make her popular, but she never seemed to mind about that. She wasn't in it to be liked, she would tell me, she was in it to repay me and Ana for our kindness, and to do whatever it took to help girls, or boys, who, through no fault of their own, found themselves in the same position as I'd found her.'

Andee sat quietly as he drank more water. She had the sense that he was moving forward too quickly, glossing over things to try and show his Kate in a good light, but there were shadows, far too much obfusca-tion for her to let it go that easily. However, for now she'd let him speak and if he didn't mention John Vic-tor again, she'd come back to it.

'Of course I couldn't help but admire her ambition,' Sven continued, putting his glass down, 'and I was more than ready to support her personal project, which she'd been working on quietly and diligently almost since her health had been restored. It was unusual, to say the least, but I was soon persuaded. Ana, on the other hand, was not. In fact she was very much opposed to it. We tried hard to persuade her to see things our way, but she never did, and I wasn't prepared to back it without her blessing.

'In the end it went ahead, but not until after Ana died.' He swallowed hard, and so did Andee. Ana had objected to Penny's idea, and now Ana was dead. Kate Trask had removed the madame from the path of her ambitions in *East of Eden* and had gone on to achieve them all, foul and depraved as they were. So how had Ana died?

'The project was not without its dangers,' Sven was saying, 'and this was a big concern to me, which is why, when we decided that we would press ahead, I wouldn't allow Kate to undertake it alone. We sought expert advice and hired people to escort her to various parts of this great continent to meet with the traffickers.' His eyes were boring into Andee's, gauging her response.

Traffickers. Her mouth turned dry, her heart began a heavy, dull thud. 'What were they trafficking?' she asked, matching his even tone.

'People,' he replied.

Again he showed no emotion, while she was finding it hard to stop herself reeling.

'Her project became very successful very quickly,' he continued. 'She gained a reputation for paying well and in cash, and she never divulged the whereabouts of the traffickers to the authorities.'

And this was a good thing? What kind of world was this man living in?

'Her operations have become more refined over the years, but they are still . . .'

Forcing a calm she was far from feeling, Andee

said, 'What kind of deal is she doing with these traffickers?'

He nodded, clearly ready to come on to that. 'She selects, she *buys*, the prettiest girls – and boys – the traffickers can offer and takes them under her wing. Everything is explained to them ahead of their departure, so if any of them don't want to go they are free to stay where they are. Of course, once they find out what Kate – or Michelle as she is for her business – is offering, they always want to come. She turns their lives around in a way that would never have happened if they'd stayed in their homelands, or with those who'd promised them a better life. This is not the only way she finds people. These days she now has many scouts and intermediaries working for her in several parts of the world. I do not get closely involved myself; she doesn't need my help, and now I am in no position to give it even if she did.'

Andee started as he waved a hand towards the open window, and Selma quickly went to close it.

'Do you need a blanket?' Selma offered, clearly concerned. 'Maybe you should take a break for a while?'

He shook his head and gestured for her to sit down again.

'You must be wondering,' he said to Andee, 'what Kate is offering these young people that is so irresistible to them. It would be easy to say a way out of poverty, a means of helping their families, we all know that is why most people leave their countries and those they love, to seek a new life. With Kate, instead of being cheated and lied to, beaten, raped, sold on to other traffickers and forced into prostitution and slavery, they are brought to Stockholm or Paris or London and installed in the various apartments we own around these cities. They are taught how to present themselves in the best way possible, so their hair is cut into sophisticated styles, their skin is given help if it needs it, they visit dentists, doctors, personal trainers, and then they are videotaped talking about themselves. They say their names and ages, where they are from, what sort of hobbies and ambitions they have, all sorts of things. These videos are then shown to couples in America, the Middle East, Asia, wherever they happen to be, to see if the girl is suitable for them. The girl's task is to carry a child for people who are unable to have children of their own. If they like the look of the girl Kate has selected for them – and they almost always do as she is very good at putting people together – then everyone meets. If they are still sure about going through with it, the necessary papers are drawn up and so it begins. Sometimes the husband will donate his sperm, or even have relations with the girl, I am told, but where that isn't possible a suitable donor is found. The fertilising process is carried out at one of the medical centres Kate owns in America. Surrogacy is legal in many states over there, as I'm sure you know.'

Whether Andee did or didn't hardly began to rate on the scale of issues being raised.

'There are so many people in the same sad position Ana and I once found ourselves in,' he continued, 'eager, desperate to have children but denied by nature.

They are prepared to pay very handsomely for someone – a healthy and beautiful young girl – to carry a child for them. If a sperm donor is being used then he too is very carefully selected. From conception the child belongs to the couple the surrogate mother has entered into an agreement with, and when she is safely delivered the infant is handed over to the happy parents.'

Instinctively knowing it couldn't be that simple, or as perfect as he was trying to paint it, Andee said, 'And the surrogate mothers? What happens to them?'

He smiled fondly. 'They are free to go home, if this is what they wish to do, or they can help another couple to have a baby, which many of them do. Or Kate and her team will help them to find jobs and places to live until they are ready to return to their families, if they have one. Sadly, some don't.'

'What sort of jobs?' Andee asked, wondering if she already knew the answer.

He held up a hand to stop her. 'This is not important,' he declared, 'and I'm afraid I am getting tired, so we really need to talk about Jonathan and why he needs your help.'

Andee gestured for him to continue.

'For some time,' he said hoarsely, 'Jonathan has been working with his mother, mainly in an administrative role, but they rarely see eye to eye. It is odd, given what she does to help others, how Kate seems to have very little maternal instinct of her own. She is not comfortable with her son, or with strong feelings, I have always known that. She is very focused on her work, which she finds much easier than many people would. Over the years I have heard her described as anything from a psychopath to a narcissist to a sadist, but I have heard many good things about her too, and it is on them that I prefer to dwell. She has brought us a lot of happiness, not least through her boys, especially Jonathan, who is the gentlest, sweetest soul you could wish to meet. It's hard sometimes to believe they are related. I think the fact that he isn't more like her is what frustrates Kate the most about him. She considers him weak, which is not the truth at all. He is as determined and strong-minded as she is, but over different issues, which is why she is rarely kind to him. I doubt she has ever told him she loves him, and this could be because she doesn't. To be honest, I don't know how capable she is of love in the way we know it.'

Certain that she wasn't, Andee said, 'Does he know who his biological father is?'

Sven's eyes narrowed as they came to hers. 'Do you?' he countered.

She could feel herself tensing as she said, 'Is it John Victor?'

He shook his head.

Experiencing an unsteadying relief, she continued to regard him, meeting his unflinching gaze with one of her own. 'Then it's you?' she said quietly.

He didn't deny it.

Andee looked at Selma.

'We never told Ana,' Sven said. 'It felt like a betrayal, to sleep with a girl I didn't know, to be able to produce a child when Ana couldn't . . . I wanted her to feel that we were equal parents. And when Kate came to join us ... It would have been too hard for Ana if she'd known the truth. She was confined to a wheelchair, she was so helpless and we were unable to be close, in a physical sense, any more. She would have looked at Kate, and me, in a different way. Please believe me when I tell you that apart from the time the twins were conceived there has never been anything of that nature between Kate and me. She is like a daughter to me.'

Putting aside thoughts of her own parents, Andee said, 'Does Jonathan know how you came to be his father?'

'He does now.'

Since there was no more to be gained from exploring that, Andee said, 'Going back to John Victor. Do you know what happened to him? I mean how he died?'

From the way Sven looked at her she could tell that he did.

'Were you the man the neighbour saw getting into a car with him, just before he disappeared?' she asked.

'Yes, that was me.'

'Was Kate involved?'

Once again he simply looked at her. It was answer enough.

Andee turned to Selma, but Selma was looking at no one.

'Jonathan,' Sven stated, bringing them back to the reason they were there, 'is protecting one of the girls from his mother. The girl, Juliette, is pregnant, and the baby has already been signed away to a couple from

Texas. The trouble is, she has decided she wants to keep it and Jonathan is trying to help her to do this. I am not sure when the birth is due to happen . . .'

'In two weeks,' Selma put in quietly.

Sven nodded. 'She should already be in the States, at one of the clinics, but as far as I am aware she is still in England, or perhaps Jonathan has taken her somewhere else by now for her protection. I think not, or he would be more likely to face his mother, or to approach you himself. The fact that he won't means the girl must still be with him.'

Andee could hardly begin to work out the implications of it all, legal, moral or emotional.

Sven waved a hand towards Selma, her cue apparently to continue.

'If the girl goes into labour,' Selma said, 'which of course she will at any time now, Jonathan will have to get her to a doctor or a hospital, which will make it easier for Kate to find them.'

'But what can she do?' Andee protested.

'She will take the baby.'

'She can't just walk out of a hospital with a baby that isn't hers.'

Selma didn't argue, nor did Sven, who was looking at her again. The answer was clear in their eyes: Kate would find a way to do it because Kate was Kate.

'You have to help him,' Sven said. 'You see, the baby is also his.'

Andee's eyes closed in shocked dismay. How much worse could this get? 'What do you want me to do?' she asked.

270

'That will be for you to decide after you've spoken to him. I imagine he is hoping your law enforcement connections will be helpful.'

'And how do you propose I do that when he won't come near me?'

'We'll make it happen,' Sven assured her. 'We just have to know for certain that you're on his side.'

Chapter Fifteen

'How do you know you can trust this Sven?' Maureen asked after Andee had finished telling her about one of the most gruelling hours she'd experienced in a very long time.

'I don't, I suppose,' Andee replied, gazing at the fountain in front of her where the water was gushing and loud, but seemed oddly far away. She was sitting on a bench in the Karlaplan, an impressive and pictur-esque setting for yet more luxury apartment blocks that overlooked a circle of soaring oaks and this giant water feature, and where a market, or art exhibition, was currently being set up on the boundary. On leav-ing Sven's home she'd insisted on walking back to her hotel, needing the time to clear her head, to assimi-late what she'd been told and what she needed to do next.

'Do you feel inclined to trust him?' her mother prompted.

Maureen seemed to be dealing with this much better than Andee was; however, Andee had been careful not to mention John Victor, or the unthinkable suspicion that Penny might have been in some way involved in the death of Ana Sylvander.

Kate Trask had used poison on Faye.

How had Ana died?

'Are you still there?' Maureen asked.

'Yes, I'm here, and yes I feel inclined to trust him,' Andee told her. 'Most of what he said makes sense, even if it wasn't the entire picture. I don't think he lied as much as omitted things.'

'If the baby is Jonathan's,' Maureen said, 'that makes it my great-grandchild, and your great-nephew, so we have to do something.'

Almost smiling at her mother's ready loyalty, Andee said, 'We'll talk about it some more when I'm back. For now, if you see him again, tell him . . .'

What should she tell him?

The question went from her mind as a message arrived and she saw it was from Penny. 'I'll call you back,' she said to her mother, and going through to the text she turned cold to her core as she saw what it was.

Pretty girl.

The picture was of Alayna's beautiful, smiling young face gazing cheekily, provocatively into the lens.

Starting to shake, Andee texted back, *What the hell are you playing at?*

Who's playing? Enjoy Stockholm, but try not to believe everything Sven tells you.

By the time Andee returned to her hotel she'd already been in touch with Alayna.

'In a casting,' Alayna had whispered down the line. 'Up next. Will call later.'

So it seemed her daughter was where she was supposed to be, and now that Andee was calmer she realised that the photograph Penny had sent was from Alayna's Facebook profile. So it was quite probable that she hadn't actually been near Alayna. Nevertheless, there was a warning in the text that Andee knew she'd be a fool to ignore. Penny would know by now, if she hadn't before, that Alayna was at Bristol Uni, and there was no telling what she might do with that information.

Determined to stop spooking herself, she went downstairs to the bar and ordered a beer. Not her usual drink of choice, but since it was in keeping with where she was she decided to give it a go.

A few minutes later, to her immense relief, as her tension was mounting again, Graeme rang.

'Do you have time to talk?' she asked as soon as she answered. 'I mean a lot of time?'

'If you need it,' he replied. 'What's up?'

Taking the phone and her drink out to the pretty courtyard, she chose a discreet table beneath a cherry tree, and spent the next half an hour bringing him up to speed with everything that was happening.

'Wow,' he murmured when she'd finished. 'I've sure been out of the loop.'

'But you're in it now and I desperately need to know what to do.'

'Well, as I see it, I'm not sure you can do anything until they put you in touch with your nephew. Any thoughts on when that might be?'

'No, but given the imminent birth it'll presumably be soon.'

'And you're still in Stockholm? Do you know where he is?'

'Probably England somewhere. I'm flying back tomorrow . . .'

'Oh hell, I don't believe this,' Graeme groaned angrily. 'Nadia's just turned up.'

'And you can't make a phone call when she's around?' Andee snapped.

'Please. This is difficult enough . . .'

'Forget it,' Andee cut in, and before he could say any more she rang off.

Minutes later she was regretting the overreaction, so after texting an apology, she decided to check her emails.

Finding one from Alayna that had apparently arrived while she was with Sven she immediately clicked on.

Boys

Interesting, but weird. The ones I checked out are mainly living in London or Paris, but they seem to travel quite a bit, and there's a kind of competition going on between some of them. They post things like: Bingo! Got it in one! Beat that. Or, Second attempt, wish me luck. Never needed more, unlike some. I've included a screen shot of some posts about 'Harry' who they seem worried about.

I'm going to say that at least half of them are gay judging by the photographs on their pages, but I don't know that for certain. No one seems to be 'in a relationship'.

How are things in Stockholm?

Love you Axxx

Andee was about to send a reply when her phone rang. 'Selma,' she said as she answered.

'Andee. I hope you are OK. I think this morning was probably quite difficult for you.'

'I'm surviving,' Andee assured her. 'How's Sven?'

'Sleeping. He was very tired by the time you left. I think it was too much for him, but as you saw, he can be very determined. Have you received details for your flight back tomorrow?'

'Yes, they've come through, thank you.'

'The driver will pick you up at eight. At the same time he will give you a mobile telephone with a number to call. I realise this must seem a little espionage-like, but Jonathan is insisting we do it this way. He wants you to call him, but he has it fixed in his head that his mother is able to monitor your calls.'

'Does this mean you've spoken to him?'

'A few minutes ago. He tells me Juliette is with him, but he won't give me an address. Hopefully he will give it to you when you call him, or at least arrange to meet you. Please tell me you are still willing to help?'

'If I can, I will,' Andee promised, 'but it's hard to know what I can do.'

'I am sure he has something worked out. He is a very smart, but impulsive young man, who is often too kind and too romantic for his own good.' She added gently, 'He means a great deal to Sven; to all of us.'

Remembering the child's drawing on the door to the den, and feeling for the boy – after all, he was her nephew – Andee said, 'Would you like me to be in touch once I've spoken to him?'

'We would appreciate that very much, thank you. And please let us know if there is anything we can do. Sven wants me to tell you that we are at your disposal in any way we can be.'

After ringing off Andee sat thinking about the call for a long time. She couldn't say why she was having so many trust issues, especially when helping the boy seemed to have no downside – or none that she could figure. Maybe it was Sven's description of Penny's career, his attempt to make it seem like some kind of charity ... For sure, helping childless couples to achieve their dreams was a good thing, provided it was happening legally, which according to him it was. However, the fact that Penny was dealing with some of the most corrupt and dangerous individuals on God's earth in order to groom and exploit vulnerable young people wasn't sitting well with Andee at all.

'But if the girls are willing,' Graeme pointed out when they spoke again later, 'then it can't, as you seem to think, be forced prostitution. And if we're going to believe what Sven told you, then she's actually saving these kids from a far worse fate.'

'I realise that,' Andee replied, putting down her fork and knowing she'd never try smoked herring again in her life, 'but it doesn't stop there. What I want to know is what happens to these girls – and boys – after they've served their purpose?'

'I'm guessing your nephew can answer that.'

Certain he could, Andee said, 'This must have happened before, a girl not wanting to give up the baby. What I'm asking myself is how does Penny deal with it? And is it the reason her son won't go near her? He must know better than most the kind of lengths she'll go to to make sure things happen her way.' She was thinking about little Michelle Cross, John Victor, Ana Sylvander . . .

Graeme said, 'You know what's bothering me quite a lot? It's that the deeper into this you go, the more she's going to view you as a threat, and that's not feeling good. In fact, it's feeling a very long way from good.'

As arranged a chauffeur came to collect Andee the following morning to take her to Arlanda airport. Although she hadn't slept well she was feeling more apprehensive than tired, not sure what to expect when she returned to England, nor satisfied that she had completed her business in Stockholm. There was so much more she'd like to ask Sven, or Selma, but neither of them had been in touch since Selma had called to tell her about the chauffeur and mobile phone. As promised, when she'd got into the car she'd been given a small package which contained a phone with pre-paid credit and a folded sheet of paper with a number that was definitely British.

'Yes, I rang it about half an hour ago,' Selma had told her, 'but there was no reply. My belief is that he will only answer when he feels sure that it is you at the end of the line. I have texted him details of the pre-paid phone which he asked me to do.'

Though that sounded reasonable, it wasn't quite enough. 'I don't understand why he'd trust you to get a pre-paid phone for him, and yet he won't speak to you.'

'He is just being extra cautious. Are you having second thoughts about helping him?'

'No, but that could change once I've met him.'

She'd needed to say that, even though she wasn't sure she meant it. She simply didn't want Sven or Selma to think she was some sort of pawn they could use in a game she hadn't yet fathomed.

Thanks to the change in the hour it was still late morning by the time Andee boarded a train for Kesterly – and she wasn't far into the journey when the pre-paid mobile rang.

Digging it out of her bag she saw the caller's number was blocked, but clicked on anyway.

'Hello?' the voice at the other end said hesitantly. 'Is that Andee Lawrence?'

'Yes. Who's this?'

'It's Jonathan Sylvander. I've been waiting for you to call.' Before she could respond, he said, 'I'm sorry. I shouldn't have spoken to you like that. I'm just very eager to see you.'

'Where are you?'

'You spoke to Sven.'

'Yes.'

'So will you help us? Me and Juliette?'

'In so far as I can, but I'm not sure what you want me to do.'

'Juliette needs to give birth safely. Please can you help us to arrange that?'

'She has to go to a hospital . . .'

'Yes, but . . .' His voice dropped out as they went through a tunnel. '. . . is having you followed,' he was saying as the line came back again.

'I lost you for a moment,' she told him.

'Do you know if my mother is having you followed?' he asked. 'I'm sure that she is, because she is hoping you will lead her to Juliette so she can take the baby. Or to me in the hope of finding Juliette. Is someone following you now?'

Andee glanced around the carriage. 'It's hard to say,' she replied. 'I haven't been looking out for anyone.' Until now she hadn't felt concerned about anyone knowing where she was; if anything, she was happy to make herself an easy target.

'Do you think you can meet me without her spies knowing where you are?' he asked.

'Probably. When and where are you suggesting?'

'Is today too soon? I can text you our address.'

'I'm on a train still two hours from Kesterly. Where exactly are you?'

'About an hour south of Kesterly, by car. I'm not sure how you get here by rail.'

'Send me the address and I'll try to be there sometime late this afternoon.'

Since her car was in the driveway at Bourne Hollow, Andee took a taxi from the station and stayed at home long enough to unpack her bag and make a few discreet viewings of the green outside to see if there was anyone trying not to be noticed. There didn't appear to be, but maybe this one was smarter than the rest. It didn't matter, she had nothing to hide, and after leaving a note for her mother, who was at the library, she drove to Kesterly police station.

'Let me get this straight,' Gould said after she'd explained why she was there. 'You want to leave your car on the Quadrant outside and take mine to wherever you're going? And I would agree to this because?'

'Because you want to help me be sure I'm not followed.'

'Am I allowed to ask where you're going, and when I might get it back?'

'I'm going to meet my nephew and I'm hoping to be back before eight.'

'This evening, or tomorrow morning?'

'This evening.'

'And if I need my car before that?'

'You are welcome to use mine.'

He didn't look impressed. 'OK. So where is your nephew? What happened in Stockholm? And do we need to start making this official?'

'Please, bear with me for the rest of today at least,' Andee urged, holding up the mobile so he could see the address of where she was going. 'As soon as I've seen my nephew I'll come straight back here with your car and tell you everything I know.'

Sighing, he reached into his drawer and pulled out the car keys. 'It's in the DCI's space,' he told her.

She blinked.

'I won it for a week at poker,' he admitted.

'You boys and the things you get up to,' she chided, handing him her own keys.

Minutes later she was driving his BMW out of the underground car park, exiting at the back of the station into a one-way street, and after taking a zigzag route through to the main road she headed for the moor, certain no one was following her.

It was close to three thirty by the time Andee drove into the caravan park the satnav had brought her to. It was garishly resplendent in its colourful spread across its few acres of the West Devon coast, and seemed to have everything a holidaymaker could want, from fish and chip shops, to Costcutter supermarkets, to a heated indoor swimming pool, to a choice of bingo halls and a loudly musical amusement arcade. There was probably much more to entertain the tourists who were swarming about all over the place, but her focus was on searching out number 68 Seaview Way.

It turned out to be one of half a dozen or so rather smart log cabins – chalets she guessed they were called – at the far end of the park, with a small wooded area separating them from a sandy beach and the sea.

As she pulled up outside a face appeared briefly at a window, and a moment later a tall, muscular young man with dark blond hair came out on to the veranda to greet her. He reminded her of Luke, not in appearance for her son was much darker, but his demeanour, his age and slight awkwardness were similar. Could that be why she felt instinctively that she cared about this person she didn't actually know?

'Andee?' he said tentatively.

'And you're Jonathan,' she responded, going to shake his hand. How like his father he was, the same almost Slavic features and arresting blue eyes.

'Thanks for coming,' he said. He spoke with an accent that was slightly American and slightly Swedish. 'I realise I shouldn't be trying to put this burden on you, but I didn't know who else to turn to. Pappa – Sven – is very sick. I don't want this to make him worse.'

'Jonathan,' a female voice called from inside.

'Coming,' he replied, and standing aside he gestured for Andee to go in first.

It was a surprisingly spacious cabin, with an overwhelming scent of pine filling the air. A large picture window looked on to the woods and sea beyond, a kitchenette took up one corner, a staircase led to a mezzanine floor, and large sloppy armchairs and a sofa were grouped around an empty wood-burner. Standing in front of the burner was a slight, nervous-looking girl with dark curly hair and violet eyes; she was so heavily pregnant that Andee had an alarming vision of playing midwife in the next few minutes.

'I am Juliette,' she said, coming forward to shake Andee's hand. She seemed so delicate, too petite to be carrying with any sort of ease. 'I am Italian. My English is not so good, but Jonathan teach me every day.' She looked at him so adoringly that Andee couldn't help feeling moved. 'Thank you for coming,' she went on. 'I hope we are not a problem for you, but we want keep our baby very much. Please will you help us?'

Slipping an arm around her, Jonathan pressed a kiss to her forehead and settled her gently into an armchair. 'Can I get you something to drink?' he offered Andee. 'We don't have anything alcoholic I'm afraid, but I can make tea . . .'

'Water will be fine,' Andee assured him, dropping her bag on the arm of a chair and sitting down next to it. In fact, now she came to think of it she was ravenous, having not eaten since breakfast, and how odd it felt to realise that meal had been in Sweden. Now here she was on the edge of Devon in a remote wooden chalet, with the sound of waves wafting in through the open window and the distant screams of playing children seeming slightly surreal.

'How long have you been here?' she asked as Jonathan brought her a glass of mineral water.

'Almost a week,' he replied. 'We are moving around and changing cars. It feels safer that way.'

Andee frowned in concern, and slight scepticism. 'Do you really have so much to fear from your mother?' she asked. 'Surely if you explain . . .'

He was shaking his head. 'Forgive me, I know she is your sister, but you don't understand what she's like. She doesn't listen to explanations, only to what she wants to hear, and with us all she wants is for us to give up our baby. If she finds us she will make Juliette go to the States . . .'

'She can't force her,' Andee protested. 'And no airline will take her at this stage of pregnancy.'

'Kate would hire a private jet and people who would make Juliette do as she wants. As far as she is concerned Juliette must give birth in the States. That way we will have no control over what happens to our baby. The law in Texas says that it already belongs to the people who entered into the contract with my mother.'

'Which you and Juliette also signed?'

He nodded dismally.

Andee swallowed more water to give herself some time. She had no idea how the law in England would view a surrogacy agreement that had been drawn up in America, and Juliette wasn't British ... However, she was European, which for the time being might protect her, if anything could. 'I'll have to speak to a lawyer to get some advice,' she told them, 'but one thing I do know,' she said directly to Juliette, 'is that Penny – Kate – will absolutely not be able to force you to go anywhere while you're in this condition.'

Glancing at Juliette, Jonathan said, 'Some of the people who work for her are not ... They are not good people.'

Realising he was alluding to the violence that could be involved, that could extend to the kind of scenes Andee would prefer not to imagine, she became aware of her protective instincts rising. 'So what exactly are you hoping I can do?' she asked him.

'I want you to help me to keep Juliette safe while she gives birth. I know she must go to a hospital, but someone must be with her and the baby at all times to make sure that no one can steal the baby away. We're afraid that the hospital won't allow this, so we want you to use your influence to persuade them that they must.'

Knowing she could probably do that, particularly if it was known that the baby was at risk, Andee said, 'And after the baby comes and it's time to leave the hospital?'

'The baby will be British,' he reminded her.

'But will your mother pay any attention to that?'

'She will have to.'

Moved by his resolve, Andee said, 'We need to speak to her . . .'

'No, she will not listen. I have tried, but she is determined to honour the agreement she has made. She always is. You don't know what happens to those who go against her.'

Remembering the Facebook pages Alayna had found that had talked about people disappearing, Andee's eyes flicked to Juliette. The girl's face had turned worryingly pale. 'Tell me what happens to them,' Andee said quietly.

Clasping Juliette's hand, he replied, 'The babies are taken anyway, and the mothers . . . We don't see them again. No one does.'

Andee's throat tightened. 'What are you saying?'

'I am saying that people who cross my mother always live to regret it.'

'Be more specific.'

'OK. She sells them back to the traffickers, or to pimps and gangsters willing to pay. This is what she does with those who do not want to carry on working for her.'

Since Andee knew as well as any detective just how rife this sort of crime was throughout the sink estates and run-down areas of Britain, indeed the whole of Europe, areas that many people only heard about on the news one day, and forgot about the next, she said, 'And those who do carry on?'

'You can do this by being a surrogate again, or by becoming an escort, as she calls it. Of course it is prostitution, but not the same as for those who go to the Serbian or Latvian gangs. Those she has no more to do with. She will not take them back, even if they beg. The ones who choose to stay she takes care of. They live in nice apartments in Ostermalm and Belgravia, she selects their clients for them – men and women – and she keeps videos and dossiers of the most powerful ones to use if she needs to.'

'You mean for blackmail?'

He shrugged. 'I suppose so, but I have never known her to do this. I think it is a kind of insurance.'

Kate Trask's modus operandi almost to the letter. Although somewhat reassured that Penny's surrogacy project meant she hadn't followed her morbid fascination with Trask in every respect, Andee's head was starting to spin.

After a while she said, 'Do all the young people come through traffickers?'

He shook his head. 'No. Some of them are from poor families in remote regions who are recruited directly by her outreach workers – this is what she calls her scouts. Deals are done with the parents or guardians and they are taken away to live the kind of life they are promised, but only on her terms. Some are students, Juliette was one, looking to make enough money to pay their fees. My mother has a very large network of scouts looking out for vulnerable young people with beautiful faces and good health.'

'How many people are we talking about?'

'Twenty, maybe up to fifty a year.'

'Are they all used for surrogacy?'

'Most, but if they turn out not to be fertile they are given the choice of becoming an escort or going back to their families.'

'And do any of them make it back to their families?'

'I don't know. Maybe some.'

Andee looked at Juliette again and wondered how much of the English she understood. Presumably she knew the story, which was why she was so afraid.

'We have thought,' Jonathan told her, 'of letting this baby go and having another, but we made it together and we already love it, and we will always know that it is out there somewhere. Giving away a child that's yours is just not possible – unless of course you are *my mother*.'

The bitterness dug into Andee's heart, along with sadness and a desire to embrace him. He wouldn't welcome it, and it would embarrass them both, so she didn't attempt it, she simply said, 'I'm sorry.'

He looked away, clearly wishing he hadn't shown his feelings.

'Tell me,' she said, 'until you knew the truth, who did you think Kate was?'

He shrugged. 'Just someone who worked with Pappa and who also lived with us.'

'You had no particular relationship with her?'

'No, because she didn't want one with me. She doesn't like children, and she never pretended to.'

'So you thought Ana was your mother?'

He nodded.

Sensing how devastating it had been for him when he'd found out the truth, she said, 'How old were you when Ana died?'

'Eleven.'

Her heart ached with pity. 'But your father didn't tell you until many years later who your real mother was?'

'He told me when he became ill. By then I had already finished university and I was working with Kate, not recruiting, but I knew most of what was going on. At first I thought it was all a good thing, but then I realised what was really happening and I told Pappa I wanted out. This was at the time he was informed by the doctors that his cancer was terminal. He felt then that he must tell me everything he knew about my other family, how my mother had disappeared from your lives when she was in her teens, how she had given us to him after he'd paid her ... Ana never knew that he was our real father. I don't know why he didn't tell her ... I think because he didn't want her to know that he was involved in supplying surrogate mothers for childless people.'

'So he started the business?' Andee asked, having already guessed as much.

Jonathan nodded. 'He helped Kate to, and she is the one who has turned it into what it is now with a specialised travel company, the clinics, the apartments

289

mostly in London where the young people stay before and after they have done their duty.'

Andee was thinking of the terrible grief he had suffered in his short life, to lose his twin brother when he was only four, then the woman he'd always believed was his mother seven years later. Now here he was, faced with the fear of losing his child. 'I'm glad Sven told you about me,' she said softly.

His eyes became desperate. 'Does that mean you'll help us?' he asked. 'We'll do anything to keep our baby, and we're afraid that if we turn to the police . . . We can't turn to them. There is a contract to say this baby belongs to somebody else, and my mother's lawyers . . .'

'I'll do my best,' Andee promised, not at all sure what her best might be.

It was as she was leaving and they were outside on the veranda that she asked, gently, 'How did Ana die?'

'She had a fall,' he replied. 'It happened at our home in Djursholm.'

'I thought she couldn't walk.'

'She couldn't. She was in a wheelchair. There is a lift at the house. One day she reversed herself into it, but it wasn't there so she fell and . . .'

Andee's eyes closed as her heart tightened. She wanted to ask if Kate had been around at the time, but she wasn't sure she was willing to hear the answer.

As Andee made the drive back to Kesterly she called Gould to assure him she'd be there within the hour, then her mother to let her know she'd be home soon.

Why on earth, she was asking herself, as she started across the wilds of Exmoor, had Penny tried to make her believe that Jonathan was the child of incest? What sort of twisted mind did she have even to suggest such a thing? The sort of mind, Andee had to accept, that could accuse her own father of abuse that had never happened.

Thinking of all she'd learned about Penny in the past few weeks, Andee decided her sister must be full of hatred or revenge for sins only she could perceive. Aside from those emotions, Penny was empty – devoid of basic human kindness, understanding and compassion that came naturally to most. Her conscience clearly didn't react the way other consciences did. Hers was unreachable, had no power over her thoughts or actions.

It wasn't hard to see why some had dubbed her a narcissist or a sociopath, for she exhibited all the signs, which meant that trying to reason with her would be like trying to reason with someone who didn't speak the same language. It wasn't possible to stir a heart that had no feeling, any more than it was possible to turn back time and hope to start again.

Andee wasn't aware of the tears on her cheeks as she took a turn towards the Burlingford estate, she only knew that there was a horrible ache in her heart as it tried to hold on to how she had felt about Penny during the years she was missing. She desperately didn't want her sister to be the person she was showing herself to be, nor did she want her mother to go through the pain of losing her daughter all over again. But it would happen; it had to, because Penny didn't want them in her life any more now than she ever had. She'd only come back because of Jonathan's attempts to turn to Andee in his time of need. If it weren't for the baby that she probably didn't even view as her own flesh and blood, she'd never have come back at all.

Quietly devastated, as much for Jonathan as for her mother, Andee returned Gould's car and drove her own back to Bourne Hollow. She'd talk to Gould in the morning; now she needed to be with her mother so they could decide together what they were going to do next.

Chapter Sixteen

Andee watched her mother going through a range of harsh emotions as she listened to what Andee had learned over the past few days, including how Penny had tried to make her believe that Jonathan was John Victor's son. It was plain from the way Maureen's eyes closed at that point that she'd lost all ability to understand what had made her younger daughter the person she was.

Andee continued gently trying to avoid distressing her mother any further, particularly when it came to confirming that Penny hadn't been lying when she'd told them she hadn't wanted to come back to them, not even after the horrific time she'd spent at the mercy of gangs.

'Does that mean she never cared about us at all?' Maureen said, seeming hardly able to believe it.

'I don't know,' Andee replied softly, trying her best to lessen her mother's feelings of rejection, failure, guilt and whatever other torturous emotions were assailing her. 'She obviously formed some sort of attachment to Sven and his wife, but how real that was . . .' Nothing would induce her to reveal her fears about Ana's death right now; she didn't even want to think about it herself.

'Do you think she cares anything for what her accusations did to Daddy?' Maureen asked. 'Oh God, if I'd known what he was going through. Why didn't he tell us?'

Her mother's pain and anguish were even harder to watch than Andee had feared. She kept trying to imagine how she'd feel if Alayna turned on her in the same way, and knew it would be devastating beyond bearing.

'Why did she hate him so much?' Maureen murmured. 'Why did she hate any of us? We were never cruel or neglectful; we were a normal, decent family . . .' She put her hands to her face. 'It has to be my fault, I must have done something, or maybe it's what I didn't do . . .'

'Ssh,' Andee soothed. 'I think we have to tell ourselves that she's just wired differently to us. We knew she was unpredictable, unusual, even before she left, and given what she went through during the time she worked for the gangs . . . The drugs alone will have had a disastrous, and lasting, effect on her, not only physically, but mentally.'

Maureen was clearly still having a hard time absorbing it all. 'How could this have happened?' she whispered. 'I just don't understand it.'

Giving the only answer she could, Andee said, 'I think for now we have to put ourselves and our feelings to one side, and consider how determined she is to get the baby away from Juliette.'

At that Maureen's eyes hardened. 'We can't let her,' she growled. 'It's not her child to take. Where are the youngsters now?'

Understanding she meant Jonathan and Juliette, Andee said, 'Not far away, and they're safe for the time being, but we need to bring them to Kesterly so we can be nearby when she gives birth.'

Maureen nodded. 'Of course. Yes, we must do that.'

'I'm going to ask Blake to collect them tomorrow,' Andee continued, 'and provided Graeme and his sisters agree, they'll stay at Rowzee and Pamela's coach house up by the moor until it's time.'

'Oh, I'm sure they'll agree. You know how soft-hearted Rowzee is, Pamela too.'

'But they mustn't know there's any sort of problem,' Andee cautioned. 'They'll only want to come rushing back from their holiday to try and help. It'll be best for everyone if they merely think that a relative of ours needs a place for a couple of weeks before his girlfriend gives birth.'

'Which is the truth.'

Andee nodded.

Maureen's eyes were suddenly bright with tears. 'To think of that dear boy and all that he's been through,' she whispered shakily, 'and now this. We have to make sure he knows we care, that we welcome him as a part of our family, because he is. Just as much as Luke and Alayna.'

Going to hug her, Andee said, 'I'm afraid the birth will only be the first hurdle. We have to work out what to do when Juliette and the baby leave the hospital.'

'They should come here. We've got room.'

'I'm talking more about the legal situation than where they'll live, but you're right, that needs to be sorted too. What we don't want is for the baby to be made a ward of the court and taken into care.'

Horrified, Maureen said, 'Is that possible?'

'It could be. I need to seek some advice.' Her eyes followed her mother's along the hall as someone knocked on the front door.

'Who on earth can it be at this time of night?' Maureen murmured, turning back to Andee.

Since it was only just after nine it wasn't that late; nevertheless their neighbours usually came round to the back door.

'I'll go,' Andee said, getting to her feet. 'You wait there. If I don't come straight back call 999.'

'You're not funny,' her mother scolded.

Still smiling past the unease that had flared with the knock, Andee went to see who it was.

'You wanted to talk,' Penny stated as Andee opened the door.

Andee stared at her hard, then standing aside she gestured for her to come in.

Maureen rose to her feet as Penny entered the kitchen. Her eyes were sharp and wary. She uttered no words of welcome, didn't even try to muster a smile.

Apparently mindful of being ordered out the last time she was there, Penny said, 'If you have any objections I can leave.' Though her tone wasn't hostile, it conveyed no contrition or sense of caring one way or another what the decision might be.

Maureen's eyes went to Andee.

Andee went to press a hand on her mother's arm, a gesture of reassurance and instruction to sit down again. After waving Penny to a chair at the other side of the table she decided against offering her a drink, and sat down too.

'So, have you seen him?' Penny asked bluntly.

'You mean Sven?' Andee countered.

'You know who I mean.'

'Yes, I've seen him.'

Penny's eyes flicked to her mother and back again. 'I suppose I'd be wasting my breath if I asked you to tell me where he is.'

'You would,' Andee confirmed.

Sitting back in her chair, Penny rearranged the gloved ends of her sleeves. 'I hope you understand,' she said, 'that obstructing me on this will serve no one, least of all them.'

Andee's eyebrows rose. 'Actually, I don't understand that. Maybe you could explain it.'

Impatiently Penny took out her phone as it rang and turned it off. 'I told you, when you went to see Sven, not to believe everything he said. The same goes for Jonathan.'

'So what should I believe?' Andee challenged.

Penny's eyes went to her mother again. It was impossible to know what she was thinking, or feeling, completely masked as she was by the steeliness of her expression. 'Tell me something,' she said to Andee while still looking at Maureen, 'have you given any consideration at all to the other people involved in this? The couple who entered the agreement in good faith? The couple who are beside themselves with fear and grief that their dream might not be about to come true?'

Andee had to admit, if only privately, that she hadn't allowed herself to dwell too much on that.

'Jonathan and Juliette knew what they were doing when they signed the contract,' Penny continued. 'They did it freely, willingly, knowing very well that they were giving the couple concerned a world of hope where before there had only been disappointment and heartbreak. They understood that these people trusted them and believed that, thanks to them, they would soon be parents.'

Her eyes remained harsh, but her tone was reasonable and calm. 'They have corresponded throughout the pregnancy,' she continued. 'Juliette has sent copies of her scans and all her medical reports. They Skyped regularly so Juliette could give them accounts of how she was feeling and show them how her bump was growing. The couple have been as involved as it was possible to be, given there is half a continent and an entire ocean between them. They have been expecting Juliette to return to the States for the birth, because that was what was agreed. They have rented two apartments next door to each other in Houston so they can be sure of Juliette's comfort in the final stages, and as close to her as possible until the baby comes. Can you imagine how they are feeling right now?' The challenge burned in her eyes.

In truth Andee couldn't imagine it, but she was more than ready to concede that it had to be terrible.

'The law in Texas,' Penny continued, 'states that the intended parents, not the birth mother, are the legal parents of that child.'

'But they're not in Texas,' Andee pointed out. 'They're here and they want to keep the child. I think British law will support their case . . .'

'I don't give a damn about British law. Juliette was paid a great deal of money to carry this baby, and there is more to come when she hands it over.'

'I don't think she's interested in the money . . .'

'She's already taken it.'

'Then she must be persuaded to give it back.'

Penny's scaly hands hit the table. 'They don't want it back; they want their baby and I am going to make sure they get it.'

Andee's eyebrows shot up. 'And exactly how are you going to do that?' she enquired.

Penny got to her feet. 'Don't cross me on this, Andee,' she warned.

'Maybe it's you who shouldn't cross me,' Andee countered darkly.

Penny regarded her with an icy contempt. 'You have my number,' she said. 'I want to know where they are by midday tomorrow.'

'It's not going to happen,' Andee assured her.

Penny walked to the door. As she opened it, Andee said, 'Doesn't it mean anything at all to you that this baby is your grandson?'

Penny turned back. 'You're a fool,' she said quietly.

'You have no idea what you're doing,' and continuing down the hall she let herself out to her waiting Mercedes.

'So where is she now?' Gould asked the following morning when he, Leo and Andee met in his office.

'I've no idea,' Andee replied, helping herself to more coffee.

'Why midday?' Leo wanted to know.

Andee simply shrugged.

'It's a bluff,' Gould stated. 'I mean, what the hell can she do? She doesn't know where they are. If she did she'd have . . . Where are they, by the way?'

Andee glanced at the time. 'Blake should be collecting them round about now to take them to Rowzee Cayne's place on the edge of the moor.'

Gould sat back in his chair, scraping a hand across his stubbled chin. 'You're right about needing to protect the young mother,' he said. 'We can't have anyone trying to force her into giving up her child, either before or after she's had it.'

'But what if . . .' Leo began.

Gould's hand went up. 'I don't care about any contract,' he declared harshly. 'We'll put the hospital on a high security alert, and I'll have someone keep an eye on Rowzee's place while the kids are there. Meantime, it's what happens to these surrogates after the births that's bothering me. Do you think it's real?' he asked Andee.

'I don't know about real,' she replied, 'but it's possible, given the contacts Penny's supposed to have.'

'In which case we need to contact the National Crime Agency, because if she's in any way involved in trafficking it's one for them, not us.'

As conflicted as Andee felt about that she didn't disagree. 'The problem is,' she said, 'we have no evidence of it. All we have is what Alayna found on Facebook, which is pretty inconclusive as it stands, and what I've been told by Sven and Jonathan. Right now wouldn't be a good time to ask Jonathan to provide us with a detailed description of what he knows. After the baby comes, hopefully he'll be ready to cooperate.' She couldn't admit either to herself or to Gould just how hard she was finding it, in spite of everything, to think of investigating and exposing her sister's activities. Given the choice, she'd find a way to force Penny to stop what she was doing and with any luck avoid all the harrowing publicity of an arrest and the revelation of who she actually was. However, it wasn't going to be in her hands, and in truth she was glad of it, for simply thinking about any young girl having to spend even one day in the kind of hellholes they were kept in made her sick to her soul.

Why wasn't it the same for Penny who'd actually experienced those hellholes?

Gould was saying, 'We found two brothels – and believe me that's talking them up – on the Temple Fields estate only last week, thanks to a neighbour coming forward. The girls are being taken care of in a rehab centre in Bristol now, and the toerags holding them are in custody here, but we didn't get them all.'

Puzzled, Andee said, 'Do you think they had anything to do with my sister?'

'I've no idea, but if she's been pushing the kids on to anyone who'll take them ... We know how much they get moved around, so it could be worth asking the girls if they know her, or have heard of her.'

'I'll get on to it,' Leo said, making a note.

Andee checked the time again. It was a quarter to twelve; fifteen minutes to the deadline Penny had set. Of course it was a bluff, but she couldn't help feeling uneasy.

Glancing at her phone as it rang, she saw it was Blake and clicked on. 'Is everything OK?' she asked worriedly.

'Yes and no. Her waters have broken.'

'Oh hell,' Andee groaned. 'Where are you?'

'On the moor, with about forty-five minutes to go before we get to Kesterly.'

Thinking fast, she relayed the information to Gould, and said to Blake, 'You need to keep coming in this direction . . .' She let the phone go as Gould reached for it.

'Stay on the main arterial road and we'll get the paramedics to meet you. Have you ever delivered a baby?'

'You're kidding me, right?'

'OK, if need be we'll have someone call to talk you through it until help gets there. Is she all right at the moment?'

'Calm. Being brave.'

Grabbing the phone back, Andee said, 'Can you put Jonathan on?'

302

Sounding hectic, Jonathan said, 'It's not supposed to happen yet.'

'It'll be all right,' Andee assured him. 'Help is on the way and we'll have briefed the hospital by the time you get there. The important thing is not to panic. Births can take a long time, so the baby's not likely to come for a while yet.'

'Will you be there, at the hospital?' Jonathan asked. 'We want you to be there.'

'Yes, of course,' Andee promised. 'My mother will want to come too. Is that OK?'

'Yes, we'd like that. Can you call Juliette's family?'

'Of course. Text me the number and I'll do it right away. Do they speak English?'

'No.'

'Don't worry. I'll find someone who speaks Italian.'

Alayna was sitting outside Carluccio's on the Cabot Circus plaza, trying to distract herself by working out her finances on her iPhone while waiting for Jay and his mother to join her for lunch. She was buzzing with excitement and nerves, and so eager to make a good impression that she felt sure she'd more likely end up making a prize fool of herself.

'Don't worry, she's cool,' Jay had promised when they'd FaceTimed that morning. 'Five minutes together and you guys will be best mates. She's like that. She's known for putting people at their ease – and you're like it too. So chill. You've definitely got the afternoon off?'

'Deff. I finish at twelve, so I'll get there early to grab a table outside.'

Given the time of day there were a gazillion people milling around, mostly shoppers and local workers, but loads of tourists too. Alayna was in love with Bristol; it was a really happening city, especially for the young. She'd love to come back after her gap year, but that would depend on finding a job, and there wasn't enough film and theatre work here to make that a realistic possibility.

She was just wondering if there was time to call her mum to share some of her nerves when a shadow fell over her, and she quickly looked up. With the sun streaming straight into her eyes it wasn't possible to see who it was, though it was clearly a woman, so had to be Jay's mother.

'Alayna?' The woman stood to one side, using her shadow to help Alayna to see her.

Alayna sprang to her feet. 'Yes, it's me,' she gushed, grabbing the woman's hand. 'It's lovely to meet you. Jay should be here any minute.'

The woman's smile was so friendly as she pulled out a chair to sit down that Alayna's spirits soared to a whole new high. 'I guess you recognised me from all the pictures Jay posts on Instagram,' she laughed. 'He takes so many.'

'He certainly does. But lovely as you are in them, they really don't do you justice.' She laughed softly as Alayna blushed. 'How long did you say he was going to be?' she asked, glancing at her watch.

'Oh, probably not long now.'

'Well, let's hope he takes his time so we can use it getting to know one another.'

*   *   *

It was just after four in the afternoon.

Andee and Maureen were at a corner table in the Starbucks coffee shop on the busy ground floor of Kesterly Infirmary. Upstairs in the maternity ward Juliette was resting through a lull in proceedings, with Jonathan at her side and a security guard at the ward entrance.

For several minutes, after bringing two lattes to the table, Andee had quietly watched her mother, knowing she was agonising over something and not sure she could guess what it was. 'So, does it feel strange to think you're about to become a great-grandmother?' she prompted gently.

Maureen continued to stare at her coffee, almost as though she hadn't heard. After a while she said, 'Everything about this feels strange.' She looked up. Her eyes were bright, almost harsh, yet Andee could sense how anguished she was. 'I don't feel like that woman's mother,' she stated bluntly. *'That woman.* This is how I'm describing my own daughter. But she's nothing like the child I lost, or the person I imagined her growing into . . . The daughter I lost . . . I failed her in ways I've never had the courage to confront.'

'Mum . . .'

'I didn't love her enough,' Maureen pressed on determinedly. 'I tried, I truly did, and it wasn't that I didn't love her at all because I did, very much, it just wasn't the same as the way I felt about you.'

'Mum, you have to . . .'

'She must have sensed it. In fact I knew she did, but I didn't know how to change how I felt. I kept trying, but . . .'

'Mum, you don't have to do this to yourself. You're not to blame.'

'Oh but I am. I'm her mother every bit as much as I'm yours, and look how different she is . . .'

'Not because of you . . .'

'Losing her felt like the punishment I deserved for not trying to understand her better.'

'But you did try.'

'Of course, but I was always so busy. I'd tell myself she didn't want to be fussed, and she didn't, she hated it. Her school reports were always erratic; I could never be entirely sure how well she was doing. Her teachers never seemed to know how interested she was; sometimes she'd try, other times she didn't engage at all. She could never keep a friend; it was as though they were all afraid of her, or just couldn't connect with her.' Her eyes returned to Andee's. 'After she'd gone I used to try and make a pact with God, *bring her back and I swear I'll be a better mother*. I'd give up work, focus entirely on her, build a relationship with her that was as special and easy as the one I had with you. But she never came back, and in my heart I think I always knew that she wouldn't. Of course, I thought she was dead, but if she wasn't . . . like you I always hoped she wasn't . . .' She shook her head impatiently. 'I'm losing what I'm trying to say, but what I mean is that if it weren't for the baby being born upstairs we'd probably never have seen her again.'

Unable to dispute that, Andee covered her mother's hand with her own and squeezed.

'I didn't have a breakdown after she'd gone,' Maureen

ran on. 'I didn't lose my way or become an alcoholic or keep going through her things day after day after day . . . That's what happens to some mothers. Well, you know that, you've dealt with enough of them. I've always despised myself for being able to cope. I mean, it wasn't easy. I was terrified. I dreamt about her all the time, I never stopped thinking about her, longing for her, jumping every time the phone rang, certain it was her, or news of her, but in the end I didn't fall apart. I coped. Daddy couldn't, but we know why now.' She fell silent for a moment, then sounding suddenly angry she said, 'Will she be able to take the baby away? I mean legally, through the courts.'

'I don't know,' Andee answered honestly. 'I'm still waiting to hear from Helen Hall.'

'The lawyer? Will she know?'

'If she doesn't she'll find out.'

After a while Maureen said, 'From what you've told me about him Jonathan seems very kind and caring. We don't really know him, of course, but he doesn't strike me as being at all like his mother.'

'I think, in his heart, he still considers Ana to be that,' Andee told her.

'And the other little boy. I wonder what he'd have been like if he'd lived. Do you know if he looked like Jonathan?'

Andee shook her head. 'Sven didn't talk about him much.'

'Twins,' Maureen murmured, almost to herself. 'I don't think we've ever had them in our family, so it must be from Sven's side.' She pressed her palms to her cheeks then pushed her hands back through her hair, leaving her skin looking taut and drained. 'Cathy Ames – or Kate Trask – had twins,' she stated, looking at Andee.

'But they both lived,' Andee reminded her.

Maureen nodded. 'One was like his mother, the other kind and gentle like his father. Is Jonathan like Sven?'

'I think he is, in so far as we know either of them.'

Seeming satisfied with that, Maureen said, 'I don't recall how the book ends, and I have to admit I'm almost afraid to find out.'

Remembering it only too well, Andee deflected by saying, 'There aren't so many parallels between the two stories, so there's no reason to think this will end the way the book did.'

Maureen nodded, apparently agreeing with that. 'Why, of all things to take did she choose that book?' she wondered.

Andee shrugged. 'To be a nuisance? She knew I was studying it.'

Her mother didn't appear to be listening. 'It wasn't a good ending, was it?' She was staring bleakly into the empty space her memory should be filling. 'You can tell me.'

'It depends how you look at it.'

Maureen swallowed dryly. In the end she said, 'Is it possible for someone to be rotten through and through, the way Cathy Ames was?'

Not knowing what else to say, Andee countered with, 'Cathy Ames was a fictional character.'

'Maybe Penny considers herself to be fictional, with all her different names.'

Andee reached for her phone as a text arrived. She was so certain it would be from Jonathan that it took her a moment to understand fully what it said.

'Jesus Christ,' she murmured, her heart turning inside out. 'Oh my God, this *can't be happening.*'

Chapter Seventeen

Abandoning her car on double yellow lines at the marina, Andee ran through the traffic towards the Grand hotel, answering a call from Gould as she went.

'Apparently Alayna left Carluccio's about one thirty,' he told her. 'She was with a middle-aged woman and young man. This allows just about enough time to get to Kesterly, if this is where she is. Still nothing to support that, unless you tell me differently.'

'I can't. Was there anything unusual about the way they left,' Andee demanded, almost colliding with a cyclist, 'something suggesting she didn't want to go?'

'Not that I've been told. No descriptions yet either. Are you at the Grand?'

'Just arrived.'

'OK. I'm a couple of minutes away. Are you sure you want to see her on your own?'

'Absolutely. If she's here.'

It would be just like the Penny she was getting to know to send her on a wild goose chase, either to give herself more time, or simply for the perverse pleasure of it.

* * *

Minutes later Andee was in the dimly lit hallway of the hotel's tenth floor, knocking at Suite Six, having been told it was where she'd find Michelle Cross who was expecting her.

If that were the case, why wasn't Penny answering the door?

She knocked again, praying with all her might that she was going to find Alayna inside and unharmed. She shuddered as she remembered the text: *Your daughter for my son.*

What the hell would Penny do to her? What was there to gain from hurting an innocent young girl – her own niece – whom she was apparently using as a bargaining chip?

Niece? Family meant nothing to Penny. She'd proved that definitively enough thirty years ago, and had carried on proving it the entire time she'd stayed away. Then there was her apparent disinterest, even contempt, for her own son, Jonathan. So why would she care about a niece?

Was it possible the other twin was still alive?

If he was then something far more threatening, even terrifying was happening than Andee could begin to imagine.

Why didn't Penny answer the bloody door?

She began to knock again just as the door opened.

'Sorry, I was on the phone,' Penny apologised, standing aside for Andee to come in. 'You're here sooner than I expected.'

'Where is she?' Andee demanded, infuriated and alarmed to find no sign of Alayna.

When Penny didn't reply Andee swung round, ready to shout at her again, but hesitated when she caught her gazing into thin air, as if she'd already forgotten Andee was in the room. Her hair wasn't in its usual neat style, but hanging loosely about her face, uncombed; Andee hadn't realised it was so . . . sparse. It made her seem oddly vulnerable, and the haunted, distant look in her eyes was baffling too. This wasn't a Penny she'd seen before. Instinctively she said, 'Are you all right?'

Penny's eyes came to hers. It was plain she hadn't heard anything Andee had said since she'd come into the room.

'I asked where Alayna is,' Andee repeated.

Penny's expression changed, showing a fleeting glimpse of surprise, even anger, before her manner dipped into coolness, as if she were perfectly in control and hosting nothing more bizarre than a tea party. 'I guess we're talking about your daughter,' she stated frostily.

Inflamed, Andee cried, 'Don't do this. I want to know . . .'

'I'm not doing anything. I've no idea where she is.'

'Then speak to whoever does know and tell them . . .'

'Andee, watch my lips. *I don't know where your daughter is.*'

'You had lunch with her today, in Bristol. You and . . . Who's the boy?'

Penny blinked, then to Andee's amazement she laughed. 'I've been here all morning, on the phone,' she insisted. 'I haven't left the room once.' As if to confirm this she held up her mobile, her knuckles showing white with the force of her grip.

Andee regarded her fiercely, still too worked up to know whether she believed her or not.

Penny turned away and went to sit on a sofa, gesturing for Andee to make herself comfortable too. She stared at her phone and fiddled with it.

Andee remained where she was.

'I have to understand from all this,' Penny said, 'that you don't know where your daughter is. Presumably she isn't answering her phone, or she hasn't turned up for a date she was supposed to make . . .'

'You sent a text,' Andee reminded her. '*Your daughter for my son.* It was a blatant threat . . .'

'Indeed! I was pointing out what it could come to if you don't tell me where Jonathan is hiding Juliette.'

Andee felt as though she was sinking, struggling, unable to get a grip on reality. 'So you were threatening to take my daughter . . .'

With an irritated sigh, Penny said, 'Wherever she is now, whomever she's with and whatever she's doing has nothing to do with me.'

So why wasn't Alayna answering her phone?

'I can see you're finding it hard to believe me,' Penny continued, glancing at her mobile again. She was clearly waiting for a call or message from someone that was setting her badly on edge. 'I don't blame you,' she continued, looking up again, 'because I am very capable of lying. In fact, I do it rather well, but in this instance I can assure you I am telling the truth.'

She was like a changeable sky, going from bright to

313

clouded in less than an instant. Guarded and restless, nervous, irritable and now she appeared so sure of herself, so contained and . . . smug that Andee was starting to feel wrong-footed at every turn.

'Who's the young man?' Andee demanded, feeling ridiculous, but she needed to know. At least she hadn't asked if it was Penny's supposedly dead son.

Penny said, 'I have absolutely no idea what young man you're talking about. Doesn't she have boyfriends?'

Andee's eyes turned hard, her mind was spinning as her phone suddenly rang, and without checking who it was she clicked on.

'Mum, what the f?' Alayna cried. 'Why's everyone calling me? Even the police have been in touch and your messages are freaking me out.'

Swallowing hard on her relief, Andee asked, abruptly, 'Where are you?'

'With Jay and his mum who're totally weirded out too. What's going on?'

'It's OK, nothing to worry about.'

'I need more,' Alayna insisted.

Andee said, 'It's just when you didn't answer your phone . . . Why didn't you?'

'I turned it off while we went for a walk around the Harbourside. Why are the police calling me? I feel such a schmuck, like my family is completely wacko . . .'

'I'm sorry. I'll explain everything when I see you. Please apologise to Jay and his mother, and call Grandma to let her know you're OK. I have to go now, we'll speak later.' After ringing off she ignored Penny's self-satisfied smirk and quickly texted Gould to let him know that Alayna was safe.

'So, panic over?' Penny asked with mock concern as Andee sank down on the chair behind her.

'You shouldn't have sent that text,' Andee told her. 'What the hell was I supposed to think . . .'

'The worst of me, of course. Isn't that a comfortable place for you?'

Their eyes locked and for a bewildering moment Andee felt her senses slipping, spiralling back into the past to who they used to be. This was her sister, the child she'd grown up with, the teenager whose disappearance had turned their world inside out . . . It seemed like only days ago that she'd vanished from their lives yet here she was, a woman in her forties with more self-possession and arrogance than seemed reasonable or right. But there was something about her today that was giving Andee pause. Somewhere beneath the harsh veneer of indifference and superiority that had never shown a single crack before, she seemed almost helpless, frightened even – but of what?

'Why are you staring at me?' Penny snapped.

'What's wrong with you?' Andee asked. 'Something's happened . . . Or you're . . .'

'There's nothing wrong with me. So shall we get down to the reason you're here. You currently have your daughter *and* my son. As far as I'm concerned you can keep both, but the baby has to come with me.'

Andee shook her head.

'I'm not asking, I'm telling you,' Penny stated. 'The

contract he and Juliette signed stipulates very clearly that . . .'

'I don't care what the contract says. If need be we'll put it to a judge, here in Britain.'

Penny got abruptly to her feet and went to fix herself a drink. It was obvious that she was still badly rattled over something that could have been about the baby, but Andee felt it was more. She hadn't put her mobile down once, and kept looking at it as though willing it to ring. Or maybe she was desperate for it not to.

'Do you want one?' she asked Andee, holding up a bottle of Perrier.

'No thank you.'

The silence as Penny filled a glass seemed to have a life of its own, drawing in sounds from the bay that had no place in this oddly functioning reality. By the time she sat down again she'd received a text, sent one in return and her manner seemed less irascible.

Eyeing Andee with a curiosity bordering on disdain, she said, 'You think you know everything, don't you?'

Since it was such a stupid remark Andee didn't bother to answer.

'In fact, you know nothing at all.'

Sounding as exasperated as she felt, Andee said, 'Is this a conversation worth getting into?'

Penny arched an eyebrow and took a sip of her drink. 'Have you ever imagined us having any sort of conversation?' she asked. 'I mean, over the years, have you ever found yourself talking to me in your mind?'

'Of course, many times. Needless to say it was never like this.'

'What was it like?'

'Does it matter?'

'I'm not sure. It might.'

Andee gave herself a moment to think, to decide whether to be truthful instead of defensive. 'OK, I used to imagine how happy and relieved we'd feel to see one another again. I thought there would be lots of tears and hugging as you told us what had been happening to you . . .'

'So I was always a victim?'

'It was hard to see you any other way, when I had no idea you'd *chosen* to leave us.'

'But mostly you thought I was dead?'

'Isn't that what we were supposed to think? The note you sent didn't leave much room for doubt.'

'Oh, yes, I keep forgetting about that. Selective memory, I suppose. Were you very upset when you thought I'd killed myself?'

'What a ridiculous question! You were my sister, I loved you . . .'

Penny's laugh was more scorn than disbelief. 'That's what you've been telling yourself?'

'It was the truth!'

'You did a good job of hiding it.' She appeared more amused than angry, which irritated Andee even further.

'We had some good times as children,' Andee pointed out heatedly. 'We laughed a lot, spent wonderful summers here in Kesterly . . .' Penny rolled her eyes. 'It wasn't all bad,' Andee almost shouted. 'In fact most of it wasn't.'

'Not for you, but you weren't me, and you had no interest in being me, or understanding what it was like to be the one who should have been a boy, who was never pretty enough or clever enough or sporty enough. The attention was always on you and you lapped it up. I might just as well have not existed.'

'And you're bringing this up now? Haven't you got over it yet? Even if it were true, and it wasn't . . .'

'Oh, it was.'

'If that's what you want to believe, then I'm afraid I can't do anything about how you perceived yourself, or the rest of us, while you were growing up. But I can tell you that in spite of what you've apparently convinced yourself, you were loved, deeply, and your leaving totally devastated our family. It was a cruel and insanely selfish thing to do to people whose only crime was to care for you . . .'

'You're not listening to me, Andee. You didn't care for me, none of you did.'

Andee wished she wasn't hearing her mother confessing to not caring enough, only an hour ago.

'You pretended sometimes,' Penny told her, 'you went through the motions, but it never rang true. I knew I was the oddball, the black sheep, the embarrassment, the one that was different and not in a good way. But it's OK, don't beat yourself up about it, because I finally discovered that I didn't mind being different. In fact, I loved it, because it was real, and because I realised I didn't care for any of you either. I really didn't. So that's why I went. I was in the wrong place with the wrong family, and when it became clear that *Uncle* John was going to make it possible for me to go, I leapt at it. He gave me a sense of myself that I'd never had before. I meant something – not to him, I've no idea what he thought about anything, but I meant something to me. There wasn't a moment, during those first years I was in Glebe Place, that I regretted taking my life into my own hands, because I was living with people like me, people who cared . . .'

Andee was aghast. 'You were a child prostitute,' she stated bluntly. 'Those people didn't care about you.'

Penny simply shrugged. 'I was doing what I wanted to with no one criticising me, or making me feel like I was a mistake or a waste of space. We were a family in Glebe Place; we looked out for each other, we had fun, we didn't need other people's approval or understanding, because we didn't belong to your rigor-mortised world. We never hurt anyone, all we did was entertain and be entertained in a way that I don't expect you to understand, because it would never have been the right life for you. You were always the one to conform. It never even occurred to you not to. You're not a rebel, a free spirit, a radical, or even an imaginative thinker. You see things through the eyes of a society that is ridiculously caught up in morals that it can't live up to. Standards that are forgotten when they're not convenient. Judgements that almost never see the other side of an argument.'

Andee was more intrigued than offended. 'Well that's a fancy little tale you've been telling yourself,' she commented. 'A very convenient fudging of what's

319

right and wrong to make yourself into the heroine of the piece.'

Penny appeared to like the response. She chuckled, sipped more water and gave an odd sort of twitch as she checked her phone again. 'There you go, proving my point,' she said. 'You look at me and judge me by your own standards that may or may not chime with mine. You see, I know that what goes on inside me is different to what drives you. I don't share your mundane sensitivities or need to be seen to be doing what you call the right thing. I am who I am, which is nothing like you and who you are.'

Unimpressed, Andee said, 'You've got no idea who you really are.'

Penny's eyes narrowed.

'You're scared of something,' Andee told her, 'maybe even terrified. What is it?'

Penny seemed to find that funny. 'There you are, doing it again,' she accused. 'Presuming you know all about me, assessing me in a way that will never get you to the truth.'

'Then tell me the truth.'

Penny's eyes remained on hers.

Andee waited, but Penny didn't speak. 'OK, then tell me this,' Andee said. 'Do you consider accusing Daddy of child molestation was a good or right thing to do?'

Apparently rattled by the question, Penny sipped her water again as she gave it some thought. 'I told you before,' she finally replied, 'I did what I needed to in order to keep my freedom.'

'So in spite of knowing what those lies could do to him, you threatened them anyway, because you and your *freedom* mattered more?'

Penny tilted her head. 'Mm, I guess that about sums it up,' she agreed.

Outraged by how matter-of-fact she sounded, Andee said, 'You hurt him so deeply that it ended up killing him. Do you have any kind of conscience about that?'

'The way he chose to deal with what I said was down to him,' Penny snapped. 'I didn't force him to keep it to himself, to internalise it like a cancer. Now you tell me this, why do you think he was so afraid of it coming out?'

Andee's eyes widened with horror as nausea churned inside her. 'If you're about to say because it was the truth . . .'

'I'm just posing the question.'

'You know very well that that kind of slur destroys careers and families, even if it isn't true. That was why he kept it to himself. He didn't want Mum to know that you'd do something so despicable; he didn't want even the slightest shadow of suspicion to fall over him, not to save himself, to save us. Even you, in case you decided to come back.'

Penny was staring out of the window, but it was clear when she looked back that she'd heard every word. 'That's an interesting assessment of what was going on his mind,' she declared, 'coming from someone who never had the discussion with him.'

'He was my father. I knew him and I know that's what he did.'

'Do you mean you *knew* him the way you *knew* me?'

'I mean he was a decent, honourable man who would never have done what you accused him of. Why don't you just admit that you lied? You have your freedom now, your life, your family, your *business*. What's the point in holding on to the lie? It doesn't serve you any more.'

'You're right, it doesn't, so I'm OK with letting it go. I lied. Are you happy now?'

Happy? For God's sake. 'Aren't you sorry for what you did?'

'If I were, would it help you to like me a bit better?'

Startled by that, Andee said, 'Only if it were genuine, and why is it important for me to like you?'

'Believe me, it isn't.'

Not quite sure where to go with that, Andee read the text that had arrived on her phone a few minutes ago. It was from her mother, letting her know that Alayna had been in touch.

Her eyes returned to Penny. To her surprise Penny had a hand to her head as though soothing an ache, or trying to shut out where she was. When she looked up her face was even paler than before, and strands of hair were sticking to her perspiring neck. Before Andee could speak Penny said, 'So you worked out what I took from you when I left?'

Deciding to go with it, Andee said, 'It was my copy of *East of Eden*?'

Penny smiled.

'Why that?'

Penny appeared thoughtful, as though she'd never

considered the reason. However, she surprised Andee when she said, 'I guess initially, it was to annoy you . . . You kept going on about the book, how shocking and fantastic it was, how you felt so many different emotions when you were reading it . . . You and Dad talked about it for hours and hours . . . It got so much on my nerves that I thought I'd burn it, or tear it up, or just throw it away. Then I decided to take it with me when I left so I could think of you searching for it, getting angry because you couldn't find it and eventually giving up and getting a new one. A bit like you'd be while looking for me. You'd give up eventually, and one of your hundreds of friends would become your new sister.'

Andee could have told her then that since her real sister had vanished she'd never had a best friend again, but Penny was still speaking.

'I didn't read it,' she was saying, 'not while I was at Glebe Place, but I was glad to have it during that fucking awful time . . . It was the only book I had, my only means of escape, I guess. It was like the characters became friends, family even. Of course I was always with other girls, we were never allowed any privacy, but most of them didn't speak English and the book kind of spoke to me . . . It had your notes in the margins. I probably read them more often than I read the book. It brought you to life for me, made me feel close to you. It was as though you were helping me to escape from that hell, even if it was only in my mind. We were sharing the book. Your notes were my thoughts, because I wasn't capable of forming many of my own; you're not, when you're in the state I was usually in. You're looking surprised.'

Andee was more than surprised. This wasn't what she'd expected to hear at all. 'I thought I meant nothing to you,' she said, and immediately wished she hadn't. There were many other things she could have said that were less mocking or accusatory or cold.

'My perspective,' Penny went on, 'along with just about everything else, changed during that time. Like the others I was desperate to get away. That was when I was sober enough to feel desperate, to feel anything at all. I used to fantasise about you climbing out of the book to come and get me, bringing Daddy with you. Even when he decided to give up on me, he must have kept a check on where I was, but he never came so I knew that I'd been right all along, he didn't care.'

Though Andee had no way of challenging her father, she knew beyond any doubt that he'd lost track of Penny as soon as John Victor sold her to traffickers, for he'd never have left her to rot in the squalid conditions used for girls forced into prostitution. It was doubtful that Penny would accept this, even if Andee tried to speak up; she'd reached her conclusions a long time ago. They were undoubtedly a very big part of why she was so badly screwed up now, and she certainly was, Andee was seeing more and more of it as the days went by.

'I don't suppose you've ever taken drugs?' Penny asked suddenly. 'Of any kind? No, don't bother to answer that, it hardly matters whether you have or haven't. You'll have dealt with plenty who have during your time with the police. You know what they do to people, how they're used like chains to keep whores in check, make them do as they're told, suffer the kind of abuse and humiliation you wouldn't inflict on an animal. Which isn't to say real chains aren't used, because they are, locked around a wrist or an ankle, sometimes even around the neck. I'm still not telling you anything you don't know? But you didn't know about the book and how much it came to mean to me, how it unlocked the chains in my mind and took me to you.'

'No, I didn't,' Andee said softly.

Penny smiled and got up to pour herself another drink.

Accepting a glass of water this time, Andee said, 'Was it because of the twins that you began to identify with the character of Cathy Ames?'

Penny's eyebrows rose. 'I suppose you could have a point there, although I have to be honest, I didn't think about them much during those terrible years. If I did, it was only to hope that John had honoured the deal and taken them to Sven. I sure as hell wouldn't have wanted them with me. If you saw what happened to babies in those places . . . Well, I guess you have. Thank God I never got pregnant again, is all I can say.'

'Did it ever occur to you,' Andee said carefully, 'that Sven might have been part of a plan to get rid of you once you'd given birth?'

'Yes, it did, plenty of times, until he came to find me. He did everything he could to make me well again. He and Ana took me into their family, not to keep, I was free to go any time I wanted, but I didn't want to leave them. For a long time I was afraid to, but eventually I got over that too. I loved being in Sweden, learning the language, getting to know the people, rising up through Sven's business.' Her eyes seemed to glaze for a moment, as her mind drifted to only she knew where. When they returned to Andee they were guarded, restless, as though she wasn't entirely sure what had been said. 'I used to read about you on the Internet,' she stated. 'When stories came up that you were involved in I'd find them and wonder what your life was like. So it's not as if I wasn't interested in you, but life had moved on, we had different families now and I didn't want the complication of becoming Penny Lawrence, the missing child. It would only set me back, disrupt my life, and yours, and what was the point in that?'

To end the not knowing? To try and heal their mother's broken heart and shattered conscience? What Andee said was, 'So you chose to become Kate Trask?'

'Kate Sylvander,' she corrected, 'but yes, Kate from *East of Eden*. I felt we were similar in some ways. Not all, but in those that had significance for me. She didn't waste time on sentimentalities. Her children were never going to be a burden to her, she didn't want any, and nor did I. I only entered into the agreement with Sven to get John Victor out of trouble. And you know how he repaid me.'

Andee didn't hold back. 'So you killed him?'

Penny's eyes bored into hers. 'Yes, I had him killed.'

More shaken than she should have been, Andee said,

'What about Michelle Cross? Why did you use her name?'

Penny sighed, and as her eyes dropped to her phone Andee felt a loosening of the tension between them. 'I told you before, it was a kind of tribute,' she said bleakly. 'She hadn't been able to live her life, so it was a way of including her.'

'Did you push her under the bus?'

Penny looked up, apparently amazed and even slightly amused. 'Wow, you really do think the worst of me, don't you? Actually, she tripped and fell. That's how it happened.'

'And you went on to be cast as the Virgin Mary in the school nativity play? A role you'd already been cast in until one of the teachers took pity on Michelle.'

'You remember that?' Penny seemed impressed. 'It was such a long time ago, but yes, I did get to play the part. She was a foster child, did you know that? She didn't have any parents, or brothers and sisters, so I don't suppose it was too hard on anyone when she went.'

Shocked, sickened, Andee didn't bother to hide it. 'Are you saying you thought it was all right to push that little girl under a bus because she didn't have a family?' she asked.

'I didn't push her under a bus. I told you, it was an accident.'

Wanting suddenly to get out of there, Andee put her drink down and picked up her phone.

'You're judging me again,' Penny told her, 'and now you're running away. We can't all be like you, Andee.

Imagine how dull the world would be if we all had the same personalities, principles, beliefs.'

'But yours are deplorable, disgusting . . .'

'Says you, because you've told yourself I helped a little girl to go and join her parents in the next life. Well, if it makes you feel any better I really didn't push her. She tripped and fell, but for all I know she did it on purpose. She hated the foster home she was in, the social workers, the teasing at school. She was miserable and to be truthful, I felt sorry for her. I knew what it was like to be in a family where you felt you didn't belong.'

Andee was shaking her head incredulously. 'You're right about one thing,' she said, 'I really don't know you and I don't think I want to.'

Penny laughed, but it was a hollow nervous sound that had no humour. 'Believe me, no one is going to force you,' she promised. 'You obviously know you'd never have heard from me again if it weren't for Sven telling Jonathan about you . . .'

'Which he did to protect him from you. His own mother.'

Penny nodded. 'Yes, that's true, but I wouldn't harm him, after all he *is* my son. We don't often agree on things, but in this instance he's got to be made to see them my way. He knows what's at stake, what will happen if he and Juliette don't honour their agreement. I'm trying to save them from that.'

'You mean from the fate that you yourself suffered at the hands of men who abused and tormented you for over four years?'

'That's right,' Penny confirmed.

'But how could you? I don't understand when you've been there, you've . . .'

'No, of course you don't understand, because you don't think like me. You hear the words, see a picture and you believe it without going into the meaning, the depth, the reality of what's actually there.'

'Then tell me what's there.'

Instead of answering Penny fumbled with her phone, checking for texts or emails. In the end she said, 'You know, I quite like the fact that you always think the worst of me. It's reassuring, makes me realise that I was right to leave when I did and not come back.'

Andee said, 'So now you're blaming me for your disappearance?'

'No, I'm not blaming you. I'm just trying to make you see how little what you think of me matters to me.'

'So why are you bothering to talk to me?'

Penny said, 'Because I'm hoping you'll end up telling me where to find Jonathan and Juliette.'

'Why on earth would I do that when you've done nothing but warn me against it.'

'Ah, reverse psychology. Is that what you call it? I'm saying one thing when I actually mean the opposite. In other words, my subconscious is crying out for you to save those foolish young people from the wicked woman who means them only harm?'

'Why don't you give me an opportunity to see you in a different light?' Andee suggested.

'Why would I do that?'

'Because you're not being truthful either to me, or to

yourself. There's a hard shell around you that's almost impossible to penetrate, or it was until it started coming apart. I don't know why, what's making it happen, but I can see it, and I just know that buried deep inside you there is a human heart that's as capable of compassion and love as mine.'

Penny's eyebrows shot up. 'Are you forgetting about Kate Trask?' she challenged. 'She was evil through and through.'

'She wasn't real.'

'She was to me.'

Refusing to go any further with that, Andee sat watching her, waiting for her to speak again. When it became apparent she wasn't going to, Andee said, 'In France, when you stopped your car to ask me if I remembered you? Why did you do it that way?'

It seemed to take a moment for Penny to recollect the incident. When she did she smiled, almost mischievously. 'I suppose it was because it appealed to me to tease you a little.'

Knowing she'd never understand the sort of mind that would see a return from the dead as a tease, Andee said, 'How did you even know I was there?'

Frowning, Penny said, 'I thought I'd explained that before. I was having you followed in case Jonathan got in touch with you. When you and your boyfriend flew to France, I felt convinced it was to see him. Apparently I was wrong. How long have you and . . . is it Graeme, been together?'

'We've known one another for a few years, but together in the sense you mean it, just a few months.'

'And you trust him?'

Annoyed, Andee said, 'Don't do that again. You tried it once before . . .'

''Her name's Nadia. He's redesigning, remodelling a house for her.'

'And?'

'I have photographs of them together. You can see for yourself how close they are.'

With a burning anger masking how shaken she felt, Andee said, 'Why are you having him watched?'

'I'm not. It just happened. When you disappeared airside at Heathrow, on your way to Stockholm, as it turned out, I thought you were returning to France. So I had someone fly over to find out.' Her eyes seemed almost soft, even sad as she said, 'I'm sorry he's not who you think he is.'

Wanting nothing more than to get off the subject, Andee said, 'You told me just now that Jonathan and Juliette know what's at stake if they don't honour the contract.'

'That's correct, they do.'

'Well?'

Penny started as her phone finally rang, and almost dropped it as she checked who it was. She didn't answer, just let it go to messages.

'What's going on?' Andee asked. 'Something's really getting to you . . .'

'It's the couple waiting for this baby,' Penny shouted. 'Their lawyers are ringing, threatening me . . .' She broke off abruptly. 'You asked what's at stake?' she said more evenly. 'And you think, probably because

331

Jonathan told you, that any girl who defies me ends up in forced prostitution, the way I did thanks to John Victor.'

'Is it true?'

Penny tossed her head irritably.

'He says girls have disappeared because they defied you.'

'It's true, they have. In fact, I could tell you where to find them, if I were of a mind to, but I really won't be until I have that baby out of here and on its way to Texas.'

Andee eyed her coldly. 'It's not up for negotiation. If the baby is born here it will be a British citizen registered into the British system, and there will be nothing you can do to get it out of here.'

'If necessary the lawyers will take care of it, but we can save all that if you would just take a break from the moral high ground and think of the parents waiting for that baby. Use your naturally bleeding heart to feel compassion and kindness for them. The child doesn't belong exclusively to Jonathan and Juliette. In fact, none of it belongs to them, because they've led these people on, taken their money, destroyed their dream . . .'

'Now isn't the time to get into the ethics of what you do,' Andee interrupted shortly. 'I just need you to understand that even if I were able to see it your way, I still wouldn't take you to them.'

'Because you're afraid of what's going to happen to Juliette after we've handed the baby over?'

'Amongst other things. She'll obviously never work for you again, and as we know what that means . . .'

'Do we? Do we know for a certainty that I sell these girls to the highest bidder? That's what you've been told, isn't it? It's what I tell them, that's for sure, but do we actually know that I do it?'

'If the girls aren't seen again . . .'

'They're not seen because they're returned to their families. I know you don't want to believe that, it won't fit with your disgustingly low opinion of me . . .'

'If you didn't behave the way you do . . .'

'Let me tell you this one more time,' Penny raged, 'I don't give a damn what anyone thinks of me. It's not important. What is, is finding girls who are about to make the biggest mistake of their lives, *before* they make it. Girls who are desperate to help their families, or to escape abuse, or to better themselves in some way . . . Girls who are more vulnerable to traffickers than they'll ever know. I make it my business to get to them first, to save them from themselves so that they'll never end up in the kind of nightmare I was stuck in for almost five years. I offer them the chance to help someone else, to carry babies for those who aren't able to do it for themselves. Jonathan will have told you that I do deals with traffickers, that I sell the girls back when they're no longer of any use to me, but it isn't true. There are no traffickers, or not that I deal with. He thinks there are because it's what I want him and everyone else to think, that I'm evil, not a person to cross. If they weren't afraid of me I'd have no power. They'd feel free to defy me, to break their contracts, to trash people's dreams, and I can't let that happen.'

Quietly stunned as she absorbed this bizarre, twisted

version of charity, it was a while before Andee could find her words. 'What about the young people acting as escorts?' she asked.

'What about them?'

'Are they doing it of their own free will?'

'Of course they are. If they didn't want to do it they'd be in other jobs, jobs that I'd help to find if necessary, or they'd be back in their own countries. They might even be working at one of three centres I've opened in Latvia, Lithuania and Belarus to provide refuge for vulnerable young people. The only condition I put on those who don't want to continue with me is that they don't ever contact anyone who stays. I don't want to destroy the image I've created of myself. They need to be afraid or they won't understand that they could ruin everything. So tell me, is this helping your troubled sensibilities? Are you feeling better about me now that I've confessed I'm not as evil as Kate Trask?'

Andee could only look at her. Her way of thinking, reasoning, even feeling was so tortured, so completely beyond fathoming that Andee knew it would be pointless even to try.

'Someone just texted you,' Penny told her.

Andee read the message from her mother and got to her feet. 'Before I leave,' she said, 'I have one more question for you. What happened to Sven's wife, Ana?'

Penny blinked in surprise, then standing up too, she said accusingly, 'You think I caused the accident that killed her.'

'Did you?'

'What if I said yes?'

'Would it be true?'

'It happened just the way I'm presuming you were told. She'd been warned plenty of times about reversing her wheelchair into the lift, but she would do things her way. Then one day, just as everyone feared, she reversed in without checking. The lift wasn't there and she plunged to her death. I was in Riga at the time.'

Andee stared at her, not sure what to say.

'It's easily checked,' Penny told her.

In silence, Andee started to the door.

Penny said, 'Are you going away feeling sorry for yourself because you don't have the sister you've always dreamt about?'

Andee turned round. 'It's you I feel sorry for,' she said, 'because you've lost sight of who you are and what means anything to you.'

Penny's lip curled.

'What you do know,' Andee continued, 'even if you don't want to admit it, is that you've made some terrible mistakes in your life and they started when you were fourteen years old,' and with a tender, sad smile she left.

Chapter Eighteen

On returning to her car Andee peeled the parking ticket from the windscreen and got into the driver's seat, oblivious to the sudden gusts sweeping the bay. Instead of returning to the hospital right away she remained where she was, her head resting on the steering wheel as she tried to process what felt like the most bizarre and difficult encounter she'd ever had.

She realised only too well that hard drugs had played a major part in distorting Penny's already irrational young mind, but knowing that didn't change how damaged it still was. The way Penny perceived the world and herself was as normal to her as it was crazy and upsetting to Andee. Even the good she was trying to do was being carried out in a convoluted and highly dubious way – this was presuming she'd told Andee the truth, and Andee was ready to believe that she had.

In fact, the more she thought about it, the more convinced she was becoming that Penny had been wanting to talk to someone for a very long time. She might claim that she had no interest in what people thought of her, but she did care what Andee thought, and realising that was making Andee want to cry.

Her sister, for all that she might deserve it, was quite possibly the loneliest and saddest person Andee had ever known. She might have been awkward and difficult when she was young, but by now she was so damaged by all that had happened to her that she had no proper sense of what was right or wrong, or even of who she really was any more. The way she'd shown signs of coming apart today, the guarded restlessness, the constantly changing moods, and cry for help that she hadn't even realised she was uttering, spoke more clearly than anything of how tormented she was inside.

For Andee, it was almost impossible to know how to go forward from here. What could she do to help Penny, or at least make her believe that she mattered and always had? Her defences were a solid wall of lies and delusions; her feelings were so deeply buried they might never be found.

Deciding she needed to speak to Sven, Andee gave herself no time to think it through, but simply connected to his number. There was no reply from either him or Selma. It didn't matter; with just these few seconds' grace she realised this wasn't a conversation to be had by phone.

Letting her head fall back against the seat, she closed her eyes and thought of how much she'd like to speak to Graeme right now. He might not have the answers, but he was such a good listener that things always seemed clearer after she'd discussed them with him. But it didn't feel like an option when she was having doubts about his relationship with Nadia. She'd have to confront them at some point, but right now she couldn't make herself and her feelings a priority.

Starting the engine, she turned the car around and drove back up the hill to the hospital. She was asking herself if she should have told Penny before she left that she was a grandmother now. Would it have meant anything to her? Or would she simply have continued to see the infant as belonging to the people who'd signed a contract they fully expected to be honoured?

Realising she needed some answers sooner rather than later, Andee put in a call to Helen Hall to find out what she'd learned so far. Then, remembering she'd left Gould at the hotel she rang to let him know where she was and, more importantly, that the baby was now in the world.

A while later Andee was holding the tiny newborn in her arms, wanting to bury herself in his irresistible baby smell and innocence. His eyes came wide and startled before closing again; his mouth was puckered and red. *Where am I?* he seemed to be saying. *What just happened?*

As she held him she felt herself understanding, far more than she had before, just how devastating it would be for the American couple to lose him. They probably didn't even know he'd been born yet; were no doubt even now waiting by the phone, more terrified than excited to hear the news.

However, how could she not support Jonathan and Juliette's need to keep him? He was theirs in every

338

way. They had made him, he carried their genes and, like any other baby born to loving parents, he deserved to spend his life with them. Even if the Americans were rich beyond belief, could give him everything he could ever wish for and love him as deeply as he deserved, one day he would want to know his real parents, and how would he feel on learning that the law had forced them to give him up?

Still inhaling the intoxicating scent of him and remembering when her own children had been born, Andee felt her mother's hand on her arm and realised she was crying.

'It's because I'm happy for you,' she told a worried-looking Jonathan and Juliette. 'He's part of my family,' she reminded them, 'and he's so beautiful and sleepy and *big*.'

Coming to take him, Jonathan said softly, 'I want you to know that we won't give him up, not for anything. I don't care what the law says . . .'

'Sssh,' Andee soothed, seeing tears of anger and defiance in his eyes. 'Don't let's worry about that now. All that matters is that he's with us, we already love him and we're going to do everything we can to keep him.'

Jonathan was shaking his head. 'You don't understand,' he said. *'We are going to keep him.* It's not about trying, or fighting, or going through courts of law. He is my son. I am his father, Juliette is his mother and no piece of paper in the world is going to separate us.'

Admiring his passion, and desperately hoping he was right, Andee watched him go to sit with a drowsy Juliette and felt her heart overflowing in the way she knew it would the day she saw Luke or Alayna's newborn baby. Jonathan and Juliette still seemed so tenderly young, and nervous, but they were parents now, proud, overwhelmed, needing the support of their families, but determined to be everything to their son. That was what he deserved. Only hours old and already he was surrounded by his mother, father, great-aunt, great-grandma, and two grandparents on the way. He was going to know the richness of being Italian, British and Swedish; he'd no doubt speak all three languages, but most importantly of all he'd be where he belonged.

Meeting Jonathan's eyes, Andee felt her heart buckling with the sorrow of Penny not being a part of this. She had no idea if it might help to heal her, or at least make her see things differently, but as the baby's grandmother she deserved to know he was in the world.

How tragic it was that they'd then have to do everything they could to protect him from her.

By late the following morning Jonathan and Juliette had taken the baby to the coach house at the edge of the moor, and Juliette's startled parents had arrived from their village home in Piedmont. Apparently they'd had no idea their daughter was even pregnant until the call had come to tell them they were grandparents. They'd believed that Juliette was spending a year in London and the US learning English, before returning to continue her studies at the university in Turin. They'd now been informed, to their horror and despair, that their daughter had accepted Penny's offer of becoming a surrogate mother because her parents' bakery business had failed. She couldn't, she said, allow them to spend every last penny of their savings to give her the education they'd never had.

Though it wasn't possible for Andee to know exactly how they felt about their daughter's decision or the unexpected addition to their family, it was plain from the moment they arrived that they adored Juliette, and they couldn't have been more eager to hold and marvel over a baby that had come as a total surprise to them. They'd already decided that they must take this little family back to Italy, where they could help with the baby while Juliette continued her studies and Jonathan found work nearby. Exactly what kind of work was apparently to be discussed at a later date, but it was clear from the wryness of Jonathan's tone as he translated for Andee and Maureen that he was more than happy to go along with the plans. What no one had yet confessed to was the possible lawsuit that would very likely prevent the baby going anywhere.

She'd left them half an hour ago, with her mother and Jenny preparing to go and stock up at the supermarket while she took the same circuitous route she'd used to get there (just in case she was being followed) to go back into town where she was due to meet with the lawyer, Helen Hall.

'As you know, this isn't my area of expertise,' Helen told her as they settled down with coffees in Helen's office. She was a slight woman, a few years older than Andee, with unruly flame hair and porcelain skin. She

was also the closest Andee had to a good friend outside her family. 'So I've been in touch with Henry Gibbs
whose speciality is family law. He should be here any
minute.'

'Have you already briefed him?' Andee asked.

'In so far as I could, but obviously you'll be able
to explain better than I can. Ah, here he is,' and she
got to her feet as the door opened for her secretary
to show in a short, wiry man with spiky grey hair,
endearingly rosy cheeks and red-rimmed spectacles.
He was wearing a jaunty bow tie and baggy blue suit
that made him look rather more like a clown than a
lawyer.

'Sorry,' he said, shaking Andee's hand, 'dressed for
the next client who's four and a half and afraid of men,
so I'm trying to play up the unscary look. Trouble is, I
don't think clowns are quite doing it these days.'

'I think you'll be fine,' Andee told him drily. 'It's
good to meet you.'

After embracing Helen, he accepted a coffee and
with a quick glance at his watch came straight to the
point. 'Personally, I've never had to deal with surrogacy,' he said frankly, 'but I've spoken to a colleague in
London, Jhanvi Best, who's had some experience,
mostly in India, and she's willing to take a look at it for
us. To get things started she's asked me to find out a
few facts from you, such as which US state the contract
was drawn up in. Do you have a copy of it? Who is acting for the intended parents in this country? And have
social services been notified yet?'

Inwardly flinching at the mention of social services,

Andee said, 'I'm pretty sure the contract was drawn up in Texas, but I'll check. No, I don't have a copy of it, but I'll try to get one. I'll also find out who's acting for the intended parents over here, and no to the question about social services. If possible we'd like to keep them out of it for as long as we can.'

He nodded his understanding. 'I'm afraid the instant it goes before a judge, probably even before that, they'll have to know, but for now we'll keep it to ourselves.'

'How soon can you get the information?' Helen asked Andee. 'I'd imagine the sooner the better?' She glanced at Henry for confirmation.

'Indeed,' he agreed. 'I'll give you my card. You can call me any time. If I'm with a client or in court I'll get back to you as soon as I'm free. Can I ask where the baby is now?'

'With its birth parents and their families,' Andee replied.

'That's good. I should think having a good support network of blood relatives will help, but I don't want to give any false hope because Americans can be pretty tenacious, not to say ferocious, when fighting for their rights.'

'As can we,' Andee informed him.

Clearly liking the response, Henry finished his coffee and got to his feet. 'I'm sorry this was rushed,' he said, shaking her hand again, 'but I thought it better for us to meet in person rather than talk on the phone. As soon as you can get the information to me I'll pass it along and we'll decide what needs to be done next.'

'Of course it all depends on the intended parents

filing a lawsuit,' Helen pointed out, gently anchoring them.

Appreciating the reminder, for everything seemed to be going so fast, Andee turned back to Henry as he said, 'Do you think there's a chance they won't?'

Wishing she could give him some hope of that, Andee said, 'I wouldn't bet on it. They don't know yet that he's been born, but we can't keep it from them very much longer.'

'No,' he confirmed, 'you really can't. If you don't own up to the birth it could be read as the parents planning to abscond. I hope they're not, by the way, because they'll be found eventually and running from this won't help their case at all.'

Ten minutes later, with those words still echoing in her ears, Andee was driving through town when Penny finally called her back. 'Where are you?' Andee immediately asked.

'Still at the Grand, where I'll be staying until you go elsewhere.'

'What do you mean?'

'Well, Jonathan and Juliette must be around here somewhere or you wouldn't be. If you move them, I'm guessing you'll go with them, so I'll follow.'

'Penny, this is crazy. They could be anywhere. I don't have to be with them . . .' Realising there was no point in pursuing that, she said, 'We need to talk.'

'Again?'

'Yes, again. I'm not far away. I'll come to the hotel.'

'*No*, don't do that. I'm busy today trying to save everything my son and his girlfriend are so selfishly destroying. Do you have any idea what it's like dealing with American lawyers? No, of course you don't, well let me tell you it's nothing short of hell, and if they carry out their threats I'll be completely ruined. Everything will be over, the surrogacy, the clinics, the refuges, everything I've spent half my life creating. My lawyer's here, so please don't come, we have a lot to do.'

'OK, then email me a copy of the contract Jonathan and Juliette signed so I . . .'

'Why? What do you want it for?'

'What do you think? Jonathan and Juliette are going to fight for their baby. You already know that . . .'

'You have to talk them out of it.'

'I don't have to do anything, but you need to know that the baby's been born. They're calling him Alexander in honour of Jonathan's brother, your other twin.'

Penny was silent, and Andee immediately regretted the way she'd broken the news.

'Congratulations,' she said softly. 'You're a grandmother.'

'For God's sake, this isn't about me being a grandmother,' Penny cried frantically. 'You need to tell me where they are. If you won't talk sense to them then I have to . . .'

'I'm not letting you anywhere near them until this lawsuit is made to go away.'

'There's no point trying to blackmail me when it's not in my hands. The Blakemores want the child they've prepared and paid for . . .'

'The other thing I need from you,' Andee interrupted, 'is the name of the lawyer they've hired to handle things over here. Please put it in the email you send with the contract,' and before Penny could protest any further she ended the call.

It wasn't until she was talking to Gould a few minutes later that she realised her big mistake. Now that Penny knew the baby had arrived it was highly likely she, or more probably the American lawyers, would contact social services with a request that they remove him from his parents to prevent them from disappearing with him. Or from harming him in some way? God only knew what they'd tell the authorities in order to get Alexander away from Jonathan and Juliette.

'And when they know he's in care,' she told her mother later that evening, 'they'll begin the most vicious attack on Jonathan and Juliette's characters to try and prove they are unfit parents.'

Maureen looked both aghast and exhausted. 'We have to talk to Penny,' she said. 'Make her see sense. This baby is her flesh and blood . . .'

'I don't think that matters to her in the way it does to us.'

'Then we have to *make* it matter.'

Wishing it were as easily done as said, Andee went to let Blake and Jenny into the kitchen with the Chinese takeaway they'd ordered to save anyone having to cook. It was often hard for her to look at Blake and not think of Graeme, and as she did so now, for the first time in a few days Graeme rang.

Liking to think it was telepathy, she excused herself and took the phone out to the hall to sit at the foot of the stairs. 'Hi, how are you?' she asked softly.

'I'm fine,' he replied. 'How about you?'

She grimaced inwardly. 'Where to start?'

'So maybe this isn't a good time?'

Surprised by the stiffness of his tone, Penny's offer to show her photographs of him and Nadia immediately came to her mind. *You can see for yourself how close they are.*

'There's something I have to tell you,' he said. 'I've been trying to think of the right way . . .'

Deciding a protracted break-up was the last thing she needed to deal with right now, she said, 'It's OK. I already know. You don't have to explain, just be happy,' and quickly ending the call she swallowed hard on the emotions twisting her heart, turned off her phone and went back to the kitchen to try to eat some food.

It happened more or less as Gould had predicted. As soon as the American lawyers knew about the baby's existence they instructed someone from their London office to get straight on to social services. The only surprise was that Penny herself rang to inform Andee of this.

'Why the hell did you let it happen?' Andee raged. 'For once in your life can't you do the right thing?'

'Right for who? For you? For Jonathan? What about me and my clients, the Blakemores? I have to consider them . . .'

'Before your own son? Before your grandson? He has the right to be with his real parents . . .'

'I'm not arguing about this any more. You won't win

347

this. You can't, so why don't you just bring the baby to me, or you'll be the one responsible for him being taken into care. Think on that; I'm not making it happen, *you* are,' and the line went dead.

Ready to explode, Andee somehow resisted the urge to slam the phone against the wall, and used it to call Henry Gibbs instead.

'OK, it'll take social services a while to act,' Henry told her calmly. 'I know this, because it always does. Do you have a copy of the contract yet?'

'I've requested it, but I'm not confident the person I asked will send it.'

'Then get me the names of the American lawyers. Jhanvi will take care of it and we'll see where that ends us up.'

'But with the time difference between here and Texas . . .'

'Don't worry, it's likely to be days, not hours, before anyone gets their act together. They'll need the court's approval for an emergency care order, and we must try to be ready for them when they apply.'

Having no idea how they were going to manage that, Andee rang Jonathan. 'Are you sure you don't have a copy of the contract?' she asked.

'I'm sorry. If I'd known it was going to matter . . .'

'OK, just tell me the name of the Blakemore's lawyer.'

To her relief, he said, 'I don't know the actual law-yer's name but it's a firm in Houston called Feinstein and Beird. They do all the contracts . . .'

'That's great. Now, please don't any of you leave the

house for at least the next two days, OK? I don't want anyone to know where you are, least of all your mother. Blake and Jenny will bring everything you need, they'll tell the neighbours you're guests of Rowzee's, and I'll always be at the end of the phone . . .'

'She might have it bugged,' he said anxiously.

'I think you give her credit for more powers than she has,' Andee told him, 'but we know that she's having me followed, possibly my mother too, so we won't be able to come ourselves. Have you explained the situation to Juliette's parents yet?'

'We're hoping it'll get sorted before we have to.'

It was a lovely thought. 'I think you need to prepare them,' she cautioned.

Later in the day Andee was once again with Helen Hall when Gould rang.

'I've just had a call from one of our guys in child protection,' he told her. 'They've been contacted by social services asking if they know anything about a missing baby in a surrogacy case.'

'Oh Christ!' Andee muttered. 'They're obviously not wasting any time. What did you tell them?'

'I stalled, said I'd ask my team and get back to them.'

After relating the call to Helen, Andee said to Gould, 'I really owe you for this. I don't . . .'

'Just tell me what your next move is going to be,' he cut in.

'We're waiting for a copy of the contract to arrive from the States. Without that it's not possible for the lawyers here to know how to proceed.'

'Well, the other side obviously already has it, so you'd better make sure they don't get it in front of a judge before your guys have seen it, or the child will be gone and you'll be fighting to get him out of care instead of being put into it.'

After ringing off Andee said to Helen, 'Can the lawyers in Texas drag this out, make sure the contract doesn't get to us until after the authorities have acted?'

Helen nodded grimly. 'It's possible. The judge won't like it, but if they can show a legally binding contract to say that the child is the subject of a surrogacy case in the United States, the court will probably decide that the child has to be taken into care to prevent the birth parents from disappearing with him.' She paused, and looked Andee straight in the eye. 'Even if the contract arrived this minute,' she said, 'I don't see how it's going to help you. They'll still take the baby away until the case has been settled, and it's anyone's guess how long that will take. It could be years.'

Chapter Nineteen

Two days later with still no sign of a contract, and mercifully no word yet from social services, Andee was in the lobby of the Grand hotel, ready to force her way into Penny's suite if necessary, when Leo Johnson rang.

'I've just had a tip from a clerk at the family court,' he told her gravely. 'The application for an emergency care order is about to go in front of a judge.'

Furious and frightened, Andee thanked him, rang off and immediately called Henry Gibbs. 'Can you get there?' she implored. 'I know we don't have the contract, but someone has to represent the birth parents.'

'I'll do my best,' he promised. 'If I can get someone to cover . . . Where are you now?'

'About to make another attempt at getting the contract.'

'If you succeed bring it straight to the court. Otherwise, I'll be in touch as soon as I have some news.'

After being assured that Michelle Cross was still in the same suite Andee didn't bother announcing herself, she just took the lift to the tenth floor and hammered on the door.

'All right, all right,' Penny snapped as she opened up. 'Anyone would think there was a fire.'

Andee looked around, found no sign of a lawyer, only a stack of papers on a desk close to the window and a laptop computer showing a screen full of text that clearly wasn't English.

'I take it you know there's a court hearing this morning,' she said tightly.

Penny's nod was brief.

'What's the matter with you?' Andee cried, throwing out her hands. 'Why are you letting this happen?'

Penny regarded her steadily. She appeared far more composed than she had a few days ago. Her hair was neatly styled, her face carefully made up and she was wearing an expensive-looking black pantsuit – as though she were about to appear in court? 'How many times do we have to go through this?' she asked coldly. 'I'm honouring the contract . . .'

'Where is it?' Andee cut in harshly. 'I need a copy *right now.*'

'What makes you think I have it?'

'For God's sake, we both know you do . . .'

'Even if you're right, it won't help you. That child belongs to Abby and Donald Blakemore. The court here will see that . . .'

'Our lawyers need to examine it.'

'They'll get the opportunity . . .'

'You mean *after* the baby's been seized by the authorities?'

'I'm told that it has to happen that way.'

Suddenly seeing red, Andee grabbed Penny by her

shirt front and shoved her against the wall. 'I want that damned contract now,' she raged. 'I'm going to give your grandson the chance to grow up with his real family, even if you won't.'

'Violence isn't going to help you,' Penny gasped. 'You don't have right on your side and if you attack me again I'll call security.'

'I'll call them myself,' Andee shouted, letting her go. 'And after that I'll call the police, the press, the whole damned world to tell them exactly who you are and what you're doing.'

Penny turned away, took a few steps, and as her head fell forward it was as though the fight drained from her. She said nothing, did nothing, until her laptop signalled the arrival of an email. It was from Selma, Andee noticed, but her mobile started ringing and seeing it was Henry Gibbs she rapidly clicked on.

'I'm sorry, the order's been granted,' he told her, 'and I've been instructed to inform the court of the baby's whereabouts.'

Andee's eyes closed as she tried to think. If she hadn't asked him to go there he wouldn't be in this position, but it was too late to regret that now. She desperately wanted to refuse the information, or to tell Jonathan and Juliette to run, but she knew very well that defying the court would be just about the worst thing they could do.

'Andee?' Gibbs pressed gently. 'You have to tell me.'

Taking a breath she said, 'Do you know Rowzee Cayne?'

'Who doesn't?'

'They're at her house.'

With a sigh he said, 'I'm really sorry. It's up to you whether to call and prepare them. If you do, for God's sake tell them not to run.'

As she rang off Andee spun round, eyes blazing with rage, ready to lay into Penny again.

Penny was at her laptop, typing so furiously it was as though she'd forgotten Andee was in the room.

Slamming the lid down on her hands, Andee seethed, 'You've got your way. They're about to take the baby . . .'

'Stop, just stop!' Penny cried, clasping her hands to her head.

'What is it with you?' Andee raged. 'You're making your own son hate you, turning the whole world against you. You say you don't care what people think of you but I know *you do*. I know that in there,' she punched a hand to Penny's chest, 'is a heart that's broken into so many pieces it's forgotten how to feel, but that doesn't mean it isn't capable. You can hide that from yourself, but you can't hide it from me. So for God's sake, help your son. Your grandson. Me, your sister . . .'

Penny shot to her feet, almost pushing Andee over.

As she turned away Andee spun her back again. 'They're on their way to get him,' she cried. 'He's an innocent child, days old, and *you* are just letting it happen.'

Penny's face was stark, her eyes so clouded by the darkness inside her that it was impossible to know how much was reaching her.

Unable to spend another minute with her, Andee said bitterly, 'I don't want you ever to come near me again. Do you hear that? As far as I'm concerned you died at the age of fourteen and you're still dead.'

After slamming out of the room she raced to the lift, took it to the ground floor and ran out to her car. She'd have to put her foot down now if she was to get to the coach house before the social workers who'd been instructed to collect the baby.

As Andee approached the coach house her heart twisted and sank. She was already too late. Three, no four social workers were remonstrating with Juliette's parents at the front gate, no one understanding what the other was saying, and fists looking as though they were about to fly.

As Andee leapt out of her car Jonathan came out of the house, closing the front door behind him. 'They're trying to take him,' he shouted at Andee, 'but we're not going to let them.'

'We have an emergency care order,' one of the social workers told her. 'If they don't let him go we'll have to call the police.'

'You do that,' Andee told her. At least it would buy them some time. Taking Jonathan's hand she held it tightly as she connected to Gould. 'It's all kicking off,' she told him. 'We're up at Rowzee's. Is there anything you can do?'

'Like what?' he asked. 'We can't go against a court order.'

'But social services are calling for backup and the

Italian parents are about to cut up rough. I need some support.'

'I'll see what I can do.'

With Jonathan's help Andee took hold of Juliette's parents and steered them back into the house. 'We'll wait until the police arrive,' she told the social workers over her shoulder, and winced as Juliette's mother screamed at them in Italian. Since it was clearly abusive, Andee quickly closed the door behind them before she could say any more.

Juliette was in the kitchen, holding Alexander and looking so terrified that Andee longed to lie and tell her everything would be all right. Unfortunately, no one had ever accused Penny of forcing Juliette to become a surrogate mother. Juliette had entered into the agreement of her own free will, as had Jonathan, and now here they were.

'Have you heard anything from your mother's lawyer, or the lawyers in the States?' Andee asked Jonathan as he went to put an arm round Juliette.

'No. No one's been in touch today, until those people outside turned up.'

'I'm sorry. I came to warn you, but obviously I didn't make it in time.'

'So what is happening?' Juliette asked in a tormented voice.

Feeling as bad as she'd ever felt when breaking the news of a death, Andee said, 'I'm afraid you don't have a choice. You have to hand him over . . .'

'No! Never!' Juliette shouted, holding Alexander tighter and making him cry.

'We can't do that, he's ours,' Jonathan told her.

'I understand how you feel,' Andee responded, as the baby's screams got louder, 'but he's not being taken to the States, at least not yet. He'll be taken to someone who's experienced in looking after babies . . .'

'But I am breastfeeding,' Juliette protested furiously. 'Who is going to feed him?'

'It's possible they'll let you continue,' Andee said, 'but only under supervision. We have to get some advice,' and taking out her phone she connected to Henry Gibbs.

'Yes, I asked for feeding visits,' he confirmed, 'and they've been granted.'

'Thank you. I don't suppose the contract's turned up?'

'No, but it's not likely to overturn anything at this stage even if it does. Are you with them?'

'Yes, I am. Social services have called for police backup and a car's just arrived outside, so I'm guessing it's them.'

'Is Blake and Jenny,' Juliette's father said, turning back from the window.

Relieved beyond words at the prospect of having two level heads to support her, Andee went to let them in, and came to a sudden stop when she saw that Graeme was with them. To her dismay she felt heat burning her cheeks as her heart lurched like an adolescent's.

With a quick raise of his eyebrows he passed her and followed Blake along the hall into the kitchen.

'What the heck's going on?' Blake demanded, hefting two bags of shopping on to the island as Jenny brought in a fresh supply of Pampers. 'Who are those people outside?'

As Andee explained, forcing herself not to look at Graeme, Jenny went straight to Juliette and the baby to wrap them in her arms. 'Don't worry, we won't let them take him,' she assured her. 'Will we?' she pressed Andee.

Wishing she didn't feel like the villain of the piece, Andee said, 'I'm afraid we don't have a choice.' Her eyes went to Graeme and quickly moved away.

Juliette's parents started shouting again, rising to a crescendo as though trying to outdo their grandson's yells, and seeming to hold Andee responsible for everything.

Using his reasonable grasp of Italian Graeme did his best to calm them down, but it took a loud knock on the front door to silence them all.

Blake went to answer, with Andee close behind.

'The police are here,' a social worker told them. 'Please don't make us take him by force.'

Afraid it might well go that way, Andee turned back to Jonathan. 'For the baby's sake,' she implored, 'please don't resist. It'll frighten him and he's already frightened enough.'

'I can't let them do it,' he cried brokenly. 'If we let him go now we'll never see him again.'

'You have visiting rights,' she reminded him.

'But for how long? He needs to be with us. He knows us already.'

'Oh Jonathan,' she groaned, touching a hand to his cheek, 'I can't tell you how much I wish this wasn't happening.'

'Once he goes to America we'll never see him again.'

'You don't know for certain that he'll go. We're going to fight for him in the courts . . .'

'We won't win. She'll make sure we don't.'

Knowing he was referring to his mother, Andee said, 'She doesn't have the power to influence a British court.'

'But I'm not British, nor is Juliette.'

'Alexander is,' she said softly, hoping with all her heart that it would count for something. There was such a long way to go, so much to sort out, but right now they must deal with the police hovering on the doorstep and one of the social workers trying to push her way in.

Juliette's eyes were so murderous as the woman approached her, and Alexander was screaming so loudly, that Andee only just made out Juliette saying, 'I will kill him and myself before I let you have him.'

Juliette's parents began shouting again, and as the social worker tried to take the baby Juliette's mother would have slammed her over the head with a poker had Graeme not swiftly grabbed it from her hand. Then the police were inside, holding Juliette's screeching, struggling parents as Juliette, yelling and kicking too, fought to keep hold of her baby.

The noise was so deafening, the scene so heartbreakingly harrowing, that it took a while before anyone heard a man's voice roaring, 'Stop! All of you *stop*.'

As silence fell, Andee turned to find Gould standing at the door with . . . *Penny*?

'She was trying to make herself heard,' Gould explained, 'so I helped.'

Penny seemed reluctant to come forward, and was quick to look over her shoulder when another car arrived.

It turned out to be Henry Gibbs.

Appearing careful to avoid anyone's eyes, Penny said, 'I have the contract,' and taking it from an attaché case she handed it to Gould. 'You will see,' she went on, 'that the law in Texas requires the embryo to be transferred to a surrogate mother a minimum of four-teen days before the agreement with the intended parents is signed. The dates on the contract, and on the medical records, show that in Juliette's case it hap-pened thirteen days before.'

When she'd finished no one spoke. Andee wasn't entirely sure any of them actually understood what had just been said.

Going for clarity, she said, 'Are you telling us that the contract is void?'

Penny's eyes still met no one's as she nodded.

Andee said to Jonathan, 'Was the baby not conceived in the normal way?'

He shook his head. 'We were both donors at the time. It happened in a laboratory. We didn't fall in love until after.'

Andee looked at Penny, not entirely sure what to make of this.

Penny's eyes were on Jonathan, but he wasn't look-ing at her.

'He's telling the truth,' Penny said, and turning around she began walking away.

'Wait!' Andee called after her, but Penny kept going.

'Does this mean we can keep the baby?' Juliette asked, looking from Jonathan to Andee and back again.

'We have an emergency care order,' a social worker reminded everyone.

Henry Gibbs took the contract from Gould.

No one moved, even Alexander fell silent, as Gibbs cast an eye over a highlighted clause of the agreement. When he'd finished, he held out a hand for the order, took it and tore it in half.

Still clearly unsure of events, Jonathan said. 'Is it all over?'

As Gould nodded for the police officers to leave, the social workers, deprived of their care order and backup, could only follow.

'We'll get it sorted with the court,' Henry Gibbs promised Jonathan and Juliette, 'but I think I can safely say that no one will be back to try and take your baby away.'

'I'll catch you later,' Graeme said softly to Andee as he left the house with Blake and Jenny.

Biting back words she hadn't even considered, Andee simply nodded, and after waiting for her mother to come inside, she closed the front door and hugged her.

'Are you all right?' Maureen murmured. 'I didn't realise Graeme was back.'

'I think he came to make sure his sister's house was still standing,' Andee told her, only half joking. 'Now go see your great-grandson. They're waiting for you.'

Maureen hesitated. 'Is it really all sorted?' she whispered. 'We don't have to go through some ghastly trial?'

Shrinking from how badly it would have affected her mother's health if they'd had to battle with Jonathan and the baby on one side and Penny on the other, Andee said, 'It's not looking likely.'

Maureen seemed to breathe. 'Where's Penny?' she asked.

Andee had been wondering the same. 'At her hotel, I suppose. Or she might be on her way back to London by now.' Seeing how anxious her mother looked, she added, 'I'll try calling her . . .'

'Maureen! You're here,' Jonathan cried, and coming to wrap her in his arms he hugged her so hard that Maureen started to gasp.

'Sorry,' he said, pulling back and wiping the tears on his cheeks.

'Oh, there, there,' Maureen soothed, clasping his handsome young face in her hands. 'It's all fine now, my love. You're keeping your baby and you're going to be such a good daddy.'

'I still can't believe it,' Jonathan choked, looking at Andee. 'I keep thinking it was a trick, and that she'll be back any minute laughing and poking fun at me for believing it . . .'

'Ssh,' Maureen chided. 'It's not going to happen.'

'You saw the lawyer tear up the care order,' Andee reminded him. 'He wouldn't have done that if he weren't confident that it has no worth.'

'But what if there's another contract and that one was a fake?'

Aching for how cruel his mother must have been to Jonathan for him to think like this, Andee recalled the way Penny had looked at him before she left. It had been impossible to know what she was feeling, but Andee knew it wasn't nothing. 'I swear I don't think she'd have come here to expose the mistake unless it was genuine,' she told him.

He turned round as Juliette appeared, and seeing Maureen she fell into the arms of her tiny son's great-grandmother.

Remembering how reassuring those arms had been for her over the years, Andee whispered to Jonathan, 'Come on, let's go outside.'

He followed her around to the back of the house where two swing chairs, a padded wicker sofa and a coffee table doubling as a backgammon board were absorbing the warmth of the early afternoon sunshine. The garden, stretching all the way to the stream that separated it from the Burlingford estate, was alive with colourful flowers. Only yesterday Rowzee had texted to say they should be cut and put in vases for her guests to enjoy.

'I'm not sure what we should do now,' Jonathan said, sitting next to Andee on a top step of the wooden deck. 'I'm afraid if we try to leave she'll suddenly spring out of nowhere and grab the baby before we know what's happening.'

Taking his hand, Andee said, 'I honestly don't think she's as bad as she tries to make out.'

Scoffing, Jonathan said, 'You don't know the half.'

'I realise things have been difficult . . .'

'She's my *real* mother. She's a *part of me*. That goes beyond difficult.' Disgust, shame, thickened his voice.

Realising that he still had a long way to go to recover from learning that Ana wasn't his birth mother, Andee searched for some words of comfort. They were hard to find when Penny had behaved the way she had, especially over the baby. He would understandably struggle to forgive that. Andee couldn't help wondering if Penny's ambivalence – to put it kindly – towards her son might in some way be connected to seeing how horrified he'd been to learn that she was his mother. No matter what she said, it must have cut very deeply to realise she was so despised.

'You're going to defend her, aren't you?' he accused.

Still holding his hand between both of hers, she said, 'I can't do that when I don't know enough about what's gone on between you, but I will say this: I truly believe she came here today to try and make you see that she's not all bad.'

Astonished, Jonathan cried, 'She fucked up a contract. That's what she came to tell us.'

'But she could have got the lawyers to do that. She didn't need to be here in person. I believe she came because she wanted you to know that *she* was making the court case go away, and that she was doing it for you.'

He clearly wasn't buying it. 'If there hadn't been a problem with that contract our son wouldn't be with us now, you have to know that. In fact, she's probably known all along that there was a problem, so she didn't need to put us through any of this. She could have made it known a long time ago.'

'Maybe she's only just checked the detail. OK, I can

see you're not ready to consider that either. Look, I can't make excuses for her, I don't know her well enough to do that, but during the short time I have known her, as an adult I mean, I've got a sense of the terrible conflict, even fear, that's raging away inside her. She's struggling badly, and what's been happening lately is clearly bringing it to a head. It's my belief that she loves you deeply, but she has no idea how to show it, she's probably even afraid to try.'

He turned to look at her, his eyes showing a tormented disbelief. 'You said it yourself, you haven't known her for long,' he replied. 'She's vindictive, sadistic . . . She's bloody *inhuman*. Even Pappa says that about her.'

'But he still cares for her?'

Since he couldn't deny that, he said belligerently, 'Alex is the lucky one. At least he got to die before he found out that she-devil . . .'

'Stop, please stop,' Andee came in gently, but forcefully. 'Your brother's death was a tragedy that you really can't use in that way. By the time your mother found out what had happened to him she had been through the kind of hell that made it impossible for her to think straight, or even know who she was any more, never mind how she should relate to anyone else. Frankly, I believe she's still suffering in ways she might not even realise herself. That's what serious drug addiction does to a person, and never forget those drugs were forced on her. Yes, she chose to leave home at fourteen because she felt unloved, unappreciated, and we are to blame for that, not her. Families, parents, get things wrong sometimes, but it doesn't mean they don't care, and in Penny's case, as a parent, she hardly knows where to begin. You know you wouldn't have been born if you hadn't been part of the surrogacy deal that Sven set up. He did the wrong thing for the right reason, and you still love him . . .'

'You have to stop now,' he protested. 'Pappa can never be compared to *her*.'

Putting an arm around him, Andee toyed with the idea of telling him that no girls had gone missing, that no one was trafficked or forced to do anything they didn't want to, but decided to save it for later. It still had to be checked, and he already had enough to process for one day. So all she said was, 'People are so complex, especially someone who's suffered the way your mother has, that we often can't even begin to understand them. I just want you to try to keep an open mind where she's concerned. I'm having to do the same, because I swear she's a mystery to me too, but as we all move forward from here one thing I know for certain is that we're going to need one another every step of the way.'

'That's just where you're wrong,' he told her, 'because she doesn't need anyone, and she never has.'

It was early evening when Graeme returned to the coach house, unannounced, and asked Andee to take a stroll with him. Knowing she'd look ridiculous to the others if she refused, Andee followed him outside, already planning to tell him that they really didn't need to have this conversation.

As they reached the hamlet, where they were greeted by the heady scents of freshly mown grass, honeysuckle and a neighbours barbecue, Andee said, 'I can only begin to imagine what a shock it was for you when you arrived here today, but at least they seem to be taking good care of the place.'

With a note of humour, Graeme said, 'I knew they would with you and your mother in charge of things, but you're right, it was a bit of a shock to walk into that chaos. I'm still not entirely sure I understand everything that happened.'

Andee had to smile. 'That makes two of us,' she confessed, 'but I guess the important thing is that the baby won't be going to the States. In fact, once Jonathan gets past the fear of this being one of Penny's cruel jokes, I think he'll be very happy to take his little family to Italy so they can be close to Juliette's parents.'

'And how do you feel about that, having only just met him?'

'Sad, because I'd like to get to know him better, and I know Luke and Alayna will want to meet him as soon as they find out they have another cousin. But we'll visit him in Italy, and hopefully he'll come to see us here. I guess my real concern right now is for Penny, and how she isn't figuring in Jonathan's plans for the future at all.'

'Mm,' he responded thoughtfully. 'There's obviously a lot of work to be done there, if they even want to do it.'

'I think she does, but heaven only knows how she'll go about it.'

'And what about your mother? How's she dealing with things?'

Andee wished she could give a proper answer to that, but all she could say was, 'I'm not sure. One minute she seems to be holding it together very well, the next she looks completely shattered – and lost, like she's not entirely sure what's happening or what she should be doing. It's been hard for her, and I'm not convinced that even the relief of Jonathan getting to keep the baby is making it much easier. Of course she's happy about that, she wouldn't have wanted it any other way, but . . .' She sighed heavily at the size of the but.

'Really it's all about Penny?'

Andee nodded, and they both waved to one of the neighbours as he returned from a walk on the moor with his dog. 'She truly doesn't know how to process the issues Penny's thrown up, and frankly I don't either. I'm not even sure we'll hear from her again now the struggle for Alexander is over.'

'But you've got her number.'

'Yes, that's true.'

After a while he said, 'Do you think she knew all along that the contract was invalid?'

'I've no idea. Jonathan's convinced of it, but if she did she'd have known we'd find out sooner or later, so why would she keep it to herself? My guess is she didn't realise until it was checked against the medical file, and that might only have happened in the last day or two.'

'Well, however it came to light, I dread to think of the kind of lawsuit she must be facing now.'

Dreading it too, Andee said, 'It won't be pretty, that's for sure, and to be honest I don't know how equipped she is to deal with it. She's not as . . . invincible as she likes to make out, and I got the feeling when I was with her the other day that she's afraid of something. Well, of course she is, given the mistake with the contract, but I wouldn't be surprised if it goes deeper than that.'

As they reached the picnic area at the end of the hamlet where a stunning view of the bay and sunset was glittering tantalisingly through the trees, Graeme offered her his hand as they descended the few rugged steps into the glade. When she was there, he kept hold of it and folded it through his arm.

'There's something I need to discuss with you,' he said, after a few moments of absorbing the beauty of their surroundings, 'and before you say you know what it is, I don't think you do . . . Why did you say that, by the way?'

Wishing she wasn't having to admit this, she attempted to sound wry as she said, 'Penny has photos of you with Nadia.'

Clearly startled, he turned to look at her. 'What photos?' he asked, apparently more perplexed than angry.

Starting to feel embarrassed now, Andee said, 'She told me you seem very close.'

His eyebrows rose with some sort of understanding as he nodded. 'And you saw these photos?' he wondered.

This was becoming more awkward by the second. 'She offered to show me, but I didn't really want . . .

She had someone following you, and I think that someone took Nadia to be me. You're going to tell me they don't exist?'

'If she had someone following me I'm sure they do, but they'd be no different to photos of me with my sisters or your mother. Affectionate, fun, although there hasn't been a lot of fun with Nadia lately, which brings me to what I want to discuss with you.'

Andee looked back at the view, preparing for the worst.

'There's no easy way of saying this,' he began, 'so I'll come straight to the point. Nadia doesn't want you working on the project any more.'

A beat after the shock, Andee felt the rejection like a slap.

'The reason,' he continued, 'is probably what you're suspecting ... I don't mean that there's anything between us, but she would like there to be. I've told her many times that it's not going to happen, but there's so much at stake with this property – in that she's paying me so well – that she thinks she's calling all the shots. She knows now that she isn't.'

Andee was very still as she regarded him closely, not quite sure of what he was saying.

'If you're not able to work on Nadia's villa with me,' he said, 'I'm not going to do it.'

As understanding reached her, Andee's jaw almost dropped. 'But all that money,' she protested. 'It's over a hundred thousand pounds.'

'I won't deny it would be good to have, but frankly I'd rather have you.'

She continued to stare at him, still trying to take it in. 'But I'm not worth that much,' she objected.

Laughing, he brought her to him and lowered his mouth tenderly to hers.

Minutes passed, birds sang, the distant sea soughed as she put her arms around him and felt so relieved and so complete that she simply ignored the text that had just arrived on her phone.

When finally he let her go, he said, 'Considering all that's been happening lately, maybe you'd better check that message.'

Seriously hoping it was something that could wait, she opened up the text. Seeing it was from Penny, she became aware of a strange feeling stealing over her.

Have you given any thought to how the book ends?

'Oh my God,' she murmured, knowing exactly what this meant, and grabbing Graeme's hand she ran like the wind to her car.

Chapter Twenty

For the second time that day Andee was hammering on the door to Penny's suite at the Grand hotel. The only difference this time was that the manager and Graeme were with her.

Her heart was thudding with fear. *Have you given any thought to how the book ends?* Kate Trask had chosen to escape her crimes, her shame and the lack of her son's love by taking her own life.

'Penny!' she shouted fiercely. 'Please let me in.'

Since she'd already told the manager what she feared, he didn't hesitate in unlocking the door, and moments later she was bursting into the room.

She looked around, hardly able to see through her panic, until finally she spotted Penny sitting in one of the window seats, staring blankly out at the sea. She was clearly very much alive, and virtually collapsing with relief, Andee cried, 'Why didn't you answer? You must have heard me knocking.'

Penny said nothing, simply continued to gaze out at the horizon, seeming not to register anything beyond whatever she was seeing in her mind.

Turning to the manager, Andee said, 'Thank you. It'll be fine now. I'll meet you downstairs,' she told Graeme.

After they'd gone she closed the door quietly and went to sit in a chair close to the window. As she waited for her heart to settle, she looked around the room and saw Penny's suitcases stacked on the floor. Whether they were already packed it wasn't possible to tell. The desk was empty, no sign of the laptop or the files that had littered it earlier.

When it became clear that she'd have to break this strangely awful silence, Andee said, 'OK, you got me here. So what now?'

Without turning round, Penny said, 'You thought I'd killed myself.'

'Isn't that what I was meant to think?'

Penny didn't deny it. 'I will, of course, leave everything to Jonathan,' she said.

Her alarm increasing to fear, Andee said, 'Have you taken something? Do I need to call an ambulance?'

Penny inhaled a shaky breath and let it go slowly. 'No, you don't need to call an ambulance,' she replied.

'So what's this about?' Andee demanded, wanting to shake her out of this peculiar stupor.

'I have something for you,' Penny said. It's a USB stick containing all the files you'll need to show where the so-called missing girls are. You'll also find details of the refuges in Riga, Vilnius and Minsk and a list of the scouts who search out the vulnerable. Everything's there, right down to the details of the students who take the opportunity to make a lot of money during a gap year. You'll even discover how much they're paid. It's easier for the boys of course, so they don't receive anywhere near as much as the girls.' She smiled grimly. 'Some of them like our set-up so much that they decide to continue being donors while working as escorts from the apartments in London and Stockholm. You can interview them if you like, ask them how free they are to come and go. All their details are there.'

Feeling faintly disoriented, Andee took the memory stick and asked, 'Why are you doing this?'

Penny's expression had no warmth, only something that looked like sadness, or possibly resentment. 'Because I'm ruined, or I soon will be, and all those young people will have to find their own way from here. I'm not sure what will happen to the refuges; it's not easy to get state funding in those countries.'

'You're assuming the Blakemores are going to sue.'

'I know they are. I heard from their lawyers as soon as the problem with the contract was revealed.'

'Which was when?'

'When I received the medical file the day before yesterday. Until then I fully believed everything was as it should be.'

Having to ask the question, Andee said, 'Does that mean you'd still be trying to take the baby if all the conditions had been met?'

Penny sighed and turned her hands over as she looked down at them. As Andee looked at them too she felt an uneasy beat in her heart. Why hadn't she made this connection before? Kate Trask had worn gloves, not to cover eczema, but to mask her arthritic joints. Did it mean anything? Maybe it was just a bizarre or psychosomatic coincidence.

'No, I wouldn't be trying to take him,' Penny replied, 'but the Blakemores' lawyers wouldn't have stopped until they had him, no matter how old he might be by then.'

'You seem so sure of that.'

'I know the Blakemores. They're very determined and desperate people.'

'Can't you offer them another surrogate?'

'I have, but after this they don't trust me, so they're going to make sure that no one else makes the same mistake. They're already petitioning to have the clinics shut down, and it won't be long before they hit me with a ruinous claim for damages.'

'And where exactly do they think all this bitterness and litigation is going to end them up? Not with a baby, that's for sure.'

'Oh, I expect they'll get one eventually, and they'll be able to boast to their friends about what they did to me, so everyone will know that you cross the Blakemores at your peril.'

After a while, Andee said, 'I can't help wondering what they'd have done if the baby had been born with a physical or mental impairment. They don't sound like the kind of couple who'd accept anything less than what they would call perfection.'

'They wouldn't have. There's a clause in all the contracts to cover that. The baby has to be in full health or the intended parents will be entitled to a full refund.'

Shocked, disgusted, Andee said, 'What would happen to the baby?'

'I can't answer that because the problem's never arisen. If it did, I guess we'd find a home for it somewhere. We'd have to if the biological mother didn't want to keep it.'

Still having a difficult time with the ethics of it all, no matter whom it might be helping, Andee said, 'So what are you going to do next?'

Penny swallowed and raised one of her flaked hands to her face.

Seeing how badly it was shaking, Andee said, 'What is it? There's more, I can tell . . .'

Penny almost laughed. 'You think being ruined isn't enough?'

'It might be, but you're keeping something back, so why don't you tell me what it is?'

Pressing her hand to her head as tears flooded her eyes, Penny said, 'Sven has been taken to hospital. He's only got days to live and I don't know how to tell Jonathan.'

'Oh Penny,' Andee murmured, going to her. She felt oddly bony and stiff, clearly uncomfortable with the physical contact, even though she didn't resist it.

'He loves his father so much.' Penny's voice shook. 'We all do.'

Andee stopped herself from offering to break the news, feeling Jonathan had to hear it from Penny.

'His father's going to die and the only parent he'll have is me,' Penny stated bleakly. 'Imagine how he's going to feel about that. He'll hate me for not being the one to die. I don't blame him for hating me. I've never done anything to make him feel any other way. I didn't want him to be my son, I didn't want anyone to belong to me and I didn't want to belong to anyone. But I do belong to Sven. He's been everything to me for as long as I can remember . . . I'm terrified of a world without him in it. I don't know how I'm going to cope. I just don't know,' she gasped desperately.

With tears stinging her own eyes, Andee tried to comfort her, but Penny wasn't listening.

'Ever since he told Jonathan about me,' she ran on, 'it's been his dearest wish that Jonathan and I should find a way to work things out. I've told him so many times that it'll never happen, that I'm incapable of what he's asking and Jonathan's not willing, but he won't believe it. He has so much faith in us . . . He thinks we'll do it for him, and I want to, I want to so much, but we've left it too late.'

'That's not true,' Andee told her firmly. 'He's still alive, and you must talk to Jonathan. Does he know how Sven feels?'

Penny nodded. 'But he doesn't know that Sven's so close to the end.'

'Then I'll take you to Jonathan now, and I'll stay with you while you tell him. I'll hold both your hands and I'll even come to Stockholm if you think it'll help.'

Penny was shaking her head. 'Why would you do that for me after the way I've treated you?'

'Because you're my sister, and he's my nephew and because I want Sven's wish to come true as much as he does.'

Penny was still shaking, seeming unable to make

herself stop. 'I've left everything to Jonathan,' she repeated faintly. 'My lawyer has my will . . .'

'Penny!' Andee cried, suddenly realising that something was very wrong. 'Penny, what have you done?'

'I lied,' Penny murmured, slumping slightly. 'I always lie.'

Trying to hold her up, Andee whipped out her phone and called Graeme. 'We need to get her to hospital,' she told him. 'Please call an ambulance,' and forcing Penny to her feet she began urgently walking her around the room.

It was just after dawn the following morning that Andee, stiff and aching from spending the night in a chair, opened her eyes to find Penny watching her from the hospital bed. Apart from the redness and slight bruising around her mouth her face was colourless and pinched; her eyes were sunken and shadowed.

Struggling to sit straighter, Andee said, 'Hi. How are you feeling?'

Penny's voice was hoarse. 'Probably about as good as I look.'

Encouraged by the humour, Andee filled a glass with water and handed it to her. 'Do you remember what happened?' she asked.

After gingerly swallowing, Penny said, 'Do you want me to thank you for bringing me here?'

Andee shrugged. 'I didn't have anything else to do.'

Almost managing a smile, Penny shifted slightly and winced.

'Headache?'

Penny nodded.

'It could be a lot worse,' Andee reminded her.

As Penny's eyes closed she raised her peeling fingers to her head.

'Do they hurt?' Andee asked.

Penny glanced at her and realising what she meant, she said, 'It's worse some days than others.' She sighed shakily. 'It's funny, isn't it, that my hands should be a problem, not like Kate Trask's arthritic joints, but still an affliction.'

'You need to let it go,' Andee said softly. 'You're not her, and nor are you anything like her.'

Penny stared off into the distance, watching ghosts only she could see. 'Who knows I'm here?' she asked.

'No one, apart from me and Graeme.'

'So it's all . . . You're still together?'

Wondering if Penny had ever known what it was to be in a romantic relationship, Andee said, 'We are.'

Penny nodded as her eyes drifted again. 'No one else needs to know about this, do they?' she said after a while.

'Not if you don't want them to.'

Penny looked at the saline drip attached to her left hand, then removing it she swung her legs over the side of the bed and swayed.

'Too fast,' Andee said, steadying her. 'And you need to see a doctor before we leave.'

'They're not keeping me here. I have to get to Sven.'

'Don't worry, they'll be glad to have the bed back. There's a shower in there. I popped back to the hotel during the night and brought you some things. They're in that bag.'

Penny stared at the holdall and seemed unable to move.

Going to her, Andee slipped an arm around her and rested her head against hers. 'It'll be all right,' she whispered. This was a new feeling, comforting her little sister.

It was a while before Penny turned to look at her. 'I've screwed up so badly,' she said, gazing into Andee's eyes, 'and I've just gone on and on screwing up.'

'So maybe you're tired of it now?'

Penny gave a small nod.

'Good, then get in the shower and when you're ready we'll take the first steps towards trying to make some things right.'

Just over an hour later, complete with all the leaflets and helpline numbers the hospital insisted they take, Andee was driving them to Rowzee and Pamela's coach house. Graeme had gone on ahead to prepare the way, while Penny's chauffeur had been summoned from the hotel to follow Andee's car. It was making Penny feel more secure, Andee realised, to know that she'd be able to get away if she needed to.

Struck again by how lonely and vulnerable her sister really was behind the façade that was slowly but surely falling apart, Andee reached out to hold her hand.

Penny didn't respond. She sat rigidly in her seat, trying to battle whatever doubts and demons were assailing

her. When Andee let her hand go, she said, belligerently, 'It's much easier when you don't care.'

Touched and amused by how like the child Penny
she sounded, Andee said, 'Really?'

Penny continued to stare out of the window, registering only she knew what as they turned on to the
coast road where block after block of affordable hous-
ing and holiday homes had replaced what had once
been vast swathes of buttercup fields and bluebell
woods. 'It's changed a lot since we were young,' she
commented, sounding offended. 'Frankly, I'm not sure
I like being here.'

Understanding that the resentment was far more to
do with nerves than genuine disapproval, Andee wondered what memories were coming up for her, and
how hard she was finding it to handle the complicated
emotions they would be stirring.

'I'm not sure she's up to seeing Jonathan this soon,'
Andee had said to Graeme earlier while Penny was in
the shower, 'but with Sven having so little time left, I
don't see there's a choice.'

'There isn't,' he agreed. 'I've looked into flights for
this evening. There's plenty of availability at the
moment, but I won't book anything until we know
who's going. I'll leave now to make sure I'm at the
coach house before you.'

After he'd gone Andee had called her mother to
tell her about Sven's deteriorating condition, and
to warn her that Alayna was intending to turn up later
in the day. 'You know what she's like,' Andee said, 'she
obviously knows something's going on and she's

determined to find out what it is. So just in case I'm not around, will you be OK with explaining about Penny?' It was a big ask, too big, but maybe Blake and Jenny wouldn't mind being there to support her.

'I'll do my best,' Maureen promised, sounding daunted. 'How's Penny taking it about Sven?'

'She's very upset. We're just about to go and break it to Jonathan. I'll come and see you before I head off to the airport.'

'So you're going to Stockholm too?'

'I'm not sure yet. I'll let you know.'

Now, as she and Penny turned at Hope Cove and started up towards the moor, Penny was gazing hard at her phone as though willing it, or even daring it to ring. Though it was on silent Andee knew it had rung at least a dozen times in the past hour, and heaven only knew how many texts and emails had arrived throughout the night.

'I should be in the States,' Penny stated. 'I've got three girls due to give birth in the next couple of weeks. I'm always there for the handover. Everyone's wondering where I am, and what's going on.'

'Isn't there someone who can deputise for you?' Andee asked.

'Maria. She runs the clinics.'

'So why are you worried?'

'*Because I should be there.*' Pressing a hand to her head, she said, 'Why doesn't Selma call? Is that good or bad?'

'You could always call her.'

Penny turned away. Clearly she was afraid to. 'I want to send a text to let him know that Jonathan and I are on our way,' she declared angrily. 'If he knew that he'd definitely hold on, but I can't until I know it's true.'

'Why not?' Andee ventured. 'Even if it doesn't go the way you hope with Jonathan, it'll make Sven happy for a while to think you're both coming.'

Penny threw out her hands. 'Why do you always know the right thing to do?'

Drily Andee said, 'I'll try to get it wrong next time.'

Penny started to press in a message. When she'd finished she said, 'If Jonathan doesn't want to go with me, I'll let him go on his own. Sven will want to see him and it's important for him to say goodbye to his father.'

'It's important for you too,' Andee reminded her.

Penny nodded, and bit her lip as tears shone in her eyes.

Opening the glove box, Andee pointed her to the Kleenex.

Minutes later they were at the gates to the Burlingford estate, only yards from the coach house where Graeme's car was parked next to the Mini Jonathan and Juliette were using.

Andee turned to Penny. In spite of the freshly applied make-up her face was ashen as she stared with dark, haunted eyes into the next few minutes.

'Graeme came on ahead to explain about the contract and lawsuit,' Andee told her. 'He hasn't had much time, but he was going to try telling Jonathan about the missing girls who aren't missing at all.'

'He won't believe it,' Penny said hoarsely.

'He'll have to when we prove it.'

Penny looked at her. 'Have you been through the files?' she asked.

Andee shook her head.

'So you don't know if I was telling the truth.'

In spite of a beat of unease, Andee said, 'I trust you.'

Penny's gaze held on to hers. In the end, she said quietly, 'You're a good person.'

Reaching for her hand again, Andee felt its icy coldness and lifted it to her cheek to warm it. The hard flakes of skin, like little signs of vulnerability, moved her deeply. 'Are you ready?' she asked softly, knowing she wasn't.

Penny glanced in the side mirror to make sure the Mercedes was still behind.

'Do you know what you're going to say?'

'No. I . . . I guess I just have to tell him.'

By the time they reached the front door Graeme had already opened it. 'Juliette's upstairs with her parents and the baby,' he told them. 'Jonathan's outside on the terrace.'

'How much does he know?' Andee asked.

'Nothing about Sven. I'm honestly not sure how he's dealing with what I told him about you,' he said to Penny.

Penny took a breath but no words came.

'I did my best,' he promised.

Slipping an arm round Penny's waist, Andee eased her inside and along the hall to the kitchen. They could see Jonathan standing with his back to the open French doors.

He gave no indication that he'd heard them come in, but simply continued to stare across the garden to the fruit orchard beyond.

Letting Penny go, Andee gave her a gentle push forward.

After two steps Penny turned back, looking as though she might flee. Andee's heart went out to her. Of all the difficult, even harrowing situations she must have faced in her life, this was clearly right up there with the hardest.

'Jonathan,' Andee said.

She saw him stiffen and for a moment she thought he was going to ignore her, but finally he turned around. His eyes were harsh, defensive; his fists were clenching and unclenching at his sides. He didn't look at his mother, only at Andee. 'Whatever she's told you . . .'

Andee's hand went up. 'You need to listen,' she cautioned. To Penny she said, 'Go ahead.'

Before Penny could speak, Jonathan spat, 'If this is supposed to be an apology I'm not interested, because you won't mean it. You're only doing it to . . .'

'Jonathan,' Andee chided. 'You really do need to listen.'

Apparently catching on to the fact that there might be more going on than he realised, his eyes shot warily to his mother and back to Andee.

Penny attempted to clear her throat. Andee could see her lips trembling and moving, but no words were coming out.

'It's OK,' Andee murmured, going to her.

'I can't do it,' Penny gasped.

'Yes you can.'

'I told you,' Jonathan growled, 'I don't want an apology any more than I want *her* as a mother.'

Andee felt Penny flinch.

Realising she needed to take over, Andee said, as firmly but gently as she could, 'What she's trying to tell you is that Sven is in the hospital. He only has days to live and she'd like you to go with her to Stockholm ...' She broke off as Jonathan backed away, shouting, 'No! I don't believe you. It's one of her tricks. This is the kind of thing she does.'

'Jonathan, you know he's sick,' Andee broke in. 'You knew this was coming ...'

'No! I won't let it,' he cried. 'He can't go. It's her fault. She made him sick.'

'You know that's not true.'

'Oh God, oh God,' he wailed, clasping his hands to his head. 'You've got to stop it, please. Please stop it.'

Going to him, Andee held him as he twisted one way then another, sobbing into his hands and calling for his father. 'Pappa, Pappa,' he gasped, stooping low as though unable to take the pain of what he'd known was coming.

Andee rubbed his back, watching Penny as she looked on helplessly.

Suddenly his head came up. 'She's lying,' he raged desperately. 'I know she is.'

Andee caught him by the shoulders and turned him around. 'Look at her,' she said, 'does she look like someone who's lying? And would she, over something like this? He means the world to her too. You know that.'

Jonathan's head fell back as he tried in vain to contain his grief. He began stomping about the room, banging his fists into furniture, even himself.

'Jonathan, we . . . we need to go to him,' Penny said brokenly.

'Not with you,' he snarled.

'Jonathan!' Andee cut in. 'Think of how much it will mean to him to see the two of you together.'

'He knows I hate her.'

'And do you think he wants it to be like that? Please, go together . . .'

From the doorway, Juliette said, 'Jonathan, we will go and we must take the baby. Sven will want to meet his grandson.'

Struggling to control more tears, Jonathan went to bury his face against her. 'Yes,' he murmured into her hair. 'He'll want to meet his grandson.' To Andee he said, 'I have to call Selma. She'll tell me if this is true.'

Feeling Penny's pain, Andee said, 'It's true, Jonathan. If you won't take Penny's word for it, *Kate's* word for it, then please take mine.'

Still unable to look at Penny, he said to Andee, 'OK, then we should go today.'

Penny managed to say, 'If you'd rather I waited a day . . .'

'No, you must go too,' Andee insisted. 'Jonathan, please don't push her out. We've no idea how much time Sven has left. Don't make it too late for her.'

Jonathan turned his back, still holding on to Juliette. Andee could hear her whispering to him in Italian, seeming to soothe and encourage him until, finally, he turned to his mother.

'Do it,' Juliette murmured.

When he still didn't move, Juliette took his arm and walked him to Penny. 'Do it,' she repeated.

Obediently Jonathan lifted his head and said, *'Kom du ocksa.'* Come too.

Andee watched as Penny stood motionless, tears spilling from her eyes, until finally she was able to lift a hand and place it on his shoulder.

To Andee's relief he didn't shrink away.

'Tack,' Penny whispered.

Jonathan turned to Andee. 'And you?' he asked. 'Will you come too?'

Andee looked at Penny, and seeing how desperately unsure she was of being able to do the right thing, she said, 'Of course.'

Andee found Graeme outside talking to the chauffeur.

'I'm going with them,' she told him. 'Juliette and the baby are coming too.'

'OK, I'll get on to the flights,' he replied. 'We'll need to sort out what to do about the baby's passport, but I think I know someone who can help with that. Will Juliette's parents be staying here?'

'No, they're arranging to go back to Italy to start making things ready for when Jonathan and Juliette join them. There's a flight later today from Bristol airport.'

'OK, I'll organise a taxi for them unless Blake's free to do it. I'll take you to Heathrow, because you won't fit all the baby paraphernalia and five people into the Mercedes.'

Andee's heart swelled. 'It might be too much for Penny and Jonathan to be in the same car for such a long journey at this stage, so Penny ought to come with us.'

He nodded agreement and glanced at his watch. 'I should get on to it, make sure you can get on this evening's flight.'

'Before you go,' she said, putting a hand on his arm, 'why don't you come too? Maybe you could show me around Stockholm.'

Drawing her into his arms, he replied, 'I'd love nothing more, but your sister knows the city far better than I do, and I think it would be good for you both to spend some time together.'

In spite of feeling apprehensive about that, Andee didn't argue, because of course he was right.

'What are you going to do now?' he asked.

'I'm taking Penny to see my mother.'

He grimaced comically. 'OK. Good luck with that. I'll call when the flights are confirmed and come and pick you up from the Lodge.'

Maureen was waiting when Andee and Penny reached Bourne Hollow, fresh coffee already made for her and Andee, tea for Penny, remembering she didn't drink coffee, and some home-baked pinwheel cookies on the table. She looked and sounded as nervous as Penny clearly was, and Andee had to admit to feeling anxious too. There was so much to say, too much for the short time they had, but it wouldn't have been right to leave without them at least trying to make the first moves back to each other.

'You should eat,' Maureen said to Penny, and knowing

389

it was her mother's way of showing she cared, Andee wanted to hug her.

'It's a new cookie recipe,' Maureen told them, 'from one of the contestants on *Bake Off*.'

To Andee's relief Penny reached for a biscuit and broke it in two, in spite of looking as though food was the last thing she wanted.

'I'm going to take my coffee upstairs while I pack,' Andee informed them. 'You don't need me to help you with this.'

Looking as though they desperately did, they watched her carry her mug out to the hall and sat staring at the door long after she'd closed it.

Penny nibbled on a cookie. 'They're very good,' she told her mother.

As Maureen looked at her she felt so lost that she had no idea what to say. All the turmoil and torment of the last few weeks was still there, it couldn't just disappear. Yet seeing Penny as she was now, seeming helplessly exposed and needy, a shadow of the woman who'd come here a few short weeks ago, Maureen realised it was as if a missing piece of herself was trying to find its way back. It didn't quite fit, kept hurting and trying to get away, but at last it felt as though she might stand a chance of getting hold of it. In this moment it didn't matter that this woman, like the girl she'd once been, had caused her mother to question herself and her feelings in the most harrowing way; or that she'd created so much doubt in Maureen's heart that the shame, the fear had been impossible to bear. Right now that child, that woman, looked broken, frightened, and in desperate need of the kindness Maureen longed to give, if she only knew where to start.

In the end she said, 'I'm sorry to hear about Sven.'

Penny's eyes went down and Maureen saw the grief go through her like a shiver. 'Thank you,' Penny mumbled. 'He was ... He is ...' She shook her head, apparently unable or unwilling to say more.

'I'm sorry not to have known him,' Maureen said. 'He sounds a very special man.'

Penny nodded. At last her eyes came back to her mother's. She swallowed hard. 'It wasn't true what I said about Dad. I know you know that, but I think you need to hear me say it,' she told her.

It was true; Maureen had needed it very much.

'I'm sorry I hurt you so badly,' Penny continued, 'and that I didn't have the courage to come back when I should have.' Her hands closed into tight, painful fists. 'There are so many apologies that it's hard to know where to begin.'

'You just have,' Maureen said softly. 'And I'm sorry too. I should have been a better mother, should have understood and listened more ...'

'I never really deserved to be loved anyway.'

Rocked by the statement, Maureen couldn't think what to say.

'It's OK, I don't ...'

'It's not true,' Maureen interrupted. 'You were loved, very much. And you still are.'

'But ...'

'Listen to me', Maureen said firmly, taking Penny's

hand, 'whatever you've done, wherever you've been and wherever you go, one thing will never change. I am your mother and I will always love you and want you in my life. That was always the case, it remains the case, and will forever be the case, so please don't ever doubt it.'

As Penny stiffened with pain Maureen went to hold her, tears running down her own cheeks as she felt her younger daughter pressing against her as though she was really, truly trying to find her way back.

'I know you have to go to Stockholm now,' Maureen went on, 'but promise me you'll stay in touch, and even come back to see us.'

'I promise,' Penny choked. 'As long as you're sure.'

'Of course I am. I don't want to lose you again.'

By the time Andee came to let them know it was time to go to the airport Penny was on her second biscuit, and sitting quietly in her chair looking for all the world like the child she'd once been as Maureen gently brushed her hair.

'She needs to look her best for Sven,' Maureen told Andee.

Andee looked at them both trying to take it in. This might feel like a dream, or something happening in a parallel world, but it really wasn't. Penny was back.

Penny was back.

She was actually here, no longer hiding behind the masks she'd created, for the moment at least she'd stopped pretending to be someone who didn't care. Maybe this was the real Penny Lawrence, the daughter and sister they'd have to get to know all over again, even as she got to know herself. Not that it was going to be easy, it would take a miracle to bring that about. With so many questions still to answer and damage to repair, it was sure to be a very long road. However, today wasn't the day to be troubling themselves with that, it was a time simply to feel thankful that things had got this far – because there was no doubt in Andee's mind that these past few weeks were just the beginning.

Acknowledgements

An enormous thank you to Gunnel Oscarsson for introducing me to the wonderful city of Stockholm. A fabulous experience and a city I'd love to visit again and again. Also thank you Gunnel for undertaking the Swedish translations.

More thanks to my dear friends Gill Hall and Ian Kelcey whose legal expertise once again guided my hand.

As usual my wonderful husband, James Garrett, provided unflinching moral support throughout the writing of this book, heroically withstanding the many highs and lows that come with creating an extreme and challenging story.

Susan Lewis

Hiding in
Plain Sight

Bonus Material

Susan Lewis

on
Hiding in Plain Sight

Dear Reader,

Having been asked many times over the last few years, 'What happened to Andee's sister?' I realised that I needed to set about finding the answer. It wasn't easy, considering how long Penny had been missing. I didn't want to turn her into the victim of some mentally disturbed monster who'd held her captive for all that time. That seemed rather predictable. Making her a victim of herself, however, was an idea that immediately interested me.

Following the twists and turns and tortured psyche of someone who'd made some terrible decisions early on in her life was both fascinating and challenging. Penny's fondness for mind games often made it hard for her mother and sister to know how to respond to her, and this was another challenge for me as I was writing. I frequently felt Penny's need to exert the power she had over her family taking hold of me, but at the heart of that power was a fear and vulnerability that ultimately makes her human.

I guess this story illustrates how difficult I find it to create a character with no redeeming features at all. I'm also constantly aware that while my books often touch on some very serious and sensitive subjects – in this instance family tragedy and mental illness – they are not intended to make anyone end up feeling frightened or miserable. It's always my aim to leave you with a smile or a sense of hope, and fingers-crossed I have achieved that here.

For those readers who are meeting Andee Lawrence for the first time, her story begins with *Behind Closed Doors*. She also features in *The Girl Who Came Back*, *The Moment She Left*, *Believe In Me* and my next book, *The Secret Keeper*. They are all stand-alone novels so don't have to be read in a particular order.

I hope you've enjoyed reading *Hiding in Plain Sight* as much as I enjoyed writing it. I'd love to hear from you if you'd like to be in touch.

With warm wishes,

Susan

Coming January 2018

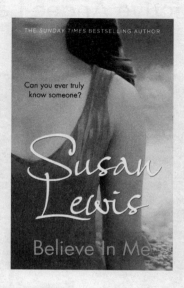

THE *SUNDAY TIMES* BESTSELLING AUTHOR

Can you ever truly
know someone?

Susan
Lewis

Believe In Me

Leanne and her teenage daughter Abby have recently been
forced to move from London back to Kesterley-on-Sea, to
Ash Morley Farm where Leanne grew up. Leanne's husband
Jack, Abby's father, killed himself over a year ago, and the pair
are still reeling from the shock waves caused by the tragedy.

Also living at Ash Morley farm is Leanne's mother Wilkie,
who is a rock for everyone, and family friend Klaudia and her
two children. Klaudia has to face the backlash of xenophobic
feeling post the Brexit vote, and is on tenterhooks to hear
whether she and her children will be sent home to Poland.

Hoping to move forward and mend the wounds her family
has suffered, Leanne decides to foster a child. And when
she's told that Daniel's father is in prison for murder, she
hardly bats an eyelid. But as Daniel becomes integrated into
the family, Leanne starts asking herself questions about his
father's conviction. Is he really guilty? With the help of
friend and ex detective Andee Lawrence, Leanne sets
out to right the wrongs of the past.

Read and revisit
the Detective Andee Lawrence
collection

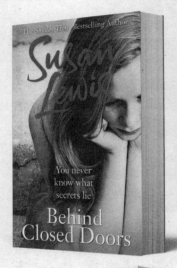

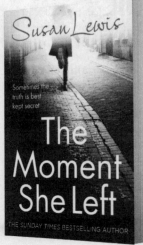

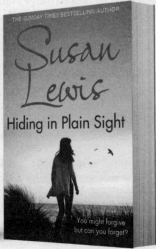

Available in paperback and ebook

About *Susan*

I was born in 1956 to a happy, normal family living in a brand new council house on the outskirts of Bristol. My mother, at the age of twenty, and one of thirteen children, persuaded my father to spend his bonus on a ring rather than a motorbike and they never looked back. She was an ambitious woman determined to see her children on the right path: I was signed up for ballet, elocution and piano lessons and my little brother was to succeed in all he set his mind to.

Tragically, at the age of thirty-three, my mother lost the battle against cancer and died. I was nine, my brother was five.

My father was left with two children to bring up on his own. Sending me to boarding school was thought to be 'for the best' but I disagreed. No one listened to my pleas for freedom, so after a while I took it upon myself to get expelled. By the time I was thirteen, I was back in our little council house with my father and brother. The teenage years passed and before I knew it I was eighteen … an adult.

I got a job at HTV in Bristol for a few years before moving to London at the age of twenty-two to work for Thames. I moved up the ranks, from secretary in news and current affairs, to a production assistant in light entertainment and drama. My mother's ambition and a love of drama gave me the courage to knock on the Controller's door to ask what it takes to be a success. I received the reply of 'Oh, go away and write something'. So I did!

Three years into my writing career I left TV and moved to France. At first it was bliss. I was living the dream and even found myself involved in a love affair with one of the FBI's most wanted! Reality soon dawned, however, and I realised that a full-time life in France was very different to a two-week holiday frolicking around on the sunny Riviera.

So I made the move to California with my beloved dogs Casanova and Floozie. With the rich and famous as my neighbours I was enthralled and inspired by Tinsel Town. The reality, however, was an obstacle course of cowboy agents, big-talking producers and wannabe directors. Hollywood was not waiting for me, but it was a great place to have fun! Romances flourished and faded, dreams were crushed but others came true.

After seven happy years of taking the best of Hollywood and avoiding the rest, I decided it was time for a change. My dogs and I spent a short while in Wiltshire before then settling once again in France, perched high above the Riviera with glorious views of the sea. It was wonderful to be back amongst old friends, and to make so many new ones. Casanova and Floozie both passed away during our first few years there, but Coco and Lulabelle are doing a valiant job of taking over their places – and my life!

Everything changed again three months after my fiftieth birthday when I met James, my partner, who lived and worked in Bristol. For a couple of years we had a very romantic and enjoyable time of flying back and forth to see one another at the weekends, but at the end of 2010 I finally sold my house on the Riviera and am now living in Gloucestershire in a delightful old barn with Coco and

Lulabelle. My writing is flourishing and over thirty books down the line I couldn't be happier. James continued to live in Bristol, with his boys, Michael and Luke – a great musician and a champion footballer! – for a while until we decided to get married in 2013.

It's been exhilarating and educational having two teenage boys in my life! Needless to say they know everything, which is very useful (saves me looking things up) and they're incredibly inspiring in ways they probably have no idea about.

Should you be interested to know a little more about my early life, why not try *Just One More Day*, a memoir about me and my mother, and then the story continues in *One Day at a Time*, a memoir about me and my father and how we coped with my mother's loss.

Memoirs by

Susan Lewis

Read the true story of Susan Lewis and her family and how they coped when tragedy struck. *Just One More Day* and its follow-up *One Day at a Time* are two memoirs that will hopefully make you laugh as well as cry as you follow Susan on her journey to love again.

Available in paperback and ebook

5 minutes with

Susan

Where does the inspiration for your books come from?

I often write about difficult issues, as you well know. I don't necessarily write from experience in these cases but I rely on listening and seeking the experience of others who might have witnessed or been through challenging situations. It's important as a writer to imagine how you'd feel if it happened to you. I enjoy doing it but sometimes it can be quite distressing – sometimes I cry, which tells me it's working. This is how I really bring my characters to life.

Do you have any peculiar writing rituals or habits?

Nothing too peculiar! I'm very strict about the hours I write, starting at 10 in the morning and going through until 5pm or 6pm, usually six days a week. Then, I love to have a glass of wine at the end of the day as I read back over what has happened in 'my fictional world' over the last seven or eight hours, socialising with the characters and often wanting to gossip about them with someone else.

What advice would you offer to aspiring writers?

Remember to listen: listen to the way people speak, to the rhythm of the words you are writing (you're most likely to do this in your head), and always give your characters room to be themselves. They'll have plenty to say if you just let them chatter on to one another, often giving you ideas you hadn't even thought of!

What is the last book you bought someone as a gift?

A variety of children's books for the recipients of the
Special Recognition Award that I'm sponsoring for the local
secondary school. They've chosen the titles themselves and what
a fascinating selection they've made – from *Diary of a
Wimpy Kid* to *The Curious Incident of the Dog in the Night-Time*
(one of my own favourites).

What's the best piece of advice you've ever been given?

If you want to be a producer you'd better write. I was
working in TV drama and this was what I was told to get
me out of the Controller's office! I took him at his word
and the rest, as they say, is history.

If you had a superpower, what would it be?

If I had a superpower I'd rescue all the children
and animals being subjected to cruelty.

What literary character is most like you?

Definitely Emma from Jane Austen's wonderful novel.

**If you were stranded on a desert island what song would
you choose to listen to, which book would you take and
what luxury item would you pack?**

That's a hard one. Song choice would have to be 'Just My
Imagination' by the Temptations. Book choice . . . *How to Survive
on a Desert Island* by anyone who's been thoughtful enough to
write such a useful guide. Luxury item: a double-ended stick
with a toothbrush at one end and a knife at the other . . .
I could give Bear Grylls a sure run for his money!

Have you read them all?

For a full list of books please visit

www.susanlewis.com

Connect with

Susan Lewis

online

Sign up to Susan's newsletter for
exclusive content, competitions and
all the latest news from Susan.

Want to know more? Visit

www.susanlewis.com

Connect with other fans and join in the
conversation at

f/SusanLewisBooks

Follow Susan on

@susandlewis